T0368966

BEHIND
CLOSED DOORS

Jasmine Kaur Dhuga

authorHOUSE®

AuthorHouse™
1663 Liberty Drive
Bloomington, IN 47403
www.authorhouse.com
Phone: 1 (800) 839-8640

© *2015 Jasmine Kaur Dhuga. All rights reserved.*

No part of this book may be reproduced, stored in a retrieval system, or transmitted by any means without the written permission of the author.

Published by AuthorHouse   12/04/2015

ISBN: 978-1-5049-6248-3 (sc)
ISBN: 978-1-5049-6247-6 (hc)
ISBN: 978-1-5049-6246-9 (e)

Library of Congress Control Number: 2015919043

Print information available on the last page.

Any people depicted in stock imagery provided by Thinkstock are models, and such images are being used for illustrative purposes only. Certain stock imagery © Thinkstock.

This book is printed on acid-free paper.

Because of the dynamic nature of the Internet, any web addresses or links contained in this book may have changed since publication and may no longer be valid. The views expressed in this work are solely those of the author and do not necessarily reflect the views of the publisher, and the publisher hereby disclaims any responsibility for them.

To my friends, Alaa El-Cheikh and Emma Fletcher. Without you, this book would have been left unfinished.

ACKNOWLEDGEMENTS

I would like to thank my friends Alaa El-Cheikh and Emma Fletcher for reading and re-reading my book and for providing me with the constructive criticism (and occasional scolding) when I needed it. Moreover, I would like to thank my editor, Rachel Starr Thompson, for her endless advice on how I could improve my book and for her incredible generosity.

I would also like to thank all of my friends and family for supporting me when I decided to publish my book. Without their support, this would have been an unreachable dream.

Three things cannot be long hidden: the sun, the moon, and the truth.
Buddha

PART 1

THE ILLUMINATION

It was half-past midnight, and rain sheeted down onto the streets of Windsor, Ontario. But the brittle wind that ran across the city, howling through the thundering sky, didn't stop the man from getting to his destination. Instead of paying attention to the icy wind slapping his face or the hard-bucketing downpour drenching him to the bone, he paid closer attention to what was ahead of him. The dim light of a building shone in the distance, standing out against the night. And he was determined to reach it.

Beside him, rows of barren trees lined the side of the pathway. Beyond them lay a blanket of darkness, mantling the unknown. Most people would have been too afraid to even come this way at such an hour. But the man knew better. He knew that whatever was out there in the shadows couldn't harm him. That was why, when he heard the crack of a twig to his side, he merely kept on walking.

Until somebody spoke from behind him.

"Grayson."

At the sound of the voice, Grayson went rigid, not wanting to turn around and face what he knew was coming for him. However, he also knew

3

he couldn't avoid the man behind him forever. So with his jaw tightening and his teeth clenching, Grayson turned to face him.

"Caden," Grayson replied, just as curtly as Caden had spoken. By his sides, his hand clenched into fists. He grit his teeth. His blood was boiling with hated for Caden—hatred and jealousy over his power and the ease with which he'd obtained it. Caden, on the other hand, detested Grayson for not trying hard enough to take advantage of the situation he was in.

He was the adoptive father of the Keeper.

Caden walked up to Grayson, not tearing his eyes away from the short man with shallow chocolate eyes. "Going somewhere?" he asked.

"Yes, actually," Grayson replied, looking up at the younger man. Of the two, Caden was stronger and *much* smarter. Both of them knew it. "So if you'll excuse me, I'm going to take my leave."

He turned and started walking away, impatient to meet Byron, but Caden simply followed. "I know what you're doing," he announced.

Grayson halted in his tracks. How much did Caden know? Did he know everything about his plans?

"And what *exactly* am I doing?" Grayson demanded, fear coursing through his veins as he realized how badly this could hinder his plans.

"Keeping tabs on the Keeper isn't going to do you any good."

Grayson wondered how Caden knew about Byron and what he was doing. How had he found out? More Importantly, did he know why he was keeping tabs on the Keeper? And if so, what was he planning on doing with that information?

He tried not to let his confusion show as he took two steps through the mud toward Caden and cocked his head to the side. "And why are you willing to tell me that?"

"Because I want to work together."

Grayson squinted up at him. Why would Caden be willing to work with him—why would somebody *that* powerful want to work with anyone like him?

"Why?" he demanded, crossing his arms.

"Grayson, you are in a position that could benefit me, and if you agree to work with me, I will give you something in return."

"I don't need your help."

"I know you want the gem."

Grayson tried hard not to shake—to hide his fear—as Caden circled around him. He wasn't sure how Caden knew this, but chances were he would try to stop him. He would want to take the gem for himself.

"At the rate you're going, you're never going to find the gem. You need a *much* better plan, and I can help you with that." He stopped walking, pausing at Grayson's shoulder. "Don't worry, I'll let you keep the gem. I want something else."

"What?"

Caden's thin lips pulled into a grin. "Reign over Planet Earth."

Grayson could feel Caden's breath on the back of his neck as he continued talking, making the hairs on his body rise. "However, I'm willing to share that reign with you. I'm willing to let you live, let you become immortal by destroying the gem. You already know I don't need its power to achieve my goal, so it'll be all yours."

Grayson's mind whirred. He had no reason to say no. If he chose to work with Caden, he could take advantage of him to get the gem and then kill him. He didn't want to share his reign over Earth. He needed all the power to himself if he was going to get the Wunissa back. He knew she wouldn't come willingly, so he *had* to bind her to him with his power. He'd hold her captive, which he could only do with the power of the gem and the submission of all those pathetic humans, who would guard her day and night and keep her from leaving the mansion he would so easily obtain once he stole the gem.

Once he stole the gem and became the most powerful creature on Earth, she could never leave him. She would always be his, and the Keeper would be dead. He would get his revenge on the Keeper, and he would have the Wunissa trapped in his grasp for the rest of eternity.

Working with Caden could be a shortcut to achieving all he dreamed of. However, he needed to sort out his options and choose the best one. If it required working with Caden, then he would do it. He would just have to be wary of Caden and make sure he protected himself well.

But first, he had to hear what Caden had to say.

"What do you have in mind?" Grayson asked.

A wicked grin stretched across Caden's face as he began explaining. When he was done, the two men departed, heading their separate ways, with a deal made and murder on both of their minds.

CHAPTER 1

THE HOT GUY

MONIQUE

SLAM!

The sound of a stall door being abused jolted me awake. I opened my eyes. I'd passed out again. Beneath my chin rested the filthy toilet seat, reeking of undigested food, urine, and somebody's time of month. I immediately got up, not wanting anyone to see me from underneath the stall door. I should have been disgusted considering my face was so close to a public toilet seat, but my mind was too hazy to care. So instead of wrinkling my nose and shrieking, I just picked up the bag that was on the floor and put it in the pocket of my sweats, knowing I needed to head to class before anyone saw me in here. If I was caught, I was done for. But I needed at least a small dose of ecstasy every day to keep me going. By the time I got home today, I wouldn't give a damn about what was happening around me. I needed it to be happy.

But when I walked out of the washroom, I suddenly didn't feel like going to class anymore. Knowing I could catch up with what I would miss in class that day, I went to my locker and grabbed my things before heading

out the school doors. Once outside, I pulled my iPod out of my pocket
and leisurely made my way to the forested area near the school, stopping
by my parked car along the way to pick up my duffel bag from the trunk.
I began to walk the path in the forest with J Cole blaring in my ears until
I reached a clearing. Once there, I set my iPod on a boulder, letting the
music blast through the area. I swung my bag from behind my shoulder
and pulled out my bow and arrows. My father owned a hunter's shop near
the outskirts of the city, so I had easy access to the weapons. I brought
my arrows to school every day—leaving them in the trunk of my car—as
I tended to skip a lot and this was what I usually did when I skipped; I
would come to this clearing and practice my shooting, hoping that I would
never have to use my skills in real life, but wanting to be prepared anyway.
I had been doing this for nearly four years now—ever since I was fourteen.

  I pulled out a target board—a new one, since my last one had been
stolen—along with some rope and securely tied the board to a tree. Once
I was sure the knots were as tight as they could be, I assembled my bow,
stringing it, and started shooting, the rhythmic clapping of the arrows
hitting the board soothing me. I could do this for ages, but I wanted to
go back to school soon because my brother—Jeremy—was on the Massey
basketball team and had a game today. Being only a year apart, we were
really close, and I wouldn't let him down by not going. He was all I had
left.

  Jeremy wasn't my real brother. I was adopted into his family the
day I was born. I didn't remember my biological parents at all and didn't
want to; if they had set me up for adoption, they obviously didn't give a
shit about me.

  I kept shooting my arrows, not allowing myself to think about
anything. Instead, I just let my anger control me as I took it out on the
target—the anger I had stored up the past four years. *All* my anger.

  I don't know how long I continued to shoot, but as soon as I heard
the school bell ring from afar, dismissing all the students for the day's end,
I pulled out my arrows from the board, untied it, grabbed my iPod, and
started heading back before Jeremy or any of my friends could notice I
had left.

  Thank the fucking lord for my freakishly good hearing.

It was when I was walking away that I saw something out of the corner of my eye that I had never seen before.

An iridescent glow at the end of a lake.

Where did the lake come from? It wasn't there before. What the hell? I came here almost every day; how could I have missed it?

Bemused, I walked closer to the lake, heading toward the glow. As I got closer, a glittering wall formed that blocked off the other side of the forest. It was translucent so I could see through it, but it still had that shimmery glow to it.

What the actual fuck?

Slowly, I lifted my hand to see if it would go through the wall. I was centimeters away when I heard a male voice behind me.

"You shouldn't be here."

My heart leaped into my throat. The air thickened. Wondering who was there, I turned around but found that I was the only one in the forest—or in my field of vision at least; I knew I hadn't imagined that voice. There was someone here. Someone had followed me. I gripped my bow and arrow tighter, ready to use them if I needed to.

"Who's there?" I called, trying hard to keep my voice from shaking. Suddenly, I heard running footsteps to my right. I sucked in a breath and turned to see who it was. Again, there was no one there. "I know you're here," I continued. "Who are you?"

"I *said,* you shouldn't be here," he yelled, sounding exasperated. I turned around. No one was there. I started shaking, gritting my teeth. Was I going nuts? Who the hell was talking to me, and *why?* Why shouldn't I be here? Why weren't they giving me a reason?

"Why are you still here?" he continued. "You need to run. *Don't* come back."

"I'm not running!"

Run, Monique. Run now, go!

"Mom?" I called out, recognizing her voice immediately. How was I hearing her voice in my head? How was I even hearing her at all? She was dead.

My mind whirled; I couldn't concentrate on what was going on.

"Run!" he ordered.

9

I heard thudding footsteps, like thousands of soldiers marching toward me, and I started panicking. I saw two lingering shadows in the depths of the forest ahead of me. Instantly, I turned, running for my life.

He's closer. He wants to kill you.

Who wanted to kill me? Why? Why was I suddenly getting these weird voices in my head?

Run!

I saw the school ahead of me, but I was still a good distance away, in the middle of a deserted street.

I ran faster.

Suddenly, someone grabbed me from behind and shoved me to the ground. I cried out as my shoulder hit the ground hard, and the pain knocked the wind out of my lungs. It was when my attacker grabbed my leg—as I tried to regain my breath—that I noticed it was a guy in a dark hood that perfectly shielded his face. There was something familiar about him, though I couldn't picture a face.

Whoever it was tried to drag me back in the forest as the voice in my head continued to shout *Run!* over and over again. With my back burning from scraping against the uneven ground, I frantically lifted my bow and arrow and tried to shoot at him. I missed. His grip on me tightened.

My heart started pounding even faster. Breathing hard, I shot another arrow and missed again, a result of my shaking hands.

I was going to die. I knew it. But I didn't want to, not like this. I wouldn't let myself die. I couldn't. I had to take care of Jeremy. What would he do without me?

I wasn't going to let this guy take me away from him.

"Let go of me, you jackass," I snarled, trying to shoot another arrow at him.

It hit him in the abdomen. Immediately he let go, roaring in pain.

I didn't waste another second. Ignoring the burning of my back and the throbbing in my leg from his grip, I shot up to my feet and ran like hell the rest of the way back to the school.

As soon as I got to safety, I caught my breath, looking at my dirty clothes and torn sleeve. I headed toward the girls' washroom, wanting to get cleaned up before I headed to the game. I was glad to find that nobody was there. Tearing the rest of the sleeve off, I pulled my leather jacket out of my bag to hide my ruined sweater. I fixed my bun, trying to calm myself down before I headed outside to meet my friends.

Okay, Brooks, chill. Thinking about what just happened isn't going to do you any good, I told myself as I took deep, calming breaths in front of the mirror. *Just calm down. Breathe in. Breathe out. Chill. You probably imagined half of that. I mean, voices in your head? The lake? It's probably just the drugs.*

It *had* to be just the drugs. This was Windsor, and *nothing* ever happened here.

Convincing myself that it had all been a hallucination, I gave myself a once-over. There were some pieces of grass still stuck in my sleek reddish-brown hair. Taking them out, I noticed that my lips and olive-coloured skin were pale from the cold, but my cheeks had turned pink. My usually narrow, deep-set green eyes were wide from what had just happened.

I looked way too crazed.

Taking a deep breath, in and out, I got rid of the mud still staining my nose. And as if it would reassure me, I smiled at myself in the mirror, watching my dimples surface on my cheeks and glaring at that little gap between my two front teeth that I'd always hated. Sighing, I headed out to meet my friends at their lockers.

I walked down the hall, seeing one of the chemistry teachers in the hallway talking to one of the janitors. I snorted humorlessly as I passed them. The entire school thought they were dating, but they would honestly make the oddest-looking couple ever: the janitor was so tall she had to duck to enter a room, and Mr. Trevino was the exact opposite—short and round. In fact, while the janitor had to duck to get through a door, Mr. Trevino had to walk sideways through some of them. At least, according to my friend Nathan.

I grinned, thinking about him. There was absolutely *no* way to describe that kid. With jet-black hair, night-sky eyes, and sandy skin, he was literally the hottest guy I knew. I mean, his face was still kind of round and boyish, but he always wore this black cap that somehow solidified his jawline. I wasn't much of a cap person, but it seriously did wonders for him. Like attracting the attention of the entire female population at our school. And some males.

But unlike a lot of girls at our school, I didn't fall in line to date guys like Nathan. Or to date at all, actually. I hated all that romantic bullshit and tended to stay away from drama.

When I reached the end of the hallway, I met two of my friends at their lockers, where they stood side by side, talking to each other. Jana was a tall, curvy Arab with straight blonde hair that fell right below her shoulders. As I walked toward her, she pushed her bangs out of the way so that they swept to the side, tucking them behind her right ear. Her hair *always* looked like she had just stepped out of the salon, no matter how bad the day was, even if it was pouring rain. Her usually golden skin looked a little sallow today, probably due to a lack of sleep, judging from the bags under her heavy-lidded sapphire eyes. But despite all the stress I knew she was under from some approaching due dates, she gave Malinda a half-smile.

Being the total opposite of Jana, Malinda was a tiny African-Canadian with a waterfall of chocolate brown hair flowing all the way down her back in tiny ringlets. She had the same type of side-swept bangs as Jana but was currently putting them up with a hairband to showcase her doe-like cognac eyes. The innocence they displayed suited her more than she would ever know.

Malinda and Jana were both really outgoing. Jana was friends with practically everyone at our school, and so was Malinda.

And then there was me.

It wasn't that I couldn't make friends. It was just that I didn't want to get close to anyone. The only two people I was really close to were Jana and Jeremy.

"Hey," I said them, approaching them with a smile on my face and interrupting their conversation. The moment I did, however, I felt a weird vibe between us. I looked at Jana, who suddenly seemed worried. I didn't bother asking her why; she freaked out a lot. Malinda and I never knew why, and we didn't bother to ask much because Jana never told us anything.

I tried to ignore the weird vibe, making myself believe I was just being delusional again. "Are you guys going to the game tonight?" I asked, excited to see Jeremy and Nathan play—Jeremy because he was my brother, Nathan because he was hot.

"Yeah, we're going," Malinda answered. "Are you?"

"Yep, screw homework; I'll do it on the weekend," I replied. Despite all the craziness that had just happened, the ecstasy was keeping me in a light mood.

"Yes!" Jana exclaimed, breaking out of her sullen state. "I love it when you go."

I rolled my eyes at her. "Why, because I create so much of a scene when the other team scores?"

"Of course! It's so much more fun with you there." Jana loved hanging out with me; she said she needed more enthusiasm in her life and I made her life more exciting. I didn't know how, but I didn't really care. I never gave much thought to our friendship. To me, it was just as natural as breathing; we had been friends for a really long time.

My thoughts strayed back to the game. I really wanted to get going to see the warm-ups, which were seriously fun to watch. Despite the fact that this school only had a limited number of hot guys, the majority of them were on the basketball team.

My mind flew to Nathan again and I smiled, biting my lip. Jana smirked. "You're thinking about Nathan, aren't you?"

Sometimes knowing each other inside out wasn't all that great.

I laughed. "Let's just get going. And don't start about me and Nathan, because there's nothing going on there."

"I seriously don't understand why you don't just ask him out. He doesn't even have feelings for his girlfriend anymore; he's been talking about dumping her for ages."

"Because," I replied, "dating is pointless. It's just drama, Jay."

She snorted, and I punched her in the arm playfully. Before she could punch me back, I grabbed her by the arm and started pulling her toward the north gymnasium.

"C'mon, let's go," I whined. "I wanna see the warm-ups."

"No, you want to see the delicious guys," Jana corrected. I smiled sheepishly, and Malinda laughed, running to catch up with us as we headed through the doors to the back stairwell.

As soon as we stepped through, we were greeted by a very excited—and hot—Nathan.

"Hey, whaddup?" he called. He was wearing his black cap backwards and held out his hand for a fist bump. Grinning, I obliged, and then the four of us started walking toward the gym.

"Ugh, I have *so* much homework," I complained. He laughed at me, and I playfully punched him on the arm. "Don't laugh. It's not funny." Just to piss me off, Jana started laughing, and I punched her for the second time that day. She punched me back, but before we could get into a typical best friend fistfight, Malinda came between us.

"Guys, stop," she giggled. "You're going to walk away with bruises on your arms."

I gave Jana one last punch—earning myself a playful glare—and then turned back to Nathan, who was still laughing. "Oh, I am so going to kill you, Khan."

He controlled his laughter and then changed the topic. "So you wanna hear something funny?

"What?" I replied.

"Mr. Travino was talking to Miss Wells today, and you should've seen the way they were acting. I saw them near the janitor's closet—*the janitor's closet,*" he repeated with emphasis, winking at me.

"I swear to God, I don't know how they're dating," I laughed as we approached the gym, "They're like polar opposites. He can't even walk through a door properly."

"Hey, you only know about that because of me," Nathan scolded.

I laughed at his absurd expression. "Yeah, I know. It's still funny imagining it."

The three of us laughed while Nathan rolled his eyes lightheartedly. "All right, I'm going to go get changed."

"'Ight. We're gonna go find a seat in the bleachers."

"Yeah, okay. Bye." He winked at us again and left just as Jana turned to me.

"He likes you," she teased, poking me in the ribs.

I narrowed my eyes at her and shoved her off. "No, he doesn't. You're being proved wrong right now. Look."

She and Malinda followed my gaze, and the three of us watched him getting bombarded by his girlfriend, Mackenzie, a girl I detested, not for dating Nathan but for something else entirely. The red-headed bitch tried to seduce Jeremy at the beach last summer. Somehow she'd found out that he'd had a crush on her and wanted to take advantage of him to fill her needs. She'd even threatened to spread some stupid rumor about him if he didn't sleep with her. But Jeremy was a good boy, and he wasn't the type to just sleep with a girl without an actual relationship. Plus, I'd kind of warned Jeremy that if he lost his virginity before he was eighteen, I'd disown him. That might seem idiotic, but I was just really protective of him. He was all I had left.

Neither Jeremy nor I told Nathan what had happened. We had decided that if he wanted to date Mackenzie, he could. Apparently he was going to dump her soon anyway, even though he was chewing her face off in front of us right then.

Ignoring Nathan and his slut, I headed up the stairs toward the gym, and Jana and Malinda followed. Once again, I was left feeling like the leader—a feeling I hated—so I took a step back and let them lead.

Just as we reached the stands, my cell phone rang. Looking down at the old Nokia, I checked caller ID. My father. I ignored it as I did every time he called. Turning off my phone, I began to search for a place to sit but was interrupted by someone calling my name over the PA.

"Monique Brooks, please come to the main office."

It was a voice I knew only too well—Mme. Simmers, the secretary. Great. That could only mean one thing: my father had called the school again, like he always did when I didn't pick up his calls. It was the one reason the secretary knew me by name and face. Jana and Jeremy, who sometimes had to drag me in to answer his calls, were known in there too.

Groaning, I turned to Jana and Malinda. "Guess my father's gonna call me home for no freaking reason again, guys. I'll see you on Monday."

"Bye," Jana said, giving me a hug. I shot her and Malinda a fake smile before walking away.

I took my time walking to the secretary's office. Mme. Simmers didn't even bother looking up when I got there, knowing I knew what button to press to answer a call. Aimlessly glaring, I picked up the phone and put it to my ear.

"What?" I demanded, leaning against the ledge.

"Monique, I need you home *right now,"* he ordered.

His voice was slurred. He was drunk again.

"And?" I retorted. "Am I supposed to listen to you?"

"Yes, you damned brat! I don't care if you want to stay and watch the game. I let you have your way too much, but not today. Get home now."

"For what?" I snarled.

"I just got home and wanted to eat something. But the plate I grabbed was dirty. Do you honestly call this cleaning, you fucking bitch?"

What the fuck? Seriously? This again? He'd called me home multiple times before, complaining about how I hadn't done something right. He *really* enjoyed pissing the living shit out of me.

"Well tough luck for you then," I snapped. He started yelling at me again, but instead of listening to his bullshit, I cut the call and headed out of the office. I wasn't going to sit through his crap. I didn't give a fuck. So instead of going home, I went back to the stands where Jana and Malinda were sitting.

"I thought you were going home," Jana said.

"Fuck him, no I'm not," I retorted, sitting down beside her. Jana and Jeremy were the only people who knew about my relationship with my father. I wasn't really friends with Malinda. She was more of an acquaintance. I didn't like getting close to people like Jana did.

"Fine, your choice," Jana sighed, turning to face the court. She didn't particularly agree with me rebelling against my father, but she didn't know how it felt to live with him. I hated him, and I wasn't going to let him control me.

We chatted casually with each other, taking in the beautiful sight of the guys before us, for about half an hour before the actual game started. As soon as the teams got into their positions, I cheered, "Yeah, go Jeremy!"

Jeremy looked a lot like our father with his ash-brown hair; chocolate brown eyes; tall, lean figure; and pale complexion. But while our father's face was intimidating and squared, Jeremy's was still kind of round and childish. He looked at me and smiled, facing the other team.

"Get outta here, yo. You be killed!" I screamed at them. I heard Jana laughing at me, but she seemed far away, just like everything and everyone else around me at the moment. I felt like I was in my own world, surrounded by pleasure and happiness. I knew it was just the drugs *really* kicking in, but I managed to pay attention to the game as it started up, and I cheered when Nathan got the ball. In less than a minute we had scored two points, and I stood up, cheering with the rest of the kids from our school.

By halftime, we were in the lead by ten points. It was when Nathan scored again that the weirdest thing happened. I stood up and started cheering for our team as usual, but I suddenly became incredibly dizzy, and was unable to stand on my own feet. Thinking it was the ecstasy, I sat down and waited for it to end.

Only it didn't.

I gripped the bench with my fingers, its iron nails cutting into the skin of my hand. My head started spinning out of control, and the next thing I knew I was falling into darkness.

~

Eyes. Grey eyes. They were watching me. Why were they watching me? They were staring at me like they were expecting something, wanting something from me. What did they want?

A face formed in front of my eyes. He was smirking at me.

He wants your power, *a voice spoke in my mind.*

But what power did I have? If I had any power at all, I would have been able to undo what happened four years ago. But I couldn't . . .

Suddenly, I was standing in my bedroom doorway, and she *was still home. Father stood in front of her, yelling, "Go, get out of this house, now! And don't ever come back!"*

She growled. "Fine, I'm leaving." Grabbing a bag from her room, she ran down the stairs. I could feel the terror again, the same panic I'd felt four years ago, the fear of her leaving me in this dreaded world alone. The pain. The loss.

"No!" I cried, running after her. She didn't stop, not even for me. Before I could do anything, she'd walked out the front door, leaving me to call after her. Father grabbed my arm, restraining me, but I hoped she heard what I screamed.

"Come back, Kay!"

I woke up screaming her name, only to be grounded back to reality by familiar hands second later. Letting my eyes focus on my settings, I realized I was in the back of an ambulance. There was a female paramedic to my left, who looked surprised as hell at my outburst, and behind me, near the front of the ambulance, sat Jana, with her hands on my shoulder.

What had happened?

Jana looked down at me. "Monique, are you all right?" she asked, her eyes wide in concern.

I was far from all right. "What happened?" I inquired, trying to avoid her question, and I could tell from her sigh that she knew it too.

She answered my question anyway. "You fainted on the stands halfway through the game."

I sat up, squinting against the light. Why was it so bright? Ugh, I felt like crap. "I did?" I asked, my voice sounding rough to my own ears.

"Yeah, it was kinda scary," I heard Malinda comment from somewhere. She was here too? I suddenly noticed her peeking back from the front of the ambulance. The look on her face said she was worried for me. She was always worrying for other people. Malinda was kind of a hysterical person, to be honest.

I blinked, looking at Jana again. It was then that I actually acknowledged the fact that I was in an *ambulance*, being taken to the freaking *hospital,* where they'd probably run a series of tests on me to see why the hell I'd fainted.

And I still had ecstasy in my system.

"I think we should go back to the school," I said urgently. I wasn't exactly sure how blood tests worked, but I didn't want them to find the drugs in me.

"You fell from the bleachers, Monique," Malinda said.

"We were sitting in the second row."

"Yeah, but it sounded like you hit your head pretty hard."

"You should still get yourself checked," the paramedic beside me added, still looking shocked at my sudden return from unconsciousness. "Just to be safe." She frowned, turning my neck gently to examine the back of my head. I squirmed, already uncomfortable from the tight space I was in and not wanting to be touched.

"Well, I'm better now, so can we please go back?"

"We should still check for a root cause. Has the fainting been happening a lot?"

"I just haven't been sleeping well because of schoolwork," I replied lamely. I highly doubted she'd believe that, but I didn't really care; I just wanted to leave the God-damn ambulance. "I'm fine."

"A doctor should still examine you—"

"You can't examine me if I don't want to be examined!" I exclaimed. "Will you please just take us back to the school now?"

She looked startled at my outburst, but I could tell she knew I was right. She turned to her partner in the front, the one driving. "Drive back to the school. She isn't willing to be examined." I could see the surprise on his face in the mirror, but he didn't say anything and just made a U-turn, heading back to the school.

Jana and Malinda didn't say anything. I knew Malinda was just too scared to speak up. I also knew that Jana knew that the fainting was just the drugs. I had told her about them, because I told her pretty much everything, but I'd been regretting it ever since. Even in that moment, she was giving me a look of disapproval.

Rolling my eyes at her motherly nature, I asked, "Did the game end?"

She shook her head. "We haven't been here long. Jeremy's still playing, although he wanted to come with us."

Good. He needed to keep playing. He was one of the best players on the team—although I can say that opinion was probably a little biased.

When we got to the school, the paramedic tried helping me out, but I just held up my hand, getting up myself. She let me leave without any assistance, but Jana and Malinda insisted on helping me back into the school.

"I'm fine, guys," I insisted.

"You sure?" Jana asked, and I nodded. "Okay, but be careful. There's still ice on the ground."

I nodded again, irritated, and she and Malinda let go of me. I really fucking hated winter. It was cold as hell, and on top of that, I didn't have a jacket on, so it was ten times worse. Thank God it was almost the end of January; I would only have to deal with this shit for another month or so.

"Malinda, you go on ahead of us," Jana said. "We'll catch up. I just need to talk to Monique alone."

I dreaded what I immediately knew was coming.

As soon as Malinda nodded and left, Jana began in a low voice, "Monique, I think you need to cut down." I looked away, not wanting to listen to this. She continued, "Look, I know why you do it, but it's not good for you. You've been taking it for four years now. That's not healthy. There're going to be consequences."

Why did I ever tell her that I took drugs?

I sighed and turned to face her properly. "I can take care of myself, Jana. Just make sure nobody finds out about this. Especially Jeremy." There was no need for him to know. It would just hurt him if he ever found out.

"I'm never going to get through to you, am I?" I shook my head, and she sighed. "Fine. Just know that you're not the only one you're hurting."

I didn't say anything back as we headed toward the gym and our previous spot, where Malinda was already sitting. People were giving me weird looks, clearly wondering how in the hell I was already back, but I just ignored them and looked at the scoreboard. We were losing. I went hysterical. "What the hell, the other team has the lead? This is so fucked up! Jeremy, get the damn ball!" I was back in game mode, screaming for our team to win. When the other team scored again, I started booing, pissed off. Just because of me, they were freaking losing. Just because I'd fainted, Jeremy hadn't been concentrating, and now they were losing. God, this was all my fault . . .

I was back in my room on my iPod touch, finally talking to her after so long. Even though it had only been a month, it felt like a decade. I stared at her face through the screen, tears pooling in my eyes as she spoke.

"You won't do anything reckless, will you, Monique? Don't rebel. It'll only make the situation even worse."

I glanced at my bag, where I kept them—the drugs I took. A sea of guilt washed over me, but it was overpowered by my pain, my obsession. The rush they gave me felt too good to stop. My palms got sweaty.

One whole month. It had been one month since I'd talked to her, and I still couldn't lie to her. Yet I couldn't tell her the truth either. I just couldn't.

I couldn't face the look of disappointment I knew she'd give me, the pain she would feel because I wouldn't listen to her.

"No, Kay, I won't do anything stupid."

Yet, I couldn't promise her anything. When I made promises, I never broke them, just like she never broke hers.

I focused on the present, not allowing myself to think of the past. I knew it would bring back the pain. My eyes fixated on the court, trying to locate the ball. I eventually found it and realized that our team was winning again. I cheered, distracting myself from the memory.

The game ended well; the score was thirty-eight to thirty us. I headed down the stands as the teams split to go their separate ways. Running up to Nathan, I congratulated him and then walked up to Jeremy to do the same. "You played real good out there."

"Don't I always?" he asked, giving me a cocky grin.

"Shut up," I replied with a light shove.

Suddenly, he got serious. "You're okay though, right?" he asked.

I nodded and gave him a reassuring smile. "Yep. Definitely," I said just as Jana and Malinda came over. "We should celebrate," I announced.

"All right, what should we do?" Nathan asked.

I grinned. "What do you think?"

Jana groaned. "Oh god, we're not going to that idiotic restaurant again, are we?"

"It's not idiotic. First of all, we get everything cheaper 'cause I work there, and second, we're allowed to get wasted 'cause no one cares if we're underage or not."

I worked at a Japanese restaurant and earned really good money for it. It was a well-known restaurant in Windsor, and we tended to hang out there a lot because all the employees were really chill and fun to be around. What was even better was the fact that every Friday my manager took a day off, leaving the assistant manager—his son, Akio—to handle things. His son was *really* chill, so all of the employees had a party after hours. There was a nightclub just off to the side of the restaurant. It wasn't part of the building, but my manager owned that as well, so all of the of-age employees were allowed to go in for free on most nights—they just had to pay for their drinks.

"Yeah, but not all of us like to get wasted, now do we?" Jana countered.

"We might get caught," Malinda added with widened eyes.

I laughed. "Do we ever get caught?"

"Just because we haven't gotten caught yet doesn't mean we can't *ever* get caught."

"Oh, come on, we'll go; there's no harm in going," Nathan argued, taking my side. "You don't have to drink. It's not like I do. And neither does Jeremy."

I smiled. "See, Nathan's with me!" I exclaimed. Jana rolled her eyes. "C'mon guys, *please*?"

"Fine," Jana agreed. "But next week, *I* get to choose where we're going to hang out."

"Great," I grinned. "We'll meet there at midnight, 'cause I gotta work my shift first."

"Nikki, can I bring Mackenzie?" Nathan asked.

I glanced at Jeremy, but he didn't seem to care. "Sure, why I not," I said, and then added, "'Ight, Jere, let's go home. See ya guys!"

I left with Jeremy, and we climbed into my white Pontiac Sunbird and drove home. Jeremy was in a ridiculously good mood and had the volume turned up all the way, singing through all the songs that played. But despite the epic game, I was full of dread. I knew that the moment we got home, we'd be faced with a really pissed-off male parental unit. I braced myself, depending on the drugs to keep me in a good mood. I prayed that for whatever reason, he wouldn't be home.

For once, my wish came true; when we got to our house—located in Serenity Circle, a neighborhood in a town just outside of Windsor—Father wasn't there, and the whole place was a *complete* disaster. My usually neat and tidy two-story house was now covered in loose papers blanketing the floor and unwashed dishes stacked on the counters. The furniture looked like it had been shoved around too. The lamp on the coffee table in the family room was on the ground, broken.

"Another drunken fit?" Jeremy asked, kicking aside what appeared to be bills to get to the kitchen.

I shrugged, not doubting that possibility, though it didn't explain all the dirty dishes. "Another night without him, I guess." I moved some dirty dishes off the island and grabbed an apple. Jeremy was already rummaging through the fridge.

"Maybe he's getting laid. I figure he needs to get some. It's been nearly ten years."

I rolled my head toward him and gave him a "Really, you just said that?" look. He widened his eyes and lifted his arms in surrender as if he were trying to block my look. "What? It could happen!"

"Uh-uh. Not like him one bit," I argued. "Getting laid is the last thing he'd be doing. He's too God-damned stiff." He didn't reply, so I changed the topic, not wanting to talk about Father anymore. "Anyways, I still have another hourish before I have to go to work. You wanna watch a show?"

"Sure, which one?" he asked as he stuffed himself with leftover pasta.

I began flipping through the channels. *The Simpsons* was on, so we settled with that. Jeremy came over and sat down on the couch as the show began.

When it was done, I looked at the time. I still had twenty minutes before I had to leave, so I grabbed some leftovers from the fridge and started eating. When I looked over at Jeremy, I noticed that he seemed kind of nervous, and I quickly realized why. "Jere, are you okay with Mackenzie being there tonight?"

"Monique, it's been a year; I can handle myself. I know you care about me, but I'm not a little kid who you have to take care of. You're only a year older than me. You don't have to act like my mother."

I sighed. "I know, Jere. It's just a habit." He didn't say anything back and just put his earphones in. I finished eating and got up to wash the dishes, my thoughts dissolving into another memory.

"Are you taking care of him?" she asked.

"Yeah, Kay, I am. I'm doing my best to take care of him."

"I'm proud of you, Monique. I know I don't have to worry about Jeremy if you're there with him. You'll be the best mother ever."

I didn't say anything back, at least not for a while. How was I supposed to tell her that was all gone for me now? How was I supposed to tell her I didn't want that kind of life anymore because there was no point? There would always be something that would hold me back. There would always be something that broke a relationship, and I didn't want to take the risk of creating new relationships with anyone. I didn't want to get too close. I knew that in the end, something would crush us . . .

"Monique," Jeremy called. I turned to face him, realizing that I had been staring at my wrist, rubbing my thumb over the solid black dot that was my birthmark. "I've been calling your name for ages. What's wrong with you today?"

"I don't know, Jere," I replied truthfully, turning off the tap and drying my hands. "But I hope I'll be better after a drink or two tonight. I have to get ready. I'll be down in five."

I headed upstairs, and once in my room, I changed into my stupid little uniform: a red blouse and white trousers. I hated wearing trousers—I was more of a sweats person—but I had to wear them. I got out the white shoes I had to wear as well and put them on. Thank the lord they didn't make us wear heels, otherwise I'd probably trip and fall to my death within a second of putting them on.

I then did my hair up properly and headed back downstairs. Jeremy was waiting for me by the front door, doing something on his phone. He had changed into something more decent and was less sweaty. I would never understand him and his quick showers; I needed my long, one-hour showers, yet he barely took ten minutes.

"Do you have the keys?" I asked.

He didn't look up as I approached him. Instead he lifted his hand, and I snatched the keys from his palm, noticing he was playing *Sims.*

I rolled my eyes. "'Ight, let's get going."

He didn't take his eyes off his phone until we were both seated in the car and the radio was blasting our favourite song. Pulling out of the driveway, I grinned as we both began rapping Lil Wayne along the way to the restaurant.

The Japanese restaurant where I worked was kind of small despite its popularity. My boss—Hiro, a Japanese man born and raised right here in Windsor—had bought the building off someone about five years ago. It had been a house, and all the renovations took roughly a year, which was good for me because the same year I was looking for a job after Kay left, they were in desperate need of employees. Because there were only a few people working when I first got the job and the restaurant had started out as a relatively diminutive business, Hiro and the old workers were pretty close. He was pretty lenient with us and let our friends chill here as long as we continued to work. In some ways, he treated Jeremy and me like his own kids. He was kind of like the father we should have had.

Anyways, the restaurant was pretty simple, with a large indoor eating lounge, a break room near the back, and a spacious kitchen that was separated from the rest of the restaurant by two swinging doors that could be seen from the moment you entered. There was also an outdoor patio, separated from the indoor eating lounge by a glass door. Just off the serving area outside was a stand we kept for music. Sometimes people would come in and play for money. Other times, we played CD music on stereos that could be heard down the street.

The restaurant was pretty close to our house—about a ten-minute drive—so when Jeremy and I got there, I still had a few minutes to chill before my shift started. Parking the car in the back lot, we walked through the back door into the kitchen. The rich smell of Japanese dishes wafted through the air toward me, and I instantly craved me some sushi. As I made my way to check in with Jeremy at my tail, I noticed the excessive amount of food being made. We had a lot more people than usual to serve today.

After I checked in, I saw one of my coworkers, Mason, and walked up to him. "'Sup, bro?" I called, and he turned to face me.

Mason was a blond with the kindest dark brown eyes I had ever seen. His face was childlike, like a cute little puppy's, but he was tall—like, *really* tall. Like ten feet tall.

He smiled when he saw me. "Oh hey, Monique; hey Jeremy. Ready for work?"

"Yep, and ready to get wasted." I laughed, and he smiled.

"Guess what?" he asked.

"What?"

He lowered his voice. "Hiro hired a new cutie, and I'm hoping he stays here after hours tonight so I can get to know him."

"Where is he?" I asked, searching the kitchen for anyone I didn't recognize. When Mason motioned toward him with his head, I spotted him immediately. His back was turned to us; all I could see was his black hair and toned body. "Did you say hi?" I asked.

"No, I was too shy."

I looked back at Mason. "Aw, c'mon Mason, you gotta have some guts to go talk to a guy. Come with me. Jere, I'll see you later. Just go chill with the others." Jeremy nodded and headed into the break room to talk to some other guys as Mason and I headed over to the new kid.

He was working with the fish, and as we approached him, I noticed that his hands were stained with some kind of sauce and that he wore a thick black band on his left wrist that neatly covered a good portion of his skin. When I could clearly see the guy's face, I couldn't help but take in every feature of him—something I didn't usually do—and I'm going to openly admit that I found him absolutely fucking smoking. He had the whole package: the tan skin, the slightly chiselled face with *the* fucking hottest cheekbones ever. His black hair was cut so it fell lightly about midlength on his forehead in wisps.

What caught my eye the most, though, was that he was wearing a slightly see-through white T-shirt over a pair of faded blue jeans. It hugged his body just enough for me to see his *full-blown six-pack.*

Holy damn.

"Hey," I said, distracting myself from his abs by wondering why nobody had given him a uniform yet—sometimes, I seriously hated the side effects of ecstasy. He looked up from the food he was making, and it was then that I noticed he had grey, almond-shaped eyes that stood out in contrast to his dark hair. Eyes that immediately widened the moment he saw my face.

Eyes like the ones I'd seen in my dream.

He can see through me.

I suddenly felt all the air leaving my body. I knew it had to be because of his abnormal reaction to me. He knew something about me. He could see me—the real me—and I didn't like it. I wanted to run like hell, but I didn't because of Mason. I was supposed to help him make conversation. Plus, I didn't want either of them to think I was scared. So, ignoring the new kid's reaction, I continued talking. "So you're the new worker here?"

He gave me a bitter smile. "Well, what do you think, Princess? Have you ever seen me here before? Am I wearing a damn uniform?"

I stifled a gasp. His voice—I'd heard it in the forest. It was the same deep, low voice that had told me to run. Obviously the voice belonged to him, but why the hell would he tell me to run? Why—?

"Are you just going to stand there staring at me, or will you actually respond? I know I'm gorgeous, but you could at least try being less obvious about it."

His voice interrupted my thoughts. I took a deep breath to calm myself down and replied, "Mason and I thought we could help you get adjusted to things and introduce you to all of the employees here. We thought we could help you make some friends and—"

"I'm not here to make friends; I'm here for the money," he retorted, glaring at me.

Why was he being so rude to me? What the hell had I done to him? Confused at his unexplainable arrogance, I frowned. I wasn't going to ponder over it for long, however; he wasn't worth it. So I said, "Okay, then, I guess—"

He cut me off again, turning to Mason. "Thanks, though. I'll come to you if I need any help." He looked back at me, that look of hatred reappearing on his face. "Can I get back to work now, or are you planning on bothering me some more?"

I turned away slowly, saying to Mason, "All right then. I'm going to head out and get to work. See ya, Mason."

"Bye, Nikki."

I walked away. I was kind of disappointed that even though I was actually being nice to someone for once, he'd given me so much shit. Whatever. At least I'd gotten Mason talking to him; that was the main objective.

But I couldn't stop wondering about this new kid. His voice was so familiar—I could swear I'd heard it in the forest. Could it have possibly been him? Was he out in the woods teasing me while I was hallucinating? But if he was real, did that mean the hooded freak was real too?

And how had I seen this kid's eyes in my dream, or whatever the fuck that was?

"Hey Monique, I got a table for you," another coworker called.

"Okay, which one?" I asked, trying to forget about the new kid. She gave me the table number and I immediately went to take their orders, deciding he wasn't worth thinking about.

SAM

If I had to pick one thing I hated with all my heart, I would probably choose being milked for answers. I didn't like people butting into my business, which was why it ticked me off to the max when Mason began asking me questions the moment Monique left.

"So what's your name?"

"Sam," I replied curtly, wanting to get rid of him. It wasn't that I hated Mason. I just really wanted to take my break soon, and I didn't want to spend it talking to the guy. Plus, I needed to make a phone call, one that I couldn't make here.

But obviously the kid wasn't going to shut up. "Where are you from?"

"The States," I replied vaguely, not wanting to give him any more information. When he opened his mouth to continue talking, I sighed and looked down at my watch in annoyance. The time had already seeped into my break. I wanted to leave. Not bothering to be polite, I muttered, "I'll be right back. I need to get something from my car."

Without waiting for a response, I walked away.

Once I was outside, I breathed a sigh of relief. I hated being pried at. I hated moving, I hated getting new jobs, and I hated being asked the same questions time and time again. But I had to do it. I had no choice.

It didn't take me long to find my old Ford Focus in the parking lot. It was trashy enough to stand out in the line of Escalades, Buicks, and Jeep Cherokees. I did see a Sunbird, though, and wondered who that belonged to—it didn't fit in with the rest of the crowd.

Looking away, I pulled out my keys and slipped into my car, taking my phone out of my pocket. My heartbeat quickened as I dialled the number, dreading the answer to the question I wanted to ask. But I needed to ask it. I needed to talk to her. I needed to know how she was, even if it killed me on the inside to find out.

When she didn't pick up, I felt a hand closing around my throat, making it harder to breathe. Something was wrong. Something *had* to be wrong. She *always* picked up my calls, no matter the time of day.

Swallowing back my fear, I dialled her number again, praying she would answer. But again, nobody picked up. This time, I was *sure* that something was wrong. With my hands shaking, I pulled out my virtencia so I could open a portal to go see her when my phone rang.

It was Maya.

Oh, thank God.

I immediately picked up. "Hi," I sighed in relief, all the while wondering why she hadn't picked up when I first called.

"Hey Sam," she replied quietly, her voice soft and soothing. I immediately felt calmer just listening to her. "I'm sorry I didn't pick up earlier. I was sleeping."

Shit, I thought. *I woke her up.* "I'm sorry," I said, my heart dropping into my stomach as guilt washed over me.

"It's okay."

"I thought something was wrong."

She sighed. "No, everything's fine."

"How are you feeling?" I asked as I put my virtencia back. I didn't really want to know the answer. I had a feeling it would be bad, that she would say she was feeling worse, that she was going to die.

"Well, it hasn't gotten worse, but it hasn't gotten better either. I'm just hoping that tomorrow's treatment will help."

"It *will* help," I assured her, despite the fact that I wasn't so sure myself.

She sighed. "I hope so."

There was a pause in the conversation, and I immediately knew what she was thinking: what if it didn't help?

"Maya," I sighed, not wanting her to think these negative thoughts. "Don't stress about this. It isn't good for your health. Just relax, okay?"

"Okay," she said quietly.

I looked at the time. My break was nearly over. I didn't want to get off the phone, but I couldn't be late getting back to work, especially now that my power of compulsion was beginning to wear off. I couldn't afford to lose my job. I needed the money. *We* needed the money.

"I have to get back to work," I said regretfully. "I'll call you as soon as I get back to the motel."

"Okay."

She was so quiet. It sounded like she was about to cry. I desperately wished I could be there to comfort her, but . . . the money.

I stifled a sigh, not wanting her to stress. "I love you," I said.

"I love you too."

It took all my effort to hang up the phone and get out of the car. It took even more effort to forget about our situation for the time being and focus on work. But I had to do this; I had to work to pay for her treatments.

At least until I got the gem.

MONIQUE

After about an hour of serving people, Jana walked into the restaurant. When I glanced at the clock, I realized it was only nine. She was sick of this place, so I guessed she was here earlier than usual to hang out with me before the others showed up.

"Enjoy your meal," I said, giving a chick and her boyfriend their food. I then walked toward Jana and gave her a hug. When I pulled back, I smiled at her. "You're here," I said lamely.

She rolled her eyes. "No shit, Sherlock," she replied. I punched her arm playfully, and she stuck her tongue out at me.

I laughed. "You're so weird. Hey, can you keep Jeremy entertained? His stupid little crush isn't here today, so he's bored."

She laughed. "Sure, I'll go."

An hour later, I had just finished delivering another order while one of my favourite songs by Maroon 5 played on the sound system. I had been nodding my head along to it, walking past the kitchen, when Nathan came through the doors of the restaurant. But I noticed he had come alone.

"Where's your girlfriend?" I asked when he approached me.

"Oh, about that . . ." he began with a heavy sigh as he draped his arm around my shoulder. I resisted the urge to shrug it off. "Yeah, I found out she was cheating on me, so I dumped her."

Damn. "Aw, that sucks, man. She wasn't worth it anyway. You're too good for her."

At that, he smiled. "Thanks."

I smiled back.

"Hey, how's your head, by the way? You had a pretty bad fall during the game. I meant to ask earlier, but you were all hyped up in game mode, and I didn't want to spoil your mood."

"I'm okay," I replied, really wishing people would stop asking me that question.

"Hey you!" someone suddenly called from behind me. I turned around to see the new kid looking at me with an expression of disgust. "Quit fooling around. Your order's ready."

I stepped aside from Nathan, annoyed. "I'll talk to you later. Jana and Jeremy are in the back if you want to go hang out with them."

He left meekly, walking past the new kid to go into the break room where Jeremy and Jana were hanging out. I scowled at the kid, glaring. "I have a name," I snapped, taking the dish from his hands.

"So do I, Green Eyes, but did you ask?"

"Fine, what the hell's your name?"

"Does it really matter?"

I sighed. I didn't have time for his bullshit. Walking away, I headed to the couple I was supposed to serve, then quickly checked on my other tables to see if they needed anything. Back in the kitchen, I gave the cooks an order and headed back out as soon as Nathan did.

"Hey, you're not staying inside?" I asked.

He made a face. "Mason was making googly eyes at me."

I laughed. I was still laughing—despite his narrow-eyed look— when Jana came rushing out the kitchen toward me with a bright look on her face.

"Did you see that new kid working here? He's *so* hot!"

I stopped laughing. "Are you kidding me? He's ugly as shit. And by the way, he's really rude."

However, when I went back to get my next order, I had to disagree with myself again. His grey eyes pierced into mine as he handed me the dish, a smirk tugging at the corner of his lips, as if something about me was amusing him.

Fine, maybe he *was* hot. But I wasn't going to admit that to him or anyone else. He didn't deserve any compliments.

"The name's Sam, by the way," he said. "You must be the overly praised Monique everyone keeps telling me about. Please tell them to shut up. It's annoying, and I really have no interest in you whatsoever."

I glared at him. "I'll see what I can do," I snapped. After delivering the dish, I made my way back to Jana and Nathan, noticing that the new kid had gone back into the kitchen.

"That kid's so messed up," I complained, still angry.

"Yeah, I heard that whole thing," Jana said. "It *was* pretty messed up. But whatever. You won't see him *every* day. And besides, he's cute, so you can focus more on *that* rather than the fact that he's fucked up in the head."

I snorted and shook my head, waiting for my next order. The restaurant had cleared up a bit, and I was glad I had a little more time to chillax. After about ten minutes, I grabbed the order from the new kid—Sam—and noticed that he was looking me in the eye with the same damn expression on his face. Rolling my eyes, I was about to leave when a voice spoke in my head.

Just you watch. I'm going to make your life a living hell.

CHAPTER 2

FLASHBACK

MONIQUE

I gasped, but it wasn't the words that stunned me. His lips hadn't even twitched—it was as if I was hearing his voice in my head. And when I looked back at him, the smirk on his face was wider before. I frowned, perplexed, but I didn't want to think about it any longer; my head was hurting.

I felt Sam's eyes boring into my back as I delivered the dishes. Thankfully, Malinda showed up by the time I got back, successfully distracting me from the new kid. I looked at the time; it was eleven already? The restaurant was supposed to close soon but the place was still packed.

I headed into the kitchen to help start cleaning up, since the people who usually cleaned were both on vacation, and I had decided to fill in for them for a while to get extra money. The moment I entered the kitchen, I noticed Mason already cleaning and then realized that the kitchen was a *complete* mess. I wondered how Nadine and Kevin did this almost every day. Sighing, I was about to get to work when I saw *Sam* still in the room. Couldn't the guy just leave? Growling in exasperation, I put my earphones in and listened to my music while I mopped, trying to ignore him. Apparently, the ecstasy I had taken wasn't enough for me to stay happy around *him*.

I was still mopping when I bumped into him accidentally, not looking where I was going. "Watch it, will ya?" I exclaimed.

"Jeez, sorry, you little brat! I'm not the one singing and dancing poorly to my music."

I glared at him. He looked pissed. "Not like *you* could do any better," I snapped. He rolled his eyes and I glowered, but not wanting to waste my time on him, I focused back on my music.

We finished cleaning the kitchen relatively quickly, and once we were done, I turned my attention to my friends and Jeremy, who were chilling with a couple of my coworkers. Walking up to them, I announced, "'Ight, let's go in."

Even though Malinda kept on whispering about how we were going to get caught, we all ignored her and made our way to the back of the restaurant and the door that led to the club, easily getting in. The club was relatively large with a standard look to it; there were two bars on either side of the dance floor and some couches off to the rear end of the place, near the VIP section. It was completely packed with people as it was every Friday; security would be tight, but since the employees knew us, we didn't have much to worry about.

I spotted one of my friends working behind one of the bars, serving drinks to a couple of men. Donna was a gorgeous Asian with deep brown eyes and tiny little curls in her brown hair. Her front bangs were coloured pink, purple, and black. This was her part-time job; she really wanted to become a hair designer but needed money to go to school, even though she was practically a professional already. She had even coloured my hair about a year ago.

"Hey Donna!" She looked up from the drinks in her hands, and when she saw me approaching, her expression brightened.

"Monique, hey!" she called back as she came out from behind the counter and locked me in a tight embrace. When she pulled away, she inquired, "What's up? How was your day?"

Donna was really sweet and genuinely cared about all of her friends. She always asked me how my day went, even though I didn't really tell her the truth about everything.

"It was okay. Just the usual," I lied flatly, and like always, she didn't notice anything wrong, but not because she didn't pay attention. It was just that *nobody* could tell when I lied.

Jana and the rest had already separated, so I followed Donna behind the counter and added, "I wish I could get out of this stupid uniform. It's *so* uncomfortable. I should have brought other clothes to change into."

"What were you going to wear while partying, a faded tee and sweats?" she asked, raising her eyebrows, and I grinned, nodding.

"They're better than this shit. I mean, who in the world would be comfortable enough to wear preppy clothes like these while dancing?"

"Well you seem to be pretty dang comfortable, considering you were dancing in those clothes not even an hour ago," a voice said from behind me. I turned around only to stand face-to-face with a grinning Sam.

I pressed my lips together. How he could change from being so hostile toward me to grinning and talking to me? Even though I didn't know anything about this kid besides his name, I knew that there was something odd about him, and I was determined to find out what it was that made him different from everyone else I knew. I mean, how the hell had I heard his voice in my head?

"Oh, hey Sam!" Donna exclaimed. I turned to face her, giving her a questioning look. "What?" she asked me, clearly mystified.

"You know this kid?" I asked.

"Yeah, I helped him get this job." She frowned, looking even more bemused than before. "Why?"

"Nothing," I muttered. "I'm gonna go."

I walked away. I had a bad gut feeling about the new kid, and something about him had my heart racing.

At the other bar across the room, I went behind the counter to grab myself a bottle of Scotch. I glanced at the bartender standing beside me, who was clearly stunned at the fact that I hadn't even asked him for a drink but instead helped myself to one. I didn't know him and he didn't know me, but from my uniform, he should have known that I worked for Hiro and not cared. When I gave him a glowering look, daring him to say something, he turned back to continue serving the others, leaving me thinking about Sam.

How come everyone was being so nice to him? What the hell did they even like about him? He was so *mean!*

I was a bit startled when I heard Nathan's voice beside me. "Hey, are you all right? You seem pissed."

"I'm fine," I snapped. I held out the bottle in my hands, offering him some. He shook his head. I shrugged, taking another sip for myself before adding, "That new kid's just really pissing me off."

"How so?"

"He just keeps on appearing out of nowhere and talking to me and he's so *mean!* I hate it!"

"Well, aren't you just like the typical bitch—gossiping about people you barely even know?"

I looked away from Nathan. Sam had approached the counter I was standing behind. I glared at him. All he did was respond with a smirk. Seriously? Why the fuck was he even here? Couldn't he just leave me alone? Fed up, I demanded, "What the hell are you doing? Stalking me?"

"Possibly," he replied, giving me a tiny nod. "Although I don't have much interest in girls like you. I would prefer someone a bit more attractive. Blondes usually. But you're not so bad, are you, Princess?"

I immediately became uncomfortable in my own skin, knowing he saw me that way. My breathing faltered, and my hands began shaking. I clenched them into fists, gritting my teeth. I'd had it. I was going to beat him up, I swear.

"Look man, why are you bothering her?" Nathan asked calmly, stepping in front of me.

"Who are you, her boyfriend?" Sam demanded, cocking his head to the side.

"No," I growled, pushing past Nathan. I shot him a dirty look; nobody ever fought my battles. "And what's it to you? Why do you care?"

He shrugged. "I don't. I'm just curious."

"Well, curiosity killed the cat, and right now, I'm visualizing *you* as that cat. So you better get out of my sight before this gets ugly. Stop pissing me off."

He smirked. "Nothing you can cook up in that puny mind of yours will make me leave, Princess."

I stepped out from behind the counter and walked up to him, putting my drink down on the counter as I did so. He stayed calm, unaffected by my temper. I grabbed his arm and twisted it behind his back. No reaction.

"Didn't you hear me?" I hissed. "I said get out of my sight *before* this gets ugly."

I increased the pressure I put on his arm, but he didn't seem to be hurting.

"You think you're so strong, don't you?" he asked calmly, cocking his head to the side.

"I'm strong enough to take you down."

"I could prove you wrong in a second if I wanted to."

What the hell was that supposed to mean? Was that a threat? What would he do to me? Was the fact that I was fighting back giving him wrong thoughts? Was I making the situation even worse? Was I putting myself at risk?

I wasn't sure, but I couldn't back down now. I couldn't let him see that he'd scared me, that I was weak enough for his words to make me back down.

My eyes were stinging, and trying desperately to hold back the tears, I ordered, *"Leave."*

"Fine," he snapped, his voice not shaking even a little. "I'll leave."

I let go of his arm immediately and stepped back from him, letting out a breath I hadn't realized I was holding in.

"But not forever," he added, flashing a smirk at me again before leaving.

I was about to walk after him and actually beat him up this time, but Nathan held me back.

"Leave it; he's not worth it."

I sighed. "Fine." I walked back behind the counter. "He just completely killed my mood. Why is he messing with me anyway?" Nathan shrugged, and I sighed again. "I need another drink." I grabbed the Scotch and chugged it down until I started to get woozy. Nathan watched me with an expression on his face that I couldn't read.

I pulled the bottle away from my lips. "What?" I spat, my voice slurred.

"Nothing, I just rarely see you this angry."

"Well, if this kid is gonna be working here for a long time, you're gonna have to get used to it. I have a feeling he's never gonna leave me alone. God, what is his problem?" I exclaimed. My heart rate was still elevated in a mix of anger and fear, and I wished it would calm down so I could actually breathe. When Nathan shrugged again, I frowned and took another swig of the Scotch, hoping it would help. It didn't. "This sucks."

"Hey, just take it easy," he said. "You'll live. You just gotta ignore him, and he'll ignore you."

"Yeah, you're probably right." I looked around the club. Music was blaring through the speakers around the room, filling the air with a techno beat.

I grabbed Nathan by the arm. "I'm bored, let's go dance."

Before he could disagree like I knew he would, I set my half-empty bottle on the counter and dragged him with me to the dance floor, finding that all my friends were already there. I started dancing with them, but Nathan soon left; he wasn't one to party much. Rolling my eyes, I decided not to call him back. I didn't care anymore. I had become a brain-dead dance bunny, the ecstasy pumping through my veins like adrenaline. The feeling gave me such a rush, and I felt myself reaching my peak. After a really weird and crappy day, I finally felt myself letting go. It felt so . . . fucking . . . good.

~

I woke up in my bed the next morning, the sun shining brightly through the window. I had a vague memory of Nathan dropping me off since he didn't drink last night. I smiled, but when I remembered what day it was, the smile left my face immediately.

It was Saturday, which meant Father would be home all freaking day long.

Instantly, I sprang to my feet and headed for my washroom. I opened the unlocked door and found Jeremy inside, brushing his teeth. Grabbing my own brush, I quickly started brushing in the other sink. I had to get out of the house before Father woke up. I needed to go somewhere else so I didn't have to deal with his shit.

"Relax," Jeremy said once he spat. "He's not here."

"He isn't?"

"No, I'm telling you, he got laid last night."

I spat. *Again* with the getting laid? "And *I'm* telling *you* he isn't the type. Do you really think the guy has sexual needs? He's too God-damned stiff." I dried my hands on the towel hung between the two sinks and added, "Anyways, I'm heading out. He'll probably be coming back home soon, and I don't want to be here when he does."

"Yeah, me too." He put his brush away and turned to face me. "I'm gonna go play basketball at Jared's; I'll take a shower when I get back."

He started to walk away, but I called after him, "Jeremy, get back here." He hesitantly turned around to face me again, clearly knowing by my tone that he was in trouble. "You can't go there just to chill. You need to get your homework done first."

He groaned. "God, why does homework have to be the one thing you care so much about?"

"Jere, you're falling behind, and I told you before, school's really important, okay?"

"Yeah, education's important. Who always told us that?" I frowned, trying to act confused even though I knew exactly who he was talking about. He sighed. "Don't play stupid with me. It's because of her. You keep trying to please her even though she left us stranded here. And even if you were to look past that, do you really think she'd be happy with you drinking and skipping school?"

"Jere, you're falling behind," I began with my eyes stinging, on the verge of tears.

He wouldn't let me continue.

"No, stop. This isn't just about the homework anymore. It's about everything you do, all the little things, including being overprotective of me. I loved her too, Nikki, but she left us. You need to stop trying to please her. Kiera's gone, and she's not coming back."

Hearing her name struck me hard in the heart. All the memories, all the emotions I had felt came rushing back to me. The horror, the pain, the betrayal I felt when she left—when Father kicked her out. Everything I felt four years ago hit me hard, all at once, and I couldn't handle it.

~

All four of us were sitting in the family room, watching TV on a bright Sunday morning. It was the weekend after my grade eight graduation, and we were all in a good mood. Well, of course, Father didn't care. He never cared about anything I did, because I wasn't biologically related to him. But Mom had adopted me, so he had to take care of me. I didn't know why he hadn't just set me up for another adoption after Mom died; he hated me.

Kiera—Kay—was proud of me, though. She was always proud of everything I did and was never disappointed in me; I always met her expectations. Even though she was my sister, she'd acted like my mother ever since the accident, even though she was only four years older than me. She understood me more than anyone else did.

"Kiera, come over here," Father ordered suddenly, a stern expression on his face, and because his forehead was creased, I immediately realized he was angry. My breathing came harder. I hated it when he was angry. Nothing good ever came out of his anger; it always led to abuse or alcohol, and he always got angry over stupid little issues that probably wouldn't annoy any other parent in the world.

"Yeah, Dad?" Kay walked over to him happily, not really caring that he seemed mad. Even though Kay knew how angry he could get, she always got along with him; she was his favourite. But it seemed that at the moment, he was very angry with her.

"Give me your phone; I need to check something." Hesitantly, she pulled it out of her pocket and gave it to him. She looked confused now, as well as slightly anxious. I wondered what was wrong.

He spent half an hour on Kay's phone while we all watched him quietly, not uttering a word. Jeremy and I couldn't see what he was doing, but since Kay was sitting right next to him, she could. I could tell from her fidgeting that she was getting more and more apprehensive by the second. But she didn't move. She didn't say anything. She just watched.

After he was done with her phone, he turned it off and walked upstairs, taking the phone with him. I looked at Kay and saw that her eyes were wide. "What happened?" I asked, but she didn't say a word. Instead, she shook her head and looked away from me, a tormented look on her face.

Night fell quickly, with all of us anxious to see what Father had done with her phone. But we didn't get to see. Instead, as soon as it got dark, we all headed upstairs to go to sleep. But even though I lay in my bed for ages, I couldn't fall asleep; I had a headache from the confusion, and my heart was pounding as the apprehension built up inside of me. Something was wrong. Why did Father take her phone?

I got up, deciding to go to Kay's room to check up on her. When I approached her door, I heard voices coming from the other side.

"I didn't expect this from you."

"Dad, I'm sorry," Kay whispered. When I realized just how hard she was crying, I figure out what had happened. It was obvious Father had found out that Kay had a boyfriend she hadn't told him about, and even though she was in university, he was still going to be angry. Not only angry, but hurt as well. I began worrying even more; Father being hurt and angry at the same time wasn't a good combination.

"Why him? Out of anyone you could be with, why him?"

"I don't know. It just happened."

"You know how dangerous he is. I don't want you seeing him ever again. I don't even want you talking to him on the phone."

"Okay, fine, I won't. But please, just don't kick me out of the house. Please."

She was begging but she shouldn't have been; she was old enough to have a boyfriend, and I didn't understand why Father thought he was dangerous. I'd met the guy, and he was just like any other guy Kay could date. She shouldn't listen to Father; she shouldn't care what he had to say. But I knew that no matter how much I explained that to her, she would never listen to me. She loved Father too much. And I understood why; he had done so much for her. He just never did the same for me.

I opened the door, unable to bear to hear Kay's sobs any longer. I couldn't stand it. I was going to cry myself. "F-Father . . . please forgive her," I stammered. We could convince him later on about letting her be with her boyfriend, but I knew he was really angry, and if either of us brought that up now, he would kick her out.

He turned to face me. "You keep out of this! This is a betrayal. I won't ever forgive you for this, Kiera!"

"D-Dad. I'm really sorry. It won't happen again. Dad, please?" Kay grabbed his hand. I walked forward and grabbed hers, trying to stop myself from crying, but I couldn't help it. Before I knew it, all three of us were crying— Kay because of regret, Father because he was hurt, and me because I couldn't see Kay cry. It was just too much to bear.

Four months passed after that horrendous night. Kay was being deprived of her life; her phone and laptop had been taken from her, and she was no longer allowed to go out. But I didn't understand why this mattered so much to Father. Kay was eighteen; she was old enough to have a boyfriend! Why was this issue such a big deal? And how the hell was her boyfriend dangerous?

"You heard that?" Kay asked when I mentioned it to her one night. I nodded, and she sighed. "Monique, Dad just thinks my boyfriend's lack of academic drive will land on us on the streets. He doesn't want to see that happen. But I can't live without him, Nikki. I think I'm going to have to move out."

I suddenly felt like I was choking. She was going to leave me here alone, with Father? "No, Kay, you can't. What will I do without you?"

She sighed. "I love him, Monique, and you know Dad's not going to let me be with him. Not as long as I'm staying here."

"Can I come with you?" I pleaded. I didn't want to live in this house if she wasn't here. Who would pacify Father when he hit me if she was gone? Who would calm his anger? I couldn't.

"No, Monique, you have to stay here and take care of Jeremy. He needs you. And . . . I can't take the both of you."

Her voice slowly began fading with sorrow.

"But—"

She cut me off. "Monique, promise me you'll stay here and live your life, not ruin it because of my mistake. Please." Tears pooled in her eyes. The sight of her crying made my heart sink low into my stomach. I couldn't stand to see her like this. I knew I had to make this promise, no matter how much it killed me.

"I promise you, Kay. And I never break my promises."

The morning after came all too quickly, and the fear of her leaving me filled me again. But Father wasn't home—he had left and we had no clue where he went.

He ended up coming home late that night. When I saw him staggering in through the front door with a bottle of alcohol in his hand, I swallowed hard. Kay and I stood in our doorways, watching him walk up the stairs.

"Dad," she started hesitantly when he reached the top of the stairs. He glanced at her with a tired look on his face. "Please, you don't know how it feels to—"

His brow furrowed, that crease of fury appearing on his forehead. I saw him clenching his fist as he growled, "Kay, I told you, no." Kay bit her lip. Realization crossed his expression. "You're still talking to him, aren't you?"

Kay wasn't that great at lying; she looked down in fear, but that made him even angrier. "Answer me!" he yelled.

She nodded once, and he immediately began shaking. My heart beat even faster, and my breath came harder. I took a step forward, just in case I needed to come in between them.

"Go," he growled. "Get out of this house, now! And don't ever come back!"

Kay's expression suddenly changed. Her widened eyes narrowed, and her eyebrows formed an angry V. Her hands were trembling, and she clenched them in tight little fists. She was angry and it didn't take me long to figure out that his stupid opinion on dating had finally started to piss her off. When I saw her expression, I realized why she had tried to convince him once more: she would rather leave in anger and have no regrets than leave sad, wishing she hadn't hurt him. At least if she was kicked out, he would blame it on himself and not on her.

"Fine, I'm leaving." She hurriedly grabbed a bag from her room, ran past him and down the stairs.

"No!" I cried, running after her. Even though I had made that promise to her, I couldn't help it; my heart was beating even faster than before. She was going to leave me in this dreaded world alone. I didn't want to feel that pain or the loss. But she didn't stop, not even for me; she just opened the front door and left before I could stop her, yet I still screamed after her, as if it would do any good. Father grabbed my arm, restraining me, but I hoped she'd heard what I'd screamed.

"Come back, Kay!"

Father shoved me to the ground, his fury overtaking him. I noticed Jeremy watching the scene from the family room. I didn't want him to see this, but I was too involved in what was going on to do anything about it. "You're not going after her," Father roared. "She disobeyed me. She's a filthy whore who will get what's coming for her. And if you respect me, you'll do as I say."

"I don't respect you!" I screamed, breaking a sweat. "You never cared about me, so why should I respect you, huh? Why should I respect a man as cruel as you? It's a disgrace to know a person like you!"

His face turned red, and he raised his arm, pulling it back and then snapping it forward just as his hand curled into a fist. As it came into contact with my hip, I heard a sickening crack and fell to the ground, whimpering and whispering desperate words that I hoped would bring her back.

"Don't leave me here alone, Kay . . . Don't leave me like Mom did . . ."

~

"Monique . . . Monique, are you awake?"

Jeremy's frantic voice brought me back to the present. I guess I had gotten knocked out somehow, because suddenly, I was on my bed and he was standing beside me, trying to wake me up by sprinkling water on my face.

"Yeah. God, stop that!" I ordered, shielding my face from the water; it was getting into my eyes. I sat up. "What happened?"

"You passed out. Your head hit the door hinge; it was bleeding a little but it stopped."

I didn't reply and instead stood up and staggered into the washroom. "I'm going to take a shower. You better stay here and finish your homework before leaving for Jared's house, or I'll beat you up."

He sighed, knowing he couldn't win this fight. "Fine," he agreed. Satisfied, I closed the washroom door behind me and turned on the shower, letting the water mesh with my tears as I stared down at the scars on my body, the results of my downward spiral, the cuts I had inflicted upon myself as a result of my pain.

I'd always thought that people who cut themselves were just seeking attention. But after Kay left, I tried to find any way possible to relieve my pain and found that I was wrong. Cutting myself relieved a great deal of my emotional pain because I was distracted by the physical, so I continued to do it. I knew deep down that cutting myself was completely wrong; Kay had always told me never to do anything so downright reckless. But I had anger management problems, and after Kay left, my resentment for my father only grew. The problem was that I could only take my rage out on myself, not on my friends and definitely not on my father. Sometimes that rage would get so out of control, would hurt so bad, that I'd want to kill myself. I still wasn't really in control of my feelings, but by cutting myself, I felt like I was. I hadn't become dependent on the cutting, though, because I found another method to control my fury, something that was more permanent, something that could get me through an entire day.

When I'd first started high school, I immediately got mixed up with the wrong crowd. It didn't take me long to give in to the kids offering me drugs, and once I got a taste of marijuana, I wanted more. Eventually, those kids got caught, expelled, and sent to rehab, and I was left with no provider. But I needed more drugs. Weed, crack, anything. I just wanted to feel better, and eventually, I did.

Five months into grade nine, I met someone new in one of my classes. His name was Tyler. He was a year older and had failed a class, but I didn't really care because he was nice to me and he listened. Unlike Jana, who I didn't talk to at the time—since she would constantly yell at me for doing drugs—he didn't scold me when I told him what I was doing. He consoled me about Kay, and he offered me even more drugs. It wasn't marijuana; it was ecstasy, but that was twenty times better. As weeks went by, he gave me more.

And then one time, when I needed more drugs, he told me to come to his house to get them. So I agreed to go to his place, willing to do anything to get my ecstasy. But when I went over, I found that his parents weren't home and that his room was full of posters. A lot of them were of women on motorcycles, and they were basically naked, with the exception of a few choice locations. I was confused. None of what I saw in his room reflected how he acted toward me. I didn't see him as a pervert. He'd never even mentioned anything remotely pervy to me at all. So I didn't understand my environment, nor did I feel safe.

I turned to leave the place, but before I could, he pushed me onto the bed. I had no idea what he was doing, but I knew none of it could be good and pleaded for him to stop as he struggled to pin me down, tying me with ropes so I couldn't leave. Soon, he was forcing himself on me, not stopping despite how much I cried.

Tyler was never the same after that. The kindness he'd shown before that day was gone. He continued to give me the drugs, but he stopped charging me money and started charging me with sex instead.

And no matter how much I hated it, I always went back; I was completely hooked on the drugs.

But Tyler had ruined my life. Because of him, I could never feel safe anymore, anywhere I went. I always felt like someone was going to jump out at me and do the same thing Tyler had done to me, only worse. That was why I started wearing baggy clothes to hide my figure. It was why the thought of dating held so little appeal to me.

Every time I went back to Tyler's place, he treated me more brutally than the time before, and I hated it. When I tried to find someone else who sold ecstasy or other drugs, Tyler found out and threatened to hurt me and Jeremy. Not wanting to take my chances, I never searched for any other dealers after that day. I just kept going back to Tyler's for more, and because he treated me so horribly, I always took more pills than usual to make Tyler's treatment more bearable. But because I also always came back feeling guilty, I took a bottle of liquor with me to drown my feelings in. I drank really heavily after things first got bad with him, but after four years of dealing with him, I got used to the way he treated me. But when I drank, I drank a lot, because that was the only way I would ever feel better.

However, I never stopped cutting myself. Sometimes I felt extreme pain and anger triggered by something around me that I couldn't control any other way, which was why I still kept a pocketknife with me everywhere I went. I just had to make sure that nobody found the knife or saw the scars.

I sighed, pulling my eyes off the light white tracks that ran down my thighs, and lifted my chin, letting the warm water run over my head as if the pureness of the water would rid my mind of all the vile memories. But all it did was camouflage my tears and crowd the air around me with loud, meaningless patter, hushing the sobs that took over my body.

It was only when I heard a crash from downstairs that I stopped crying and straightened up. I immediately got out of the shower, quickly got dressed, and rushed downstairs just as I heard someone yelling.

Father. He was home.

I had to make sure Jeremy was okay.

Father was in the kitchen, standing in front of Jeremy, pointing to what looked like a shattered bowl. "Do you not know how much that set cost?" he screeched, his chocolate eyes wide in fury. His brown hair was neat and tidily brushed back like always, perfectly framing his intimidating square face—well, intimidating to others, anyway. I wasn't scared of him—most of the time, at least. It was only when he was angry enough to physically abuse me that I became petrified. I didn't know what to do then; I couldn't stand up to him because he was a thousand times stronger than me.

But his words were harmless. There was no meaning to them. They were just letters put together in anger in an attempt to terrorize his victims. I never felt threatened by them; instead I felt angry. In fact, what he said next pissed me off so much that I decided to act out a bit.

"Clean that up right now!" Father ordered. His voice was slurred. I sighed when I saw Jeremy cleaning the mess with his bare hands, and I grabbed a broom to help him.

"Spoiled little brat can't do anything right," Father muttered. I was close enough to smell the booze in his breath as he spoke.

I stood up, throwing the broken pieces of glass away, and then turned toward him. "Actually, *Grayson*," I said coolly, using his first name to piss him off, "if he was spoiled—which he clearly isn't—it'd be your fault. I wouldn't even be complaining about it if I were you."

He growled, narrowing his eyes at me. "No, it'd be your fault. You and that other disobedient little brat."

"If you're talking about my sister, you need to get your damn facts straight, because neither of us spoiled him. The three of us actually took care of and understood each other, something that you failed at doing."

Before I could see what was coming, he had slapped me across the face. Hard. The sound seemed to echo throughout the house, and the pain of it resonated through my body. It stunned me. Usually I could see it coming.

"Don't you *dare* call her your sister," he snarled. "You are *adopted*; you are *not* biologically part of this family!"

I came out of my stunned and scared state then, so sick of him telling me that I was adopted and making me feel out of place.

"I don't freaking care!" I shrieked, my entire body shaking. "No matter what happens, I'll still consider her a sister and love her like one! Nobody, not even you, can change that!"

When I said that, I actually saw the fury rising in his expression before he punched me in the stomach. I doubled over in pain, making it easier for him to strike me again with a shove to the ground. I backed away from him with my heart racing as he stalked toward me.

Suddenly, Jeremy put himself between us. "Stop it," he shouted, making me break a sweat. Was he trying to get himself killed?

Before I could stop him, Grayson grabbed Jeremy by the shoulders and shoved him to the ground. Jeremy landed flat on his ass on the other side of the kitchen and grunted in pain. But I couldn't focus on him any longer because Grayson was coming closer to me.

Now with a knife in his hand.

CHAPTER 3

DIVIANO

MONIQUE

"You will never speak to me like that again," Grayson growled.

And then I saw it—the murderous look in his eyes. He didn't just want to hurt me anymore; he wanted to *kill* me.

I swear to God, his eyes were red.

He drew the knife back and struck at me. I screamed and moved to the side just in time, but he was still able to nick me in the side of my stomach, tearing my shirt and drawing blood. Hissing, I scrambled back, but he was advancing fast. I was breathing harder as I sprang to my feet. I *needed* to get out of there.

This man was going to kill me.

He took another swing. Shrieking, I dodged, holding up my hands in defence. Jeremy was on his feet, and he grabbed my car keys from the key hanger, distracting me enough for Grayson to make contact again. He pushed me to the ground, making my entire body sting with pain. It was then that Jeremy threw something at his head, which shattered as it hit him. I quickly moved out of the way before any of the broken glass could hit me.

Grayson roared in pain, forgetting about me for a moment, giving Jeremy and me enough time to grab our bags and run like hell toward my car outside. We could hear Grayson screaming after us, but we had already left the driveway by the time he got out the door. Without hesitating, I sped onto the highway, wanting to get far away from that man as quickly as possible.

"Are you okay?" Jeremy asked.

I shook my head, catching my breath. It was the first time I had spoken the truth when answering that question in years. "No. He tried to kill me, Jeremy. He was going to kill me."

"I can't believe he would do that. I know he hates you, but murder?"

"Did you see the look on his face?" I continued. "His eyes were red. He had a knife. He was going to kill me."

"Monique, are you sure you're in the right mental state to drive? His eyes could *not* have been red."

"I don't care what mental state I'm in!" I exclaimed. "I need to get the hell out of Windsor! I can't live here anymore. I won't go back. I *can't* go back."

"Where will we go?"

I shook my head. "I don't know. I just need time to clear my head."

"So where will we go for today?"

There was really only one option.

I turned on the radio, increasing the volume as I picked up speed. "Chatham. We're going to Aunt Carrie's."

~

In about an hour, we reached the brick house deep in the city. We weren't that close to Aunt Carrie. In fact, we hadn't seen her in two years. So, Father would never expect us to go to her place, and Aunt Carrie was always really welcoming. I knew she would take us in pretty much immediately. She reminded me of Mom in that way. Plus they were both very kind. I always thought it was because they grew up together; they were cousins and lived in the same house down in Texas. But while Mom had moved to Toronto for university and then come to Windsor after graduating teachers' college, Aunt Carrie moved to Chatham after her second marriage. That was why she still had a Southern accent.

Aunt Carrie was a natural blonde with curly hair that fell to her shoulders when it was let out. But when she opened the door, I noticed that today, it was straightened and up in a bun. Her heavy-lidded electric-blue eyes were framed with light freckles and tanned skin. She held a paint brush in her hand and wore paint-stained overalls. She was obviously repainting the house. At thirty-five years old, she was raising a daughter all on her own, as her first husband had died in a car accident and her second died serving the country.

"Hey, Aunt Carrie," I greeted her, fidgeting with my hands. I was still in a bit of an internal frenzy, but I kept it together. "Me and Jeremy needed to come to Chatham for this school project and were wondering if we could stay at your house for the weekend, if it's all right with you."

She sighed. "Well, I was doing some painting, and the house is really messy . . ." she began.

"Oh, we just need a place to stay for the night; we'll be out all day," I assured her. "I'm sorry we didn't call ahead; we had another place to stay, but it fell through at the last minute."

The worry immediately left her face, and she smiled. "Oh, okay then, that's fine. I haven't gotten to work on the second floor yet, so it's not messy. Why don't you two come on in and settle in upstairs?"

"Okay, thanks," I said as she stepped aside to let us in. After we took off our shoes by the door, she led the way upstairs. There were four rooms in total, one of them being Carrie's, one of them her daughter's, and two guest rooms. Jeremy and I chose a room each and set our stuff inside.

Carrie was practically rich, and her house was fucking amazing. It was what I wanted my future house to be like, and the room I was staying in that night was simply *amazing*. It was double the size of my room back home and had a washroom attached to it that I had all to myself, complete with a steam shower. The bed was cream-coloured with a matching dresser and cabinet. There was a window just opposite the door that lit up the entire room and made the walls, a soft shade of gold, glow.

Once I put my bag away, I went into the room Jeremy was staying in for the night. This one was much simpler; it had peachy walls and a small bed like mine with just a dresser. The room also had a walk-in closet and a washroom, but they were much smaller.

As I looked around the place, I noticed that Jeremy was nowhere to be seen. Frowning, I called his name. "Jere?"

He popped his head out of the closet.

"What are you doing in there?" I asked.

"Monique, come here," he said quietly, looking more befuddled than I felt. I obliged, and when I was standing right beside him, I saw him staring at what looked like a square carved into the wall.

I cocked my head to the side. What the hell?

Bending down, I popped out the drywall and saw that behind the carved hole was a tunnel made out of steel, large enough for one person to squeeze in and make their way through on their hands and knees.

But it wasn't just the tunnel that confused me. Sitting in front of me, just at the edge of the hole, was a small, rectangular box. Even though I knew it was wrong to snoop around, I still took the box in my hands and opened it.

There was nothing but a small knife inside, although it looked much different from a regular knife with the exception of the smooth silver material. It had an odd-looking handle to it that looked like it was made out of wood, but it was blue, and it felt a lot sturdier. The handle also had a small, blue, globular object that seemed to be lodged inside of it. The object gave off some light, as if the thing ran on batteries, but when I checked for a battery holder, I found that there was none. All I found were intricate lines carved into the wood and four concave spots for my fingers to lie upon. The hilt was oddly shaped too, with one side of it shorter than the other. The longer one was pointier and made out of the same blue wood as the handle. It resembled a stake and was the complete opposite of the shorter side of the hilt, which was made out of silver. There were intricate blue lines swirling around it—and a little lid.

I lifted it. Out of the hole escaped some blue steam that Jeremy—whom I'd aimed the opening at—immediately started choking on.

My heart jumped. I closed the lid, and the steam instantly disappeared.

"What the hell was that?" Jeremy asked, catching his breath.

How the fuck was I supposed to know?

Grimacing, I blurted out the first thing I could think of. "She's a bookworm; I bet you anything this is just a replica of something in a book she read. She probably got it for a high price, so she probably hid it here to keep it safe."

That had to be it. I mean, what else *could* it be? But even if this *was* related to some book, what the hell was with the tunnel? And where did it even lead?

Curious, I lay down on my stomach and wormed myself into the tight space; it was smaller than it looked. While Jeremy waited for me, I looked around and noticed three different directions I could go. Choosing the path that went straight ahead, I crawled forward through the tunnel. Darkness quickly engulfed me. Blinded, I pushed myself forward until my face hit something.

"Ow, *fuck!*" I cussed quietly. I felt around with my hand and pushed whatever I'd hit with my face. Drywall. I gave it a shove, and light suddenly surrounded me. I was in another closet.

When I moved forward to grab the drywall I had popped out to put it back in place, I felt something hard hit my chest and looked down to find another rectangular box. Although I was crammed into the tunnel, I had enough room to prop myself up on my elbows and open it. Another one of the knives, or whatever they were, was inside. But this time, I noticed words written on the thin silver blade. When I peered closer, I also realized that none of them were in English. What the hell?

Putting the knife back in the box, I grabbed the square piece of drywall and popped it back into place before heading down another path in the tunnel. I was hit in the face again, and when I pushed against what had hit me, I found myself in another closet. There was a rectangular box there as well, with the same knife inside.

Even more bewildered than before, I went down the last path and saw that this one led to the closet of the room I was staying in, with yet another box containing a knife. Raising an eyebrow, I quickly crawled my way back to Jeremy's closet to figure out what was going on.

He was kneeling in front of the hole when I approached him, but he got up and moved out of the way so I could get out. When I straightened up, breathing hard, he asked, "What happened?"

"There were pathways inside that led to each of the other bedroom closets. They all had a box with another one of those things in it," I explained, pointing to the knife he was holding in his hand. Taking it from him, I turned it in my hand and noticed a word written near the top of the handle: *Diviano.*

What the hell? What did that even mean? I searched for the definition on my phone but found none, so I went to Google Translate and typed the word in, trying to detect a language. Nothing came up.

"But what the hell is it?" His eyes widened. "*Hey,* maybe Aunt Carrie's a witch."

I rolled my eyes. "One, she'd have a wand, not a knife, and two, that's crazy. There's no such thing as witches and wizards or whatnot. That's idiotic."

I typed the word *Diviano* into Google itself, but nothing useful came up.

I sighed, giving up. "Like I said, it's probably something from a book we don't know about. Just forget about it."

I was about to put the knife back in the box when suddenly, a blue light shone out of the end. My heartbeat spiked, and I dropped it. "What the hell was that?"

Jeremy's eyes were wide, but all he said was, "Maybe it has a little button or something, and you accidently clicked on it."

I was about to agree when the blue light spread and created a circle on the floor, flaunting a place that reminded me of paradise. The area displayed was full of jade-green grass and crystal-clear water in lakes.

"And a ghost clicked that button?" I asked sarcastically.

The image disappeared. I sighed. All this confusion was making the blood rush to my head, giving me a pounding headache. "Okay, this is stupid. It's probably a toy. Let's just put it away."

He agreed, and after I put the knife and the box back where we had found it, he popped the drywall back in. We had just turned the closet light off and walked back into the room when we heard footsteps coming up the stairs. Immediately, we jumped onto the bed, and Jeremy quickly pulled his books out to make it seem like I was explaining something to him.

"So basically, all you do is move this around, and you'll have the domain of the function," I explained just as Aunt Carrie came in.

"Are you guys settled in?" she asked.

I turned around, pretending to be surprised. "Oh, Aunt Carrie, I didn't hear you come in. Yeah, we are."

She smiled. "That's good. "I was going to make Anissa a snack soon." Anissa was her daughter. "Did you guys want anything to eat?"

"No, we're good."

"All right, then. If you need anything, you can just ask me. I'll be downstairs."

"Okay, thanks," I replied. Her smile widened, and she walked away. The moment she did, I got up off the bed.

"Where are you going?" Jeremy asked.

"I'm going to the library. You wanna come?"

"Do you think it's safe with Grayson out there?"

"I highly doubt he'll think we're here," I reminded him, despite still being a little worried myself. But I didn't want to be confined in a house forever because of him. "You coming?"

He paused to think for a second. "No, I'm gonna stay here," he replied eventually. "Maybe I can get something out of Carrie."

"No. You can't do that. What are you going to tell her, that we were snooping around? She'll never let us in the house again. Plus, you *suck* at lying, so if you have to lie about why you're asking questions, you're going to screw us both over. If we're getting anything out of her, I have to be here because I'm the *only* one out of the three of us who's good at lying."

I included Kay in this even though she wasn't here; I knew he would understand who I was talking about.

"Got it?" I added, wanting to make sure he didn't do anything stupid.

He sighed. "Fine, but I'm still gonna stay here."

I raised an eyebrow at him in suspicion but gave in. "Okay, but if you do anything stupid, you know I'll beat you up." With that, I turned and left, grabbing my bag from my room before I headed down the stairs. "Aunt Carrie, I'm going out!" I called.

"Okay, bye!" she shouted back.

In my car, I put the key in the ignition and blasted the radio, speeding my way to the library. I was a little paranoid, looking around me for Grayson's car, but I kept telling myself that this was the last place he'd be looking for me. Besides, he wouldn't kill me in the middle of a busy street. So with that in mind, I tried distracting myself by directing all my attention to finding the library.

Coming from Windsor, I had expected the Chatham library to be relatively small. I mean, Windsor is a really small city, and is mostly known for the bridge that connects it to Detroit, but Chatham is even smaller. To my surprise, though, the library was a surprisingly adequate size. The ceiling was high, and there were a fair amount of books too. I idly wondered if the library had anything on Diviano or the knife we'd found. Maybe I could find the book that the knife was based on . . .

I walked up to the librarian at the front desk, hoping I didn't sound like a complete idiot. "Excuse me; do you have a book on something called Diviano here?" After checking her database, she shook her head and looked back down at whatever she was reading.

I heard a quiet laugh from behind me and turned around to see the new kid from the restaurant sitting at a desk.

Sam.

I took a step back, as if distance would let my breath come back and would rid my body of the surprise I tried hard not to show. What the hell was he doing here?

"What?" he asked, raising an eyebrow at me when I didn't say anything; I was in too much shock.

"Are you *stalking* me?" I demanded, narrowing my eyes at him. I noticed he still had the black band around his wrist.

He shrugged. "Most people would lie and say no, but I'm not most people. So *yes*, actually, I *am* stalking you. Although I prefer the term 'following.' Stalking sounds too . . ." He looked away from me, seeming deep in thought. "Disturbing," he finished with a smirk, looking back at me.

I suddenly felt like heavy hands were wrapped around my neck, cutting off my air supply, and I took another involuntary step back. "I swear to God, you better back off or I'll beat you up."

His smile widened and he laughed again, but this time, his chuckle was shorter. "I *highly* doubt your ability to do that."

I raised an eyebrow at him. "Are you really trying to provoke me? Because I'll do it, I swear."

He got up from the chair he was sitting in and slowly made his way toward me. I tensed. Still smirking, he quietly asked, "You really want to know what Diviano is?"

I completely forgot about our argument the moment he mentioned Diviano. Did he really know what it was?

"Uh, yeah, *kinda*," I replied like it was obvious.

"Then come with me," he ordered, motioning toward the exit doors with his head. I stood still. He rolled his eyes. "What?" he demanded.

"I'm not going anywhere with you; I don't trust you. Tell me everything here."

"I can't. There's a reason that lady you just spoke to had no clue what you were talking about; it's because not everyone knows about it," he elucidated. "If I explain everything here and those *humans* overhear our conversation, we're pretty much dead."

I laughed humourlessly. Was this guy insane? Did he have some sort of mental problem? Maybe he was schizophrenic. *"Humans?"* Are you trying to tell me that you're some kind of supernatural creature or something? A vampire? Is that what this is? Well guess what, buddy, I'm not falling for that shit."

"Oh, so we're *buddies* now?" he replied, raising his eyebrows. "I guess that means you should believe me when I say that *you're* not human either. You're just like me."

He was nuts. He *had* to be. "Oh *please*. Just shut up and tell me what the hell is going on."

"Come with me and *then* I'll explain."

After a good stare-off, I decided that nothing insanely horrible could happen. He couldn't attack me or anything; I would kick his ass if he even tried. Plus, I was ridiculously curious about what was going on. So I agreed tightly. "Fine." He flashed a smile at me and walked off toward the exit. I followed him. When we got outside, I spotted a Tim Horton's near the library and added, "But first, I'm getting an Iced Capp."

He glanced sideways at me, looked back in front of him, and sighed. "Fine, Princess."

I grimaced. "Stop calling me Princess."

"You have too many requirements, Green Eyes. I'm starting to regret this."

"You're the one who came up to me in the first place. I could have figured this thing out on my own."

He laughed humorlessly. "No, you couldn't have. You were asking a damn *librarian* about Diviano. If you were smart enough, you'd realize she wouldn't know shit about it."

Seriously? Couldn't he just tell me already? "What *is* Diviano?"

"I'll tell you once we get out of here."

I rolled my eyes but didn't say anything back.

We approached the doors to Timmies, and I opened the door, walking in. He followed and stood beside me in line. From the corner of my eye, I noticed he was about a head taller than me.

"Stop looking at me like that," he suddenly commanded.

I raised an eyebrow at him, confused. He had an emotion on his face that I couldn't read, and it was bothering me. "Looking at you *how*?"

"Like you're *dissecting* me."

Rolling my eyes, I just looked away from him to face the front of the line. When it was my turn, I bought an Iced Capp. He didn't bother getting anything, so once I got what I wanted, we left. "Where are we going?" I asked.

"Bus station. We're taking a bus back to my place in Windsor."

"Uh, no, I'm not leaving Chatham," I retorted, stopping in my tracks to my car. There was no way in hell I was going to his house.

He gave me an exasperated sigh. "Relax; we'll only be there for a while. We just need to go somewhere private for what I want to show you."

I swallowed hard as my heartbeat picked up. What did he want to show me? Was he lying about Diviano so he could get me alone in his house and hurt me?

"You're scared, aren't you?" he asked, reading me easily despite how much I tried to hide my emotions.

"No," I lied. "Why the hell would I be?"

He rolled his eyes, laughing incredulously and crossing his arms. "Seriously? You're really scared of me? After all that shit you gave me about beating me up?"

I didn't reply because that was the truth; I *was* scared. Despite the fact that I had my arrows and I knew I could kick his ass, my heart was still hammering hard in my chest.

"Seriously, Monique, I'm not going to rape you or anything. I have no interest in you. Trust me."

I was left petrified the moment he mentioned rape. Why the hell had he chosen that word instead of anything else? Instead of *kill?* Instead of *harm?* Did he somehow know about my past? Had he read me *that* well? Was he trying to scare me?

I suddenly found it harder to breathe as the memories took over. I tried desperately to drown them out, but the image of Tyler's face with his hideous smirk wouldn't escape my mind.

"Monique?" Sam called, bringing me back to the present. I focused on him again and saw that he'd raised an eyebrow. "Can we get going?"

I took a deep breath, calming down as I escaped the memory. "Why should I trust you not to hurt me?"

"Because you're my half-sister—*adopted* half-sister," he replied with disgust oozing from his voice.

"What?" I nearly shrieked in surprise. I lowered my voice. "I don't even know you; I can't be related to you!"

"You're *not,*" he replied. "Just because my mother adopted you doesn't make you biologically related to me. Anyways, the point is I'm not interested in you, and you should trust me enough to come with me to my place so I can explain Diviano to you. And if it makes you feel any better, I have a girlfriend."

"No, I don't care about that," I interrupted him, shooing away that topic. "How the hell am I your half-sister? Adopted," I added.

"Grayson's my stepdad. My mom had me before she married him."

"How old are you?"

"Seventeen."

"You're lying," I said. "My sister's older than you, and she's my mother's daughter. My mom couldn't have had you before marrying Grayson."

"It's called cheating, ever heard of it?" he snapped. "And honestly, does it even matter? The whole point of me telling you this was so you wouldn't freak out about coming with me. Now can we hurry up, or will I have to drag you and make it seem *more* like rape?"

Would he stop using that as an example?

He raised his eyebrows at me, waiting for an answer.

I agreed, only so that he would stop mentioning rape. "*Fine,* I'll come," I snapped, but I was still suspicious. "I'm warning you, though; if you dare try anything on me, I'll knock your brains out. I know karate." It was a lie, but I didn't want him thinking he could hurt me.

He laughed. "*Aww,* you know karate? How adorable. Please tell me more about how *unskilled* you are in self-defence."

I clenched my fists. "I am *not* unskilled." He didn't reply but stared me down silently, and I suddenly couldn't look away from him. The next thing I knew, he was reaching for my bag, but before I could stop him, he had it in his hands. When he saw my shocked look, he laughed, handing me my bag back.

"Fuck you," I cussed.

"Just be glad you're completely safe, Feisty; nobody can kill you, at least not now."

I frowned. "What do you mean?"

He sighed. "Look, we'll talk about this at my place. I don't want anyone overhearing us."

"Fine, let's go. But we're taking my car not the bus."

"Okay." We walked to my car and sat inside. When I started the car, the radio immediately began to blast music. Smiling as Drake came on, I started driving, speeding back to Windsor.

We drove in a silence that seemed all too awkward to me. I noticed when I glanced over occasionally that he was on his phone, doing something I couldn't see and couldn't care less about. He seemed unaffected by the silence between us, while I, squirming in my seat, had to turn up the volume of the music in order to drown out his presence. The only time we spoke was when we were approaching the city and he was giving me directions to his place.

His place ended up being a motel room, and a crappy one at that. Although I wondered why he was living in a motel, I didn't really care. I was paying more attention to my heart rate, which I was desperately trying to slow by taking deep breaths.

But I broke into a sweat when he closed and locked the door after we walked in.

I watched as he sat down in a chair by a small table. "Sit," he ordered, motioning to the chair in front of him.

I sat down. "Okay, start talking."

"Jeez, someone's impatient," he replied. I raised an eyebrow but didn't say anything back, waiting for him to start talking so I could quickly get out of here. When he saw my annoyed expression, he rolled his eyes. "Okay, fine. I'll explain. But first promise me something."

Oh my God, will you just get on with it? "Okay, fine. Whatever."

He gave me a judging look, and just when I thought that he wasn't going to say anything—that he'd just lured me here with lies after all—he said, "You have to sit through *all* of this. You can't leave before I'm done talking, and you can't tell anyone about this."

"What about my brother and my friend?"

He visibly thought about it. "If they can keep their mouths shut."

"Okay, fine. Shoot."

"You're going to think I'm crazy—"

"I already do."

He pressed his lips into a thin line, paused, and then said, "Neither of us is from Earth. You could kind of consider us aliens to this planet."

What the fuck?

"We're from a world called Diviano. It's a small planet that orbits the earth. Point 5 percent of Earth's population is from Diviano."

Did he honestly think I would believe this? Forgetting my fear, I laughed and countered, "*Okay*, smartass, if this planet orbits Earth, how come that librarian and other 'humans' don't know about it?"

"Because it's invisible to the human eye and to scientific instruments." I didn't believe him, but I stayed silent, wanting to see what other ridiculous lies he could come up with. "Anyways, as I was saying, we're a more advanced version of humans. We have supernatural powers, like mind reading and telekinesis."

"Bullshit."

"Are you seriously doubting me, Green Eyes?" he asked. "I can compel you to do anything I want you to."

I laughed again, humorlessly. He was *unbelievable!* Did he seriously think that I would believe him?

"*Try* me," I taunted.

So he did. He looked me in the eyes, and I tried to look away but suddenly found that I couldn't. Yet instead of cringing away from his piercing gaze, I stared right back at him, keeping my expression unscathed.

He spoke quietly but dauntingly. "Give me your Iced Capp," he decreed.

His irises turned blue.

I'll admit, I was suddenly at a loss for air, and his words had my brow furrowing, but his command had no effect on me. Even though his eyes were changing colour, I blamed it on the delusions the drugs were giving me. There was *no* way in hell this could all be true.

"No," I retorted without any difficulty. He sat back in his chair in obvious confusion. When he didn't say anything, I stood up and announced, "You're a fake. I'm out."

I was just about to leave when he called, "Wait."

I stopped in my tracks, turning back around to look at him. "What?" I demanded.

"You promised me you wouldn't leave until I was done talking."

I sighed and sat down, knowing I had to keep that promise. I *always* kept my promises. But I wasn't happy about it. Crossing my arms, I leaned back in my chair and asked, "Why are we even on Earth if we're from a different planet?"

He glared at me in obvious annoyance but explained, "Because we started off on Earth, and some decided to come back when it was safe enough to."

"What do you mean by safe? Why wouldn't it be safe?"

"Some millennia ago, there wasn't any world called Diviano; we all lived amongst humans for centuries. But our population was scarce and shrinking because humans would kill us out of fear—we had superstrength, and that scared them. We had no powers like we do now, but we were much stronger than regular humans."

I scoffed. "Right. Then how did they manage to kill us?"

"Numbers. They were able to gang up on us, since there were a lot more of them than there were of us. It was a dark era of death, and because of it, we separated from humans by creating an entire world of our own with the help of our leader, Queen Amora."

"Okay wait, hold up. A *queen?* And how did she create an entire world?"

He scowled. "She could do an incredible amount of magic. She could make things disappear and create stuff out of thin air. She used that magic to form our planet. Obviously it resulted in some orbital and climate changes on Earth, but this happened so long ago that none of these changes were recorded, and soon the humans forgot all about us. And yes, Queen Amora was our leader for an entire millennium. She was immortal."

"Was?"

"Will you just let me finish?"

"Okay! Fine!"

He sighed and then continued, "After about a century on Diviano, Queen Amora became even more powerful. The environment changed throughout this time and became more mystical. As it changed, she became more magical herself and acquired all Divianan powers existing today. But not wanting to be selfish, she took a little bit of her blood—and a bit of everyone else's blood—and locked it all in a gemstone created from nature's belongings—"

"What do you mean, belongings?"

He rolled his eyes. "Meaning all the magic she was surrounded with. She took some from the wind, the soil, the water, and from naturally created fires—like from lightning storms. Creating the gemstone allowed her to channel all her powers to all Divianans. The queen also created portals to get to Earth from Diviano and back."

"But didn't you say that 'humans,'" I air-quoted, "were trying to kill you?"

"Yeah."

"Then why the *fuck* would she create portals to come back to Earth?"

He shrugged. "She was apparently involved with someone on Earth."

"Who?"

He narrowed his eyes at me. "I'm not God. I have no idea. I'm just reiterating what I know."

"Okay, but why are you talking in past tense?"

"Because she disappeared about a thousand years ago. We have no idea where she is."

"How'd she disappear?"

"We're not exactly sure. All we know is that whatever happened was done by the hands of Daeblo, which are creatures kind of like us but stronger. They're complicated to explain and aren't around much today, so not even many Divianans know about them."

I raised an eyebrow at him. "Would you care to elaborate? If you really want me to believe you, you can't be so vague about everything."

He clenched a fist; I knew I was getting on his nerves, but I didn't really care. "They were like us when we all lived on Earth. But when the queen created Diviano, these people decided to stay back. Nobody forced them to come, but the queen warned them that they would be killed. When they wouldn't budge, everyone left through the portals without them. They stayed back because they believed that feeding on humans would make them stronger. So that's exactly what they did. They hid out in caves and forests and attacked any human they would come across. The worst part is, it turns out they were right. They eventually became much more powerful than we are, and I'm guessing that when the queen created portals, they found her when she came back to Earth. Either that or they found their way onto Diviano and attacked her. I'm guessing that's how she disappeared."

"Okay, so now you're going to tell me that you need help finding her or something because of some stupid reason like how special I am, right?" I asked, giving him a bitter smile. I read books; I knew how these things worked. But I also knew this was all a bunch of bullshit and that he was just fucking with my mind.

"No," he replied. "I'm not telling you this so you can help me find her. I'm telling you this because I need something from you."

"What?" I demanded. What did he want? Sex? Was all this a lure to get me here alone with him? Did he make all of this up? He didn't look like he was smart enough to do that, but I wasn't going to rule out any possibilities.

He leaned forward, and his gaze intensified. "The gemstone."

"What?" I asked, even more mystified than before. "That gemstone you were talking about earlier—the one with the blood? I don't have it!"

"I know you don't have it right now. But you'll get it soon enough, and I need you to give it to me when you do."

I gaped at him. "Why am I going to get the gemstone?"

"Because this world that I just told you about, you are its Keeper. You are its protector."

"That's bullshit!" I exclaimed. "Even if this stupid world *is* real, I can't be its protector. I literally *just* found out about Diviano! And even if I am its *Keeper* or whatever, why the hell do you even want this stone?"

"You are in the worst position to protect the damn stone, and I want to keep it safe, that's why."

"How am I in the worst position to protect it?"

"Because your father wants it."

What in the world did Father have to do with all this?

Sam went on, "He wants to destroy it to become immortal and obtain all Divianan powers. It'll make him the most powerful being on Earth *and* on Diviano. But destroying the gem will also result in the death of all Divianans."

What? Grayson wouldn't do that. He was cruel to me, but he wouldn't kill that many people just for power and immortality. He wasn't a murderer.

Yet it was crystal-clear he had been trying to kill me today.

"How will it do that?" I asked.

"Remember how I said that the queen took her blood and everyone else's and locked it in the gem?" I nodded. "Doing that connected everyone on Diviano to that gem, along with their descendants. Destroying the gem will kill anyone whose bloodline is contained in that gemstone."

Why the hell was I even believing all this was real? I couldn't just accept this without some kind of proof?

I shook my head. "You need to prove to me that this world even exists."

He rolled his eyes. "Fine," he snapped and then pulled out a knife similar to the ones I had found at Carrie's, but without the intricate hilt.

"This is what I wanted to show you. It's called a virtencia," he told me before tapping the end of it against the table. A blue light came out the end, creating a circle exactly like the one in Jeremy's closet, with the same paradise displayed inside. "That's Diviano," he continued. Taking the virtencia, he flipped it in his hand so that he was now holding the handle instead of the knife portion and cut through the circumference of the circle. The action let out a sizzling sound like fire would make when it burned out. The appearance immediately became more watery, and the circle seemed to flow in shallow waves. I cocked my head to the side just as he grabbed my hand.

Immediately, my mind went on hyperdrive, and I looked up at him, realizing how different of an effect his touch had on me than it should have. Instead of feeling the urge to pull my hand back, I simply felt my pulse quicken.

Anxiety flooded through me.

He looked up at me. "Don't—" he began but then cut himself off, sighing. "Stop biting your nails. Do you have any idea how distracting that is?"

"I'm sorry, okay?" I exclaimed, pulling my other hand away from my mouth. "I do that out of nervousness."

"You're nervous?" he asked. I nodded. "Well, *don't show it*. If you distract me again, I'm going to lose my concentration, and we might end up somewhere dangerous."

What the hell was he talking about? I bit my lip.

Not pulling his eyes away from mine, he continued, "Don't freak out. I'm going put my other hand in the portal, and we're gonna teleport. It'll be easy."

Teleport? WHAT? I thought, freaking out, doing exactly what he'd told me not to do. But before I could ask him to clarify what he meant, he placed his free hand in the circle—or as I now knew, the *portal*. Instantly, I felt a tugging sensation as I was suddenly lifted off my feet and felt myself falling down.

I screamed, closing my eyes as my entire body began shaking. My stomach was churning, my head was throbbing, and my ears were ringing. My heart felt like it was going to pop out of my chest, and I couldn't breathe. I felt like I was falling down from a mountain, and no one was there to save me. What the hell was happening to me? Why the hell hadn't I just walked away when I could have? Oh man, I was so stupid!

I continued cussing until I hit a hard surface with a thud. I moaned in pain and felt around with my hands, only to realize I had fallen on grass. Blinking, I got up off my stomach.

It was then that I heard a quiet laugh from behind me. I turned around to see Sam grinning at me. He was on his feet and didn't look hurt at all. His clothes were perfectly clean, unlike mine, which were now stained with mud and grass. "I should have told you to stay upright," he said. "Welcome to Diviano."

With shaking hands, I pushed him away from me. "Where the hell did you *fucking* bring me?" I screeched.

"You try to beat me up and you'll regret it," he threatened, seeming unaffected by my push. But his words just had me shaking even harder. I was about to shove him away again, but before I could, he grabbed my wrists and pushed me to the ground. "What did I tell you?" he hissed, standing over me. I tried not to cringe back, wanting to hide my fear. "You dare try to beat me up, and you'll regret it."

I shot up to my feet quickly. "Get me back to Windsor. I don't want to stay here!" I yelled, punching him in the face. He was making me more and more angry. I didn't like being beaten up; I'd had too much of that already.

When I punched him, I saw the fury boil up in his eyes. Before I knew what he was doing, he had grabbed my arm and twisted it behind me so that my back was facing him. He wrapped one arm around my neck. When I bit it, he let go, and I took the chance to turn around and throw another punch at his face. He stood ramrod straight, seemingly unharmed. I threw a kick at his side, but he grabbed my leg and flipped me, throwing me onto the ground again.

I held back my scream as my entire body throbbed in pain, not wanting him to know that he was hurting me. Instead, I reached for my bag and grabbed my bow and arrows from it. But before I could use them, he threw them on the ground, pinned my arms behind my back as he got me to my feet, and spoke in my ear.

"Stop it," he snarled, and I could tell from the sound of his voice that he was clenching his teeth. "You have no reason to be pissed at me. I'm simply telling you what your dad should have told you years ago but didn't." Breathing hard, I struggled to get out of his hold, but he just tightened his grip. I started shaking, wanting desperately to go back. "Stop struggling and take a look around you, Monique. We're not on Earth anymore. Look at everything here and *then* tell me if you believe me or not."

I didn't want to, but I couldn't do anything else at the moment; I couldn't even move an inch without Sam allowing me to. So I did as he said and looked around me, finally noticing my surroundings.

We were in a field—off the side of a colonized street—with clean-cut grass that was jade green and feather-soft. There was a small lake nearby that looked perfect for swimming in. The sky was a clear blue without a cloud in sight, and the sun shone brightly down on us. There was a forest to my right with the most beautiful and unique trees I had ever seen. Instead of the typical brown bark, these trees were blue, at least on the outside; from some broken twigs lying around, I noticed that the inner layers were the brown I was used to. The leaves on the trees were oddly shaped as well. Some were perfect circles, while others were zigzags. Most had an orange tint, but some were pink. Odd-looking things of various colours grew on the treetops. Some were long and round, log-like, but others were flat, looking like squished balls. When a gentle breeze moved the leaves, a sweet smell was sent over to me, and I wondered if they were fruits, or maybe flowers. Some of them—like the really tiny curled cylinders—looked like they could be flowers.

This place was paradise—an easily habitable environment like Earth, but much easier to breathe in. Even standing there seemed easier, despite Sam's grip. I felt lighter, like I was floating, but when I looked down, I saw my feet firmly planted on the ground. I felt much more alert, more aware of everything around me than I had ever been back on Earth. I felt better, livelier, revived almost.

I felt like I belonged.

But then I saw something that completely killed the beauty of this place. Across the street from where Sam and I were standing were two little kids playing with each other. The girl was disappearing and appearing in different locations on the road. The boy had what looked like a toy spear in his hand and was trying to hit her with it but was failing miserably. I moved my attention away from them to see that there were more kids of different ages in the field they were standing in, practicing fighting skills as well. I looked past all of them to a soaring, medieval-looking building—a fortress perhaps—made of red concrete with brown trimmings. There were no windows on the entire thing, so I couldn't see inside the building, but a sign outside it read, *Mediralis Defidium Disciplacion Centriates.*

Mediralis Defence Training Center.

How the fuck did I figure that out?

Confused, I turned my attention away from the building to see a whole street, full of what looked like restaurants and shops, all made of the same type of material as the training center. But each one was painted in a different colour. People were walking around everywhere, and I half-expected to see some weird-looking creatures among them, but I didn't. Everyone looked like normal humans, but they were all doing weird stuff. One guy was carrying a bunch of boxes, but he wasn't *physically* carrying them—he was using telekinesis. Others were just teleporting from one spot on the street to another. Focusing on their faces, I saw that they all had strangely colored eyes—some red, some purple, some yellow. But despite all of that, they looked *so normal*, laughing and talking amongst themselves.

I wanted to believe I was just imagining this, that I was having a vivid hallucination and that Sam was part of the hallucination too. I didn't want to believe that I had some kind of big responsibility to take. But this didn't feel like a hallucination. Nor did it feel like a dream. Still, I closed my eyes momentarily in the hopes that I was imagining it all, but when I opened them again, everything in front of me was still there, and the people were still using their powers.

Holy fuck these people were *real*. Everything around me—this stupid world called Diviano—*existed*. Could it possibly be true that I had more to me than I thought there was? All my life I had thought I was just a useless waste of space, complaining about my fucked-up life. But apparently, I possessed a stone—a gemstone—that held this world together. And apparently, if I didn't protect that stone, every single one of these people in front of me would die. Could it be possible that I actually had some meaning to my life? I hadn't believed Sam at first, thinking that everything he was telling me was just insane, that it could *never* happen. But honestly, what the hell did I know about my background? Just that I was adopted, and it wasn't like Father had told me anything about those circumstances, and I'd never asked my mom because I was too young to care. He'd kept me in the dark my entire life. What if Sam *was* right? What if I *was* part of this weird world called Diviano?

"Let me go," I demanded.

"Are you going to try to hit me again?"

"No."

He complied, and I turned around to face him. His brow was furrowed, and he still seemed annoyed, but he was calmer than before. I began walking toward the road ahead of us, filled with dozens of people and, as I soon noticed, no cars.

There were, however, carriages with people on them, being pulled not by horses, but by these weird creatures. They had four muscular legs and a swinging tail like a horse, but their fur was silver and they had two horns on their heads. Their snouts were smaller, and their ears *much* larger. Each one carried an aggressive expression, but when I saw a woman getting off a carriage and petting the animal, the look on its face softened, and it seemed to smile.

"What's that?" I asked, pointing to the horse-like creature.

"It's an animal, called a chequo," Sam told me, walking up beside me. "The livestock our ancestors brought with them changed too because of the mystic atmosphere."

My eyes widened. "They brought livestock with them?"

"Well, they kind of had to. The queen could create all the plants around us with her magic, but creating a life form like that was too much. Where are we going?"

"I want to see more of this place, and you still have more explaining to do."

"What more do you want to know?" he inquired as we crossed the street, sounding annoyed.

"Why are there no cars here? Haven't you people discovered them yet?"

"Cleanliness," he replied simply, lowering his brow. "We want to minimize pollution and try to keep things the way the queen would have wanted them."

I looked up at the training center as we passed it. "What's Mediralis?"

"It's the territory we're in," he explained. "Diviano is split into territories, each one named after and representing a specific power, with the exception of the one we're in now. This is the central territory of the planet, or the *main* territory. Mediralis. It's the smallest of them all, and the people who work here are in charge of keeping everything else on the planet running smoothly. It's kind of like the headquarters."

"Is the planet really so small that it's only divided into territories and not countries?" I asked, seeing a shopping center to my right. There was a parking lot reserved for carriages, with a single person inside each one of them. Drivers, I assumed. The whole lot was covered so the creatures had some shelter from the sun while they waited. I noticed that the parking lots here were relatively small, but considering the amount of people around us, it made sense.

"Yeah," Sam replied.

"Okay, so why do the territories represent each individual power?"

"Each territory deals with certain jobs based on their powers. Like most law firms and courthouses are in Farum, which represents the compulsion power. The majority of people who live and work there have a compulsion power. The government doesn't force people to take those jobs and living environments, though—they don't want anyone to feel confined. They want everyone to be happy to avoid conflict."

"Government?" I asked, seeing a newspaper stand outside a store. I stopped walking and grabbed one, surprised to find that they were free.

"They want everyone to have easy access to information," Sam explained. "And yes, we have a government. We have a mayor for each city, who becomes the representative for the territory he or she comes from. We have three governors, but they don't have much power. Generally, the representatives for the territory make collaborative decisions, since they're the ones who actually know what's going on in their respective communities, and the governors are there to settle any conflict. And then there's you."

I looked up from the newspaper I had been skimming through. "Me?" I squeaked. How was I part of this system?

"Holding the gem makes you the most powerful person on this planet and on Earth. If you destroy it, we all die, but you obtain all of its powers and become immortal."

71

"Then why do they choose some random person to protect it? That sounds like a very fucked-up plan."

He sighed. "The gem itself chooses its Keeper. It essentially finds the purest heart to take care of it, but changes its Keeper every three years to keep itself from being found."

Pure? I thought. Pure my ass. I wasn't pure. I was *far* from pure. I was probably less pure than the devil himself.

"So who will give it to me?" I inquired, not wanting to think any more about just how *pure* I was. "The previous Keeper?"

His jaw twitched. "It'll show itself to you."

"But wait," I said, now confused about something else. "If the gemstone changes Keepers to keep itself from being found, are you saying that people don't know who the Keepers are?" He nodded. "Then how do you know I'm the next Keeper?"

"Because every single time a Keeper is chosen, the name writes itself on a special plaque in the main governmental building here in Mediralis. It's made of the same stone the gemstone was created from, which is why the name automatically appears there."

"And it's kept there so that nobody but trusted people will see it?"

He nodded. "Yeah, it's heavily guarded."

"So how did you and Grayson find out that I would be Keeper?"

He smirked. "I broke in."

Of course. "And they didn't notice?"

"No, they did. I got arrested, but I broke out. I'm assuming Grayson did the same."

"And you can just stand here freely even though you're a criminal?" I demanded, horrified at the idea. These people clearly didn't take the protection of their Keepers seriously.

He leaned toward me with a smirk still on his face. "I'm not stupid, Green Eyes. Of course they want me. They're just looking for someone by the name of Seth Garrity, not Sam Crowman. And I made sure to completely alter my appearance before I broke in in case I *did* get caught."

"How'd you break out?"

"Easy diversion. They only had one guard on me and didn't suspect that I would have a metal implant. I ripped it out of my skin to pick the lock."

I cringed at the thought. "Why did you have a metal implant?"

His grin widened. "I had it in my arm. Just a wire close to the surface. Compelled a human surgeon to put it there beforehand, in case I got caught. Of course, after I broke out, they decided to make the death penalty immediate for any criminal activity that involved the gem and our planet's Keepers, instead of waiting a few days like they did for me." He grinned, seeming all too proud of himself.

I rolled my eyes and dropped the topic, focusing on the real issue here. "And you're saying Grayson wants to destroy it to become immortal and powerful, right?"

Sam nodded, and I kept walking until we found ourselves in another forested area that seemed to stretch out for *miles*. We'd gone past civilization. This place *was* small. "How does it make you immortal?"

"Because it has the queen's blood in it, and she was immortal."

"But if everyone's blood is mixed inside, how come everyone isn't really powerful and immortal?"

"Because to get that power and immortality, you have to break the stone and drink its contents."

I frowned, pausing in my tracks again and turning to look at him. He seemed tired, but I didn't really care. I still had more questions. "You said destroying the gem would kill everyone here."

"Yeah."

"Grayson wouldn't do that. He's cruel and he wants *me* dead, but he wouldn't kill so many people."

"Okay, but let me ask you this: does Grayson hate you?"

"Yeah," I replied, confused as to where he was going with this.

"Then why the hell would he adopt you if he didn't know you were going to be Keeper and if he didn't want the gem?"

"He adopted me because my mom wanted to adopt me."

He scoffed. "Couples usually have to agree on things like that, shitbrain. You really think *my* mom would have won that argument? Plus, Grayson could have easily put you up for adoption again after she passed away."

I thought about it, trying to find something to argue with because I honestly didn't want to believe that Grayson had only adopted me to get the gemstone. And if that was true of him, what about Mom? Was she only using me too?

I pushed that thought aside. I *knew* Grayson wanted to kill me. But it was different killing one person versus thousands. How could I trust what Sam was saying?

He sighed. "He's not going to stop until he gets the gem. He'll take your life for it. He'll find a way around the protection you have on you that makes you immortal until your time as Keeper is up, and then he'll kill you to get the gem. If not for everyone else, at least try saving your own life."

"How?" I inquired, not understanding where to go with all this information. "How can I save my life? Should I move?"

"Moving won't do anything. He'll just figure out where you're hiding, and he won't stop until you're dead. You need to kill him first."

"But that's murder," I stammered, running a hand through my hair. "Can't we get him arrested?"

"What if he escapes?"

I didn't reply. I would be killing my father. I would be committing murder. I didn't know if I could do that. I mean, he'd made life hell, but Grayson *did* raise me—

No, he didn't raise me. He hurt me. I couldn't remember him caring for me even once. What was the point of caring if he died or not if he didn't care about me at all? I needed to protect myself from him, not cower away from all of this.

"So basically, I either kill him or let him kill me, and all these people," I realized in frustration. Behind us, people walked back and forth along the street. The distant sounds of their casual chatter, laughter, and the quiet trotting of the chequo swam through the air, seeming to easily find their way into the woods where we stood.

Sam nodded. I sighed, realizing he was right, despite how much I hated to admit it to myself. Grayson would eventually find me, and he would kill me. I'd seen it in his eyes. The only way to avoid getting killed myself was to kill him.

But I wasn't ready to do that. I wasn't ready to kill.

"How am I supposed to do that?" I asked, averting my eyes.

"You need to train to fight so that you *can* kill him. You need to get stronger. I'll train you. What you need to do is leave that house immediately.

Don't go back. I don't care what for. There's nothing important enough there to risk your life going back for."

"Where will I stay?"

"Somewhere there is someone who is capable of protecting you until you can protect yourself."

My immediate thought was Jana. "My friend's house is loaded with security cameras, and she always has the system on. But it's not far from my house."

"Where are you staying while in Chatham?"

"My aunt's place."

"If you talk to her and make sure she understands your situation, then her place might be best. You want to get as far away from Grayson as possible."

"But school . . . work, my life," I realized.

"Will be gone if you don't drop it all, at least for a while."

He was right. I needed to get out. "Okay." I nodded, though I still wasn't set on the killing. But I could at least get stronger to protect myself, right? "So when should we start training?"

"As soon as possible."

"Okay. I'll call you. What's your number?" I pulled out my phone and added his number as he voiced it. "I should be getting back before it gets even darker," I said, noticing how dark it was getting around me. Plus, I needed to make Jeremy aware of the situation we were suddenly immersed in.

"It's not that late in Chatham. The time is different here. You just didn't feel any change because of the enchantment of the portal," he explained. "But we *should* get back. I have work in a little while. I'll be off at midnight, so call after twelve."

Using the virtencia, he made another portal and grabbed my hand a second time. Soon we were back at his motel, and I quickly left. He came with me because I wouldn't be able to defend myself yet, and I wanted to get safely to Carrie's.

"So what powers can we have?" I asked on the way there, still wanting to know more and wondering what it would be like to have all the powers he had already talked about.

"There're a lot. Teleportation, telekinesis, mind reading. There're Trackers, who use people's scents to locate them, and Cloakers are kind of like their rivals, since they can hide people from Trackers. They're really rare. So are Resurecters—people who have the ability to bring others back from the dead. And that power has certain limitations. Plus, it's generally not the best idea, since it can have physical consequences for the person being resurrected."

"Like what?"

"Like a nonfunctioning heart, which just kills them again. Or a part of them could be missing, like an organ. It can be dangerous if not done right. There's also compulsion, which is the power I have."

I scoffed. "It doesn't seem to work."

"It does work; it just didn't work on you."

"Why not?"

"I'm not one hundred percent positive, but my guess is that it's because you're the next Keeper. If I could compel you, I could easily ask you to give me the gem when you get it, and you'd hand it over without a fight. You must be protected somehow."

That *did* make sense, and I felt a sudden sense of relief knowing I couldn't be compelled. "What about mind reading?" I asked. "Would a person with that power be able to read my mind?"

"I guess not. But that doesn't mean Grayson can't get the gem from you. I really think you should give me the gem once you get it. I'll be able to protect it much better. I'll give it to you once you've killed Grayson and you're strong enough to protect yourself."

I didn't reply immediately, because I didn't know whether to agree or disagree. I knew he probably *was* in a better position to protect it, but I barely knew Sam. What if he had some ulterior motive for wanting it? What if he was just as bad as Grayson? If this thing really held all of our lives, I couldn't just hand it over to him.

"I'll think about it," I said, but really, I wasn't going to. I knew I couldn't give it to him, because despite his being in a better position to protect it, I couldn't trust him not to destroy it himself. I trusted myself more, and if I became stronger, I *would* be able to protect it, even from Grayson.

I hoped.

We eventually got to Carrie's. After getting out of the car, Sam came around to my side and said, "You really should start preparing soon. Call me tonight."

I nodded. "I will, but I have to settle a few things first." Mainly, I had to explain this all to Jeremy and talk to Carrie about staying at her place. Plus, I had to inform Hiro that I wouldn't be able to work for a while. Hopefully, he'd rehire me when I could start working again. "We'll start tomorrow. I'll call you," I added.

He rolled his eyes, clearly annoyed for some reason, but he left without another word, walking down the driveway. I didn't know where he was heading, especially on foot, but I didn't care. I had my own life to worry about.

CHAPTER 4

REVELATIONS

SAM

I ended up having to take the bus back to Windsor from Chatham after escorting Monique to safety. I needed to call Cole and let him know about my progress, but I waited until I was back at the motel, not wanting anyone to overhear our conversation.

He picked up on the second ring. "Hey man, what's up?"

I sat down on the couch, tired as fuck. "She's in. I told her. But I need to train her. She's vulnerable, and I can tell she's scared as hell of her dad. This isn't going to work out if I don't get her to start training soon."

"So get her to start," he said simply. "I'll look into a few Divianan training locations around Windsor to see if they're safe enough for her, but you might also want to take her to Diviano a couple of times so she can get to know the place. It'll be vital if you end up in a fight there. Oh, and she's damn good at archery," he added.

I was about to ask him how he knew that, but then I remembered he had Tracked Grayson near Monique's school and gone to warn her about him. Thanks to him, Grayson hadn't been able to get his hands on her yesterday afternoon. But Cole just *had* to be idiotic about saving her by using my voice and not his own. Him and his damn power to imitate voices perfectly . . . She'd been looking at me weirdly all day yesterday.

"Yeah, I'll keep that in mind. Have you got a hit on Cameron and Warren?" I asked, putting my foot up on the torn ottoman. Cameron was my younger brother, and Warren was my father. I didn't talk to either of them after my dad kicked me out of the house. He'd been trying to Track me down and kill me for the past six years, but I was trying to keep a step ahead of him. Cole, a friend of mine from high school, was helping me with that.

"I've tracked Cameron to England. He hasn't left the country for a week, but I don't know if he's been traveling within it. I don't know where your dad is yet, but I'll find him soon. I don't think he's near you."

"Thanks, Cole. I owe you."

"No problem, man. It's the least I could do; I know you have a lot going on. How's Maya?"

I put my head in my hands. "Better than before," I answered, glad I finally had some good news to share. "Things are starting to look up. But the condition she's in . . . she's paranoid about it negatively affecting me."

"Everything will work out, Sam. Just have hope. You said things are looking up, so be happy."

"I'll try. Thanks again, Cole."

"Don't mention it. I have to go, but I'll talk to you later."

"All right, bye."

He hung up on me, and I put my phone away, staring at the picture in front of me on the coffee table. I picked it up, rubbing a thumb over Maya's flawless face. My memory of her worn-out expression from one week ago crossed my mind. I squeezed my eyes shut, trying to drown it out, and got up, throwing the picture back on the table before I thought too much of it again. Grabbing my gun, I stuck it in my waistband and headed out the door, slamming it shut behind me.

MONIQUE

When I got back to Carrie's place, I rang the doorbell, not having a key with me, and seconds later, she opened the door. "Hiya, Monique, you're just in time for dinner. Did you get your homework done?"

"Yeah, most of it," I lied with a fake smile on my face. "I'm gonna go put my stuff upstairs, and then I'll come help you set the table."

"Okay," she responded. I walked past her, going up the stairs to put my bag in the room I was staying in and then heading toward Jeremy's. I found him sitting on the bed with the virtencia in his hand.

"I have something to tell you," we both began at the same time, and then we burst into laughter, despite the situation we were in. After we quieted down, I said, "Okay, you first."

"So I was examining this thing while you were gone when it started shining blue again. I held it up to look at it more closely, and the door slammed shut. Just like that!"

"Okay, not really that big of a surprise compared to my day," I said. When he gave me a bewildered expression, I explained everything that had happened, including finding out that Sam was his half-brother.

"I really think I should talk to Aunt Carrie," I added when I was done.

Jeremy's eyes were so wide, it honestly looked like they were about to pop out of their sockets. "Yeah, you should. God, Monique, this is awful!"

"I know. Listen. We're not going to go back home. I can't even go back to Windsor. But I don't want *you* to leave your life too. I don't want to drag you into this mess. You're not in as much danger as I am, because he doesn't want to kill you, but I'm guessing Grayson will try to contact you and ask you where I am. So I'm not going to tell you. Jana will come here tomorrow to pick you up, and you can stay with her until I figure this out."

"I don't want to leave you here by yourself!" he exclaimed.

"I won't be alone, and it'll only be temporary, just until I can figure out how to get rid of Grayson," I replied. "Sam thinks I should kill him, but I'm not ready for that. I can't kill him, despite the fact that I *know* he wants to kill me."

Jeremy's eyes grew wider, if that was even possible. "Murder? He's asking you to commit murder?"

"I'm not going to, Jere. I can't."

"But then how will you get rid of him?"

I sighed. "I'm not sure, but I'll figure it out. Don't worry about me, okay?"

"How can I not? You're in danger."

I shook my head. "I'll take care of myself, I promise. And like I said earlier, I'll talk to Carrie. We have people who can help us. You don't need to worry."

"I'll try not to," he said.

Just then, Carrie called from downstairs, "Kids, dinner's ready!"

"All right, Aunt Carrie," I responded and then turned back to Jeremy. "We'll talk about this later. C'mon, let's go down to eat. I'm *starving*."

He agreed, following me out the door and down the stairs to the kitchen. I realized when we walked in that I'd lost track of time and hadn't helped her set the table.

"Oh, I'm sorry, Aunt Carrie," I said. "I got distracted and forgot to come downstairs to help set the table."

She merely smiled at me. "It's all right; I'm used to it."

I realized what she was implying and suddenly noticed that my cousin wasn't anywhere to be seen. "Hey where's . . .?" I had forgotten her name again.

"Anissa?" Carrie filled in, and I nodded feebly. I hated it when people knew what I was thinking, but I hid my annoyance. "She's gone to a friend's birthday party."

"When is she coming back?"

"Tomorrow," she sighed, and I realized that something was going on between Carrie and her daughter.

"Is something wrong, Aunt Carrie?" I asked.

"No, nothing at all," she assured me, giving me a smile. But I could tell it was fake. "I'm fine." Changing the topic, she began, "Now, I cooked both chicken and steak, and of course I have something vegetarian for you, Monique." I smiled, and when she served me a heaping plate of pasta, I began eating in silence. So did Jeremy. In fact, we had dinner in complete silence, all of us busy with our own thoughts.

After we were done eating, we put our dishes away and went off in our own directions. Except my direction was with Aunt Carrie; I felt bad for her and wanted to know what was wrong. Plus, I really needed to talk to her about the situation I was in.

"Aunt Carrie, do you need help with anything?" I asked.

"No, I'm fine," she said a bit too quickly.

"Are you sure?" I pressed. She looked away at something, but then turned back around to face me. It wasn't really obvious, but I'd always been really perceptive, and I noticed the tears in her eyes. She was crying but smiling at the same time, trying to make it seem like everything was all right when clearly something wasn't. And I had a feeling it had something to do with Anissa.

"I'm fine," she insisted. "You don't need to take care of me, Monique. I know you've had a habit of taking care of Jeremy ever since your mother died and Kay left, but I'm your aunt. I should be taking care of you, not the other way around."

"Does age really matter, Aunt Carrie? You're my mother's cousin, and Mom would want you to be happy. She was like your older sister, and she always tried to keep you happy. As her daughter, shouldn't I step in for her?"

She smiled, holding my cheek gently like my mother used to when I was little. "You're a good child, Monique; you have good values, just like your mother. Please don't change that."

"I won't," I said quietly, trying hard not to flinch. I wasn't used to being treated nicely—at least not by family—and it was making me uncomfortable; I didn't know how to react.

When she let go of my cheek, I began talking again. "But you being Mom's cousin and me being your niece, don't you feel the need to tell me what's going on?"

She sighed, the smile gone now. "It's nothing, I—I just made a mistake." I waited for her to continue, and she did. "I gave Anissa everything she wanted. She has so much freedom, but I'm afraid that by giving her too much, I've spoiled her. Now she won't take no for an answer. Whenever I try to say no and set some ground rules, I just can't do it, because then she gets angry and I can't stand her being mad at me. I wouldn't even mind so much, but some of her friends—I'm worried she's going to end up in trouble, and I won't be able to stop her."

If Anissa really *was* hanging out with a bad group, it had to be because of her stepfather, I was sure. His death had been so recent, and despite the fact that I didn't know much about their family dynamic, I was positive Anissa's relationship with her stepdad wasn't like mine and Grayson's. But I had no idea what would make her change. I had no idea what to say that would help. But I could tell that Carrie was waiting for a response, so I quickly threw some words together and hoped for the best. "I'm sure if you talk to her calmly and explain to her why she can't have everything she wants, she might listen to you. She might just need an explanation"

"Maybe," she agreed and then smiled. "Thank you, Monique, for trying to help. It's so funny how you and your mother are so alike, even though you're not even blood related. You're exactly like her."

"She *did* raise me," I countered.

She nodded in agreement. "All right, you can go study or sleep if you want. You're probably tired after being out all day."

"Yeah," I replied. I was going to tell her what had happened but after hearing all she had to say, I couldn't do it. I didn't want to stress her out even more than she already was. I knew my issue was *huge*, and it honestly freaked me out knowing I had lived nearly eighteen years with a man who was just waiting to kill me. But I knew I would feel guilty stressing her out even more, and I didn't want to deal with it. Plus, staying with Carrie and Anissa could put them in danger if Grayson ever found out where I was. I didn't want to do that to them. I still couldn't go back to Windsor though, so I would have to stay somewhere else, on my own. I didn't really know where I could stay at the moment but I knew I could figure it out.

"I'm going to go finish the rest of my homework," I said, lowering my eyes.

She smiled and picked up a brush to start painting again. "Okay."

As soon as I was in my room, I ran to my bag, pulled out my stash of ecstasy, and popped a pill in my mouth to relieve myself of the stress I was feeling. All the day's events came crashing down on me all at once, when I had time to breathe, and it was too much. Plus, Carrie reminded me too much of my mother. She reminded me too much of Kay. She reminded me of what I wanted to forget. I couldn't stand the loss. The littlest things set me off, and I hated it. I hated myself for it. I just wanted to start over.

That was when I realized I was almost out of drugs. The pill I had taken was the second last, and I needed more. But Tyler lived in Windsor, where I couldn't go if I wanted to stay safe.

Oh fuck *safety,* I thought bitterly as the severity of my situation hit me again. I needed more drugs, and I didn't care if I died while getting them.

I pulled out my phone, my hands shaking as I dialled Tyler's number. "Hello?" he answered on the second ring.

"Are you home right now? I need more," I said in a hushed voice.

I heard the excitement in his voice when he responded. Fucking guy couldn't even get a girl. "Yes," he replied. "Come on over right now."

"'Ight, I'll be there in an hour. Bye."

I hung up, and staring at the last pill in the bag, I took it. It was the extra that I needed for what I was about to endure.

Heading into Anissa's room, I tried to find something appropriate to wear to get what I needed. She had a bunch of dresses, but they were all too short on me. I found a longer one that would go to my midthigh at least and grabbed some matching heels from her shelf, hoping they'd fit. Snatching a pair of hoops from her dresser, I headed back into my room to change. When I was done, I walked outside and opened the door to Jeremy's room, popping just my head in. "I need to head out for just a sec."

He frowned. "Is it safe?" he asked.

"Yeah," I lied. "I'll still be in Chatham. If Aunt Carrie asks, tell her I got a text from one of my friends and that it was urgent. I'll be back by midnight."

He just nodded. I walked down the stairs, grabbing a house key from the key holder beside the front door before I left the house. Once in my car, I started it, letting the radio blast as I drove off into the dark night.

SAM

After calling Maya to check up on her before she went to the hospital, I created a portal and headed to Diviano again, landing in the house I shared with my friend Griffin and his fiancée. Noticing when I walked by their bedroom that they weren't home at the moment, I headed to the backyard to work out. There was only a small section near the back of it that I could use—that and a shed. Every other square inch of it was *covered* with exotic plants.

Griffin's fiancée was seriously nuts.

I had just gone inside the shed to use the punching bag I kept there when my phone rang. When the number came up as unknown, I frowned but picked it up, knowing that nobody could track me to this location from their phone.

"Hello?"

"Hi, Sam."

Jana.

"How did you get my number?" I demanded, wondering who could have given it to her. Nobody I knew would do that, unless it was Monique. But what reason would Monique have to give Jana my number? She didn't even know Jana was Divianan.

"Let's just say it came to me in a vision."

Great. I'd completely forgotten about her damn visions.

"I just wanted to forewarn you. I know you don't want the gem to protect it, and if you dare cross the line and try to get it from Monique, I will kick your sorry ass."

I rolled my eyes. "You don't scare me, Jana."

"You really want to take your chances with me?"

I really didn't; I had no idea what she was capable of, and her visions gave her an advantage. But I didn't let her know that. "You can't do anything to me. You're powerless."

"I may not be as strong as you, Sam, but I have brains and information. I know about Cameron and your dad. I also happen to have Cameron's phone number."

She what? Was she *threatening* me? "You wouldn't tip them off."

"Oh wouldn't I?"

I was just about to respond when I spotted Cole walking out through the back door of the house.

"I don't have time for your empty threats, Jana." I hung up and left the shed, joining Cole outside.

"We have a problem," he began immediately, and I noticed he was holding papers in his hand.

Great. "Now what?" I sighed.

Without saying a word, he handed me the papers in his hand. It was information on the Diveratus Mundoversum bond.

"I hacked into Grayson's computer. He was searching that up," Cole said.

Fuck no.

My throat tightened. I swallowed hard. "He can't know about this," I hissed, looking back up at him. "Has he approached Maya yet?"

"No," Cole assured me, and I found it a little easier to breathe. "But that doesn't mean he won't. You really need to pick up your pace and kill the man."

I clenched my teeth, shoving the papers back in his hand. "I should have *already* killed him. I shouldn't have waited for Monique. I should have already done it, when you found him—"

"Hey," Cole said, placing a hand on my shuddering shoulder. "Sam, you *know* the risk you'd be taking by doing that. You're not at your best, not with—"

He cut off, looking over the fence at the neighbour's house. Lowering his voice, he continued, "Not with Maya being ill. You can't risk your life like that, especially when it's tied to hers."

"Then *you* help me."

He shook his head. "You know it's not the same. You need *Monique*. If trained right, she'll have enough power to take him down in a second. She's your only hope."

Fucking hell! With shaking hands, I turned around, pacing around the backyard with my hands in my hair. I was stupid not to have started training Monique immediately, when she was still over at the motel. Now Grayson was not only one step closer to killing her, but he was going to kill me too. And not just me, he was going to kill Maya. I couldn't let him do that. I wouldn't.

CHAPTER 5

X

MONIQUE

I came home stumbling, taking swigs from the liquor bottle in my hand. I don't know how I managed to get myself back to Carrie's house without crashing my car, but I didn't really care; I was too focused on the fact that all the lights in the house were off and everyone must have gone to sleep, which meant I had no way of getting inside.

"Ugh," I groaned, staggering toward the front door. I hastily tried the doorknob, and when it didn't turn, I sighed, my head spinning like crazy. To stop myself from falling, I leaned my forehead against the front door, wondering how the hell I was going to get back in.

"*Shit*," I said, taking another drink from my bottle. I was about to walk back to my car to sleep in there when I shoved my hand in my jacket pocket and felt a key. With a start, I remembered having taken a house key before I left and giggled, shoving it into the keyhole. Opening the lock was a struggle since I was so God-damn dizzy, but I still somehow managed to get inside before the cold could numb me even more than it already had.

Smiling widely, I gently closed the door behind me, trying not to make any noise. But since I didn't have enough sense to take off my heels before climbing the stairs, they made a clattering noise as I went up.

When I reached the top of the staircase, Jeremy came out of his room with dishevelled hair. Obviously I'd woken him up.

"Hey JereBear!" I whispered a bit too loudly.

"Monique, are you drunk?" he asked, raising an eyebrow. When I didn't reply, too focused on trying to get my damn heels off, he continued, "And why are you dressed like a freaking hooker? Did you go out?"

"Mhmm," I replied vaguely and then yawned, stretching my arms out as I did so. Losing my balance, I nearly fell back down the stairs, but Jeremy caught me just in time and held me up. I grinned up at him. "Thanks, man," I said and patted his shoulder gently. "Well, I'm tired. I'm gonna go to sleep, and so should you. Don't want to wake up Aunt Carrie."

He looked worried. "Let me help you into your room."

I laughed. "Jeremy, I'm fine."

"Where did you even go?"

I had enough sense left to lie. "Clubbing."

His forehead creased. "Alone?" I nodded, and he sighed. "And you're drunk. You do realize you could have gotten into a car accident?"

"Well, I didn't. Jere, I'm fine, just tired. I just need sleep."

He hesitated before letting me go and heading back inside his room. I stopped struggling with the heels, deciding to take them off once I got into my room so I could sit down to do it. I slammed the door shut behind me, too preoccupied with not tripping to give a damn about the noise I was making. Oh, how I hated wearing heels . . .

When I turned around, Sam was standing in front of me. "Holy fucking shit!" I screamed, tripping and nearly falling to the ground. But before I could hit the floor, he steadied me and then shoved me against the door. Covering my mouth with his hand, he leaned over me to hold the door shut, that stupid band still on his wrist. I was about to bite his hand so that he'd let go of me and I could yell at him when I felt the door opening behind me. He immediately pushed it shut again, his body twice as close as it had been before.

I felt an unfamiliar buzzing between us.

What the fuck was going on?

"Monique, is everything all right?" Aunt Carrie asked from the other side of the door. My eyes widened as I realized that she'd probably heard me cussing, but I spoke calmly when Sam uncovered my mouth.

"Yeah, it was just a bug. Startled me. I killed it," I lied.

"Okay then," she said, sounding unsure. "Good night."

I heard her leaving and was about to start screaming at Sam when he covered my mouth again. He leaned in closer to me, and I widened my eyes, not used to being so close to anyone other than Tyler. It felt so fucking different. "She's still here," he whispered in my ear, so quietly that I could barely hear him.

God, I needed another drink. But I couldn't move, so I focused on the ecstasy running through my veins instead, loving the funny tingling crossing all over my body.

He uncovered my mouth after a second, and I took another drink from my bottle before setting it down on top of the cabinet beside me. Then I turned to him. "What the hell are you doing in my room in the middle of the night?" I demanded, but I was still kind of ditzy, so I played with a strand of thread at the end of my scarf as I talked. "Do you know how creepy that is? It's freaking stalker-like! Unless," I added, smiling, "it's because you want me, isn't it?" I giggled quietly, winking at him.

He gave me a hollow laugh, shaking his head. "You do realize you make absolutely no sense, right?" I frowned, glaring at him through my lashes. He looked away. "Anyways, sorry to ruin your little fantasy, but that's not why I'm here."

"Then why *are* you here?"

"We need to start planning Grayson's death," he answered.

I groaned, stomping my foot on the ground like a little girl. "*Oh*, but why *now*?" I whined. "I'm dead tired, and I wanna go to bed."

"Does it look like I care?" he demanded. His hands were in his pockets, and he glared at me on an angle. "We need to plan his death, and *you* need to train."

"You just needed an excuse to come into my room. You know you don't have to lie." I leaned toward him, my body tingling all over. "I'll give you anything you want," I whispered in his ear.

When I pulled back, grinning, I saw that his eyes were turning a bright crimson. Shock immediately filled me. "Whoa, your eyes just turned red! What the hell?"

"Our eyes change colour depending on our mood," he said through gritted teeth. "Red means anger."

"Well, why are you angry?" I asked, slightly dizzy. I needed to sit down, but he was blocking my way to the bed.

He leaned in closer to me. "Why do you *think*?"

I shrank back against the door, looking into his brooding eyes as they slowly turned back to grey. They were penetrating, as if they could see right through me. But in that moment, I enjoyed it. I *wanted* him to know that I felt the buzzing between us getting stronger, especially everywhere he was touching me. And as I stared into his eyes, I felt an even stronger pull toward him.

I wanted to kiss him. Right now.

I leaned forward, grinning with anticipation. Placing my hand on his shoulder, I ignored his confused expression as I stood up on my tiptoes. It was when I was inches away from his face, tilting my head to the side, that he realized what I was doing.

"What the hell?" he demanded, shoving me off. My back hit the door with a thud that sent sharp pain up my spine. I pouted. "I have a girlfriend, and could you just be serious for *one* God-damn second? Grayson is one step closer to killing you."

"Yeah, but I'm wasted."

"Do you not care at all?"

To be honest, I really didn't. I was too high to care, but I couldn't tell him that. So instead I said, "Just get out. I want to sleep."

He narrowed his eyes at me in obvious frustration, but to my surprise, he listened, heading toward the open window. Seriously? Was this dude really going to *Twilight* me? Gaping in disbelief, I stopped him in his tracks. "Oh *please*, stop tryna show off and go use the God-damned stairs."

He turned around to face me. "Or what?" he taunted, making a move toward me.

"Or I'll kick your ass." He didn't reply but just rolled his eyes, opening the bedroom door. He headed out and down the stairs, and I followed, trying not to make any noise.

After Sam left, I locked the front door and made the journey upstairs again, trying not to make any noise.

As soon as I made it back to my room, I closed the door and locked it, getting out of the stupid clothes I was dressed in and slipping into something more comfortable. Jeremy was right; I *was* dressed like a hooker. But I guess doing what I did to get my drugs did make me a harlot. Still it wasn't like I *liked* doing it. I hated it, but I didn't have any other way to get my ex. Tyler wouldn't take my money, just because he couldn't get a girl. Then again, I couldn't really blame him; he was as ugly as shit.

Grabbing my half-empty bottle of Scotch, I shoved it in my bag to save for another night and then collapsed on my bed, falling asleep immediately.

~

I woke up around twelve the next day, my head throbbing from a killer hangover. I groaned, turning onto my stomach and shoving my head under my pillow, not wanting to get up. But when the previous day's events came floating back into my mind, I suddenly became completely alert.

I needed to talk to Jana about what happened.

Sighing and trying to ignore the ache in my head, I grabbed my phone from my nightstand and dialled her number.

She answered on the second ring. "Hey, what's up?"

"I have a lot to tell you," I said and then recited my story.

Her reaction was a *lot* different from Jeremy's.

"Holy crap man, that's so neat!" she exclaimed through the phone. I winced, pulling the phone slightly away from my ear. "You could like completely run the world with your power! But it really sucks about your dad."

I was a little surprised that she believed my story so easily; Jana wasn't the type to take shit from others and believe everything she heard, not even from me. But I guessed she knew that I wouldn't make something like this up. I *couldn't* make anything like this up, even if I tried, so it made sense for her to believe me.

I sighed. "Yeah, I know."

"Plus, I can't believe Sam thinks you should kill him! I'm fairly certain you could make do with just protecting yourself somehow, you know, like building your strength and learning self-defence. And you're seriously going to be living away from Windsor? I know you're in danger, but you'd be safe at my place."

"I just don't want to take any chances," I explained. "But I was wondering if Jeremy could stay with you. It'll only be temporary."

"Yeah, it's no problem."

"Great. I'm not going to come back to Windsor at all, though, so I was wondering if you could pick him up and take him back to your place. I'll text you the address."

"Sure, I'll leave right now. See you in an hour."

"Bye." I ended the call and took a shower before I went downstairs to find Carrie painting the living room.

"Aunt Carrie," I began, "we're going to be leaving in an hour. Thanks for letting us stay the night."

"Not a problem. You're always welcome here. Take some leftovers with you when you leave, okay?"

"Okay," I said.

Jeremy was eating some of those leftovers at the dining table. I sat down beside him. In a hushed voice, I said, "Jana's going to be here in half an hour to pick you up."

"What about you?" he asked. "Have you found a place to stay?"

"I'll be fine. Don't worry about me, okay?" He nodded, and I got up to grab my stuff from upstairs. I ruffled his hair as I left, and when he patted it back down into place, I grinned.

I had just texted Jana Carrie's address and told her to text me when she got here when I remembered Sam. He'd been here last night. Why? I tried to remember our conversation but couldn't. Still, I decided to call him. The sooner I could start training, the better.

"Hello?" he said when he picked up on the third ring.

"Hey, it's Monique."

"Finally decided to call me, did you?" he said, and I could hear the annoyance oozing out of his voice.

"I was sleeping," I muttered.

"How could you sleep knowing that Grayson's one step closer to killing you?"

"He's what? How do you know that?" I demanded, even more freaked out than before. He'd told me that last night? How had I *not* remembered that? Even if I *was* high and drunk, I should have remembered something that serious.

"One of my friends hacked his computer and figured out that Grayson knows how to get around the protection that keeps you alive."

I still couldn't believe I had forgotten.

"When do you want to train?" he demanded.

I checked the time. It was almost one. "How about two o'clock?" I still needed to get myself and Jeremy out of Carrie's house as well as find a place to stay.

"Okay. Where should I meet you?"

"At the library from yesterday," I said. He hung up after a clipped, "Okay, bye."

Putting away my phone, I grabbed my bag and was about to head down to see if Jana was here when I remembered the virtencias Aunt Carrie kept stashed in her walls.

I knew it wasn't right to take Carrie's stuff, but I figured a virtencia would help me out. I would probably need access to Diviano, right? And I had no idea if Sam had an extra one he'd be willing to give. So supressing my guilt, I popped open the hole in the closet and grabbed the virtencia from the box inside.

After putting the drywall back, I headed down the stairs just as I saw Jana's car pull up in the driveway. I went out to meet her, closing the door behind me. "Hey," I greeted her, giving her a hug as she approached me.

"I have to tell you something," she said the moment she pulled away.

Oh, God. Now what?

"What is it?" I asked, biting my lip.

"Well, it has to do with the whole Diviano thing you were talking about earlier." She paused. I waited a little impatiently for her to continue, and finally she did, looking me in the eye. "Okay, the thing is, I've actually known about Diviano for a while now."

What the actual fuck?

"My parents told me about it when I was pretty young, because they wanted me to be able to easily adapt to everything. The thing was they told me not to tell anyone about it so I didn't, but I figured I could tell you now since, well, you *are* the Keeper. And I kind of found out last night that you were Keeper too," she added, fidgeting with her hands. "I sorta have visions that tell me this kind of stuff. I saw you and Sam together, while he was explaining stuff to you. I just didn't want to be the one to bring it up, because I wasn't sure if you wanted to talk about it with me. So I just waited for your call."

"So you're a part of this world too?" I asked for clarification, still not used to using the new terminology. She nodded. "And you have visions?"

Again, she nodded. "Of the future and past, yes," she said.

"How come you don't have weird eyes, though? How come I don't? And what about Jeremy?"

She laughed. "Our eyes aren't always weird colours. They depend on our mood. I just started wearing contacts at the age of five, which is when they start changing colour. My parents wear contacts too. And don't you remember telling me how Jeremy needed glasses at a really young age but was forced to wear contacts instead?"

The moment she mentioned it, I remembered how confused I'd been at the time. It wasn't normal for a doctor to recommend contacts for a kid at the age of five.

"What about me?"

"Your eyes have never changed colour. It's because you're Keeper. Keepers' eyes never change colour so that they'll be protected from humans if they're born and raised on Earth. But you can force your eyes to change colour to blend in amongst Divianans." She paused as I took all this in. "I'm really sorry I didn't tell you."

"No, it's totally understandable," I said. "I'm just a little surprised. I mean, how often do you come across a whole new world with people who have freak powers and then find out your best friend is part of it as well?"

"Not often." She grinned, but she lost her smile pretty quickly. "There's more," she admitted.

What more could she possibly have to say? I waited again, and she continued, "I kinda sorta know Sam."

"How?" I asked.

She bit her lip, hesitating before finally answering, "He's my ex."

I swear to God, my jaw literally dropped. She nodded, giving me a sheepish smile. "I didn't tell you since it all happened and finished so quickly, and I didn't really think it was a big enough deal to talk about. Plus we kind of weren't talking at the time. We had that fight, with you doing, um, ex and all."

I remembered, though I didn't want to. My heart sank, and I changed the topic. "But why would you be with someone who's such a jerk?"

She made a face at me, shuffling her weight to her other leg. "I met him at a party, and honestly, Monique, all I was thinking about when he asked me out was how ridiculously hot he was. I was sixteen and I barely knew him, but I didn't care about anything else so I just went for it. It only lasted a week. When we went to my friend's birthday party, I realized I was a rebound girl. He'd dated my friend beforehand, and when she dumped him, he looked for someone to distract him. I was that someone."

"A friend from Diviano?" I asked.

She shook her head. "No, she's human. Her name's Maya. She used to live in Rochester, but I don't know where she is now; I haven't talked to her in a while. I hope she's okay." Jana frowned.

"What do mean, you hope she's okay?" I inquired, befuddled. "What's wrong with her?"

"She was sick. She was at the hospital all the time. I think she had some immune system problem or something, but I'm not sure. I lost contact with her. She moved away so suddenly and I didn't even have her email, let alone anything else. So there's no way I can contact her again."

"Couldn't you ask Sam for her number?"

She gave me a clipped laugh. "Monique, you have no idea how much he resents me. That guy will run across the city stark naked before doing me a favour."

"Why does he hate you?"

"I bitched out at him for treating me like a rebound girl, which made my friend—his old ex—pissed at him."

"That's a stupid reason to hate someone."

She smiled at me. "Yeah, I know. You're okay with this though, right? The whole me dating Sam and not telling you thing?"

"Yeah," I replied. "It's all good."

She smiled. "So where's Jeremy?"

"Upstairs. I'll go get him," I said and then headed back inside just as Jeremy walked down the stairs. "Come on," I urged. "She's waiting for you."

"Sorry," he said as he slipped on his shoes and coat and followed me outside. "Hi Jana."

"Hey Jere," she replied, smiling at him. "Okay, we should get going." She gave me a hug. "I'm really going to miss you."

"I'll miss you too, but I'll call you guys every day. And this is only temporary, remember that," I reminded them as I hugged Jeremy.

"Stay safe," he said.

"I will. I promise."

SAM

It was just after one in the afternoon and I was at my motel, getting ready to go train Monique, when my cell phone rang. Preoccupied with grabbing a change of clothes out of the drawer, I picked it up without checking Caller ID.

"Hello?"

"I'm coming home, Sam," she announced.

A wave of contentment flooded over me when I heard her voice.

And then I realized what she'd just said.

I dropped the clothes in my hand on the ground in surprise. "Really?" I whispered, breathlessly. She was coming home? Did that mean everything was okay now?

"Yes, I'm leaving LA soon. My flight will arrive in Detroit around midnight tonight. Would you be able to pick me up from the airport?"

"Of course," I replied. "Maya, I'm so happy. Is—is it fixed?"

"It's fixed, Sam," she assured me, her voice barely above a whisper. But I could still hear the smile in her words as she spoke. "I'm finally cured."

It was suddenly like I could breathe again.

I sat down on the edge of the bed, laughing with overwhelming gratitude. "Maya, I can't wait to see you."

"I know, Sam. But we should get off. I've got a plane to catch, and you still have to go to work, remember? Just because I'm okay now doesn't mean you don't have a living to make."

I'd cancelled my shift today, but she was right. I still had a living to make, only now, I could finally go to school. I could do anything I wanted to do without anything getting in the way. As long as Cole kept track of Warren and Cameron, I was free.

And now that Maya was cured, I didn't need the gem anymore, which meant that I didn't have to worry about dealing with Monique anymore either. I could leave Windsor with Maya, and we would finally be happy.

MONIQUE

It didn't take me long to find a motel to stay in, hoping this whole thing wouldn't take long so they wouldn't charge me like crazy. After checking in, I went to go meet Sam at the library. When he didn't show up by two o'clock, I decided to call him. He didn't pick up.

"Are you fucking kidding me?" I cussed. Fidgeting in impatience and irritation, knowing I needed to learn how to protect myself, I decided to call him again. When he still didn't pick up, my frustration rose, and I called a third time. I ended up calling him seven times before he finally picked up.

"What do you want?" he demanded.

"Um, *to train*," I reminded him.

"I can't train you anymore."

The words just hung there for a second. I became immensely confused as well as scared. What the hell had changed within the past hour and a half to make him not want to train me anymore? More importantly, if he wasn't going to train me, who would?

"Why not?"

"I just can't. Find somebody else to train you. Don't call me again."

With that, he hung up, leaving me listening to the dial tone, wondering how the hell I was supposed to survive now.

CHAPTER 6

THE GEMSTONE

SAM

I woke up the next day to the sound of birds chirping and a gentle, warm breeze drifting in through the open window. Blinking my eyes open to bright daylight seeping into the hotel room, I turned onto my side to look at Maya sleeping beside me.

I smiled when I saw her. She had taken her wig off when we'd gone to sleep last night, but she looked just as striking without it. Her flawless skin was so pale but so beautiful. I caressed her cheek gently, unable to remember the last time I'd felt this relaxed, this carefree.

I was so glad I'd left Windsor when I did. I was so glad that I'd convinced her to stay where she was, that I could come to her. I was so glad I was able to relax. I was glad I could let everything go. I was finally done fighting.

I got up quietly, careful not to wake Maya up, knowing she still needed to rest and recover from her last treatment. Heading out to the balcony, I quietly ordered room service, asking them to bring up some food in an hour. After hanging up, I leaned on the rail and stared down at the view. People and cars swarmed through the streets below me, buzzing back and forth as they carried on with their busy lives. I saw businessmen on cell phones and a cameraman filming something as he walked down the street. Out in the distance, mountains lined the hazy blue skyline, and palm trees swayed with the breeze.

I fucking loved LA.

I also loved the warm feel of Maya's arms around my waist as she came up behind me. I smiled, turning around to face her. She was wearing a gigantic grin on her face as she leaned up and kissed me. I kissed her back. I'd missed the soft touch of her lips against mine.

She pulled away all too soon and quietly murmured, "Happy birthday."

MONIQUE

Sam was a total ass.

After he ditched me to fend for myself—breaking his promise to train me—I ended up having to call Jana back to Chatham, a little bit hysterical and not sure what to do. She immediately agreed to get a professional trainer to help me build my strength, but because Jana believed she could protect me just fine at her house, I ended up going back Windsor after all.

I spent all day cooped up in Jana's house, protected by a security system, and my presence there led her to convincing her mom to get extra security. Her mom got three new surveillance cameras installed the same day I decided to move in and hired a personal bodyguard for me, making me glad her parents were in on all this Diviano stuff. Jana's mom was really sweet and understanding about my situation, and I was really grateful for that. But she was rarely home for her daughter. Neither was Jana's dad. They both lived busy lives; Jana's dad was the mayor, and her mom worked as a TV reporter, so she travelled a lot. I was just lucky she was still home when Jana brought me to her house; she was leaving in an hour to head out to Winnipeg.

On the bright side, Jana was crazy rich. Her house was probably the biggest I'd ever been inside, and it was incredibly elegant. The guestroom I was staying in had its own washroom and walk-in closet, which was twice the size of mine back home. It had ready-made shelves inside, designed for specific wear. There were shoe holders, plastic necks to hang scarves on, and plastic hands for gloves. The room itself was probably the size of a normal master bedroom, with pot lights in the concave ceiling. The queen-size bed sat in front of the washroom, which contained a four-by-four standing shower. When you pressed the right buttons, it released steam and mist. There was also a single-seater Jacuzzi in there, which Jana told me they'd added "just because."

So yeah, when I woke up that day, I found myself in a pleasant environment, and the female—as I'd requested—bodyguard that stood outside my room made me feel safer than I had in days. The clock sitting on the mahogany nightstand beside me told me it was nearly twelve.

At least leaving my life behind meant I could sleep in on a school day.

I yawned, stretching in my bed, feeling like royalty. Throwing the covers off, I went into the washroom and brushed my teeth. I then took a shower and changed into some of Jana's clothes, since I wasn't going to go back for mine. That unfortunately left me in jeans, but since I wasn't going anywhere and wouldn't be seen by any guy besides Jeremy, I didn't mind.

It was when I was walking out of the grand washroom that the weirdest thing happened. The moment I opened the door to the room, I was filled with a sudden pain in my chest, right where my heart was. It was excruciating. I felt like my heart was being pinched, but it wasn't just my chest that was hurting. So were my left shoulder, arm, and hand. My wrist especially was burning, and I stared at the mark there, the one I had always assumed was a birthmark. It had always been a solid black dot, but the moment the pinching at my heart worsened, it morphed, making the pain in my wrist even worse. I cried out, dropping down to my knees as my legs gave out. My immediate thought was that Grayson had used some kind of magic to hurt me from wherever he was. But the moment the security guard barged in, and the moment I saw what the dot was morphing into, I realized I was wrong.

The black dot had changed to form a wicked design of intricate dark blue lines that extended out of the central image of a stone.

The gemstone.

The moment I realized what was going on, the pain stopped and the gemstone started liquefying from the center of the tattoo, recreating the small blue image on my wrist, including the lines that surrounded it. Only the lines were now black vines, sharp and twisted.

The gemstone was now floating in the air, waiting for me to reach out and grab it. But I was too shocked to. I'd known that I would be getting this stone since Saturday, but I hadn't given it another thought since. So it wasn't like I had any expectations. That was why seeing it stupefied me. I had no idea what to do. I just kept staring at it, admiring its beauty. The blue, diamond-shaped gemstone sparkled in the sunlight and gave out some light of its own. It was rotating in front of me, creating rainbows on the walls around me, giving the room an eerie but beautiful glow.

But it was so small. Just by looking at it, I could tell it would easily fit it into the palm of my hand. How could something this tiny be so powerful? How could this *tiny* little thing hold the lives of everyone on a whole damned planet? How was that even possible?

I was so stunned and mystified by this little thing in front of me that I didn't even notice that the bodyguard was inches away from me until I saw her reaching for the gem. Suddenly feeling protective of this thing, I was about to grab it, but before I could, she had slipped her hands through the vines and wrapped her hands around the gem.

The vines immediately tightened around her wrist, the thorns puncturing her skin. She screamed in pain but didn't let go. I watched in horror, wondering if that would happen to me too, as the vines tightened even further. Blood was streaming down her arm, and her hand was turning blue, forcing her to let go. The moment she did, the vines loosened up, her blood still dripping off the little thorns. She fell back on the ground, her eyes going wide as I saw the skin of her wrist turning black. Whatever had caused it to do that was clearly spreading, as soon, the rest of her body turned black as well. The next thing I knew, her chest had stopped moving, and I realized with a shock that she was dead.

It was the first time I had seen someone die in front of me, and it left my heart pounding loudly in my ears and my body shaking uncontrollably. I could hardly comprehend what had just happened. Had it killed her because she tried to steal the gem?

I didn't have time to think about all of this. I was now unprotected. Breathing hard, afraid that somebody would barge into the house and attack me any second now, I grabbed the gem—which was floating again—not wondering for a split second whether the vines would kill me too. Fortunately, the moment I grabbed the gem, the vines disappeared. I was left feeling the surprising warmth of the gem in my hand and an overwhelming feeling of gratification—a feeling of fullness. Despite the danger I was in, I suddenly found it easier to breathe.

I shoved the gem in my pocket and quickly called Jana. I knew she was in class, but she'd told me last night that I could call her anytime. She didn't pick up when I called her, but about a minute of freaking out later, she called me back. She must have had to step out of class to talk to me.

"Hey, is something wrong?" she asked.

"The bodyguard's dead," I said. "The gem appeared in front of me and she was there. She tried to grab it, but it killed her somehow."

"Don't move. I'm coming home right now." She immediately hung up on me, leaving me waiting in anticipation for a good ten minutes. And in those ten minutes, I got another scare as the body of the woman in front of me disintegrated into ashes.

My heart leaped up into my throat. "What the fuck?" I cried. Where did her damn body go? What just happened?

I heard the front door opening, and forgetting about the body, I poked my head into the hall to see Jana coming up the stairs. Her eyes were wide. Glancing into the guest room, she asked, "Did the body already disappear?"

"Yeah, what the hell was that?"

"That's what happens when we die. It's normal. But only when it's a supernatural cause. That includes a Divianan killing another Divianan. If we die naturally or are killed by a human, then our bodies remain." Seeing my obvious confusion, she explained, "Mom hired a Divianan because she didn't want humans asking questions if anything happened." She pulled out her phone. "But I guess that backfired—she must have wanted the gem for herself. Okay, I know the company Mom spoke to. I'll get you another bodyguard, a human this time. It'll probably take a while for her to get here, though, so I'll stay with you until she does."

I didn't object, since I didn't have any other protection and I still didn't know how to fight. Cussing Sam again, I left Jana alone as she made the call and pulled out the gem, realizing that from this moment on, I would constantly be in danger protecting this thing. Seeing how that bodyguard had gone for it made me realize just how much people wanted it, and if they found out I had it, they would immediately start hunting me down. Unfortunately, the only physical skills I had were in archery, and that wasn't going to do me a whole lot of good since I'd only practiced shooting still targets. And chances were that the people attacking me weren't going to stand still for my convenience. I mean, I'd hit a moving target once, but I was sure that was just luck.

Basically, I was screwed. I definitely needed to train.

So I did. After getting me a human bodyguard, Jana went back to school, but when she came home, she hired a personal trainer to come help me every single day. Jana also decided to join me in order to help protect me. Jeremy asked to join too, and although I didn't want him getting caught in the middle of this, Jana convinced me that he'd be better off honing his strength as well.

"Look, I don't want to worry you," she said that same night. "But if Grayson finds out you're cooped up here, and if he gets in, if he hurts Jeremy to get to you, it'll just be better if he can defend himself. You're not encouraging him to join the danger by allowing this; you're saving his life."

She was right, though I didn't want to think about Jeremy getting hurt. But I had to take precautions; I had to keep my mind open to possible dangers, despite how much it sucked.

That realization wasn't the only thing that sucked that day. The text message I received from Nathan the second I finished eating a tasteless dinner also had me sighing.

Did you skip school again?

I simply replied, *I'm sick.*

I had just finished slipping into my PJs when he texted me again. *I'm coming over.*

Groaning because I really wanted to sleep, I texted back, *Don't. I'm really not feeling well.* When he agreed, I headed out of the washroom and went downstairs to say goodnight to Jana and Jeremy with my new female bodyguard following me. I found them in the living room, sitting side by side on her ginormous white leather couch, doing homework.

I sighed. I totally forgot about school.

I walked in, immediately feeling minute in comparison to the room, which had a soaring ceiling and a crystal chandelier hanging high above us. There was a fireplace against one wall with brownish bricks surrounding it and a ledge beneath it that had pictures placed on it. Up above the fireplace was a flatscreen TV, which had been left on idly to create some background noise.

I sat down beside Jana and asked, "What did I miss at school today?" She took her English binder out of her bag for me, and I flipped through it to find her notes on *The Great Gatsby*. But I got bored fairly quickly and gave the binder back to her. I then addressed the issue that was really on my mind. "Jana, I'm never going to be able to fight. I'm pretty much dead already."

She put her books to the side and turned to me. "Don't think like that. Look, this trainer is amazing. She'll teach us everything we need to know to get stronger and how to defend ourselves. Plus, you're lucky, since being Keeper gives you all that extra strength."

My jaw dropped. "What?"

She frowned. "Sam didn't tell you?" I shook my head. "You're born naturally stronger than the rest of us. It's protection. And you'll pick up everything really quickly. Trust me, for you, this is going to be a breeze."

It turned out that building my strength wasn't a *breeze* like Jana had assured me, but it *was* easier than I'd expected it to be. The trainer—who was a human—was ridiculously surprised at how much cardio and weight training I could keep up with. I mean, it wasn't like I could lift a thousand pounds or run ten miles without stopping, but I definitely had more endurance than somebody with my level of physical activity should have had. And I could carry much more than she had estimated by looking at my physique.

The trainer was surprised to find that Jana and Jeremy were stronger than they looked too—since they were stronger than humans—but not as surprised as she was with me.

Within a week, she'd built my endurance and my strength, teaching me some blocking techniques as well, but I still felt like it wasn't enough. Having been on the receiving end of Grayson's abuse, I knew his strength, and I felt as if the skills I had would only be enough to fight a random passerby, not him. Not Grayson.

Unfortunately, I was proved right.

SAM

I had a week of bliss with Maya in LA. All we did throughout that week was lie in bed lazily while she rested, enjoying the view of the city from our balcony. We ordered a crazy amount of food and enjoyed every bite, letting the credit card bills rack up. I'd pay it off with the money I was no longer putting toward Maya's treatments.

It felt good to let loose.

But like all good things, our time in heaven didn't last very long.

I woke up Friday morning to find Maya vomiting in the toilet in the washroom of the hotel room. The air around me thickened, and I tried to convince myself that all this had to be the result of food poisoning as I rushed to her side, but it was useless. "Maya," I called as I knelt down beside her, wrapping an arm around her shoulders as she finished vomiting.

"I'm okay," she assured me, her voice cracking. She was shaking.

"You're not okay," I said, feeling angry, annoyed, and worried at the same time. Was she honestly sick again? Had the doctors not checked her properly? What the hell was wrong with them?

I helped her stand up, and it was then that I noticed how weak she was. Her legs were shaking, and despite her protests, I wouldn't let her go as she washed her mouth out and brushed her teeth. I didn't trust that her legs wouldn't give out on her.

Oh God. Please let it be a stomach bug.

She pulled away from the sink and closed her eyes, looking dizzy. "Sam, you can let go of me," she sighed, turning to reach for the face towel. I handed it to her, but instead of letting go, I felt her forehead.

"Your temperature's running really high."

"It's probably just a bug," she insisted, pulling the towel away from her face.

It was then that I saw the streak of red on the towel. I looked back at Maya, my throat tightening. She had a nosebleed.

This was all too familiar.

With my eyes stinging, I whispered, "Maya, open your eyes." She obeyed. When her eyes landed on the towel, they widened. She touched her still-bleeding nose gently, and her forehead creased. Her eyes became watery. "It's not a bug." She swallowed, and a sob escaped from her mouth. My heart dropped low in my stomach, and I tried hard to keep my tears down as I spoke to her. "We're going back to the hospital. I'm going to talk to that idiotic doctor of yours, and you're going to get yourself tested again."

She continued crying, looking down at her feet. I kissed her on the forehead.

"We don't have the money."

"I'll *get* the money. Don't stress about that. We just need you healthy."

She finally agreed, and after grabbing her something to eat from the hotel, we called a taxi and went to the hospital she was getting treated at. Once we got to the floor she used to stay on, we asked the lady at the front desk to take us to her doctor.

"I'm sorry, but he left for vacation earlier this week, and his replacement is with another patient right now."

My hands shook. "I don't care who he's with," I retorted as Maya squeaked beside me, "We'll wait." I ignored her, not wanting to take any chances with her health, and continued, "You will get us to the doctor, and you will do it *now*." I could tell she was about to object, so I ended up using my compulsion power. I didn't care if I would lose it as a consequence. Maya needed to see a doctor.

The lady finally complied and led us to the doctor's office. She proceeded to go find him, and finally, after fifteen aggravating minutes, he came in. He was clearly annoyed, but I didn't give a damn about his mood. I just wanted him to run tests on Maya that instant, and I used compulsion when I needed it.

By the end of the day, Maya's tests were all done, and they had finished analyzing the information. We were called back into his office near six that night.

"I don't know how your doctor could tell you that you were cured," he said bluntly. "If anything, your disease has gotten worse within the past week. Even if this were a relapse, it could never have gotten this bad this quickly. You need to start treatment as soon as possible, ideally now."

Bullshit. It was absolutely total bullshit. How could the doctor misdiagnose her like that? Was he even qualified to call himself a doctor? If the disease was so bad, how had he missed so many signs when he last ran tests on her? It didn't make any sense—

Unless he was bribed to lie. It had seemed too good to be true when Maya first told me she was cured. Maybe because it was. We'd spent nearly four years trying to pay for her treatments, and not once had she been fully cured, so what were the chances of her becoming cured now? Obviously, her doctor had to be bribed. There was no way he could make that big of a mistake when diagnosing her, especially since he had such a prestigious reputation within the hospital.

And who else would bribe him but Grayson? He clearly wanted to get rid of me, and what better way to do that than to send me halfway across the continent to relax with my girlfriend while he dealt with things back in Windsor, like finding out how to get rid of the Keeper's protection? Grayson must have known that I would be training Monique to kill him so I could take the gem, and he clearly needed me out of the way so that he'd have more time to find a way around her protection.

But if Grayson had bribed Maya's doctor, he must have known she was sick.

How had he known?

I needed to find out. I needed answers, answers I would only get in Windsor. I needed to go back to Plan A and get the gem, meaning I would have to deal with Monique again. I didn't want to, but there was no other way.

I had to go back to Windsor. I had no choice.

MONIQUE

I had just finished showering after another day of training when I heard Jeremy cussing from the living room. Ignoring my bodyguard, I rushed down the stairs to find him sitting in front of the TV. His eyes were wide, glued to the screen, his hands held to his mouth in shock.

Wondering what the hell was going on, I looked away from him and focused at the screen in front of me.

A woman was giving a local news report on five teenagers who been found dead in the river. Apparently, one kid had been going missing per day for the past week, and they had all just turned up dead in the Detroit River, with their wrists slit and their bodies drained of blood. Not only that, but their organs had been removed from their bodies, which were then stitched up.

"Of the five kids, four of them were local," the woman said. She then proceeded to list their names.

"This is horrible," Jeremy muttered, looking disgusted.

I wasn't listening to him. A knife had pierced my heart when she listed off the last two names.

Donna Wu and Mason Lloyd.

Donna and Mason were dead?

Before I had time to fully process everything, my phone buzzed in my hand. I looked down to notice a text from an unknown number that sent a chill up my spine.

I know you're hiding. Come meet me, or you're going to find another one of your friends dead.

Grayson.

This *had* to be him.

I *had* to kill him.

This wasn't a matter of protecting myself anymore. He'd killed two people I actually cared about, and he was willing to kill more. Jana and Jeremy were in danger. I *had* to go meet him, despite the fact that I wasn't prepared at all to fight him. I didn't have a choice.

"Monique, I don't like the look in your eyes," Jeremy said, but I ignored him and began walking toward the garage door. "Where are you going?"

"I need to make a phone call," I muttered. I knew he'd try to stop me if he knew the truth. Unfortunately, my bodyguard followed me out. Already shaking, I turned to her and said, "Go back inside. I'm not going anywhere. I just need to make a call."

"I'm being paid to stand right by your side," she replied.

"You want money?" I demanded. I reached into my pocket and got out my wallet, thrusting a twenty in her hand. "Here. Now leave."

"I don't take bribes, ma'am."

Gritting my teeth, I used the only battle skills I had and punched her in the face before she saw it coming. It didn't do much, only swayed her a little, but it gave me enough time to open the garage, run to my car, and hop in. She reached my door an instant later, but I just locked it and put the car in reverse, heading out of the driveway. I saw Jana coming out of the house, but I ignored her and sped off into the snowy night before they could follow me.

It was when I was alone that I let the events of that night run through my mind, amplifying my rage and making my hands shake.

How *dare* Grayson kill my friends? How *dare* he end *their* lives to get to me, to get to the gem? How *dare* he use them as a lure to get me out of the house? Was he really that selfish? Was he really that cruel? Killing others to get power . . . it was ridiculous. It was *insane*. He was a monster.

No. A monster was an understatement. He was worse, much worse. Monsters had no reason to kill, but Grayson thought did. He had selfish reasons, and he was willing to kill innocent people to get to me.

This was all my fucking fault.

I shrieked, slamming my fist into my steering wheel, my heart dropping low into my stomach as I realized that their deaths were on *my* hands. He had killed them to get to *me*. If I hadn't tried to hide, if I had just handed myself over to him, he wouldn't have killed these people. He wouldn't have killed my friends.

I wasn't going to let him kill any more people. If he wanted to see me, he would. And when we met, I was going to kill him. He wouldn't get away with this.

I found myself driving to the woods near my school and parked my car some distance away, where neither Jana nor Jeremy would spot it. I then walked into the forest as I made my call to Grayson.

"I thought you would call soon," he said when he picked up.

My entire body shook hard. "If you dare touch another one of my friends, I'll—"

"You'll what?" he laughed. "You'll kill me?"

"I'll do exactly that."

"I have so much more power and strength than you do. You cannot possibly kill me."

"Oh yeah? *Try* me. Come to Oakwood Park and prove to me that I can't."

With my breath coming hard, I hung up. My temperature rising, I picked up a rock and threw it at a tree with an indignation I had never felt before.

Nobody could hurt my friends and expect to live.

Nobody, not even Grayson.

CHAPTER 7

THE PUSH

SAM

"I have to go back to Windsor, Maya," I said after we went back to our hotel room.

"Sam, *no*, you're not going back," she insisted as she packed up her stuff. We had to leave as soon as possible and get to a motel. If we were going to be paying for her treatment, we couldn't stay here any longer. "We can both get jobs here; we don't need the gem."

"But how can you work when you're sick?" I asked. "I'm not going to let you work when you need your rest."

"I'll manage."

I grabbed her by the shoulders before she could bend down to pick up a shirt that had been lying around. "No, you won't. You can't. Let me compel them," I pleaded. "As long as I keep compelling them, they'll give us the treatment for free."

She sighed, shaking her head and walking away from me. "Sam, we are not having this conversation again. Not only is your power going to wear off quickly, it simply isn't right. It's not fair."

"It's taking advantage of what we have."

"And it isn't fair to others who are in the same situation as us, yet don't have the same advantage!" she exclaimed. "You do that all the time! You get jobs like that, and you get other stuff like that too. It's wrong, Sam. Like today," she added. "I get that you care about me and want the best for me, but what you did wasn't right! Compelling that lady and the doctor—"

"Okay," I interrupted, not wanting her to get worked up. She needed to relax; she shouldn't have been stressing. "I'll let it go. And I won't do it again."

She sighed, looking really tired. "Thank you. Now help me pack up."

We left within the next hour and found a cheap motel close to the hospital. We had just settled in when Cole called me. Dropping my bag off near the entrance, I closed the door and answered his call. "What's up?" I asked.

"Did you hear?"

I frowned, confused at the frantic tone of his voice. "Hear what?"

"Someone killed *five* teenagers in Windsor, one a day the past week, taking their organs out. When I noticed that two of them were your coworkers, I hacked into Grayson's computer to see if I could find anything that told me that this is on his hands. It was. But I found something worse."

"What?" I asked, unable to think of what could be worse than death.

"He's sucking up the spirits of these people and feeding them to a Daeblo in exchange for power."

I swallowed hard, realizing that he was going to use that energy to kill Maya, me, and Monique. But before I could verbally react, Cole continued, "I didn't think it was just a coincidence that he killed *two* of your coworkers, and I figured it had something to do with Monique. She got worked up about it. I figured she would, so I headed to the park where I found her practicing archery last week. I got someone to Track Grayson, and he told me he's headed there too."

"He's going to try to kidnap her," I realized. Maya had been changing her clothes but halted when I spoke, looking confused and a little scared.

"Or kill her, if he's found a way around the protection."

"Find out if he has. I'm heading there right now." Monique wouldn't be fully trained within a week, even if she did find a proper trainer, and now that Grayson was gaining power through the souls of other people, she was in even more danger. And if he was able to kill her, Grayson would destroy the gem right away, and I would lose my chance to save Maya's life.

I had no choice but to save Monique. I'd made a mistake in letting her fend for herself, and now, there was a chance I'd have to pay for it.

MONIQUE

I walked toward the clearing in the forest, holding my bow and arrows in my hand. It was quiet here this time of night, especially in the winter. The summer sounds of grasshoppers and crickets chirping to one another were absent in the cold, brittle air surrounding me. I watched as a squirrel scurried past me to find shelter from the falling snow under a tree, and it wasn't like I spoke squirrel, but seeing his head dart back and forth and hearing his quiet chattering, I assumed he was scared. Scared to be out alone in the cold. He had to fend for himself, just like I had to fend for myself after Kay left.

For six years after Mom had passed away, Kay had been the one to take care of me. She was like a mother to me. She'd taken me school shopping, given me advice when I needed it, and even though Grayson wouldn't spend a single penny on me, Kay had given up all the money she had to throw me a birthday party every single year. I missed her, now more than ever, because if she were here right now—if she hadn't changed her number, if she hadn't decided to break off all contact with me—I knew she would be right here with me, supporting me through all this. She would help me take down Grayson even though it would kill her, because it was the right thing to do.

But she'd abandoned me, just like Mom had. She'd left me like Mom had, even though they'd both promised me they would never leave.

I realized as I stopped to watch the squirrel just how much I was craving a family at that moment, now more than ever. But I wasn't going to go back home, because Grayson wasn't my family; he was just a man who had abused me my whole life. I loathed him, and although I'd known him my whole life, I wanted him dead.

Murderer, I seethed to myself. He wasn't going to get away with this. I wouldn't let him.

I was going to kill him.

Suddenly, I heard the crack of a twig to my right. Gasping, I turned, dropping into the fighting stance my trainer had taught me. But it had turned out to be just another squirrel. Breathing a sigh of relief, I straightened up and relaxed a little.

Until I felt a thick, hairy arm locking around my neck.

I screamed as he began choking me. Immediately knowing it was Grayson, I squirmed beneath his hold. But I was quickly losing air, slowly becoming lightheaded, and despite using all of my effort to try to pull his arm off me, I was completely unsuccessful. He was too strong for me—even stronger than I remembered. I wouldn't be able to take him. I'd made the stupidest mistake of my life.

I was becoming lethargic; my body was shutting down. My eyes were slowly starting to shut. I was falling into unconsciousness.

Until he was suddenly pulled off me.

I heard a thud and roar of pain and turned around to see that Grayson had hit a tree. My heart beating wildly in relief, I looked to my left to see a portal closing behind the person who had just saved me.

Sam.

He looked really annoyed and twice as pissed off, and from the look of disgust he shot me, I knew a lot of that emotion was aimed toward me. But he soon pulled his attention away from me and sauntered toward Grayson, who was getting up now. Before he could fully straighten up, Sam punched him in the stomach, and Grayson doubled over. Sam took another swing at him, this time at his face, and then grabbed Grayson by his collar, pushing him against the tree. He looked Grayson dead in the eye with such immense fury written on his expression that it scared *me*. I stayed back, watching from a safe distance.

"You're a pathetic coward," Sam seethed.

Grayson laughed, and when he bared his teeth, blood dripped down his chin. "It was the smartest move I've ever made in my entire life.

I was able to distract you, and now I have more than enough power to kill you."

Sam's grip on Grayson tightened, and he pushed Grayson harder into the tree. "You're despicable. She had nothing to do with this—"

"But you do," Grayson countered as I wondered who they were talking about. "And it is because of you that she has *everything* to do with this. Because the first step to destroying someone is finding their biggest weakness. And that's exactly what I did."

Grayson's grin widened as Sam's expression flared with increased rage. "Tell me, Sam, who's with her now?"

Realization crossed Sam's face, and Grayson laughed maniacally. Sam's eyes widened as terror seemed to take over his entire body. Grayson didn't waste a single second, taking advantage of Sam's shock to knee him in the abdomen. Sam's grip visibly loosened, giving Grayson the opportunity to get out of his hold and throw a punch at his head. He accompanied the punch with a shove to the ground and then pulled out a gun.

My eyes widened. He was going to kill Sam. Sam couldn't die. If Sam died, I was *screwed*. Not only would I be left alone with Grayson, I would lose an ally I desperately needed. Sam could *not* die.

"One little mistake and your entire world disappears," Grayson boasted, cocking the gun and aiming it at a still-recovering Sam. "You'll see your girl in hell."

No!

Running as fast as I could, I threw myself right into Grayson, knocking into him the moment he pulled the trigger and taking him down to the ground. I fell down beside him and groaned in pain, rolling my head to the side to see that the bullet had lodged into Sam's arm.

Damn it.

And then suddenly, Grayson was on top of me, immobilizing me with his weight, holding both of my hands in one of his as he punched me in the face. I tasted blood in my mouth as the pain rang through my body, but I stayed silent as I tried unsuccessfully to push him off. I squirmed as he placed both of his hands on my throat. My eyes went wide when he started squeezing and choking me again, but before I could become lightheaded, I put my hands on his chest and pushed with all my might. I couldn't budge him one bit; he was as solid as a rock, sturdy and unmoving.

But I needed to survive. I needed to kill him. I couldn't let him strangle me. I couldn't let him kill me, and I couldn't let him kill anyone else. I needed to get him off.

Move! I willed him to move with my mind, hoping it would do something. But it didn't, and I knew in that moment that I was done for. If he couldn't kill me now, he'd take me and hold me hostage until he could. Either way I was dead. Either way, I wouldn't be able to protect the gemstone, and when Grayson destroyed it, Jeremy and Jana, everyone I cared about would die.

I couldn't let that happen. I couldn't let Grayson win this battle. I had to fight back with all my might. I had to avenge my friends.

Move! I pleaded again, starting to become lightheaded as I tried hard to push him off. I could see victory in his eyes, and it made my entire body shake. Driven with rage, I shoved hard.

In that moment, I felt something like snakes crawling under my skin. A second later, I saw a blue light shoot out of my hands as he flew back against the clearing, skidding across twigs and grass. Gasping for air, I got up on shaky legs. I stared at my hands, unable to focus on anything else. What the hell was that? What the hell had shot out of my hands and made him fly like that?

I remembered Sam saying something about us having powers, and then I remembered that guy in Diviano who was using telekinesis to carry boxes.

Was that me? Do I have that power too?

I couldn't believe it. Despite how much craziness I'd experienced this past week, I couldn't believe I had this power, or any powers at all.

An overwhelming sense of excitement washed over me as I realized the advantage this could give me. I smiled.

I looked up from my hands only to notice Grayson sauntering toward me again. Before I even saw it coming, he punched me in the stomach with incredible force, and I doubled over in pain. He grabbed at my neck to choke me again, and I grasped his wrists, trying to pull his hands away with no success.

And then suddenly, Sam was back up on his feet. He wrapped an arm around Grayson's neck, pulling him away from me. It was when I could finally breathe that I noticed that Sam's arm was bleeding like crazy. He looked like he was about to pass out, but he had enough energy left in him to shove Grayson to the ground and jam his foot into Grayson's rib cage. Grayson roared in pain.

"You pathetic," Sam seethed, "little son of a bitch. Tell me what you did to her!"

Grayson laughed as he recovered, but I could tell laughing put him in pain. He didn't reply, however, which just seemed to make Sam angrier. He kicked Grayson again, this time in the stomach, over and over. I gaped as Grayson continued to laugh even through his pain. He was completely crazy, downright insane. And Sam was going to beat him to death.

I didn't stop him.

Suddenly someone behind me covered my mouth with their hand. My heartbeat spiked, but before I could utter a sound or try to pull away, the person stuffed a wet cloth under my nose. I breathed in something sweet—and a wave of dizziness made my legs give out beneath me. An arm came around my torso, immobilizing my limbs, and despite my weak struggling, whoever it was quietly dragged me away.

Soon, the person laid me down beneath a tree, blocking my view of what was going on in the clearing. But I was still conscious, for whatever reason. I could still hear everything and soon heard Sam snarl, "You better tell me what you did, or I swear I'll—"

I fought against the dizziness and realized Grayson wasn't working alone. The man who had drugged me was going to drug Sam too.

I couldn't let that happen.

My head was still spinning, and I felt incredibly weak, but I somehow conjured up enough energy to yell, "Sam, run!"

Immediately, I heard running footsteps approaching me. Staggering to my feet, I started running, steadying myself against the tree trunks when I needed to, and praying that I wouldn't slip on the snow. Just when I heard a second pair of footsteps behind me, I was grabbed by the arm, only to be released a second later when Sam punched the guy and pushed him away to give us both more time to run. We quickly ran out of the clearing and safely back to my car before Grayson's partner came running out.

I was driving away even before he could reach my car, not daring to look back.

SAM

I knew we weren't safe even though we were in a car now. Grayson wouldn't give up this easily, and now he had an accomplice. I didn't know why anyone would want to help him gain power, though I didn't really care. I just wanted them both dead. But with Grayson having obtained this much power, I couldn't kill them by myself. As much as I hated to admit it, I would need help. But all I fucking wanted to do was go back to the woods and beat the shit out of Grayson for taking Maya.

He was a monster.

I needed to find her. I didn't know how long he'd keep her alive, knowing he wanted me dead. Killing a human in the midst of his Divianan killing streak would dilute the power he gave to the Daeblo, but I didn't know when he planned to end that streak. Plus, he was working with someone else, who could easily get the job done for him.

No, Maya, I thought as I pulled out my phone. I needed to call Cole and tell him to find her, and fast, but when I pulled it out, I noticed that it was dead.

"Damn it!" I cussed, wanting to throw my phone out the window. My luck was the worst.

"They're following us," Monique said, ignoring my outburst. She stepped on the accelerator just as I looked in the side-view mirror to see a dark car gaining on us. I could just make out Grayson's face in the passenger seat, but I couldn't see who was driving. Ignoring that fact, I pulled out my gun, and leaning out the window into the snowy night, I pulled the trigger. The bullet hit a tire on their car. They immediately went skidding down the road.

Ignoring the pain shooting up my arm, I sat back down. I rolled the window up as the snow on my shoulders slowly melted. "Can I use your phone?" I asked Monique.

"Why?" she demanded.

"Mine's dead."

She pulled out her phone and clicked a button. "Mine's dead too," she said, a minute after it didn't turn on. "Just wait until we get to Jana's house."

It didn't even register in my mind that she'd told me where we were going. I didn't care. All I could think about was Maya begging for help, begging me to get her out of wherever she was. And now I was going to have to wait to talk to Cole, wait to find out where she was.

I needed to leave. I needed to find Maya. I needed to get her to safety. But how? I didn't know where to start.

If I hadn't left her, she would've been safe.

If *Monique* hadn't gone stalking into the woods like an idiot . . .

"If you knew you weren't properly trained," I began with gritted teeth. I had the urge to punch her in the face, but I held it back. That didn't stop me from shaking, though. "Why the fuck did you go after Grayson?"

"He killed—"

"I don't *care* if he killed your friends!" I boomed. "That's not a good enough reason to act out as rashly as you did, even if you did know how to fight! Do you know how many people are counting on you?"

"I did exactly what you did."

She was right. The moment I'd found out that Grayson took Maya, everything and everyone else seemed too minute to focus on. That was why I hadn't noticed the guy helping Grayson until it was almost too late. If I hadn't been so invested in hurting Grayson, I would have heard him approaching me. If it hadn't been for Monique's warning, I probably would have been dead.

But Maya . . . I needed to find her.

"Listen, I don't know who Grayson took, but it's obvious you care about her," Monique said, and I looked away. I didn't want to hear this from her. She didn't know anything.

Maya, where are you?

"I'll help you find her."

I looked back at Monique in surprise. "Why the fuck would you help me?" I demanded. I'd been a jerk to her and left her to train and fend for herself a little less than a week ago. I didn't think she'd forgive me that easily.

"Because despite the fact that you're a total ass who completely ditched me after promising to train me, I can't beat Grayson without you, and I'm pretty sure you can't do it without me. And if he's teaming up, then so should we. But *you*," she added, pointing at me and narrowing her eyes, "can't ditch me again. *You* need to stick by me and train me so that not only can we defeat Grayson, but we can find your friend too."

She was right. But I needed to talk to Cole first. I needed to hire a damn Tracker. But with my fucking phone being dead, and Monique's too, I couldn't do anything besides flip nervously through radio channels. Unfortunately, nothing could calm me down. I would just have to wait until we got to Jana's house and pray to God that in the meantime, Maya wouldn't die.

This was all my fucking fault.

MONIQUE

Jana was going to kill me for putting myself in danger when I got back to her house, but the thing was, she was our only hope. I had no idea how we were going to kill Grayson when he had so much power and was working with someone else, and Sam seemed too impaired to think at the moment. Plus, Sam was bleeding out, although it seemed like he was completely immune to pain. And Jana knew more about Diviano than I did and could probably think of something.

But when I let us into the house, it seemed too quiet.

"Jana?" I called, walking past the foyer and into the living room. I was surprised to see Nathan sitting on the couch.

He got up when I came in. "Where were you?" he asked, his brow furrowed. He had a worried look in his eyes, but I ignored it, needing to get the first-aid kit.

"Out," I replied vaguely, going past the staircase to get to the linen closet. "Where're Jana and Jeremy?"

Sam didn't give Nathan a chance to talk. "Where's the phone? I need the phone."

I rolled my eyes and turned back to face him after grabbing the kit. "You're bleeding out. You don't need the phone; you need a doctor, but the hospital's too far."

"I don't need a doctor! I need the damn phone!"

I slammed the closet door shut. "Hey!" I cried when I saw him walking around, searching for a phone. "Do you *want* to die? You've lost enough blood as it is. Sit your ass down and let me help you, or do it yourself. You can't get the girl back with one arm."

His eyes blazed red, and I noticed him clenching his fist. "You don't understand. I need the phone."

I sighed, grabbing Sam by his good wrist and dragging him to the kitchen. "Nathan, give him your damn cell phone, would you?" He followed us into the kitchen and handed Sam his phone.

"Get out," Sam muttered, sitting down at the island as he dialled a number on Nathan's phone. Nathan immediately left, but I stayed put, opening up the kit. When I didn't leave, Sam demanded, "Are you deaf? I said get out."

That was it. I'd had enough. Just because he was injured didn't mean he had the right to treat everyone like crap. With my blood boiling, I lifted my arm to throw a punch at his face, but he effectively blocked it with his good hand, twisting my arm. Pain immediately shot up to my shoulder.

I hissed.

"Nice try. Just because you're telekinetic doesn't make you the almighty." He glanced at the open kit as he took off his jacket and then, to my surprise, pulled the bullet out of his wound with his bare fingers. "Now get out."

I rolled my shoulder back, trying to get rid of the pain. "You're wasting your time arguing with me," I said, grabbing the peroxide. He pressed his lips into a thin line before giving up and finally making the call. I stayed silent as the person on the other end picked up, focusing on the task at hand.

"Hello?"

"It's Sam. He took her. Kidnapped her when I came back to Windsor. I have no idea where she is. Find her. Please."

Sam sounded like he was about to cry.

"I'm on it."

The guy hung up, and Sam put the phone down.

121

"You're lucky the jacket you were wearing prevented the bullet from lodging itself really deep," I said.

"Why are you doing this?"

"Because frankly, I could use the extra set of hands in strangling that man." I put the gauze dressing down and grabbed Nathan's phone from the island. "Clean this up," I added as I left.

I found Nathan pacing in the living room, looking more worried than before. When I walked in, he looked up, and I gave him his phone. "Jana and Jeremy went out to find you," he said, answering my earlier question. They said you just picked up and left after you saw the . . . the news, and they were worried. They called me and told me to stay here in case you came back. And . . . what happened to his arm?"

They hadn't told him why I left, had they? No, they obviously wouldn't. He was clueless about Diviano.

I ignored his question. "My phone's dead. Call them and tell them I'm here. Tell them to come back ASAP. I need to go change," I added, looking down at my drenched clothes. I hurried up the stairs. By the time I came back down, having changed into more of Jana's clothes, Nathan and Sam were talking. But they stopped the moment I showed up.

"I called them," Nathan said. "They're on their way."

"Thanks." Not wanting him to ask any more questions, I added, "You can go home now. You probably have tests to study for."

"I don't want to wait for Jana," Sam said, interrupting our conversation. "She's taking forever, and—"

Sam was cut off by the doorbell ringing. He immediately unfolded his arms and went to open the door. Before I could move to see whose face was behind the deep-voiced "Hey," Sam had stepped out and closed the door behind him. Wondering if he was going to ditch me again, I walked toward the double doors and pulled aside the curtains shielding the side windows. Unfortunately, the porch lights were turned off. All I could see was darkness.

"Who is it?" Nathan asked.

I turned around to face him, letting the curtains fall with my hand. "I don't know."

"What was he talking about earlier? Why is he waiting for Jana? And what happened to his arm?"

I suppressed the urge to roll my eyes. Why was he even here? Why would Jana call him here? He was getting in the fucking way.

"Nothing, Nathan," I sighed, heading toward the stairs to get my phone charger.

He followed. "Are you pissed at me?"

"No, I'm just tired."

"From what?" he asked, giving me a nervous laugh as we approached the top of the stairs. "You've been gone from school for a week. What could you have possibly been doing that made you tired?"

"Why do you have to know what I'm doing all the time?" I demanded with an exasperated sigh. Why was he so God-damn interested in what I was doing with my time? Why did he care? Couldn't he just leave me alone for two freaking minutes while I grabbed my stupid charger? And why had Jana left me the burden of having to answer his ridiculous questions?

He followed me into the guest bedroom as he answered, "I'm just wondering. It's not like you. Not to mention the fact that last Friday, you were ready to rip Sam's throat out and now you seem to be such good friends—"

I grabbed my charger from the nightstand and cut Nathan off, turning to face him. "We are *not* friends. I haven't spoken to Sam since last Friday. He showed up tonight and we kinda just got thrown together, okay?"

He didn't reply, but the confused and kind of angry look on his face disappeared, immediately replaced by shame that he was clearly trying desperately to hide. He looked away. "What's wrong?" I asked.

"I—" He sighed. "Nothing. I'm sorry."

What the hell was he was apologizing for? Confused, I asked, "For what? Nathan, what's wrong? Why do you look so upset?"

He blatantly stared at me as I waited impatiently for him to speak up, hating the suspense he was keeping me in. But when he shook his head and opened his mouth to finally talk, all he said was, "It's not the right time. You're busy."

"Well, fuck it. That doesn't matter. I want to know what's wrong. I want to know why you look so upset, so stop making me wait and just tell me."

He sighed. "The thing is . . . I really don't know how to start this. It's different with you than it was with anyone else. *You're* different. I know you're not the dating type, but . . ."

Oh man. Great. So this was finally happening. I immediately felt uncomfortable in my own skin, wondering how exactly he would phrase this and what I would say next. I suddenly wished I hadn't constantly ignored Jana's teasing and had asked her what I should say if this ever happened.

He trailed off, shoving his hands in his pockets. I waited for him to continue, digging my own hands into the pockets of my jeans.

Letting out a breath, he resumed, "The thing is, I really like you Monique, more than a friend. I've had feelings for you for a while now and have been meaning to ask you out; I just didn't know how."

God damn it! *Really?* We'd been friends for four years, he'd dated so many other girls, and *now* he was showing feelings for me? Couldn't he have asked me sooner? Four years ago, I would've agreed to go out with him for sure—I had liked him at one point, before I met Tyler. But now, I was too scarred. The things Tyler had done to me forced me to stop shying away from reality. Yeah, it was Nathan—I had known this guy for four years. But the only reason I'd been able to tolerate him without getting scared was that we were never alone together.

Up until this moment.

Now that I was alone with him, I was hyperaware of everything single move he made, every breath he took, wondering if this was all just a stupid ploy to get me in his bed. What was to say that Nathan wasn't just more persistent than Tyler in making it seem like he was a good guy? That way, if I told anyone if he raped me, nobody would believe me.

I knew I couldn't say yes. Even if he didn't rape me, sooner or later, the relationship would all just be about sex. No matter how much I knew it would hurt his ego, I *had* to say no.

But I also knew the guilt would eat me alive. I didn't want to hurt his feelings and have it ruin our friendship. I didn't want to look at him every single day and be reminded of the look on his face if I turned him down. I didn't want to be reminded of the fact that *I* had caused our friendship to falter by saying no.

But I also didn't trust him enough to say yes. A relationship entailed being alone together, and I knew I wouldn't be able to stand it. I didn't want to feel any more of the terror that rumbled beneath my skin in this moment.

I had no idea what to do, what to say. I didn't want to deal with this right now, when I had so many other things to focus on, like the fact that Grayson was trying to kill me, Sam needed to train me and was chilling outside with God knew who—or had totally ditched us again—and Jana still wasn't back. Nor was Jeremy.

I couldn't concentrate. I couldn't think.

"Monique," Nathan called. I finally focused on him. He looked more nervous than he had a mere minute ago. He was staring at me with panic swimming in his wide eyes, no doubt caused by my silence. My heart dropped as a sea of guilt washed over me. But instead of responding to him, giving him a definite answer, I walked away, heading into the washroom and locking the door after me. I turned on the fan to drown out any noise he could possibly make and looked into the mirror.

My eyes were just as wide as his, my expression matching the terror I felt. He obviously had to know I didn't feel the same way if I'd looked this petrified in front of him. What he didn't know about was the guilt, and not only that, but the feeling of abnormality.

Any normal person would have been able to respond right away. Any normal person wouldn't have taken so long deciding to give him a yes or no, because normal people didn't have to deal with the fear I lived with. They didn't have a hard time trusting others. For everyone else, it was a matter of wondering if they wanted to try it out with a friend or not. But I wasn't everyone else. I wasn't normal, because of my past, and to top that off, I was part of some stupid world called Diviano and had obtained a stupid gem that contained some stupid power that I still didn't understand. I was an abnormality in this ordinary world, and even though Jana would understand why I felt out of place amongst normal people, she wouldn't understand that I still felt like a freak with her, Jeremy, and Sam, because she didn't have a father who was trying to kill her. Not only that, *she* hadn't been raped. *She* had never been a drug addict, so she would *never* understand why I felt so out of place.

I hated the fact that I couldn't trust any guy, even a guy I had been friends with for years. I hated the fact that my disgust for Tyler was overridden by my addiction to the drugs I took. I hated the fact that I couldn't protect myself from him, that I couldn't protect myself from Grayson, that I was the reason Mason and Donna were dead. I hated myself for the power I had, knowing it had landed me in this position. If I wasn't a Keeper, Grayson wouldn't have adopted me, and I would have been raised in a different family. I could have avoided Tyler altogether, never needing drugs to eradicate the pain I felt from the death of my mom or the fact that my sister had left me to deal with my abusive father on my own. I would never have to take it out on myself when I faced the anger I felt, knowing that safety had always been a 911 call away but never being able to make the call because of the chance that Jeremy and I would be split apart, that I wouldn't be able to take care of him. If it wasn't for this stupid stone, I would be normal. I would be sane. I would be unscarred.

I would be happy.

But that wasn't the case. My luck sucked too much for me to ever be happy. And it was that realization that caused the tears surfacing in my eyes to spill over and flow down my cheeks. It was that realization that caused the defeat that soon had me flat on my ass, sobbing into my hands as I prayed desperately to whatever power was listening to take away the pain. For this to all be over.

For my death to come more quickly than it should.

SAM

The fact that Cole showed up at Jana's house pretty quickly after I called him—even using a portal —could only mean one thing. He hadn't been successful. The furrow in his brow and the worry in his eyes was confirmation.

"Just hit me with it," I ordered once we were alone outside on the driveway, next to his car.

He sighed. "Sam, he's using a Cloaker. The Tracker couldn't find her scent, and I know that could mean she's dead, but you would know if she had died. So he *has* to be working with a Cloaker."

He was right. I would have felt it if she died. My hands shook, and I swallowed hard. Why had he kept her alive this far? Why hadn't he killed her yet? What did he want from her?

"Why would a Cloaker work for him?"

"It's probably not voluntary. My guess is he's using the Daeblo to compel people for him. Listen, Sam, he knows about the Implizma Piezeau bond."

I raked my hands through my hair, my breathing coming harder.

Noticing a light turning on in the house, I thought of Monique inside.

This was all her fault. If he didn't want to get to her, he wouldn't want to get to me. And if he didn't want to get to me, he wouldn't want to get to Maya.

I lowered my hands, gritting my teeth. "This is all her fault," I seethed.

The moment I spoke, I felt my head burning as if it were on fire. "Argh!" I cried, a dozen needles poking into the sides of my brain. I felt my eyes rapidly changing colours, and my vision blurred. I fell to the ground, my knees giving under me as the pain intensified.

"Sam?" Cole called frantically, dropping down to his knees in front of me. "What's wrong? What happened?"

I immediately realized why Grayson hadn't killed Maya. "He's torturing her. He has to be."

"What are you feeling?"

"Needles," I gasped, trying to think through the pain. The needles were still there, poking me everywhere, piercing through my skull. "Burning," I added and roared in pain as it became worse.

"He took her to Diviano. Her brain is unable to take the enchantment."

"She's going to die," I realized, and immediately, I felt my heart in my throat. Sobs were threatening to take over as my eyes began stinging. She was going to die. He was going to take her out of my life in a split second.

"No, she won't. We're not going to let that happen."

"This is all Monique's fault. He wants her."

127

"It's not her fault, Sam. I don't want to explain this to you again. She didn't purposely put herself in the position she's in. You can't blame this on her, and if you want to find Maya, you're going to have to tolerate her. She's our key to beating Grayson, to finding Maya."

I didn't reply, unable to think through the fury, the pain, the fear.

Suddenly, the pain stopped.

My vision cleared up, and I saw Cole kneeling in front of me. "You okay?" he asked as the burning went away. The poking of the needles simmered down to a dull ache.

"The pain stopped. Why did it stop? Did she die?"

He shook his head. "I have no idea," he said. But I could tell he was thinking that she had.

JANA

When Jeremy and I got back to my house, I noticed Sam standing outside on my driveway next to a tall, dark-haired guy and a black Cruze. The moment I saw him, the fury I had forced myself to forget bubbled back up my throat, and as I got out of my car, I snarled, "You fucking asshole."

Jeremy stopped at the front door, but I gestured for him to go inside. When he left, I walked up to Sam with my blood boiling.

Ignoring the fact that he looked like he was ready to cry, I slapped him across the face, *hard,* and pulled my hand away to find that he now had a red mark on his cheek. But there was no pain in his expression. He just looked startled as the mark slowly waned. Unsatisfied, I was about to punch him but was suddenly grabbed from behind.

"Hey, hey!" the other guy cried, holding on to my arm. "What the hell are you hitting him for?"

I turned around to face him, immediately feeling tiny in comparison to the man looming over me. It wasn't like he was eight feet tall or something, but he was *seriously* buff. Even though he was wearing an undone peacoat, I could see the muscles of his arms threatening to poke out from the black material.

I looked up from the Toronto University sweatshirt he was wearing underneath the coat to actually look him in the face and was met with surprisingly warm, russet eyes and Adam Levine's dark locks.

Trying to keep my mind off how frigging attractive he was, I retorted, "Who the hell are you?"

"I'm his friend. Now would you mind telling me what the hell you're hitting him for?"

I crossed my arms and raised an eyebrow, not appreciating his hostile behavior, even though it wasn't surprising given my own. Plus, he was Sam's friend. Hostility should have been a given. "If you're his friend, you should know what an ass this kid has been to *my* best friend, Monique."

"Seriously?" Sam muttered from behind me.

I turned around to face him and lifted a finger in his face. "No, *you* don't get to talk! You're such an *ass*! If we didn't need you to train her, I would be kicking you off my property this minute. Unfortunately, that's not the case, so get the hell inside." I turned back to his friend, who looked a little less pissed than before. The angry V that had shaped his eyebrows was now gone. "As for you, if you can't provide us with anything useful, I suggest you leave before I serve you with a restraining order."

I had just turned to lead Sam into the house when his friend spoke again. "Okay, I'm sorry for yelling at you. I get why you're pissed. I would be pissed too, if I were in your situation. And I know Sam can be an ass, but if you're going to need him, then I *can* provide you with something useful."

I decided to stay and listen, folding my arms and giving him an unimpressed look—even though I was surprised that he had actually apologized. I'd figured if he was Sam's friend, he would be just as rude.

He motioned toward Sam. "I can provide him with comfort. His girlfriend was kidnapped—"

Oh jeez. "I took care of it," I snapped.

They gave me identical questioning looks as Sam asked, "How?"

I thought of Monique, waiting inside. Not wanting to repeat myself, I replied, "I'll explain inside." I then turned to his friend. I didn't see what harm he could do in helping us catch Grayson, and he *was* something pretty to stare at. So I added, "And as long as you can keep your friend in line, you can come inside too."

MONIQUE

When I heard a door opening and voices coming from downstairs, I immediately tried to stop the tears from flowing, taking deep breaths and washing my face with water, though it did no good; I still felt icky. As I left the washroom, Nathan was nowhere in sight, but that didn't keep the tears from wanting to resurface.

I was still trying really hard not to burst into tears again when I headed down the stairs to see Jana coming inside with Sam and a guy I didn't recognize. He looked around my age—maybe a couple years older. His large brown eyes were framed by thick eyebrows and high cheekbones and shadowed by his brown Adam Levine hairstyle. He was wearing dark jeans and a University of Toronto sweater underneath a peacoat that he took off as he made eye contact with me.

I looked away, curious as to who the hell he was and what he was doing inside the house. I looked to Jana for answers, but she was busy rapidly talking to her maid, who left the house immediately after Jana was done.

It was then that she looked at me.

Her expression, which had held a mix of emotions including anger and frustration, immediately melted to just one: relief.

"Do not *ever* run off like that again," she warned me as I came down the stairs to meet her. She pulled me into a tight hug, completely ignoring Nathan and Jeremy, who had just walked into the foyer from the living room.

My stomach churned as I saw the pain in Nathan's eyes, and I immediately looked away, pulling away from Jana.

"I'm sorry," I replied. "I shouldn't have done that. I wasn't thinking straight. But we have bigger issues going on right now."

"I know," she said, looking at Sam and completely ignoring the model beside him.

"Grayson's gaining power by killing these people. They were all Divianan," she added. I glanced at Nathan, who didn't appear to be confused by this term or startled by what she was saying about Grayson. He just continued to have that look of despair stretched across his face. I wondered if perhaps Jana had told him about our current situation, but I also remembered her telling me that her parents didn't want her talking about Diviano with humans, which had me even more bewildered. If Jana had gone years without telling me for that reason, she definitely wouldn't take the risk with Nathan.

"Oh shoot," Jana said, noticing my confused expression. "I forgot to tell you, Nikki, but Nathan's Divianan." I looked at Nathan, who averted his eyes when I did. "I found out when we first met. He read my mind when I happened to be thinking about something Diviano related and confronted me about it."

"I'm sorry, *what?*" I demanded, not thinking I heard her right. "Did you say he *read* your *mind?*"

"I'm a mind reader," Nathan said quietly, and immediately, my heart went racing. That meant he'd known exactly what I was thinking upstairs, including my train of thought when I was deciding whether to reject him or not. That meant he had to know I no longer trusted him. But it also meant he had to know *why,* which was good in a sense, because then he could feel less hurt about it. But it made me more vulnerable in his eyes. Plus, I couldn't stand the thought of not having my privacy.

"I can't read yours, though," he added.

I remembered Sam's theory about me being immune to some powers and relaxed.

"Um, sorry to interrupt," Jeremy began. "But who are you, exactly?"

He was looking at the model, who responded in an incredibly deep voice. "I'm Sam's friend. Cole."

Cole held out his hand for Jeremy to shake, but Jeremy ignored it, looking between Sam, Cole, and Cole's hand. He was clearly sceptical, which was good. Any friend of Sam's was worth being wary of. I didn't understand why Jana had let him into her house.

"Can we get back to the point here?" Sam demanded as Cole dropped his rejected hand.

"Yeah, you were saying that all the people Grayson killed were Divianan?" I began, looking at Jana. She who nodded in response. It took my confused brain a moment to put the pieces together. "That means Mason and Donna were too?" Again she nodded. What the fuck? Who else did I know who was Divianan and hiding it?

"Can you explain how you saved Maya?" Sam urged Jana, looking really impatient. He had his hands in his pockets and was shifting from foot to foot.

"I didn't *save* anyone, exactly," Jana said. "I simply made me it harder for Grayson to kill her. I got a vision of some guy taking Maya from her motel, but I couldn't get to her in time. So I took Jeremy and went to a Wunissan instead. I created a bond between her and Nathan so that as long as Nathan lives, Grayson won't be able to kill Maya. So she's safe, at least for now."

"Why Nathan?" I asked. "And who's Maya? And what's a Wunissan?"

"Sam's girlfriend. Grayson kidnapped her," Cole answered.

Sam gave him a dirty look.

What the hell was that?

Jana turned to me. "A Wunissan is a man with a gift to create, break, and discover bonds. They also have various other abilities. As to why I picked Nathan, I had to think of someone Grayson wouldn't suspect of being bonded with her, in case he figures out what I did. But I also needed someone who would be willing. A human would have been less obvious, but there's always the possibility that in order to protect him from Grayson, we'll have to take Nathan to Diviano. The enchantment on our planet is too much for a human brain—so much so that it will kill them. So it had to be Nathan, which is why I let him in on what was going on."

And yet, Nathan still couldn't comprehend why I was so tired. Did he not understand the toll this whole thing was taking on me?

Jana turned back to Sam. "But this bond is only temporary. It'll last a month at the most, and considering the fact that it's weaker than normal since the Wunissan wasn't that experienced, I doubt it'll last longer than half that time."

"How'd you do it?" Cole asked. "Don't you need the blood of the person you're creating the bond with?"

"It wasn't hard to get. The motel was covered in Maya's, and Nathan was willing."

At her words, terror painted Sam's expression. His eyes widened, and his body went rigid. He stopped shifting and instead went to sit on the couch behind us.

"Wait, hold on," Cole said. I could tell from the way he glanced at Sam that he was clearly worried for his friend, but instead of comforting him, he asked Jana, "You said you went to a Wunissan?"

Jana nodded.

"Does he know how to track people?"

"I'm not sure. I never met him before, but again, he didn't seem very experienced. I didn't have the time to search for a more experienced one since the bond had to be created quickly."

"Why?" I asked.

"Blood has to be as fresh as possible if the bond is going to work. I know a Wunissa though, here in Windsor, and would have gone to her if I'd been able to create another portal."

I was so confused. "What do you mean?"

"Our virtencias need an hour to . . . charge, in a sense, after creating portals. It takes a ton of energy to create one," Cole answered.

"Yeah, so I went to LA to scrape a bit of Maya's blood off the furniture in the motel and had to find a Wunissan in LA to do the spell, since my virtencia needed time to charge and regain energy."

"What gives them energy?"

"What did Sam even explain to you?" Jana asked.

Sam, who had been leaning forward with his head in his hands, abruptly stood up. "Why does that even matter right now?" He sounded royally pissed at both me and Jana. "You can criticize me all you want later, but we *need* to focus. Every second we waste, Grayson is using to get stronger." When he earned the silence of our group, he asked Jana, "Does the Wunissa in Windsor know how to track people?"

Her brow furrowed. "Yes, but why would we need her when we could just hire a Tracker?"

"Grayson's Cloaking Maya," Cole interjected while Sam visibly boiled with impatience. "I hired a Tracker to find her, but he couldn't. So he tried Tracking Grayson instead but couldn't find his scent either. He's Cloaking himself too, so we need a Wunissa or Wunissan to find them."

"What's the difference?" I asked.

"Female versus male," Jana explained quickly and then turned back to Cole. "But I'm still confused. I assumed Grayson called you out. Isn't that why you left the house?" she asked me.

"Yeah."

"We retreated, Jana," Sam sighed. "He's gained too much power, and he's not working alone anymore. We couldn't fight him. But we have no idea where he is anymore. He could have used a portal and gone to Diviano, and if he found a permanent portal, he could have already teleported back to Earth, even somewhere halfway across the world."

"Permanent?" I asked.

"Some portals are sealed up—usually in a doorway—by a spell," Jana clarified. "Gets rid of the need for a virtencia. They only last on Diviano."

Cole shook his head. "The point is, we can't meet him head-on because he's built up his power, but we need to find out where Maya is, and my guess is that she's wherever he is. And if she isn't, then at least we can find *him* and kill him."

"Can't we just call him out now and team up on him?" Jeremy asked.

"I don't think he'll come out now," I replied. "He's probably realized that Sam and I will be working together, and if he knows who's Divianan around here, then he'll know Jana's with us too."

"And if he knew about Maya," Cole added, "he must know about me. He won't face us now, not all together. He missed his chance."

Jana sighed. "Okay, I'll take Jeremy and go to the Wunissa. We'll need his blood to find Grayson. I would take you too, Monique, so I could explain some stuff Sam didn't along the way." Jana glared at him, but he didn't seem to be bothered by it. He just gave her his own mean, impatient stare. "But you need to train. So I suggest *you*," her eyes narrowed as she continued staring at Sam, "get on that and start training her like you said you would, and try not to be a dick. And feel lucky that I'm letting your mistakes slide."

On that note, she turned to Jeremy and led him out the door. I was immediately filled with a restless tension as I was left alone with three guys inside this house, one who was totally pain-stricken yet obviously into me, and two whom I trusted even less than the boy I thought was my friend.

"I have to head home for something," Nathan muttered. "I'll be back." He left not a second after Jana, and I was able to breathe easier. But I still felt intimidated as I stared up at the two guys towering above me.

They were clearly close friends, and I didn't trust either of them. I didn't know what their intentions were, and I didn't want to find out.

Plus, I *knew* I would feel much safer dealing with just one of them.

I cleared my throat. "Cole, is it?" He had turned to say something to Sam, but he faced me when I spoke.

He smiled and gave me a pleasant, "Yeah." But I didn't let his kindness shake me. I didn't trust it to last.

"Get out," I ordered. The smile quickly vanished from his face, replaced with a bewildered expression. "Sam needs to train me, and it's not necessary for you to be here."

"Well, his girlfriend was just kidnapped, and I think he deserves some support."

"I don't care."

"This isn't your house. You can't kick him out," Sam cut in.

"It's much more mine than it is yours. When Jana leaves this house, *I'm* in charge. And I said, *Get. Out.*"

I expected Cole to put up more of a fight, but he didn't. He just gave me a confused look and sent Sam a silent message before walking out the door, leaving Sam and me alone.

JANA

"You know," Jeremy began once we'd hit the road, "I can't believe that just a week ago, both me and Monique were just two ordinary kids with a crappy parent. The fact that we were so easily and quickly pulled into all of this still shocks me."

"Yeah, it's a lot to get used to," I replied as I took a turn on the road, thinking about the unease I'd felt in that room when I'd walked in. It wasn't just the angry tension between Monique and Sam, which I'd expected. It was also the discomfort I'd felt radiating from Nathan. Something had happened in the time we were gone, but I wasn't sure what. That bothered me. I was used to knowing *everything*. My visions had made me so accustomed to knowing the pasts of people I didn't even know and the futures of those who mattered the most. So when something came up that I didn't anticipate, or that I couldn't figure out immediately, it made me want to scream and throw rocks at something.

In that moment, I wanted to throw boulders the size of rockets at Sam.

God, he was a dick. I mean, I understood. His girlfriend had been kidnapped. He had no idea where she was, and he was freaking out because he loved her and obviously didn't want to see her get hurt or die. Point taken. But he didn't have to be such an ass to us all the damn time. He didn't even explain Diviano to Monique properly, and then he got angry when I tried to fix his mistake. Who did he think he was? The way he acted reminded me of my three-year-old cousin.

"Jana?" Jeremy called.

"Hmmm?"

"You didn't answer my question."

Shoot. "Sorry, I zoned out. I didn't hear what you said."

"I asked if you think we'll be able to defeat Grayson."

I sighed. I had no idea. The way Wunissa tracking worked was very different from regular Tracking. It didn't give you an exact location, just a relative one. The most we were likely to get out of this was a city, but that was better than nothing. Even then, it would still be more difficult since we wouldn't just get Grayson's location from the Wunissa. We would get Kay's as well. Warlock tracking would find any living parent and sibling of the one whose blood was being used. We would have to split into two groups and pray we found Grayson before he left the city the Wunissa would give us. We could only hope it wasn't a big city and that he would stay in one location while we scoped out the entire place, along with the other locations we would receive.

But I didn't tell Jeremy all that. I didn't want to make him nervous about all of this. He had enough to deal with knowing his father was a psychopath who was trying to kill his sister. I wanted to keep feeding him hope so that he would have the strength to keep fighting. So I answered, "We'll find him. I promise."

We made the rest of the journey in silence as he visibly chewed on my words. When we finally got to the Wunissa's house, we rang the doorbell, and she soon answered the door.

With tousled brown hair falling down the length of her back and cold, emerald-green eyes, Alice was easily the most beautiful woman I had ever met in my entire life. Her golden brown skin was glowing under the porch lights that shone down upon us, and her pouty red lips greeted us with a warm smile. She was wearing a simple white half-sleeve dress with white heels and white earrings. She was a flash of blinding white, a woman of elegance who stood out against the darkness of the night.

"Good evening, Jana," she said in a smooth, savvy voice. "Come in."

We walked in, and I could tell that Jeremy seemed intimidated by her and her beauty, petrified even. It kind of made me smile, remembering that my reaction had been exactly the same when I first met her.

After Alice closed the door behind us, she led us downstairs to her study. We passed an antique red mahogany staircase that spiraled upstairs, and we went down another, this one going down straight. Within moments, we were surrounded by the warm, peach-coloured walls of Alice's study and sat down in front of her desk, made of holly.

"What can I do for you two?" she asked, looking straight at me.

"We need to track down his father," I explained, motioning toward Jeremy, who was staring at Alice's bookshelf, which was filled with tons of spell books.

"What is your name, child?" she asked.

He didn't answer. He seemed to be lost in everything around us.

"Jeremy," I called.

He turned to look at me. "Sorry. What happened?"

"Alice was talking to you," I said. He looked at her, glancing down quickly and muttering a quick apology.

Alice smiled. "It's all right. Newcomers always become distracted here. I need to know your full name, darling."

"Jeremy Rolland Brooks."

"Okay. Give me your hand please," she said. He complied. "I will need your blood in order to find your father, but first, I must tell you, this spell will also find your mother and all of your siblings. It will not find the dead. Furthermore, I will simply be able to give you a general location and will not be able to tell you who is where. You will have to judge that for yourself. Is that okay with you?"

He nodded, and she smiled. She then grabbed a small knife and black pad from her drawer. Wiping the knife on the pad, she explained,

"Sanitation." Jeremy nodded in understanding. "Are you ready?" He nodded again and laid his hand on the table.

Alice grabbed his wrist. Slowly and gently, she cut across the palm of his hand.

"Ah," he hissed, but he didn't complain any more than that. Murmuring a quick apology, she collected his blood in a black bowl, and once she had enough, she gently wiped the blood away. The moment she did, the cut began healing.

Jeremy pulled his arm back as Alice looked into the bowl, holding it in both her hands. She closed her eyes, and the room was awashed silence. The Wunissan I'd gone to earlier that day had spoken the spell he'd used out loud, but Alice was so experienced that she could apply the same level of concentration and devotion to her spellcasting without verbalizing the words. This was truly a gift of hers, a gift I sometimes envied.

The next thing I knew, she was listing off locations.

"You have family here in Windsor," she said. "Two people, actually. You also have two family members in Diviano: one in Caprimo, the other in Peligrum. Both cities are in Mediralis."

"I have four living family members?" Jeremy asked, startled. He and I exchanged surprised glances.

"It appears so."

"Well, we know Sam's here in Windsor, so we can cross that off the list," I said. "And we know two are Kay and Grayson."

"So who's the extra?" he asked.

I shook my head "I have no idea."

MONIQUE

"You didn't have to kick him out," Sam said once Cole left. "He hasn't done anything to you."

"He's friends with you, and that's enough. Now *train me*. If I'm going to kill Grayson, I need to have some skills under my belt."

He sighed and rolled his eyes but gave in.

He owed it to me.

We decided to head to the backyard despite the chilly weather, stopping in the kitchen to get water bottles.

"Can you throw a good punch?" he asked me after setting our bottles down.

I thought I could, so I said, "Yeah."

"Okay. Punch me."

I raised an eyebrow, surprised at his directness.

"You heard me. Go ahead, punch me. In the face."

I did as he said. Clenching my first, I threw a punch at his face, but it did no good; even though I hit him, his posture remained steady and he didn't seem affected by it at all.

He raised his eyebrows. "You call that a punch? *This* is a punch." Before I saw it coming, he smacked me in the face with a hard fist and sent me stumbling back as sharp pain ran through my cheek. My skin starting stinging, and I stared at him in disbelief.

He smirked. "Still think you're as tough as nails?"

I gritted my teeth and pulled my hand away from my burning cheek. "Instead of picking on me like some school bully," I seethed, "why don't you tell me how I can make my punches *better*? How I can become *stronger*."

He seemed to understand that I was right, but he didn't admit it. "You should have been able to learn more in a week, shitbrain. Now curve your arm a bit more first and then straighten it out just before you make contact. Like this."

He grabbed my arm abruptly, startling me, but before I had time to react, he mimicked the motion with my arm and then let it go. Despite my moment's fear, I quickly memorized what he'd done and tried it on him, curving my arm a bit more and straightening it out just before I made contact with his face. This time, his stance wavered slightly, but again, the punch didn't seem very effective.

He sighed. "Great. At this rate, you'll *hopefully* be strong enough to kill Grayson by the time the world ends."

I glared at him. "I'm sorry, all right? It's not my fault I'm not prepared! I tried to build my strength, but I'm not a freaking vampire or something, okay? My strength and skills aren't going come by feeding on blood and dying just because I'm Keeper. So stop treating me like crap!"

The fury in his expression rose, and that was saying a lot, considering how pissed off he was before. But instead of fighting back like

I expected him to, he simply took a step toward me and said, "You wanna fight? Fine. Go ahead. Take your anger out on me. Punch me, kick me, whatever. I don't care."

So I did. But it wasn't much. I couldn't even get him down to the ground. He just stood there, looking extremely bored as he stared down at his hands, as if he were examining something important. The fact that I was having no effect on him whatsoever made me want to scream! While I'd thought I had gotten stronger with practice this past week, apparently I hadn't.

Or maybe he was just stronger than my trainer. I wasn't sure, but I was hoping it was the latter.

After a while, he rolled his eyes, and the hands he had been examining came down to his sides. "Stop," he ordered. I stopped. "You're stronger than the day you tried to hurt me in Diviano, but you still have nothing in you."

I took a step toward him, crossing my arms. "You're *not* helping."

He mirrored my move, towering over me. With a poke in my chest, he said, "And *you* need to start doing some exercise. Cardio, weight training."

"*Which* I have been doing, in the time you were gone. Jana has a home gym in the basement. Weights, elliptical, everything. I've been using it all."

"Clearly not enough. You're still stick thin. You've got no muscle," he commented, holding my arm up.

I jerked it back from him and cocked my head to the side with a glare. My blood was boiling like crazy, and I felt those snakes surfacing again. "If you're so almighty, why don't you give me some advice then, *dick?*"

He flashed me a bitter smirk. "God, I hate you. You and Goldilocks both." He turned away, grabbing his jacket from the lawn chair. "You know what, I don't need you to do this. I don't need you to find Maya or to kill Grayson. I'll do it on my own."

He walked away, which pushed me over the limit. The snakes shot out to the surface of my hands, and he fell to the ground but got right back up. Turning around, he taunted, "That all you got?"

"No," I snarled, picking up my bow and arrow. He waited, crossing his arms, which just made me angrier. How dare he act so chill when I was so mad? He was *so* going to get it. Setting my arrow on the bow, I shot it at his chest, but he moved to the side and snatched it in his hand. Without breaking eye contact with me, he snapped the arrow in half.

I gaped. "Do you know how expensive those things are?" I exclaimed.

He shrugged. "No idea. Should I care?"

He was pushing it. He was totally asking for it!

The snakes surfaced again.

Control, I reminded myself. It was a distant thought, but it was still there. *I can make him go anywhere I want. All I have to do is control it.*

I knew that was what I needed to do, but I wasn't sure how to control my power. How could I simmer the snakes? How could I move him whichever way I wanted to?

Drop it. Go for the punch.

I ran at him. He didn't move out of the way but let me take him down. It was too easy! Why was he letting this be so easy? Gritting my teeth, I punched him in the face, but it didn't seem to hurt him much. He just smirked.

Form, remember?

I didn't have enough time to make the thought into an action because the next thing I knew, I was underneath him, and he was slamming a fist in my face.

"Oof," I moaned as I tasted blood in my mouth. My jaw was throbbing.

He was about to throw another, but I recalled some of the techniques my trainer had taught me and used them, as my arms were still mobile. I grabbed his hand, twisting it, but it seemed to do nothing. He just moved to using his other hand. This time, I was ready and blocked his fist, locking his arms in a crisscross.

"Well, you have much more arm strength than I anticipated," he said, breathing hard. "Thanks to the lovely Suzanne Collins."

I frowned, not appreciating his *The Hunger Games* reference. "I use it as a way to protect myself okay? And conceal-and-carry is illegal in Canada, remember? So arrows are better. And besides, I *did* build my strength this past week."

His smirk just widened. "You just let yourself get distracted." Before I had time to realize what he meant, he'd freed himself of my grasp and quickly immobilized my arms by pinning them above my head.

I couldn't move at all.

"Besides," he continued, seeming to enjoy all this, "you drink alcohol. *Underage.* Why the fuck would you care about possessing a gun illegally? So really, why *wouldn't* you carry one? It's better protection too."

I grimaced, pushing away a memory I didn't want to relive, especially in that moment.

But my resistance wasn't enough.

"Don't you dare walk out of here!" Tyler boomed.

I cringed back, my hand on the bedroom doorknob. "I can't do this anymore," I sobbed.

"I don't give a shit! You cannot *go to anyone else, you hear me?"*

I turned the knob but paused when I heard something clicking behind me. Turning back around to face him, I realized he was now holding his brother's gun in his hands.

My eyes widened, and I was suddenly finding it harder to breathe.

He walked toward me. My hands trembled. Placing the cocked gun against my jaw, he threatened me with a puffy face. "If you walk out, if you find someone else, I will kill you and *your brother. Never forget that. You're* mine. *Only mine."*

Tears sprang to my eyes.

"And distracted again," Sam muttered, throwing another punch at my face. The pain fully immersed me into the present as I tried desperately to find a way to get out of his hold.

Legs.

I was only immobile from the waist up. I tried kneeing him in the back, but it didn't seem to do any good.

I squirmed beneath his hold, and he rolled his eyes. "If you could get your legs wrapped around my neck, and if you were strong enough, you could either flip me or try choking me." I lifted my legs but wasn't flexible enough.

"Another thing you should improve."

142

"What?" I asked, confused.

"Flexibility. Speed and strength aren't everything. What have you done in a week?"

Damn it! All he was doing was criticizing. When was he going to teach me anything? Baring my teeth, I tried once more to get my legs up, and when I failed, I felt the snakes coming to the surface again.

"Ah-ah!" Sam said, twisting my hands so they were facing the ground. I hissed in pain. "Work without it."

"How did you know I was about to use my power?"

"Your eyes change colour. Dead giveaway. Every power has its disadvantage. If you're willing to listen, I suggest you get contacts."

And then he let go of my hands, getting up. I was immediately able to breathe easier and stretched out the kinks in my muscles.

"Key thing is," he said, taking off his jacket, "know how to improvise with your surroundings. If you lose a weapon, know how to look for one around you without getting distracted. Can't find one, know how to use your fists—and your legs. Sometimes your head. You could have gotten out of that position in at least four different ways. I was hoping you would figure at least one out."

"Is this how your training is going to go every single day?" I asked, feeling a bruise forming on my cheek.

He took a step toward me, and I got up on my feet. "No. It'll get rougher each day." Great. "But I'm going to be teaching you something different each day too. I'll teach you some combat techniques and focus on your form today. We'll do cardio and weight training tomorrow. And your supernatural strength is there. It's just been hidden for the past seventeen—"

"Almost eighteen," I corrected.

"—years," he continued. "The point is, you need to know how to channel it. That doesn't mean you don't need the rest of this training, though. You need to know how to use it effectively, and you can always improve the strength that's already been given to you." He cracked his knuckles. "Now, are you ready?"

I wasn't, but I nodded anyway. I would do anything to become better prepared to take down Grayson. And the moment I agreed, Sam began explaining and demonstrating. He taught me about half a dozen different moves, including jabbing, cross-punching, and side-kicking. The last thing he taught me was axe-kicking, which had me flat on my ass in a matter of seconds, as I was unable to get my leg as high as I needed it be while keeping my balance. Instead of being nice about it, though, Sam just started laughing.

I scowled as I got back up. "Fuck you."

It was precisely that moment that Jana and Jeremy came back.

"Hey," Jana said as she walked up to us. After looking around the backyard, she frowned. "Where are Nathan and Cole?"

"Nathan left," I explained.

"And she kicked Cole out," Sam continued for me.

Jana looked confused, and if I wasn't mistaken, a little disappointed. "Why'd you kick him out?"

I shrugged. "We didn't really need him here."

"Did you find Grayson?" Sam asked.

Jana immediately began explaining. Apparently, they'd found four living individuals, two in Windsor, two in Diviano, which just confused the living crap out of me. How did we have four living family members? It didn't make any sense.

"Do you think Mom's alive?" Jeremy asked me when they finished explaining. His voice was filled with a hope I didn't enjoy. He couldn't hope about that, *ever*. Hoping would only deliver him pain.

I shook my head. "We buried her body, Jere. We saw it minutes before they lowered her coffin into the ground."

"But I thought you said our bodies disintegrate when we die," he countered.

"Only when it's a supernatural cause, remember? Mom died in a car accident. It can't be her."

"Then it's another sibling?"

"Guys, can we figure this out another time?" Sam cut in. "We have to find Grayson."

"Okay," Jeremy muttered.

"We should start in Diviano," Sam continued.

"I agree," Jana said. "But I still think we should check Windsor out too. Grayson might move around. We should split into two groups."

She sighed in frustration. "It's just going to be really hard to find him this way. I have no idea where to start looking."

"Then we call him out," Jeremy suggested.

Sam sighed. "We already discussed why that wouldn't—"

"No, I mean, *lure* him out. You know, use his own medicine on him. Give him something he wants, or take something he has."

"Your sister," Jana said. "He loved her to death."

I shook my head. "I don't think that'll work. First of all, we don't know where she is or how to find her. Secondly, even if we *can* find her and she contacts him somehow, he'll know why. It's been so long since they've talked."

"Then we scope out all areas and hope we get lucky?" Jeremy suggested.

"I honestly think searching Windsor is pointless," Sam said, clearly getting more and more frustrated by the second. "With all the murders going on, the police are looking for a suspect and he won't want to take the chance of getting caught. So, he *has* to be on Diviano."

"But these locations are all so temporary," I complained.

"He wants the gem," Jeremy began, and from his expression, I could tell he was formulating an idea. "Would we be able to make a replica of it and hang it out, kind of like a worm on a fishing line?"

I liked the idea, but Jana clearly didn't. "I don't think he'd fall for that. He knows we wouldn't give up that easily. And anyway, Monique isn't strong enough to take him on alone, and if we're all with her, he'll know it's a trap. He won't take the bait."

"Look, our best shot is to just out check those two Divianan locations," Sam insisted. "If we keep waiting, he could just relocate. We need to move *now*."

"Sam's right," Jana agreed. "We need to take advantage of the information we *do* have. I suggest splitting up, but I also think Monique should stay here and continue to train with Sam."

"I can't just let you do everything!" I exclaimed.

"Hell no," Sam snarled at the same time. "I'm coming with you."

Jana sighed. "Nikki, All I'm saying is you're not strong enough to take him on, and if he sees you out and unprotected, he *will* attack. I don't want to take that chance. Plus, if Grayson gets the gem, we're all dead."

"It won't be any different if you go. He'll know you guys are there on my behalf, and he will *definitely* attack you guys and get my location out of you, or force you to bring him to me."

"Jana, call Nathan, You go with him," Sam began, ignoring everything I'd said. "Jeremy, I'll go with you."

"For the last time," Jana exclaimed, "you're staying here and training Monique! You owe it to us." He opened his mouth to argue but she didn't give him the chance to talk. "We'll find your damn girlfriend! Now call your friend so he can go with Jeremy."

"I am *not* going with his friend."

"Oh for God's sake, I'll go with Cole, okay?" Jana sighed, running a hand through her hair. "You can go with Nathan. You'll be safe with him; he'll be able to spot a trap. Sam, call Cole." Again he tried to argue, but she wouldn't let him. "Jeremy, call Nathan. I gotta talk to your sister."

Jana pulled me into the house without any more warning, and I wondered what this could be about.

"What?" I asked as she pulled me upstairs to the guest bedroom, shutting the door behind her.

"What happened while I was gone earlier, looking for you?"

I frowned. I wasn't sure how she could have figured out something was wrong. "Why, did something seem wrong?"

"I saw the look on Nathan's face. He seemed upset, and he left when Jeremy and I did. There was an awkward vibe in the air, and I got the sense that there's something going on between you two. But there can't be, not right now. We're going headfirst into some serious danger, and we *need* to be able to trust each other. You two need to trust each other, and I need to be able to trust the both of you as well. This is *not* a good time for secrets, nor is it a good time for drama. So spit it out and be done with it. Get it off your mind."

I sighed, not wanting to tell her what had happened. I knew she wouldn't be pleased with how I'd reacted. But she was right, and not only that, I *needed* to talk to her about it—I needed her advice on how I should handle things with him from now on, and I needed a clear head if I didn't want to get myself killed. So I told her, "Nathan asked me out."

Her eyebrows shot up.

"What?" I asked.

"Nothing. I mean, I could tell that he liked you, I just didn't expect him to actually tell you."

"Why not?"

"Well, for starters, you showed no romantic interest in him. I thought he knew you didn't like him back, so I figured he wouldn't tell you."

"Well, he did," I snapped.

"What did you tell him?"

"I didn't say anything," I said. "I was in too much shock to respond. Eventually, I just walked away. I didn't know how to respond, so I didn't."

"Oh, well, no wonder he was upset." She sighed. "You could have been nicer about it."

"I didn't expect it!"

"Even after I constantly told you he liked you?"

"I wasn't taking you seriously. I didn't think you actually knew. I thought you were just guessing."

She shook her head. "Even if you didn't expect it, you could have responded so much better. You need to apologize to him. We can't have this going on between you two right now."

"I will," I sighed. "And I *do* feel bad. I just wasn't sure what to say . . ."

She placed her hands on my shoulders. I lowered my head, my heart dropping into my stomach. I hadn't meant to hurt him. I just couldn't think straight. And my eyes were stinging again as I thought about the whole thing, but I knew crying wouldn't help. It would just make me weak. I couldn't cry any more than I already had. I had to be strong. I didn't have time to think about how I'd affected Nathan. I had to keep my mind focused on the bigger issue here.

Jana hugged me and I hugged her back, but our embrace ended quickly because just then, the doorbell rang. We immediately pulled apart, and she led the way downstairs. When I saw that Jeremy was letting Cole in with a glare, I glanced at Jana, who seemed uneasy.

I stopped her at the top of the staircase. "What's wrong?" I asked quietly.

"Nothing," she murmured, but I wouldn't have it, especially when Cole looked at her and she immediately looked away. I turned her to face me, giving her a no-nonsense look. Eventually, she sighed and gave in.

"Is it bad," she whispered, "that I feel attracted to the friend of the biggest douche in the world?"

I laughed with relief, having expected something much bigger. "No. He's hot. I get it. Just don't trust him."

"He seems a lot nicer than Sam."

"I know. But we know nothing about him. The only reason I didn't object to him helping us is that I know he wants to get to Grayson just as much as we do, to find Sam's girlfriend. So be careful with him, okay?"

"Okay," she agreed. "Continue training with Sam."

I nodded, and we headed down the stairs.

"Ready to go?" Cole asked Jana. She nodded. "We're going to Peligrum."

"Okay," Jana agreed. I gave her a smile as she created a portal and he took her hand. The moment he placed his hand in the watery entrance, they were vacuumed in, taken to a completely different world.

"Nathan will be here any minute," Jeremy said.

"Okay." I didn't want to be here when he showed up, so I simply hugged Jeremy and said, "Be safe."

He smiled when I pulled back. "I will."

I found Sam bouncing a softball off the outer wall of the house in the backyard. He was stoic, but he seemed really angry, throwing the ball with a force I wouldn't have thought was possible before I met him. He didn't notice me when I stepped outside but continued throwing the ball. When I was about a yard away from him, he threw the ball harder than before and smashed through a couple of bricks. The ball landed in the little hole Sam had created and remained stuck.

And in the moment of silence that followed, his fear became evident. Lost in his thoughts, he was completely unaware of my presence, and he dropped his guard. His breaths became shaky. The anger vanished from his expression, and panic took its place.

I stifled a sigh. Why was he so scared? I mean, I understood that he didn't want to die. None of us did. But the way he'd reacted to his girlfriend being kidnapped . . . it wasn't ordinary. No man could possibly care that much about a girl, not unless she was family. Especially not a jerk like Sam. I just didn't understand.

I shook my head, not wanting to get a headache trying to figure him out, and narrowed the distance between us.

"Good going," I snapped.

His expression hardened as he turned to face me. "What do you want?"

I sighed, crossing my arms. "Okay, I get it, Sam. You're worried. All of our lives are on the line here. But you're not the only one who's stressed. And even if you were, being stressed doesn't give you the right to be a dick to everyone. So stop acting like a princess. And if you really want to find your girlfriend, *train* me. At this point, you *need* me strong."

"Why did *I* get stuck with this job?"

"Because you promised me you would train me."

He rolled his eyes. "Fine. Then let's get to this."

JANA

"I'm sorry about how things started off with us," Cole apologized once we landed in Peligrum. Unfortunately, the moment we landed, I was blinded by darkness. Only the stars twinkling in the sky gave off light, but it was very minimal, and the moon was hidden.

There were no streetlights either. They didn't have them anywhere in Diviano except near hospitals, the only places that were fully equipped with technology on this planet, since it was about saving lives. That, and military bases. Everywhere else, saving energy and watching out for the environment were priority.

"Yeah, I'm sorry too," I agreed. I then changed the topic; we had more important things to focus on than our first encounter. "We need a map," I realized. "We should have brought a map and a flashlight. I've never been here before."

"I have, don't worry. It's an easy town to navigate."

"Even in the dark?"

"Relax. I have night vision. Just follow my lead."

But it was hard to see him in the darkness, as my eyes were still adjusting, and he quickly realized that when I bumped into him as we headed on our hunt, trying to be as quiet as possible.

"I'm sorry," I whispered.

"That's okay. Maybe it'll help if I hold your hand. You good with that?"

My heartbeat picked up, like it had when we held hands to get here. "Yeah," I replied, and he held my hand as he led the way. It didn't take much longer for my eyes to adjust, but I enjoyed the butterflies I got from my hand in his, so I didn't say anything. I just continued walking beside him, secretly admiring his looks in the dim light. I mean, I couldn't see much besides his silhouette, but it was enough to make me smile.

"We're lucky this is just a small village," he said quietly.

I looked around us. We were on a deserted street and were surrounded by nothing but trees on one side and acres of agricultural fields on the other. There didn't seem to be too many places Grayson could hide here.

I sighed. "Jeremy and Nathan got the capital. It's going to be so much more difficult for them to scope out the place. Hopefully we'll be done quickly and can go help them out."

I had wanted to take the bigger city originally so the search would be easier on Jeremy and Nathan, but I figured Cole had a good reason for coming here instead, which was why I hadn't objected to his decision.

He cleared his throat, suddenly seeming nervous. I was curious but I didn't ask.

"This place is mostly agricultural," Cole said. "The only reason I can see him coming here is for a place to stay the night. But that man doesn't seem to rest."

Speaking of resting . . .

"What time is it?"

"Three in the morning here. It was around one on Earth."

One I could deal with. I wasn't used to three, and our bodies took no time adjusting to the time change, because of the enchantment that came with teleporting. So I was already tired, but if Grayson didn't rest, neither would we.

"I'm just glad the sun will be up soon,' Cole continued. "Grayson won't be able to hide much if it's light out."

The fact that Diviano orbited around Earth meant that the planet was entirely hidden from the sun at certain times of the year and remained in total darkness all day all across the planet. That would happen about a month from now. A few months later, we'd be exposed to the sun and would experience the day just like people did on Earth.

"It's so stupid that Monique became the Keeper just before one of the most dangerous times of year," I said. Evil prevailed during the months of total darkness. That was when all evil on the planet was at its strongest. "You'd think nature would be smarter."

"The last Keeper died early," he explained. "It threw the cycle off."

I frowned. "What? How do you know?"

"I've been hacking into Grayson's computer. He was reading about his death. The Keeper's protection disappeared, and he was shot in the chest. He died on the spot. If it hadn't been for his early death, Monique would have gotten the gem sometime in June or July."

In other words, Monique's luck sucked.

"So where do you think Robert would be?" I asked, changing the topic again.

"Somewhere he can hide—a warehouse, maybe, or a barn, or an empty storefront, assuming he doesn't own a house here."

"And what if he does? We break into each one to check?" This was such a stupid plan. I understood that it was our only option, but it was so inefficient. It wasn't going to work. For once, I had no hope.

"Well, the good thing about a small town like this is that everyone kind of knows each other. Fortunately, I know a couple who lives here who might be able to help us out."

Okay, so there was a plus. Maybe that was why he'd chosen this town.

I let go of his hand and picked up my pace. "All right, where do they live?"

He quickly caught up with me. "See that house down the road?" he asked, pointing to a little corner lot surrounded by weird plants. In the darkness, they made strange, creepy shadows up the side of the small white house and crawling across the lawn.

"The one that looks like it came out of *Alice in Wonderland*?"

He laughed. I couldn't help but grin. "Yeah, that one." Fully adjusted to the light around me, I started walking faster. He kept up. We passed by all the dark houses on the road and eventually found ourselves on a path going through the tropical garden that led to the front door of the white stone house.

Cole knocked on the wooden door, and minutes later, a little light flickered through the window beside the door. Candlelight. After a few more seconds, I heard locks being unlocked and then a sleepy man in PJs opened the door.

He appeared to be in his mid-to-late twenties and could easily have been a friend of Cole's, but the look in the man's blue-green eyes gave me a different impression. A fatherly—or brotherly—impression.

"This late, Cole?" he asked in a deep voice. He ran a hand through his messy blond hair. "Is something wrong?"

"Yeah. I'm really sorry to bother you, Griffin, but it's Maya."

Griffin continued to ignore me, giving Cole his full attention. He seemed much more awake as he hesitantly asked, "She's not . . . dead, is she?"

I frowned. Was Maya still sick? And if she was, was it really that serious?

"No, but she's in trouble." When Cole's words were met with Griffin's confused and worried gaze, he began explaining as we were both ushered inside, past an open dayroom with three plain white couches and into a dining room with a circular wooden table. We sat down as Cole continued explaining, and Griffin listened intently even as he walked around, getting more candles to fill the room with light.

Once Cole was done, Griffin sat down, and after looking at the picture of Grayson Cole had pulled up on his phone, he put his head in his hands, clearly tired out. I sympathized. I felt like I'd been up all night, and my eyes were starting to droop. Cole seemed to be high on some sort of drug that kept him up and alert at this hour.

"I still can't believe you know the Keeper," Griffin murmured through his hands. And then he looked up. "But back to the point, most of the houses in this town are occupied, none of them by the man you're tracking. Some are in the process of being built, and a few haven't been sold yet. I can help you figure this out. I just need to get a map."

"You have one?"

"Sam was given one when he was helping out with the construction team for extra money. I'll go get it from his room."

Sam had a room here? Okay, so Griffin knew Sam too. But this guy was a lot nicer than Sam, kind of like Cole. How did Sam end up the way he was?

My thoughts ended when Griffin left the room. I immediately put my head down to get some shut-eye while we waited. I hated that I was so tired, but I couldn't do anything about it. It was the stupid portals and their enchantment.

I sighed and had just closed my eyes when Cole spoke up. "I'll make some coffee for when we get out of here." I didn't reply but drifted off.

I was gently shaken awake by Cole what seemed like only seconds later to see that Griffin was walking back from the hallway with a map in his hands. But when I looked at the clock on the wall above us, I realized that half an hour had passed.

I didn't feel any more alert than I had before. If anything, I felt even more tired.

"Okay," Griffin began as he sat down on the table again, unfolding the black-and-white map. He'd brought a pen with him too and began crossing off several houses.

"These are all occupied by people I've personally met. None would be the type to leave their homes unguarded." He continued crossing off a few more houses. "After that Possessed man went on a killing spree, everyone here took their security up a notch. In our village, we've all gotten Wunissas to create special systems that will immediately—and temporarily—paralyze an intruder until we can get back to our houses and take care of it. So we shouldn't even consider these."

He had crossed off his entire neighborhood and moved on to the other two, crossing off at least five houses in each, with seven to spare in total. Five in one and two in the other.

"I don't know who lives in these houses." He pointed to three of the ones he hadn't crossed off. "And then there are these four still being built. One of them is just bare bones, so it would be obvious if someone was in there. The other three are nearly finished but haven't been sold yet."

He pointed to a street just past a park shared by all three neighbourhoods. "Past this street are farmhouses you could check out. They're usually unguarded, but the animals in the barns can get quite noisy if intruders show up. They can sell you out right away. On this street, there's a grocery store here that you could scope out. There's a storage warehouse for machinery parts about a kilometer down. There's a school here. And then there's a family-owned restaurant here. The rest of the street leads into a different town." He looked up at both of us with his worried blue-green eyes.

"The only reason I can see anyone hiding out in a town like this is that nobody would expect it. But there's also the risk of being seen and called out. You have to figure out what this person is more likely to do, assuming that he's assuming you're following him. Will he take the risk of getting caught, thinking you'll go the other way? Or will he choose to go to the city and take the safe route, hiding amongst a larger group of people? Either way, it's going to be difficult to find him, and I wish you luck. If you need anything else, *please* ask. Don't forget we're in this together."

~

"Grayson's a coward," I said when we walked out of the house. We were going to hit the farmhouses first, because although they were farther away, there were fewer chances that a break-in would be noticed out there. "I honestly think he'd hide in a big city."

"He's also pretty smart," Cole countered. "He knows exactly what we'll do. He separated Sam from Monique so she would be unprotected and untrained, and when that failed, he knew exactly how to reel Sam back in."

"Okay, but wait," I began. "He also lured Monique out of hiding the same day. If he had thought it through, he would have realized that bringing Sam to him the same night Monique went to go see him would result in Sam saving Monique, so he wouldn't be able to kidnap Monique and hold her hostage until he could kill her."

"I don't think that was his fault. He couldn't have anticipated Sam coming back when he did. And Grayson knew he could still kidnap Maya if he had to, with the help of someone else. No doubt he paid a human to do it. I don't know why any Divianan would help him, unless he lied about his purpose for doing all this, or the person who did the kidnapping didn't ask for one. Or he could have used compulsion."

"But if he's so smart, why didn't he kidnap Monique sooner?"

"He didn't have to. He was *raising* her. If Sam hadn't shown up when he did, she never would have learned the truth until it was too late."

"Of course," Cole continued as we jumped over a fallen tree to get to the other side of the dirt path, "maybe he's being a coward and a smartass at the same time." I frowned, confused. He quickly explained, "He knows Monique and knows you too. He probably knows how intellectual you are and realized that we would automatically think he'd be here, because most people would think that he'd go into the city. Assuming that, he's probably evading us by hiding in the city."

"You mean, he's using cross-cross-psychology."

He shrugged. "Something like that."

"Or he could just be jumping towns to dodge this problem."

"And that's assuming he thinks we're following him."

This was all making my head hurt. Finding Grayson was going to be impossible like this. We needed another method, something that wouldn't take so long and possibly cause the death of more Divianans along the way, if he chose to get more power through the killings.

But what else could we do?

"This is going to be really tedious," Cole sighed.

I could not agree more.

~

By seven o'clock, we'd thoroughly searched every empty farmhouse, outbuilding, and barn without difficulty—well, except for when we woke an animal that started mooing like crazy after she saw us. We immediately bolted, not wanting to be seen by the face that no doubt belonged to the running footsteps we heard soon after. Thankfully, we got away and then scoped out the shops on the streets. We had a security problem with a restaurant after picking the lock but received the sympathy of the woman who owned it once we explained to her that we had gotten lost and just needed a place to sleep for the night.

When we approached a large warehouse on the outskirts of town, Cole decided to go down with temporary paralysis after breaking a window, and when the owner came down to see what was going on, I attacked him from behind, knocking him out. Given that the owners themselves showed up at the restaurant and the warehouse, we expected the same to happen at the next store we checked out, but I guess since it was a chain, it had much better security regulations. Two police officers showed up instead. Fortunately, we got off as a couple just looking for a place to hook up for the night. They didn't take us too seriously; actually, they laughed in our faces, but Cole and I shrugged it off. All that mattered was that we were able to get out of the situation.

All three places confirmed one thing— Grayson could not possibly be there. The stores seemed untouched, and judging from the owners' expressions, it was the first time—that night at least—that someone had tried to break in and gotten caught.

We tried the unfinished houses next, which thankfully didn't have security. Unfortunately, we didn't find Grayson.

But we did find something else.

"Somebody's clearly been living here," Cole muttered as we walked into a room of the last house we checked. There were a bunch of clothes lying around on the finished hardwood floor, clearly belonging to a teenage boy, judging from the band T-shirts and long black jeans. There was also a blue sweatshirt lying on top of a bag thrown in the corner.

Just as we stepped toward it, we heard the shower running in the next room. We looked at each other. Figuring this was a cue for us to continue searching, we did and found more clothes in the bag, plus something useful. A wallet.

"Riley Worcester," I read out loud, looking down at the photo of a teenage boy on the license. He was definitely around my age and had long hair that fell onto his forehead. But I couldn't tell what color it was, since the card was faded out.

"Windsor, Ontario," I mused, wondering what a boy from Windsor was doing here. I didn't think that was a coincidence.

"Listen," Cole said quietly. Focusing my attention on the bare white wall he was motioning toward, I realized that the person in the shower was singing.

"It sounds like 'Fall Out Boy,'" I commented, and Cole grinned, clearly amused by all of this. I'll admit, it was a little funny, and Cole's smile practically had me melting, but I didn't have time for singing boys. We needed to find Grayson.

"I suggest we wait until little Bieber is done with his personal concert, and then we can interrogate him. It's a little sketchy for him to be staying here, and like you said, he's from Windsor. Can't be a coincidence."

He was right. This was our first find, and we needed to carry any possible lead to Grayson all the way through. So when Cole sat down, I sat down on the floor too.

As soon as I was sitting, my body began relaxing, and my eyes started drooping.

"I need more coffee," I muttered.

"Get some sleep. I'll wake you up when he's out."

I would have agreed if I didn't have Monique's warning to be careful ringing in my head. But I honestly didn't understand why she was so worried. We all had a common goal here, so I didn't expect Cole to attack me. Plus, Cole had many chances to get at me all night. If he wanted to, he would have hurt me already. So I didn't think he would try anything if I fell asleep.

But I had another reason to stay awake. "No, I've already gotten a good half-hour. If you want to rest, go ahead. I'll keep watch."

"I'm an insomniac."

"Really?" I asked, trying hard not to stare at his biceps as he crossed his almond-coloured arms in front of his chest. I'd never met anyone who actually suffered from insomnia.

He laughed. "No. I slept in all day yesterday, that's all. I won't be crashing until later today."

"Don't you have school?" I asked, staring at his university sweatshirt.

I guess he saw me looking at it, because he glanced down at it as well. "Yeah, but sometimes, you just gotta shove school to the side, especially when it's a matter of life and death."

"That's nice of you, to ditch everything and come help your friend find his girlfriend. I mean, you're putting a lot on the line here."

"Sam's not the only reason I'm here. Maya's my friend too."

I understood. It was hard not to become friends with someone like Maya. Despite the fact that it had been years since I'd met her, I remembered just how compassionate she was, and talented. She really had a thing for artistry.

I couldn't blame Sam for falling for her.

"You and Sam dated once, right?" he asked.

"Very briefly. I quickly realized I was a distraction from the real issue—his breakup with Maya."

"You knew her?"

I nodded.

"So you know she's human."

Knowing what he was getting at, I sighed and replied, "Yes, so I know why Grayson wants her head."

He gave me a worried smile and opened his mouth to respond, but he halted when the water stopped running. The singing continued, however.

"We both attack, or you distract and I attack?" Cole asked.

"Latter," I whispered. "Cut off his air supply."

He nodded, and we quickly got into position. Cole hid in the room down the hall, on the other side of the washroom. I stayed just inside the doorway, waiting for the kid to come in. That way, he would be distracted enough for Cole to sneak up on him. It would be easier this way, not having to attack him head-on and possibly cause an injury. We were planning on interrogating him, not hurting him.

Well, we would if we needed to.

A couple minutes later, the washroom door opened and the boy stepped into the room, whistling to himself as he walked in. His head was down, and he was straightening up a towel in his hand. In his other hand were dirty clothes. He wore another band T-shirt and black jeans. His hair was multicoloured, different shades of neon blue—light, dark, electric, teal—and purple mixed in with what I was fairly certain was his natural black. His eyes were a bright, electric blue, and when he finally looked up and saw me standing in front of him, they widened to the point where I half-expected them to come out of their sockets.

"Hi," I said with a smirk.

He looked like he was ready to bolt out of there, and if Cole had given him another second, I knew he would have. Unfortunately for Riley, Cole grabbed a hold of him from behind, swiftly cutting off his air supply. Riley pulled against Cole's arms, but Cole was too strong for him to take down. Eventually, Riley's widened eyes began fluttering closed, and soon he was out.

Cole gently let him down on the ground and turned to me.

"We don't exactly have anything to tie him up with here," he realized just as I did.

"We'll go back to my house," I suggested, and he agreed. And so we took a portal, dragging the kid with us.

MONIQUE

Despite how much I wanted to keep training, knowing I needed to get strong quickly, Sam forced me to go to bed at one o'clock by refusing to train me anymore that night. His reasoning was the constantly recited "You should be getting eight hours of sleep every night." My personal trainer had been telling me that too. Only Sam twisted the saying to make it uniquely his own: "If you don't want to end up looking like barfed-up squash when you face Grayson, you need to get enough sleep. Not only will it keep you alert, it'll allow your body to relax. And stop eating crap," he added when he saw me grabbing a Twix bar before bed.

I seriously felt like I was on an episode of *Weight Watchers*.

Sam slept over that night, not trusting that Grayson wouldn't barge in here and try to kidnap me as well. Jana had fired my bodyguard, and no one else was in the house, so the only protection I had was him, the security system, and my minimal fighting skills.

"Wow, I didn't think you'd actually care," I teased him when he told me why he was staying the night.

"I don't," he retorted, not to my surprise. "You're just another problem needing to be taken care of."

I expected him to be rude. But not *that* rude. I didn't understand why he hated me so much, and it bothered me that I didn't know. But I knew that no matter how much I pried, he wouldn't give me a single word of the truth.

I didn't sleep well that night, knowing Sam was in the house. Despite the fact that I had locked my room door and he was downstairs on the futon in the living room, I didn't trust that he wouldn't come in and take advantage of our being alone together while I was asleep so I wouldn't fight back. He could easily put me in bonds in case I woke up as well.

But he didn't. All night, I would doze off and wake up at any little sound, but the sounds were never him coming into my room. They were never him at all—just sounds of the house settling and stuff outside, nothing alarming. Yet I still couldn't sleep properly. By the time eight o'clock hit and he came to knock on my door, I was still exhausted.

"Get up," he ordered from outside like we were in some sort of military boot camp. The sun wasn't even up yet, and his wake-up call just ruined my mood.

But I got up. I headed into the washroom and brushed my teeth. I then went down some Cheerios, but before I could even pour them into a bowl, Sam showed up out of nowhere and grabbed the box from me. I noticed that the thick band was still on his wrist. I wanted to ask why he wore it all the time but I highly doubted he would give me an answer, so I didn't bother.

"Not these," he said, putting the box back in the pantry beside me. He opened the stainless-steel fridge and got out some strawberries, handing me the container.

"Just these?" I asked.

"Dice them," he ordered and walked away, doing something at the stove. I realized he was making both me and him oatmeal.

I fucking hated oatmeal.

Fifteen minutes later, we were sitting on the black marble island on barstools, eating delicious strawberries and nauseating oatmeal.

"This is disgusting," I muttered, pointing to the oatmeal. He ignored me, doing something on his phone that I couldn't see. But I could see his expression, and he looked impatient. Worried. "How do you like this?"

"I don't. But it's good for you."

"A lot of other things can be good for you too."

"Will you stop complaining and just eat?" he demanded, giving me an annoyed look. His face held more fury than before, and it scared me how quickly his temper could rise. It made me think of how similar he and Tyler were, and my mind was immediately flooded with memories of Tyler losing his temper on me when I wouldn't do what he wanted me to do. I could still feel the sting of every slap, the throbbing pain I'd feel the morning after. And it scared the crap out of me knowing that Sam could do just the same.

Trying to control the fear that had my heart beating like a jackhammer, I picked up my bowl and left, choosing to eat in the living room instead.

I had just sat down to eat, quickly drying away the tears that had surfaced, when Sam walked in. I averted my eyes but didn't leave, because I didn't want to give him the impression that I was trying to avoid him while I got my fear under control. I didn't want him to know I was scared at all.

He sat down beside me, and it pissed me off to find him smirking. "I scared you, didn't I?"

"Like hell you did," I snapped.

"You're lying."

"And *you* overestimate yourself way too much."

He opened his mouth to say something else but was cut off by the sound of a portal opening up. And then, through the watery, translucent opening stepped Jana and Cole, who was carrying an unconscious teenager with wicked hair on his back.

"I didn't think necrophilia was your thing," Sam joked.

"That's not funny," Jana snapped. "There are ropes in the shed out back. Go get them. Monique, get me that chair." She pointed to a chair in the dining room, just past the plasma TV on the other side of a glass wall. We did as we were told, and once I got the chair, Cole sat the kid down on it. Seconds later, Sam came back with the ropes, and Cole tied him up.

"Why?" I asked Jana, figuring that one word itself would be self-explanatory.

"He was in an unsold house in some random village, alone, with barely anything on him. Plus, he's from Windsor. We searched everywhere else for Grayson in the town, and he was our only plausible link. We figured we'd better have a chat."

"What have you gotten out of him so far?"

"Besides the fact that he *loves* 'Fall Out Boy,' nothing."

Well, she didn't have to tell me that. The T-shirt this kid was wearing was self-explanatory.

"And he loves singing," Cole added with a grin. Jana rolled her eyes at him but was clearly amused by something too.

"Name?" Sam asked with his arms crossed, not paying any attention to the clear chemistry going on beside him.

I hoped it was just attraction, though. I didn't want Jana trusting any of Sam's friends, or Sam himself.

"Riley Worcester," Cole answered.

"Age?"

"Sixteen."

I half-expected Sam to accompany those questions with their siblings: height, place of birth, etc.

Soon, the boy bobbed his head into consciousness, his eyes blinking open. He squinted against the bright light above us at first, but when Jana dimmed it, his bright blue eyes immediately widened at the sight of us. Particularly when he looked at me.

"No, no, *no*," he began, struggling against his restraints. He nearly tipped the chair over, but Cole quickly caught it, stabilizing it with his strength so that Riley couldn't hurt himself—or us.

"I did everything I could to get away from you," he continued. "How did you find me?"

I was *ridiculously* confused, and I could tell the others were too. They were also waiting for me to respond, so I did. "What are you taking about?"

"Don't play dumb with me! I'll call the police; I'll file a restraining order. I don't want anything to do with you!"

"Sorry to burst your bubble, shitstick, but you're tied up. You can't exactly call anyone or do anything else, for that matter."

Jana gave Sam a glare that told him to shut up.

"I have absolutely no idea what you're talking about," I told Riley truthfully. "Who do you think I am?"

He narrowed his eyes at me in clear inspection, but moments later, shocked realization crossed his expression as he looked me up and down. "You're not her."

"I'm not who?"

He didn't answer my question, clearly still freaked out by the situation he was in. "Who are you? What the hell do you want from me?"

"Tell us where Grayson is," Sam demanded, though I highly doubted just *asking* was going to work.

I was right.

"I have no idea who you're talking about."

But Riley was lying. It was clear; the nervous look in his eyes gave it away.

Sam persisted, uselessly might I add. "Of course you do. Tell us where he is," he seethed. I saw his irises turn a blinding blue like when he was trying to compel me, but just like that time, it did nothing.

Riley glared at Sam. "Your compulsion is useless on me. I've been on my own for a month now. I know which rituals to perform to make myself immune to your powers."

Sam ignored his explanation and shook the chair the kid was sitting in. "Where is he?"

"I already told you! I don't know! Now stop bugging me about it and let me go!"

Sam's hands shook as he turned to Jana. "Are you even sure he's working for Grayson? He's so lanky. I highly doubt he could even throw a good punch, and I'm fairly certain Grayson would choose someone more capable of protecting himself."

"Not if he wanted to choose someone inconspicuous," Cole said. "Who knows what Grayson wants him to do?"

"I still think Grayson would look for someone a *bit* stronger."

"I may not be strong, but I'm much smarter than you assholes," Riley snapped, and I realized that in the moment we had turned our attention away from him, he'd figured out a way to untie himself and had bolted out the seat, running like hell past me toward the front door. But Sam had longer legs and was much quicker. Within a second, he was in front of Riley and had shoved him to the ground *hard*, only to lift him up by his shirt collar a second later.

"Listen, *punk*," Sam snarled, lifting the now wide-eyed, scared-as-hell kid into the air above him like he was as light as a feather. "We are trying to save lives here. So you better stop acting like an idiot and give us answers, or I swear I will take your paper-thin body and shove it down a shredder."

He shoved Riley back into the chair amongst our little circle and gave him a death stare.

"Okay," Riley gave in, his voice shaking. "I'll give you the truth. I know a man named Grayson. But I have no idea where he is. He just gave me some things to do, and in turn, he gave me money and a place to stay."

"What stuff did he tell you to do?"

"Get information."

"What information? And why couldn't he get it himself?"

When Riley didn't answer Jana's question, Sam lost his patience and pulled out a gun I didn't even know he was carrying. My eyes widened as he put the gun to Riley's head, and Cole held Riley back in the seat so that he couldn't move, the ropes having been deemed useless.

Sam tapped his feet impatiently as he spoke to the more-than-terrified kid in front of us. "Start talking, otherwise you become useless to us and we kill you."

I looked at Jana, who seemed to be perfectly fine with all of this, and wondered why. Sam would murder this kid, I was sure, and although he was helping Grayson, Riley didn't seem guilty enough to deserve to die.

"Please don't kill me," Riley begged.

Sam pushed the gun harder into his temple. "Then start. *Talking.*"

"He'll find out if you hurt me. He'll come and kill you."

"We're already on his kill list. We literally have nothing to lose."

Riley visibly gulped. Sam cocked the gun. Immediately, Riley began talking.

"He needed information on a spell."

"What spell?"

"Compulsion. He's building an army and needs to use dark compulsion to do it."

"Why did he need you for that?" I asked.

"Because it's not easy information to get. It's hidden in the government resource center, and he wanted me to read the information, memorize everything to do with the spell, and report it back to him."

"Why wouldn't he just ask you to steal the book?" Jana asked.

"In case I got caught and they took the book back. That's why he didn't do all of this himself. He didn't want to get caught, and I have photographic memory, so it was more efficient sending me. He didn't tell me any of this, though. I only realized when I *did* get caught. They were going to execute me, but he sent a suicide bomber to blow up the door of the cell I was in."

"Why would anyone do that?" I mused out loud.

"Compelled."

"Does Grayson have a compulsion power already then?" Cole asked.

Riley shook his head. "Teleportation. He's working with a guy who has compulsion—someone he's paying back by feeding him power in the form of stolen souls."

"Daeblo," Sam muttered.

I wasn't following. "So why can't the guy he's working with just compel him an army? Why does he need some spell?"

"It doesn't work that way," Cole explained. "Natural compulsion doesn't last very long. Only twenty-four to seventy-two hours; so memory erasing or permanent control aren't viable options. Which is generally fine because compulsion is usually only used by the law to get the truth out of people."

He shot Sam a look, but Sam ignored it.

What the hell was that about?

Cole continued, "There *are* ways to take away memories and convince people to do certain things, like fight in war over a lengthy period of time. But it requires dark magic that involves a lot of killing. They keep this kind of information on lockdown in the government resource centre to keep it out of reach of people like Grayson, who are trying to kill us all by destroying the gem."

At that, Riley's eyes widened. There was *no* way he was faking that kind of fear. "He's trying to kill us?" he squeaked.

Sam paced the room with his hands in his hair as Jana asked, "What did he even tell you?"

"Nothing. He just told me to do something in return for money and a place to stay. I didn't care because I just needed some shelter and food."

"And he set you up in an unsold house? Where are your parents?" Cole inquired.

Riley looked down at his feet. "Dead. Car accident."

The air became thick with uncomfortable silence. It was Cole who finally broke it by saying, "I'm sorry," which just made me angry; I would never in my entire lifetime understand that response.

Riley's face hardened. "Don't be. They were pricks."

Sam was still pacing, looking frustrated. "Daeblo," he murmured again.

"Wait," Jana said, bringing us back to the topic at hand. "Did you actually end up giving Grayson that spell?"

"He wanted it and I wanted shelter, so yes. But I swear, I had no idea he was trying to kill us all by taking the gem."

She turned to Cole. "If Grayson can compel hundreds of people with this information, doesn't that mean he can take over the military?"

My heart beat faster at the thought, but Cole quickly simmered my fear down by shaking his head. "Doubtful. Militants have to go through a ritual every morning to protect themselves again powers like compulsion, even Oscubris." He looked at me. "Which is the proper term for dark compulsion."

"How do you know all this?" I asked.

"I was in the military with Sam for roughly two years."

That explained the abs.

All of a sudden, I heard a loud crash and nearly jumped ten feet in air. Turning around, I realized that the vase on the dining table was gone, and there was broken glass everywhere on the floor. Sam was breathing heavily.

"It's useless!" he roared. "Tracking him is useless! He can teleport! He's working with a Daeblo!"

"How do you know that?" Jana asked as I recalled the information Sam told me about them.

"Feeding someone stolen souls? What other creature feeds off the living that way? The Daeblo feeds on souls. He feeds on the bodies of humans, of Divianans. We can't kill a *Daeblo*! There's no possible way!"

"Unless he's in a vessel," Cole mused, looking more terrified than before. "Riley, do you know if he's in a vessel?"

"I don't even know what a Daeblo is," Riley replied, shaking his head.

Jana sighed. "Well, this is perfect."

"He could feed off of *her*," Sam continued, pacing again. "He could be—"

"Okay," Cole cut in, raising his voice. "We need to think straight right now. It's the only way we're going to figure this out." He was giving Sam a look, but it didn't seem to do any good. Sam was still foaming. "So we don't have any information on the Daeblo, whether he's in his true form or a vessel. We can't kill him, but we do know Grayson's building an army. So we know he's planning on confronting us eventually, when he's gained more power. He'll have to anyway, if he wants Monique. But he doesn't know that we know about his army. He thinks it'll just be the six of us. But if we ditch the tracking and start building a force to counter him, he won't see it coming. And Divianans will fight with us once they understand the stakes. In the meantime, we need to make sure he doesn't help this Daeblo get any stronger, which means no more souls. So the next time he murders, we need to be there. The feeding has to happen soon after the killing, meaning if we show up in time, we can prevent the Daeblo from feeding. Not only will we save lives, it may give us a winning chance."

"We won't be able to fight a Daeblo," Jana countered.

"But we need to try to save as many lives as we can. If we can stop this Daeblo—go as a group, restrain him, and maybe hold him hostage—Grayson won't have anyone to sacrifice those souls to. Hopefully."

Jana sighed. "Okay, fine. I'm in." Sam doubled her agreement but seemed even more impatient than before. He seemed . . . scared.

I shook my head, looking away from him. He was confusing me more than this conversation was. "Can't Grayson just infinitely gain power by killing people instead of getting the gem?" I asked.

"He'll always be on the run," Jana said. "And he won't be immortal. Plus, it's not the same kind of power. It will eventually reach a plateau, no matter how much, or who, he kills."

Sam was clearly impatient. "Are you good with this plan?"

"Yeah," I replied.

Jana turned to Riley. "Where do you stand on all of this? Are you going to help us, or are we going to have to lock you up in the basement, *with* a guard?"

"I'm helping you," he said without a thought. "I wouldn't have agreed to help him if I knew what he was up to."

"You should have realized it," Sam snapped.

"I *just* found out about Diviano. Not even a month ago, I was living at home with my parents. It was after they died that I found out. From *Grayson*."

"Ease up, Sam," Cole said.

Sam ignored him. "I'll turn on the TV and set up a Google Alert in case Grayson kills on Earth again."

"I think one of us should alert someone on Diviano to keep an eye out over there."

"I'll call some people I know," Sam said.

"I'll do the same," Jana pitched in, and so did Cole.

"I don't know anyone but Grayson," Riley muttered.

"It's okay," Cole said. "I know enough for the both of us." He grinned at Riley and then walked away as he put his phone to his ear.

He also winked at Jana as he did so.

Jana, who was now blushing.

Okay, what was going on here?

I needed to go upstairs to set up a Google Alert on my laptop, but I didn't fully trust Riley just yet. I looked at Sam, who was dialing a number on his phone. Noticing that Riley was aimlessly staring at his hands, hopefully from guilt, I called, "Sam." He looked up at me, and I motioned toward Riley with my head. "Watch him," I mouthed. He rolled his eyes but nodded.

I dragged Jana along with me as I left. "I need to talk to you," I said quietly, and she followed me the rest of the way upstairs without complaint.

"What is it?" she asked once we were in the guest bedroom.

"What the hell is going on between you and Cole?" I demanded.

She looked utterly confused. "Nothing, why?"

"Um . . . he winked at you?"

She blushed again. "That was nothing. If you think we kissed or something, we didn't. We didn't do anything but look for Grayson all night. We didn't even sleep."

I immediately forgot all about Cole. "You need to sleep."

She smiled. "I'm fine. I need to call some people first, and then I'll rest."

I chewed my lip. "Okay, but don't wear yourself out. And don't trust Cole, okay? He's Sam's friend; he's probably just hiding how much of an ass he really is so he can get into your pants."

"Monique, I will be *fine*," she assured me, placing her hands on my shoulders and giving me an even look. "You just take care of yourself. And get Sam to continue training you. This thing is getting more out of hand than I had ever imagined it would. I don't know when Grayson will come after you again, but it's really important that you be ready."

I sighed. I knew she was right, but I was worried for her. I didn't want her to get hurt like I had.

"Be careful," I reminded her, and she nodded.

"I will. I need to go make those phone calls now. Oh, and I should probably call Nathan. Which reminds me," she added, "I need to get you a new phone from Diviano."

I frowned. "Why from Diviano?"

"They're specially designed so you can call between planets."

"They don't have lights, yet they have super high-tech cell phones?"

"Through black markets. I'll explain later. Set up that Google Alert."

I nodded, and she left. The moment she was out of the room, I turned on my laptop and set up a Google Alert for any recent murders on Earth that matched the description of Grayson's killings.

Soon after I was done, I heard Jeremy's voice through the open door and found him and Nathan standing in the foyer. When Nathan saw me, he immediately averted his eyes. It was Jeremy who asked me for all the details as I walked down the stairs. Trying hard not to let the guilt that I felt for hurting Nathan distract me, I explained all we had learned.

"An army?" Jeremy exclaimed with eyes as wide as the moon. I nodded. "That's crazy. Grayson's crazy!"

I sighed. "I know. How was your night?" I added.

"We just walked around uselessly all night. Didn't find a trace of him," Jeremy answered with a hint of annoyance. "Can I at least go sleep now?"

I smiled, but this whole situation was worrying me. What if Grayson tried to kidnap Jeremy like he'd kidnapped Maya? Was there some way to send him away without putting him in more danger?

Maybe if we hired what they called a Cloaker . . .

I decided to see what Jana's opinion was on that. In the meantime, I replied, "Yeah, of course. I'll call you down if anything changes."

"All right, thanks." He headed up the stairs, leaving Nathan and me alone in the foyer.

I sighed.

I really needed to apologize to him, but I also had to train . . .

I just had to make this quick.

"Listen, Nathan," I began. I really wanted to make amends right now so it wouldn't remain awkward between us. I didn't want to be thinking about this while I was trying to keep my head clear to kill Grayson. But before I could continue, Sam called me from the living room.

"Hey, Everdeen! Do you want to keep training, or would you rather make out with your boyfriend?"

I growled, squeezing my hands into fists. I was so *sick* of him and his stupid *Hunger Games* references! He'd been at it all last night, and I was through with it. Not only that, I was so *done* with his stupid commentary, and I especially didn't want to hear him talking about me and Nathan like we were a couple. It was seriously pissing me off! I wanted him gone. He was *such* a jackass!

Walking away from Nathan with my blood boiling, I headed over to where Sam was standing near the entrance to the kitchen, and before he saw it coming, I punched him in the face. *Hard*. Hard enough that I heard his nose cracking beneath my fist.

"Ouch," Cole commented from somewhere in the room.

I snapped my head toward him. He was standing next to Riley, having just put away his phone. Riley still looked upset, but I didn't give a shit about his guilt right now. "Zip it, asshole, or you're getting it next." I was pleased that Cole looked startled—not scared, but startled was good enough for me at the moment. "And stay away from my best friend. I know your pretty face doesn't match up with your *real* personality, and I don't want her getting hurt. If I ever see you trying to pull a move on her, you'll be dead before you know it."

I turned back to Sam, who seemed just as startled as his friend, only a bit more annoyed. "As for you, if you *ever* call me another stupid nickname *ever* again, I'll punch that puny little brain of yours out your ear and shove it down your throat."

He supressed a grin. "Well, I don't know what I can promise you—I mean, it depends on what your definition of stupid is."

I laughed humorlessly. "I think the whole universe would stand on common ground for that issue. *Anything* you would come up with would be stupid. Now stop talking and *train me*. It's the only thing you're good for."

Before he could say anything else that would make me want to rip his heart out, I shoved past him and headed into the backyard. Nathan could wait. I needed a fight, and in that moment, I was more than glad Grayson was willing to give me one.

PART 2

THE OBLITERATION

CHAPTER 8

TRUST AND ALLIANCES

COLE

What Monique had said made me really uneasy. I wasn't used to people being rude to me. If I was nice to people, they were generally nice to me. Nor did I ever have a problem gaining trust, so I wasn't used to not being trusted. I didn't like how it made me feel, and what made it worse was that I was fairly certain the distrust she felt toward me was because of Sam. It was even worse knowing that if I didn't earn Monique's trust, it would be hard getting Jana's as well. That was the way it worked with best friends. Not only had I experienced that myself, I had experienced it secondhand with my sister and her group of friends. So yeah, I knew how this system worked, and I knew I would need to get around it if I wanted to ask Jana out. Of course, I knew she was into me. That wasn't hard to figure out. But she would never agree to date me if Monique didn't trust me, which meant I had to figure out how to *make* her trust me.

After Monique and Sam headed outside, Riley trailed after them. Monique's friend, Nathan, sulked in the living room. I'd figured out something had gone south between him and Monique, but I couldn't really give him advice without seeming like an overly perceptive creep. So I let it be and went upstairs, looking for looking for Jana, who came out of a bedroom while I was going up the stairs.

"Oh hey," she said, flashing me a winning smile. It was such a contrast to the look she'd first given me, but that interaction was understandable. I hated having met her that way but couldn't do anything about it now, so I let it go.

I smiled back at her. "Hey back," I replied, now standing on the same step as her. She clearly noticed how close we were, but it didn't seem to bother her.

"Did you need something? A place to rest for a while? You must be exhausted."

"Actually, I was looking for the bathroom. Riley's using the one downstairs," I lied smoothly.

"I'll walk you to it. It's a little further down." I looked away from her and actually took note of my settings, realizing just how large this house was. There was a guest bedroom near the staircase, but it was essentially the only room close by, besides a laundry room further down on the other side of the hall. Around a sharp turn at the end of the hall were a few stairs that led up to another level, with a master bedroom to the right, its double doors taking up half the wall, and two other bedrooms to the left, with a washroom in the middle. Across from the stairs was just a simple closet.

"Here it is," she said, motioning toward the bathroom with a little wave of her hand and a bounce of her feet. I grinned, amused by her little nervous gestures, and stepped inside. She flipped the switch when I couldn't find it.

"Thanks," I replied.

Her smile widened. "No problem."

She was about to turn away, but I didn't know when I could get her alone again, so I just said it. "Your friend doesn't like me very much, does she? Monique?"

The smile immediately fell off her expression, and I wondered what was up. "Don't take it personally," she responded. "Monique's not very trusting of anyone."

"Is there a specific reason why . . .?" I trailed off, hoping I wasn't prying too much, but she didn't seem to notice a thing.

She shook her head. "I'm not sure. She wasn't always like this, but I don't know what it was exactly that changed her. She's been like this for a while now, and she hasn't changed in those four years. It's become practically impossible to get her to make new friends because of the way she is."

So in other words, it was going to be next to impossible to get her to trust me.

"Why?" Jana asked, cocking her head to the side. "Are you interested in her?"

I didn't know Jana well, but having spent an entire day with her gave me enough insight to know that she wasn't stupid enough to really believe that. I knew she was trying to get a more solid reaction out of me, something that would tell her if I was just a flirt or if I was actually into her. But I didn't want to let her know yet, not when I didn't have her best friend's trust. I didn't want to rush or screw things up.

So all I said was, "No. I prefer blondes." I gave her a little smirk and then closed the door, leaving her to chew over what I'd said.

SAM

Training Monique was a fucking pain in the ass.

Training Monique while a sixteen-year-old idiot who had just put your entire planet at risk watched every move was even worse.

Doing all that while constantly thinking about your dying girlfriend probably being tortured just for some psycho's amusement felt like death.

I would have preferred to experience death ten times over than go through all of this once. Unfortunately, that wasn't an option. I was being forced to do this, not only by Monique and her group of idiotic friends, but also by that little voice in the back of my mind that kept reminding me that this would get me to Maya. And I really wanted to find Maya, but three hours into training had mentally worn me out. I was finding it hard to focus on the task at hand knowing Maya wasn't safe.

I kept imagining her in a dark room, with one dim light and no windows. The room was cold, underground, and just plain inhumane. I prayed to God she wasn't in a location like that. Hoping she was alive, but not suffering.

This was killing me. I needed to get her to safety. But that wasn't going to happen unless we found Grayson.

Damn it, if Maya's family wasn't dead, no doubt we would have found her by now with the help of that Wunissa.

This was all my fucking fault.

"When can I start using my power?" Monique asked. I came back to the present to find her breathing hard, stretching her arms out as Riley took a sip of his water.

"Later," I replied. "Your power can be blocked, so we can't rely on that."

"Can I take a break?" Riley whined.

Please.

"Go ahead," I said, and then turned back to Monique as he left. "Can you go some more?"

She rolled her shoulders back. "Let's do it."

I immediately shoved her to the ground and she gasped, clearly not expecting that. But I didn't give her a second to breathe. I dropped to my knees, flipping her on back and twisting her arms behind her. She squirmed beneath my hold, but it was useless.

Legs. I sent the thought to her, remembering to skewer how it sounded so she didn't realize it was me.

She kicked a leg back and shoved hard against my back. She only got in a nudge.

"Sam," I heard Cole call, and I let go of Monique, standing up. He approached us as Monique got back on her feet.

"Go catch your breath," he said. "Find any locations where we can gather a counterforce. Jana's house won't work. We need more training ground. I'll take over from here. And order pizza."

"Okay," I said. "Just another half an hour out here. Then take a break before focusing on weight training."

He nodded, and I walked away, but I could still hear what they were saying. "Have you done the uppercut yet?" Cole asked Monique.

"Yeah," she replied.

"Okay, show me." I heard her hit him as I walked into the kitchen and pulled out my phone. His voice drifted after me. "It could be a little better. Here, I'll help you."

I had just finished dialing the number when I glanced out the window to see Cole grabbing her arm to show her, but she snatched it away. "Don't touch me," she snapped, and I rolled my eyes. Cole wasn't going to be successful trying to help her.

"Relax, I'm just trying to show you the correct form."

I could tell Monique didn't approve, but she had no reason to fight him. So she didn't say anything, and Cole went back to correcting her form—not only her arm, but her posture as well.

"Naples Pizza," the woman on the line said. I quickly ordered something, but the moment I hung up, I got a sick feeling in my stomach, wondering if Grayson was starving Maya to death.

Fighting the urge to throw up, I racked my brains for another way to find her as I pulled up a map on the desktop computer in Jana's study.

This was killing me.

I sighed, looking for any large, secluded areas in Windsor and the cities nearby, but I became distracted when I heard Cole talk again. The study had a window facing the backyard, and I could see them from here. Thanks to my other power, I could also hear them through the closed window.

Monique was now practicing the moves I'd taught her on him, but she clearly wasn't enjoying it.

"Why do you hate me so much?" he asked her as she tried cross-punching him. He dodged, and she tried jabbing.

"I don't hate you," she admitted when he grabbed her fist and spun her around. He now had his arm around her neck in a chokehold, but she easily got out. His grip was too loose. "Hate is a strong word," she continued, pulling away from him to look him in the face. "I just don't trust you. There's a difference. And I've got good reason not to trust you. Like right now, you're not helping me. That chokehold? You're not even trying to pose a threat. You're not giving me a realistic situation to handle. So if you're not trying to help me, what the hell are you doing? What do you want from me?"

"I'm not giving you a realistic threat because I'm trying to focus on your form, not your strength. Strength is going to take ages to improve. I'm not using my full force on you so you won't have to focus on your strength. You'll focus on your form."

Of course he had a reasonable explanation. He always did, for every single action he took. He never did things without reason.

His explanation threw Monique off, and I could tell she didn't like it. It made me smile, knowing that he was putting her through hell, but I knew he didn't mean to. Cole never liked hurting anyone. Although, he should have made an exception with Monique. She had stolen my mom from me, my mom, who wanted to protect her instead of me. My mom, who left *our* perfect family to join Monique's fucked-up one. All to protect her from Grayson.

"Let's try kicks now, okay?"

Monique agreed, now focusing on her legs. She tried to take him down again, but watching her do that with her kicks was even more pathetic to watch than her trying to do it with her fists. She could barely take down a feather, let alone a two-hundred pound male.

"Why don't you trust me?" Cole asked a little while later. I frowned. What was he trying to get out of her?

"I have no reason to," she replied simply.

"You also have no reason *not* to trust me."

She sighed and stopped fighting. "Is this why you're out here? So you can get answers to all the questions in your head?"

"No, I'm just curious."

"I don't trust you because you're friends with that jackass." She motioned toward the house but didn't look this way to see me. Cole did, though, and he looked kind of annoyed now. "I don't trust him, and therefore I don't trust you."

"What has he done to you?"

"Well, besides being a total prick, he clearly wants the gem for something, and I know it's not to keep it safe from Grayson like he told me. So yeah, I'm onto him. You can go report that to him now, since I'm sure he sent you out here."

"He didn't," Cole replied.

"Yeah, right."

"Sam's not like that. If he wanted something out of you, he would have confronted you himself."

Which was true, but she still didn't believe him. However, instead of giving him some snappy response, she began walking toward the house.

"Hey, I'm sorry," Cole called after her. She stopped in her tracks. "I'll stop prying. Come back, and I'll continue helping you."

"I'm tired."

"You're lying. You were walking away with an energy you wouldn't have if you really *were* tired."

She clearly didn't expect him to notice that, and I could tell it bothered her. I half-expected her to come inside so she wouldn't have to deal with him, but she didn't. Instead she walked back and continued training.

I stopped watching and went back to searching the Net, but I didn't find anything solid anywhere nearby. I sighed, leaning back in my chair in defeat just as a text popped up on my phone. It was a Divianan I knew, agreeing to help fight. I thanked him and was about to turn my screen off but halted when I saw the picture of Maya on the background.

I heard her cries in my head again and squeezed my eyes shut, as if that would drown my imagination. But it didn't. I couldn't stop picturing her crying her eyes out, screaming for someone to help her. Building this army wasn't going to be a quick job. It would be ages before I saw her again. In that time frame, her bond with Nathan could break, and even if it didn't, she'd go so long without her treatment . . .

Oh, God. Her treatment.

"Who's that?" Riley asked.

I hadn't heard him come in, and he startled me but I tried not to show it as I opened my eyes and gave him a glare.

"What do you want?" I demanded.

He pointed to my phone screen. I turned it off.

"I was just wondering who that was."

Getting angrier by the second, I stood up, towering over him, not wanting him asking any more questions about Maya. "Get lost, shitdick, or I swear I'll—"

"Throw me down a shredder?" he demanded, looking way too amused.

"I'll lock you up in the basement. And this time, it won't be ropes tying you down. It'll be snakes. *Tiger* snakes."

"Your threats are just that. Empty, useless threats," he countered. What the fuck did he want from me?

"Yeah?" I seethed. "You think so?"

The kid held his head high. "I know so."

But he didn't know me at all. He didn't know how pissed I was at the moment or how impatient I was to find Maya. And he did *not* know my strength.

It was those factors that led to my fist in his face. I heard a crunch, and he roared in pain, holding his face in agony as blood from his nose seeped through his fingers. "Like I said," I snarled. "Get. *Lost.*"

He immediately left, heading out into the hallway, and I heard his little feet running toward the bathroom, probably to wash up. It was precisely that moment that I heard Monique laughing outside, and my attention immediately went elsewhere.

That girl *never* laughed.

Guess Cole just wanted to work his magic again.

MONIQUE

Cole and I went at it in silence for a pretty long time, still working on my hand-to-hand combat skills. It was completely exhausting, so after a while, we took a break.

It was then that he said, "I don't want to freak you out, but yesterday wasn't actually the first day I saw you."

What the hell was that supposed to mean? I didn't think he meant he'd seen me randomly on the street. "When did you first see me then?"

"A little over a week ago. I was with someone who was Tracking Grayson down before he started working with a Cloaker, and we realized he was headed toward a school. I wasn't sure why until I saw you heading into the woods nearby and him following you. So I followed the both of you there and gave you a heads-up."

Unable to contain my shock, I let my jaw drop. "That was *you?*" He nodded, giving me a sheepish grin. "But I heard Sam's voice," I remembered aloud, now more confused than ever.

"I have the power to mimic voices," he said, starling me by using my own voice. He laughed, no doubt at the expression I carried on my face, and sat down on the grass. I followed suit. "And I can see in the dark."

It was then that I realized I'd never asked him what powers he had.

I wondered what powers Riley had.

I wondered what powers *Jeremy* had.

"But why did you mimic Sam's voice?"

"Because I found it hilarious imagining the look you would have on your face when you eventually met him. And I found it even more hilarious knowing how confused he'd be as to why you were looking at him so weirdly until I told him." His grin widened. "Of course, that landed me with a bruise on my arm, but it was worth the laugh."

Despite my previous repulsion toward him, I found it amusing how he took pleasure in the smallest possible moments. I found myself grinning. "Is that what you do all day with your power? Mimic people just for the laughs?"

"Pretty much."

It was then that I realized how different he was from Sam. How the hell were they even friends, when Sam was so dead serious all the time—not to mention angry—while Cole seemed so calm, even in the worst situations? Like right now—how was he even grinning?

How was *I* even grinning?

"You're thinking about how Sam and I are so different, right?" he guessed aloud.

How did he know that?

I decided to answer truthfully. "Yeah."

"We're actually not that different," he replied, and I wasn't sure how I felt about that. After spending a little more time with Cole, I found that they didn't seem similar at all. But Cole's character could be some sort of an act. But if it *was* an act, why would he tell me this?

"Sam isn't that bad of a guy; he just lets his emotions get the better of him, and it clouds his judgment. Like right now, he's worried about his girlfriend, and it's making him impatient and angry. He's taking his frustration out on other people, like Riley. And you. But he cares."

I shook my head. "No, he doesn't. He *hates* me."

"It probably seems like it. But he *does* care. He just hides it. He's really a big softy who just wants to appear tough. Like he's . . . the Macho Man," he finished off in Sam's voice.

Just then, I heard someone yelling from inside the house, but I was too focused on what Cole just did to care. I found myself laughing and Cole grinned, glancing toward the house.

"I'll be right back," he said.

"Okay," I replied, and he stood up, heading inside. I followed him shortly after, now curious as to what had happened earlier.

I noticed Cole walking upstairs as I headed inside the living room. "Where are you going?" I asked as I approached him.

"Washroom. Bottom one's occupied."

I looked down the hall. The bathroom light was on, and I heard the sink running. Ignoring Cole, I headed down the hall to see Riley inside, washing his hands and tipping his head back. His nose was bleeding. It looked broken, and he seemed to be in a lot of pain.

"What happened?" I demanded.

"What do you *think* happened?" he retorted, his voice off because of his nose.

It wasn't a hard guess. "Sam punched you?"

"All I did was ask him who the girl on his phone was."

I rolled my eyes, grabbing a stack of tissue papers. "Tilt your head forward," I said.

"What?"

"Just do it."

He complied, holding the papers underneath his nose and letting the blood drain out. Grabbing him by the wrist, I led him to the living room and sat him down on the couch, making sure he kept his head tilted forward.

Just then, Jeremy came down the stairs, reminding me that I need to talk to Jana about getting him a Cloaker. "Hey," I said.

"What happened?"

"Broken nose." I turned back to Riley. "You're lucky I know how to deal with this."

Jeremy had broken his nose as a kid by tripping and falling, and I had been there when our old neighbor fixed it up for him. Last year, Jeremy got hit with a basketball to the face when he wasn't paying attention, and I fixed it up for him.

"Is it going to hurt?" Riley asked as I felt around his nose for the right spot to push against.

"Like a bitch," Jeremy replied. "Hey, by the way, where'd Nathan go?"

I didn't know, and I didn't want to know. It was too awkward between us at the moment. Fortunately, I didn't have to answer, because just then, I heard footsteps coming into the room and Sam saying, "He went home, but he's still calling around to find people to join us."

I ignored Sam, finding the right spot on Riley's nose. "Don't jerk your head back," I told him when I did. "I'll count down from three, okay?"

"Okay."

"Ready?"

"Yeah."

He seemed scared, but I couldn't do anything about that. "Three . . . two . . . one."

I turned his nose and heard a crack as it straightened out. Riley hissed in pain, and I pulled away to find his eyes closed. "When you can, open your eyes and look at me." He took a few seconds and then did as I said. I frowned. "Okay, it's still a bit crooked. I'm going to have to do that once more."

"Fucking hell," he muttered but prepared himself. Again, I counted down from three, and once I straightened it, I stepped back. I waited until he was able to look me in the face and then smiled.

"It's straight. You feeling better?"

"It still hurts, but yeah, thanks."

"Wow, you're like brother and sister already," Sam sneered. I ignored him, but Riley didn't.

"You're an ass."

"Do you *want* me to break that nose again?"

"Sam, just shut up," I sighed. I didn't care if he was impatient and pissed about his girlfriend. He didn't have the right to take it out on other people.

Just then, the doorbell rang. "That's probably the pizza," Sam said. I was about to offer to get it when Cole came down the stairs and opened the door, grabbing the two medium pizzas and paying the guy. Jana came downstairs soon after, appearing rested. But before she could get lured in by the smell of the pizza being carried into her elegant dining room, I pulled her aside and explained my issue with Jeremy to her in the guest bedroom.

She gave me a calculating look, taking a second to think before she replied, "Okay, I'll see if I can find a Cloaker. They charge a lot, though."

"I'll work extra for the loss after this is all over."

"Okay. I'll get back to you when I've found one."

I smiled at her. "Thanks." She smiled back, and we went down to eat with everyone else. As soon as we were all seated with food on our plates, I voiced the questions I'd thought of while training.

"Riley, what powers do you have?"

He looked up at me from his pizza slice, seeming befuddled by my random question, but answered me anyway. "I'm very aware of others' emotions. But I've always been like that, so I don't know if that's a power or if I'm just really perceptive."

"It's a power," Cole replied. "A form of mind reading, in a way. Used mostly by therapists to calm patients down. It's a cool power to have." He turned to Jeremy, asking the question I had been planning on voicing. "Jeremy, what's your power?"

Jeremy looked taken aback, and I realized he must have not thought about it before. "I have no idea. Is that a bad thing?"

"Not at all. People's powers develop at different points of their lives, and usually people who live on Earth develop them later on, because of the lack of the mystical environment. I only developed night vision when I joined the military, but I had the ability to mimic voices at a very young age."

"I'm sure you'll discover yours soon," I assured Jeremy.

Riley asked Jana and Sam what their powers were, as well as mine. But the topic was quickly dropped when Jeremy asked, "Why do your virtencias look so different?"

We all looked at him, but I was the only one who wasn't confused. I clarified his question. "Yeah, our aunt has a bunch of virtencias in her house, but they don't look like yours. See?" I pulled the one I'd stolen out of my pocket and held it up for everyone to see.

Sam pulled his out too. "Yeah, the hilt is different. I've never seen that before."

Jeremy and I looked at each other. Why did Carrie have these things?

"Carrie, right?" Jana asked. I nodded. "Why don't you just ask her why these look different?"

I bit my lip. "Because she would realize that we were snooping around, and that I stole this."

Cole frowned. "I'll look into it later, if you don't want to talk to her. But if she knows things we don't, she could be an asset. She could help us out."

I didn't really want to drag her into this. I knew what happened could affect her and her child too, but I didn't really want her to know how much crap we were in because of me. "I think we can handle it without her, right?" I replied.

"We'll try. We'll only bring her in if we need to," Jana said.

"But if she can speed up the process—"

"Sam," Cole cut in. "Leave it."

Sam scowled.

"Anyway," Jana began, "we still need to arrange a place for everyone who joins us to gather. We can't have the gathering here. Cole and I talked about this, and we think it's best if we stay on Earth. Most Divianans we know live on Earth anyway, and getting around from motels to the training ground will be much quicker."

"Where will we gather, though?" I asked.

"Sam's looking into it," Cole put in. "We also need to find out how many people we're going to have to ask to join. We have no idea how many people Grayson is compelling to join him, and we need to be prepared."

So Cole spent the next two hours trying to hack into Grayson's computer using a virus, while Sam had me go into Jana's gym, run a couple miles on her treadmill, and then do some weights. When we came back up and I finished showering, I headed back into the dining room to find out that Cole hadn't gotten anything useful out of hacking, and the only other way to get the information we wanted—plus Maya's location—was to find out where Grayson was hiding. We were spinning around in circles, and it was making me dizzy.

"Monique, he took advantage of the fact that he knew you personally to bring you out of hiding when he killed your friends," Cole said after his useless hacking. We were still all sitting around the mahogany dining table with untouched snacks Jana had laid out for us.

I had been so busy since the murders that I'd hardly thought of them. When he mentioned them, I immediately felt like I was drowning in the pain and the anger I had felt just the day before. Wondering where he was going with this and wanting to get this conversation over with, I replied, "Yeah, and?"

"We should use the fact that *you* personally know him to defeat him." He glanced at Jeremy as well. "Do you know what kind of places he could be hiding out at?"

"He was always at bars," Jeremy said. I nodded in agreement.

"Anywhere he could spend the night? Or somewhere he could keep information?"

Jeremy and I looked at each other from across the table but couldn't think of anything.

"Monique, I know you tried to spend as little time with Grayson as possible," Jana began, "but you really need to think. Try to figure out where he would be. Think back to the times before your sister left."

I knew she had mentioned Kay purposely so I'd go spiraling down Memory Lane and come back with something useful. And the mention of Kay brought so many unwanted memories, memories I had tried so desperately to erase from my mind but couldn't. Memories of a time I still missed. Memories of her buying me clothes, taking me places when she finally had her license. Memories of watching movies together. Happy memories that in a single instant turned brutal when Kay left. Left me to protect myself from Grayson. Left me defenceless to his blows. She'd left me to hurt, to wake up in the middle of the night when he would come back home from God knew where to reprimand me about some stupid issue, like unscrubbed toilets or uncut grass.

I would wake up and find him at the foot of my bed in dirty clothes.

"Grass stains," I remembered out loud. "Dirt." Sam rolled his eyes. It wasn't enough. Because even if the place Grayson would go to every night for the past four years was where he was spending his nights now, grass and dirt were everywhere.

"His hunter's shop," Jeremy put in suddenly. "He used to go there all the time. It's not that far and it's super convenient for him; he could run the shop and do all his scheming at the same time."

"But he can teleport," I objected. "Why would he stay so close to home when he can go anywhere he wants at any given time?"

"He can't teleport on Earth," Cole explained. "It's one of the limitations of the power. And he can't teleport between planets with his power either. No one can without a virtencia."

"But if he suspected we would fight back, he wouldn't want us to find out where he's spending his time or keeping information. And the hunter's shop is *so* obvious."

"I don't think he did suspect we would fight back," Sam interjected. "I don't think he expected me to confront you and train you, otherwise he would have kidnapped you a long time ago."

"Okay but why would he do all his scheming in plain view?" I asked.

"It's very likely he has an office in there," Cole replied. "Wouldn't you know? Haven't you ever been inside? You own a bow and arrows. Surely you must have gotten them from there."

"Yeah, I've gone a few times, and I never noticed anything. But I never needed to wander far."

"We should still scope out the area," Jeremy said.

"I suggest you and Sam go." Cole looked at Jana and explained his reasoning. "Jana, your visions could be used as an advantage, and Monique, Riley, and Jeremy could use some more training before they go out somewhere where Grayson could easily be."

Why would Cole be staying back instead of Sam?

That distrust started to slip back.

"I agree," I said, wanting to find out what he really wanted, and since Jeremy would be here, I knew I wouldn't have to worry about Cole taking advantage of me.

"Okay we'll go. I need the address though. I have no idea where it is."

I gave Jana the address for the shop, and she wrote it down on her phone. Minutes later, Sam and Jana left.

"All right, let's get training," Cole said. "Riley, Jeremy, I suggest you go down and use Jana's gym. Monique, you and I will go to the backyard."

He was separating us? He definitely wanted something out of me, but I wasn't sure what. Suspiciously, I followed him outside.

"Okay, I sent them down so we can focus on your power for the moment," he began, giving me yet another reason to ignore my distrust. Although it did give me a reason to get a little excited. I could finally figure out how to use this damn power. "Plus, now it's dark enough that people won't see things flying up in the sky."

"All right. So what am I going to be doing to strengthen my power?"

"Actually, you need to learn how to harness it first. Sam told me he riled you up and used your anger as a trigger for your power, but you're going to have to learn how to use it without getting angry." He picked up a twig from the ground. Placing it in his open palm, he held out his hand. "Lift this."

"How?" I asked.

"Concentrate. You're going to have to channel a part of your brain that you've never really used before. This is something only you and other people with your power will know how to do. I wish I knew another telekinetic who could help you better, but I don't. I'll do the best I can to help you, though."

So I tried, and it took all of my concentration and willpower to make the twig move. It was different now, weirder, since the snakes crawled from my brain, through my skin, and to my hands *much* more slowly than when I was angry. And unlike when Sam was fueling my anger—perhaps because I was now actively channeling my power—my hands glowed with a blue hue I had only seen the first time I used it.

The snakes made it all the way to my hands, and instantly, Cole was thrown back across the backyard.

I immediately lowered my hands, and unexpected guilt flooded through me. "Oh my God, I'm so sorry!" I squeaked.

He rubbed the back of his head and sat up. "It's okay. I expected that to happen. That's why I made the guys leave, and why I suggested I train you instead of Sam. He wouldn't have tolerated that."

I grinned, realizing he was right, and he smiled back. "Let's try this again, okay? Try controlling it this time. Don't let it take over you."

I tried doing as he said, but the moment I focused on the stick on the ground and that part of me clicked into place, the snakes crawled, only at top speed this time, and I threw him off his feet again. On the bright side, the stick moved too, but not in the way I wanted it to.

"Again," he said, and so I tried, failing time and time again, until finally, an hour later, the stick lifted in the air and Cole stayed planted, though a little bruised up.

"Perfect. Now try moving it."

I followed his command, but the stick just rammed itself into Jana's shed. Great. First the dent the softball had left in the house, now the hole I'd created.

"Um," Cole began, taking a step back. He looked a little scared. "Try moving your hands slower."

Realizing just how dangerous my uncontrolled power could be, I felt an unexpected sense of admiration at the fact that Cole was willing enough to stay back and be the one to teach me this.

This time, I was more careful when he laid another stick in front of me, making sure I used a little less speed moving it. Only I was now focusing too much on speed and not on the power I was harnessing. The stick quickly fell to the ground.

I spent two full hours trying to focus on harnessing my power without much success. Eventually, I just began wondering why Jana and Sam still weren't back. I wanted to call Jana to make sure they were okay, but Cole wouldn't let me.

"They might be hiding, and their phones could give them away, if they didn't get a chance to turn them off."

So I grudgingly put my phone away, and Cole let me vent my worry by flinging things across the yard, something I found enjoyment in, and release. He also let me use my arrows as he focused on Jeremy and Riley still down in the basement. But the moment he left, my mind wandered off to Jana again, wondering where she was and what she and Sam had found. If they had even found anything. And what if Grayson had caught them? What if they were already dead?

SAM

Grayson's hunter's shop turned out to be a thriving little store and not a personal hideout like I'd expected it to be. It was on a main road on the outskirts of the city with just a few other buildings nearby, so I was surprised it got a decent amount of attention. When we went inside, we noticed about a dozen people walking through the aisles, hunting for weaponry. But we didn't notice anything suspicious. Even the single employee there seemed completely ignorant.

"Evening," he said, greeting us with a friendly smile. "Is there something I can help you find?"

"No, thank you," Jana replied with a smile just as wide. He nodded, looking away. Trying to look casual, we made our way around the entire store without finding an office.

"Trapdoors," Jana whispered just as I was thinking it. I nodded. "Where do you think one would be?"

"Back of the store or behind the front counter."

The back of the store contained nothing. We patted every single surface and found nothing suspicious. So Jana asked the cashier for help, keeping him busy near the back while I looked through the area near the counter.

Nothing.

I headed back to where Jana was just as she thanked the employee for his help. Once he left, I told her, "There was nothing there."

"I figured. It's in the back. Kind of found out from him just now."

"How?"

"I have my techniques." When she grinned, I rolled my eyes. No doubt she'd flirted her way to an answer.

We headed into the bathroom, a place we hadn't given a second glance. It was fairly spacious—spacious enough to conceal a door leading into another room. The only thing that gave it away was the oddly placed window that showed nothing but a back alley. The ledge contained a concealed button that was disguised as a little painted image of a gun. When we pressed it, the wall beside the toilet mutated to look like a door, and a silver door handle showed itself.

Just then, there was a knock on the door to the washroom. "Hey!" It was the employee. "I know you two are in there! Only one person in the bathroom at a time." We immediately opened the office door and ducked inside. "If you don't come out, I'm going to come in myself. I'm giving you ten seconds." We closed the door as soon as we were in the office but could still hear him yelling.

Ignoring him, we turned around to find a small space that contained nothing but a desk and a computer. No papers. The drawers didn't even have locks on them. There was nothing here.

We suddenly heard someone in the washroom. Making a snap decision, we hid in the foot area of the desk. But when we sat down, we realized the floorboards weren't sturdy.

We'd found it.

We lifted the rug to find a trapdoor. Praying to God it wasn't locked, I pulled the handle.

It opened.

"Guess he didn't think anyone would get this far," Jana muttered as we headed down the steep steps. I closed the door above us just as I heard someone walking into the office.

There was no light down in the humid stairwell, and unable to see, we stayed close to the trapdoor, which I held down so that the employee—if he found it—would consider it locked. Soon, he was pulling hard on the door, but he gave up after a while.

"Is he gone?" Jana whispered.

I heard footsteps leaving the room and then a door closing shut. "Yeah."

"Okay, good." She pulled out a flashlight. "I brought one just in case something like this happened," she explained when she saw my surprised—and relieved—expression. Leave it to her to foresee everything.

With the flashlight guiding our way, we descended the steps, enclosed tightly by muddy walls. The ground we hit was pure dirt, which explained Monique's description. There was no grass, but Monique might have been mixing different memories.

We stayed quiet as we walked down the corridor, which was only one person wide. Jana led the way, and I stayed close behind her, straining my eyes to see. Eventually, we came across another door.

And of course, it was locked.

"Now what?" I asked. She shook her head, chewing her lip, clearly just as confused as me. I could tell she was trying to think her way through this, but we didn't have time for brainstorming. Squeezing past her, I tried breaking the door down, but no matter how hard I shoved, it stood sturdy.

"Damn it," I cussed.

"Sush."

I looked at Jana. She was pulling out her phone. "What are you doing?"

"Calling that Wunissa I was telling you about. If we can sneak her in through the office window, she can open this door for us."

Unfortunately, she couldn't get a signal. We moved closer to the trapdoor. Still no signal. With heavy sighs, we climbed back out into the office assuming the employee wouldn't come back and we'd be safe. I slowly and quietly opened the door and heard absolutely nothing, so we got out.

But the moment I stood up, I was hit hard in the back of my head, and before I had time to process the pain, everything went black.

~

When I came to, I noticed that I was tied to the chair we had pushed aside to access the trapdoor. Jana was out cold too, tied to another chair in the corner of the room.

The employee was sitting on his own chair in front us with a gun in his hand.

For the first time, I noticed what he looked like. He was probably in his early thirties. His hair was a dirty blond, and his dark brown eyes were cold but knowledgeable—full of wisdom.

"About time you woke up. Hi, Sam," he said. At the sound of his voice, Jana's head rolled. She blinked her eyes open as I wondered how he knew my name. "Morning, Jana." When he called her name, she immediately became more alert, probably thinking the same thing I was.

"Who the hell are you?" I demanded. I knew we had been tricked into coming this way. He'd probably known that the door down in the tunnel was locked and that we would come back up, unsuspecting.

But why hadn't I heard anything from him when we came back up? Why hadn't I heard shifting, or breathing—*anything*?

"My name's Byron," he answered without a fight. "And in case you're wondering," he added, training his eyes solely on me, "Silencing rituals. That's why you didn't hear anything from me that I didn't want you to hear."

My heart hammered hard. How did he know exactly what I was thinking? How did he know so much? "What do you want from us?"

He ignored my question. "You guys are here for information, right? Let me guess." He shifted, resting his head on his arm.

"You both want to know the size of the army Grayson is trying to create, and *you* want to know where your girlfriend is. You also want to know what's behind the closed door."

"How do you know all this?" Jana demanded.

He got up and untied her, something I didn't expect him to do. And then he gave her a key. "Go find out for yourself."

She looked up at him like he had just told her the sky was pink. "This is a trap," she said. Of course it was a trap! Otherwise, he wouldn't be giving her the key after going through all the trouble of tying us up.

"It's not a trap."

She hesitantly grabbed the key. "Jana, don't go," I warned her. "You're going to die down there." But it was as if she didn't hear me, compelled by his confusing nature. She left, leaving the trap door open behind her. "At least let me go with her," I said, wanting to get out of these ropes. I cussed silently, wishing I had the skill Riley had.

"No. Because whereas she won't smash my skull, you would. You don't trust people easily and that's understandable, but you also don't think clearly. Plus, I don't think you *want* to see what's down there."

"What is it?" I asked, uncomfortable with how much he knew about me. "If I don't want to see, then just tell me."

"Sam, do you want to see your girlfriend alive?"

Obviously!

"Yes," I replied.

His eyes narrowed. "Then you have to do something for me."

This was *definitely* a trap.

"What?"

He went back to sit on his chair. "Two years ago, Grayson hired me to come work here. He treated me like a friend, and I let him. I was depressed. My child had recently been diagnosed with leukemia."

Leukemia . . . did he know what Maya had?

But he was Divianan, and Divianans didn't get cancer. We *couldn't.* We were built differently.

"I'm not Divianan like you are," he explained. "I simply went through the Silencing ritual. And I go through it every day because of what I'm about to tell you." He paused, looking down at his hands before continuing. "I trusted Grayson blindly when I met him, because I wasn't in the right mind-set to think clearly. I even invited him into my home a few times for dinner." His expression hardened. "A year later, he kidnapped my wife and my two kids and told me the only thing I could do to save them was to be a spy for him. He told me to spy on Monique. And you."

He was the reason Grayson knew about me and Maya.

Which explained how he knew about me, Maya, and Jana, and how he knew us so well.

"I don't know where my family is, but my child's condition is worsening; he's missing his treatment just like your girlfriend is missing hers. I'll tell you where she is, and I'll happily give you any other information you want to know. But only after you find my family."

Skeptically, I asked, "How come you can't?"

"About the same time he kidnapped my family, Grayson put me under and got a tracking device inserted into my brain. I have to take photos of everything, everywhere I go, because except for going home to sleep and getting groceries, I have to be following you, Monique, or anyone closely related to you at all times. And I don't want him tapping into my cell phone to find out I'm calling a Tracker. So I need *you* to do this. The moment you get them back, I will give you your girlfriend's location."

"How do I know this isn't a trap?" Although I already knew I would do it—I would do anything if there was a chance it could save Maya—I still wanted to see how he would respond, how he'd prove to me that it wasn't a set-up. I wanted to be sure.

"You don't."

"Then I won't do it."

"Of course you will. I've been following you around for a year. You'll do anything to save Maya. But in case you need more motivation . . ."

He pulled out his phone and got up to stand in front of me. Opening up an app, he showed me the video that was playing on his screen. "Live feed," he said.

It was Maya. She looked all but lifeless as she slept on the dirt ground of the place where she was being held captive. The only thing that gave away the fact that she was alive was the light rising and falling of her chest.

She looked so drained. Her face had grown paler and her lips had dried out. She looked exhausted and in pain, and I suddenly realized that whoever she was with wasn't going to be giving her pain medication either.

I couldn't look at her any longer. I needed to eradicate her pain. I needed to get her out of there. I needed to get her home, wherever home was, and keep her safe. I couldn't bear to have her looking like that, looking so lifeless, especially when she was already dying.

Maya, I thought desperately, *I'm coming for you.*

CHAPTER 9

VICTIM'S DECLARATION

JANA

I half-expected to be attacked the moment I stepped over the threshold of the hidden room. But I wasn't. Instead, I was merely surrounded by darkness, the only illumination coming from my flashlight. I was barely able to see a thing, so I felt around for a light switch and quickly found one right beside the doorway.

What I saw frightened me to death.

I was surrounded by a line of pictures hung up above me on a string. There were pictures of me, Monique, Jeremy, Sam, Cole, and Maya. I wasn't sure why this guy was stalking us, and it creeped me out to the max to know that he had been watching my every move. I wondered how he did it before I finally took notice of the large black screens in front of me, a row of them like something you would see in a surveillance room. I turned the screens on and was immediately presented with a bunch of live video feeds.

I soon realized that this guy was tapping into cameras everywhere—the surveillance cameras at Massey, the Japanese restaurant Monique used to work at, and a hospital. But what bothered me the most were the live streams of places like Monique's room, which looked so eerie now that she hadn't been there for over a week, and various spots in my house.

How had he gotten cameras inside my house without my family noticing?

My heart went racing at the thought of some sadistic killer entering my home, but was soon met with a more pressing issue.

Grayson must have known all of our plans, all along. We were trying so hard to outthink him without realizing what a big screw-up this all was.

We were going to lose this battle unless we took Byron out.

I wanted to bolt out of there and kill him myself. But my conscience got in the way. Killing was not my way of life. If someone deserved punishment, I'd always believed that arrest and prison was good enough. But now I wasn't so sure. If we wanted to save Monique's life—and the rest of the Divianan population— Grayson needed to die. And if we wanted to kill him, then Byron had to go too.

We would never get an advantage over Grayson as long as this guy was watching.

Yet I still didn't immediately go up, because something else caught my eye.

Off to corner of the field of screens was a small one containing a video of Maya, lying still on the ground of a damp-looking room. It was dark, but I could still make out her barely breathing body, and her face contorted in pain. There were two men standing beside her, clearly keeping her from leaving—like she would have the strength to—and preventing anyone from rescuing her. But they seemed brain-dead. No, brain-dead wasn't the right word. Brain*washed*. Compelled. Grayson had compelled them to stay with her, and no doubt one of them was a Cloaker, masking her scent so it would be impossible to find her.

But Grayson wasn't in the frame, and I realized I had no idea how far a range a Cloaker could cover.

Maybe Grayson was working with two.

I ignored that thought as I realized that the place where Maya was looked all too familiar.

Of course Grayson wouldn't think to keep her in a random location, because he didn't expect me to see this. But if he had, if he wanted Byron to show me this, then he wanted it to be an easy recall location so that we would fall right into the trap. Whatever it was, it didn't matter. The point was I knew exactly where she was.

It was the little hole in the wall—next to a familiar cabinet of wines—that gave it away. Stuffed with little rocks, it gave me flashbacks of a simpler time, when Monique and I were little and would hunt the playground near her house for rocks. A rock collection we'd hid to keep safe.

Maya was being kept in Monique's own house.

Down in the cellar, where no one would hear her screams.

~

I went back up the stairs and tried my very best to appear calm about this whole situation, not wanting to let Byron know I'd recognized where Maya was being held captive. But when I went upstairs, I noticed that Sam was untied and Byron was giving him information.

"He's gathering a small army, roughly two hundred."

Two hundred? If Byron wasn't lying, we were screwed. Two hundred was pretty big for a small army, given the population of Diviano. It would be nearly impossible building a counterforce to that.

He continued, "I haven't told him that you're gathering one too. He can still look through the videos I have of you in the surveillance room, but I've been deleting some files bit by bit so that I don't appear suspicious."

"Why are you helping us?" I demanded.

"I'll tell you once we leave," Sam replied quickly and then turned back to Byron. They were both still sitting in their chairs.

Byron continued, "I've been giving him some information so that he doesn't suspect I've been helping you guys all along. I told him what you did with the tracking, and he specifically sent Riley where you would find him. I overheard some of their conversation but wasn't able to figure out what exactly he wanted Riley to do—or why," he added, glancing at me. I stared back in horror. We needed to get Riley out of the house. We had to warn the others. "But Riley's smarter than he lets on, and, unless he's being compelled, he'll quickly figure out which side is the better one to be on."

"I am going to *kill* that kid," Sam snarled.

"I wouldn't. If you play the right cards, he could be an incredible asset rather than a liability."

"Okay, is that all?" I interrupted, not trusting this guy. "Because we have things to take care of."

He glanced at Sam, a silent message passing between the two of them. Great. So now they were best friends. Why was Sam trusting him?

Eventually, the two of them stood up. To my surprise, Byron ripped up the ropes that had been on the ground with a pocketknife I didn't see him pulling out. He then threw the chairs to the side and smashed open the window with one of them. Finally, he shoved the desk to the side and held his palm out toward me. "Key."

I handed it to him. He turned to Sam. "Punch me. Grayson will know you came in because of our security cameras, and I need to make it seem like you got away despite my best efforts to stop you."

Sam did as asked, and on Byron's command, we climbed out the window and ran the rest of the way to my parked car to make it seem like we were running from Byron.

Once we got in, I turned to Sam. "Why the hell are you trusting him?"

"His family's being held captive. He told me he'd give me all this information, if I promised to find his family and rescue them. Then he'll give me Maya's location." He gave me more detail on the situation and then said, "I know it could be a trap, but I have to take my chances. I'll go alone if you guys aren't willing to take the risk."

Still breathing a little heavily, I replied, "Sam, that doesn't matter now. I know where Maya is."

He looked at me as if I just turned into a potato or something. I told him what I'd seen.

"It could be trap," he said. "But I don't care. I'll take my chances. Let's go now."

"Wait. We need to take care of Riley first. Plus, what if Grayson's there? We need to make sure he's not home . . ."

I mentally smacked myself. We'd checked everywhere for Grayson, but we didn't think of the most obvious place he could be. None of us even suspected he could just be at home, resting, while people he'd used Oscubris on did his work for him.

And the Cloaker . . .

"What is it?" Sam asked.

"What if he's been at his house this entire time?" I replied, explaining my theory. I could tell he wanted to boot himself in the ass for it too. Two of Jeremy's relatives had been in Windsor the night we tracked him. One of them had probably been him. And we'd gone searching the ends of Diviano instead of looking in our own backyard, so sure he wouldn't be here that we didn't even bother to check.

"Okay, so if he *is* home, then what?"

I sighed, starting the car. "Let's group up with the others and think of a plan."

MONIQUE

When Jana and Sam finally came back in one piece, I was so relieved that I threw my arms around Jana the moment she walked through the front door.

"I thought you were dead."

She laughed, but not wholeheartedly. "Please. I wouldn't go down that easy." And then she gently pulled away. "Okay, we've got work to do."

So we grouped up in the dining room. The moment we did, Sam pinned Riley to the table facedown, holding his arms behind his back.

"What the hell, man?" Riley cried, and for good reason. I didn't think Sam was still suspicious of him. The kid hadn't done anything stupid in the time we'd had him here. So why was Sam getting all offensive on him now?

Jana surprised me by being the one to respond. "What information have you given Grayson?" she demanded.

Riley looked shocked, his eyes growing wider than they already were. Any more wide and they'd be falling out of their sockets. But I couldn't blame the kid. I was just as shocked, and from the looks of it, so were Jeremy and Cole. "What?" he squeaked.

"Don't play stupid. We know that Grayson wanted you to come here for a reason, so tell us what the reason was and what information you've given him. Which reminds me . . ." Jana got up off the table and went to the other side of the living room, looking around for something. Eventually, she stopped near a vase full of flowers on the ground and pulled an artificial flower out, tearing it apart.

Mechanical.

What the hell was going on?

"Camera," she explained. "We're being watched. I'll explain everything once Riley tells us how much he's told Grayson."

He didn't crack, so Sam pushed him harder into the table, making Riley wince in pain. I shouldn't have felt bad for him, since he wasn't on our side according to Sam and Jana. But I found it hard not to; the kid just seemed so innocent.

Sam, even more impatient than before, threatened, "I swear, I'll give you another broken nose, and this time, Monique won't be nice enough to fix it."

I'd never expected him to call me nice, *ever.*

"And I think a dislocated jaw will go along with that pretty well," Sam continued. "A broken hip sounds pleasant too."

"Okay, okay!" Riley exclaimed. "Enough with the threats. I'll tell you exactly what happened as soon as you let me go."

"Not a chance, Houdini. The moment I let you go, you'll either run or poof yourself out of here with whatever magic you carry in those hands. So tell me everything before I carve your face into this table."

Riley, whose face was firmly compressed, now looked pissed but gave in. "He told me to spy on you, tell him what you were planning on doing."

"Lie. He has someone watching our every move already."

"I know, but he also wanted me to lead you in the wrong direction. He told me to make sure you didn't start gathering an army, and I figured it was because he was building one of his own and didn't want competition. I was going to do it until you told me what he was really after. Now I'm thinking that an army is the best option we've got."

"How much have you told him about what we're doing?"

"I told him that tracking failed so we're brainstorming to find another solution. I also told him you were trying to hack into his computer to see what he's up to, but that was about it. I didn't tell him about the army. I've just been giving him enough so he'll keep sending me money."

I wondered when and how he was getting the money delivered to him; he must have gone out and met Grayson somewhere without us noticing.

"How do we know you're telling the truth?"

"You don't!" Riley grunted.

"Then I guess we should just lock you up."

"Let him go, Sam," I sighed. I could tell from the look on Riley's face that he was telling the truth. There was a sincerity in his eyes that just gave it away. Plus, I was sure if Sam kept his face pressed into the table any longer, Riley's face would have swirly designs permanently etched into his skin.

Sam let Riley go, and the kid rubbed his shoulders as he straightened up. And I was right: he did have carvings in his face, but they were slowly waning.

Sam still seemed pissed, however, and he turned to me. "If he screws this thing up, I'm blaming it on you," he snapped. I ignored him as he sat down beside me.

Riley sat down on my other side. "Thanks," he muttered.

"Just because I saved you from a permanent tattoo doesn't mean we won't constantly be watching your every move."

"You better prove yourself worthy of keeping," Jana added. Riley nodded, lowering his gaze. "All right, back to the main problem. There's this guy named Byron who's being blackmailed by Grayson to spy on us. Monique, you have a camera in your room back home," she added. "Just thought I should let you know."

What. The. Actual. Fuck.

She then turned her attention back to the issue at hand. "Riley, do you know him?" Riley shook his head. "I figured. There's a lot of strength in numbers, but for people like Grayson, it's only when those numbers are divided. That way nobody can team up against him—but that's what we just did. And we're going to keep doing that. I got texts from a few more people who are flying to Windsor soon, but in the meantime, I'll explain what else we found out."

And so she dove into her story, telling us about Grayson's plans and how Maya had been in *my* house this whole time.

Not to mention the fact that Grayson had probably been in that house this entire time too.

"I don't think we should go in until we can check out all the threats," Cole put it, looking directly at Sam. "I know you want to save her as soon as possible, but we need to be careful about this if we don't want to wind up dead."

"And I hardly doubt he'd even hesitate to kill us now that he's compelled more people to help him, especially since he has such little morality he'd keep even an ill kid hostage," Jeremy added, looking extremely pissed about that. He wasn't the only one. It made me sick to my stomach thinking about how Grayson was willing to do that. It made me sick knowing that he was willing to kill so many others too, for his own selfish reasons.

"I have an idea," Riley began. "To check out all the threats I mean. But it'll kind of be dangerous."

"Okay, shoot."

"If we can get a really quiet toy helicopter that runs on remote control with a camera attached to it, and if we can get that camera inside the house, I can drive it through the entire place to check for threats."

"Okay, done. I can help with the techy stuff," Cole added.

We all agreed, and then Riley said, "We should get the stuff now."

"Let's go."

The two of them left, and Sam continued training me while Jana and Jeremy got some rest for the night.

"What did Cole do with you while I was gone?" Sam asked once we were in the backyard.

"He helped me channel my power."

"Okay, show me what you can do."

It wasn't much, but in the time Cole and Riley were gone, Sam helped me control my power a little more, training it to obey my speed and direction. But it all ended in a huge headache. I was just hoping that soon, controlling my power would require little to no effort, and fewer painful headaches.

"With enough practice, you'll be able to use your power to move things through eye contact alone," Sam mentioned when I was taking a quick break.

My eyebrows shot up. "Say what now?"

His lips tugged up into a half-smile. "Eventually," he added. "Don't get too excited. Does Grayson know about this power at all?"

"I don't think so."

"Good. Use that to your advantage. It's better if he underestimates you. That way he won't see this coming, and you'll be able to take him down with a simple snap of your fingers."

Just imagining that left a smile slowly spreading across my face.

~

I woke up Jana and Jeremy when Cole and Riley came back roughly two hours later, finding that they had gotten something else while they were out too.

"Use these earpieces," Cole said, handing each of us a small black object that hooked easily onto our ears. "It'll let us communicate at far distances without ever having to touch our phones; plus, they can be hidden well and give us an advantage in a battle. If we all use these, we can become the eyes and ears of everyone else on our side."

"Did you get these from Earth?" Sam asked, looking confused and shocked.

Cole laughed. "Of course not. Nobody on Earth would be able to come up with this kind of technology."

"Are you saying you got it from Diviano?" I asked, and he nodded. "But everything seems so old-fashioned there. How do they have better technology than we do?"

"It's not like using modern-day technology is prohibited there. It's just not encouraged, which is why it's not available to the public like it is here. They have advanced technology in hospitals and military bases, and special centers for professionals who need it. You've seen one side of Diviano, Monique. You still have so much more to see." He paused and then added, grinning, "Plus, we got these from the black market. They're too high-tech to be sold to civilians legally."

He then looked at Sam and Riley. "You guys are good for hiding them. Me and little JereBear over here are going to be at a bit of a disadvantage, but I think we'll be okay."

Jeremy was clearly annoyed by the nickname, but I just grinned.

Cole noticed and grinned at me. "You're good for now, but you might want to let out your hair when you go out." He looked at Jana, whose hair was already down, gave her a look I couldn't decipher, and then turned back to Riley. "We should get on assembling this thing."

He held up the two bags in his hand, and they walked off without another word. Jeremy refused to stay up any longer so he headed back to bed. I was exhausted too, but I knew I wouldn't be able to fall asleep. My mind was still running on hyperdrive, knowing I needed to get stronger *fast* and that we needed to hurry up the building of our army if we really wanted to defeat Grayson. Plus, we hadn't found training grounds yet. There were just too many issues getting in the way of my sleep.

Jana seemed to be having the same problem. After Jeremy left, she sat down beside me at the dining table. "Do you want to go work out? I'll come with you."

"You guys should sleep," Cole said, laying out the pieces of their device.

"I can't," I replied.

He sighed. "Just try. We might need you to fight after this is done, and you guys should be well rested." Jana mirrored my look, but eventually, we agreed and headed upstairs to try to catch some sleep.

God, I just hoped this would all be over soon.

COLE

Riley and I were the only two awake for the rest of the night, running on coffee and Coke we found in the fridge. Sam went to sleep an hour after the girls and Jeremy. He had been pacing around the entire time, clearly impatient to go save his girlfriend, but it wasn't going to do him any good.

"You're just going to tire out, and then you won't be able to rescue her tomorrow."

After I told him that, he crashed on the futon, snoring loudly while Riley and I continued to burn calories throughout the night in the dining room, assembling our surveillance chopper. Unfortunately, when we flew it, we found that it was noisier than we thought it would be. With heavy sighs, we set on fixing that problem.

By 5 a.m., we'd managed to make the helicopter as quiet as it possibly could be by dismantling and reassembling it. We'd also synced the camera to my laptop so that we could get a live feed using Bluetooth.

We tried out the machinery, made sure it flew well, and then grinned, satisfied with our work.

"Maybe you are more than skin and bones," I teased after we were done. Riley just rolled his eyes, but something in his expression told me he took that to heart.

SAM

Cole woke me up at around five-thirty in the morning, and after telling me that he and Riley were done making their special, techy device, we decided to head out before the other three even woke up.

But we had no idea how we were going to get the thing into Grayson's house, so we paused in our departure and woke up Monique, who came downstairs with sleepy eyes and bedhead hair.

She thought hard about it, clearly, but all she said was, "Nathan dropped me off the last night I was there and didn't lock the door that connects the balcony to my room. But Grayson probably made sure every door and window was locked, and knowing him, he probably set the security alarm as well. So I have no idea how you'll get in."

"I can fix that," Riley said excitedly. "I've been sneaking out of the house since I was like two, and I can easily turn off systems from outside the house. I just need a laptop and half an hour, tops."

Riley immediately went to work his magic. Monique looked at the helicopter sitting on the coffee table in the living room, which Riley had creatively named the HellCam, with judging eyes, and said, "Wake me up if you need any more help."

As if she had helped at all.

She left, and like Riley said, all it took for him to break through the house alarms was half an hour. As soon as he was done, we left for Monique's house, taking Cole's Cruze there. Cole decided to take the risk and pick the lock on the front door before running back to his car, which we had parked down the road. Needing to stay concealed, we parked behind another car. Thankfully, Riley could still control the helicopter from there,

Cole luckily came back safely after opening the door and placing the helicopter just past the threshold. Once we had an opening, Riley took control of the HellCam by watching where he was going through Cole's laptop.

"Are you sure you have control?" I asked with my heart thumping loudly.

"Relax," he said. "I've been playing video games from the moment of conception. I know exactly what I'm doing."

He wasn't bluffing. He maneuvered the house easily, stealthily sneaking into each room on the first floor. There were a couple men appearing dazed in the kitchen and a few in the living room. All compelled. Plus there were two guys guarding the door to the basement and two down in the cellar with Maya. When he drove the HellCam to the upper level, we noticed that all the bedroom doors were open except two. One of them seemed to be unoccupied. The master bedroom, however, had loud snores seeping out through the cracks of the doors. Someone was clearly in there, and my guess was that it was Grayson.

"Shit guys, Grayson's sleeping," Riley exclaimed. "It would be the perfect time to attack right now."

I looked back at Cole, and I could tell he was thinking the same thing I was—there was no way in hell Grayson wouldn't have somebody keeping guard while he was sleeping.

"The blinds are closed aren't they?" Cole asked, leaning past me to see.

"Yeah. All of them are," I answered.

He leaned back in his seat. "Christ. We have no way of finding out whether he's got two men in there or fifty guarding him while he sleeps."

"I highly doubt he'd have fifty," Riley replied.

"We know for sure that he has nine men in the house," Cole mused out loud. "We're already outnumbered, even if we call the other three."

"And what if we aren't?"

"I'm not risking chances of a failure, Riley," I responded with impatience. "I need to get Maya out of there as quickly as possible."

She needed her treatment.

"But how are we supposed to get past Grayson? He could wake up, and like you said, there could be others keeping guard. Should we wait until he leaves?"

"No. He might take Maya with him."

"Smoke grenade," Cole answered simply. "You and Riley sneak into the cellar and take down the guards there. If he wakes up, I'll let you know. I'll drop a smoke grenade to slow him and any others down if I can't kill them."

"Okay," I said. "Let's go get that grenade."

~

An hour and a half later, we'd come back with the grenade. Riley used the HellCam again to make sure there were no new threats but didn't find anything.

"Perfect," I said.

I was about to get out of the car when Riley mentioned, "Shouldn't we call the others?"

Cole sighed. "Riley, we have no idea how many men are there. We could easily be killed, and we can't take the chances of Monique getting captured. We need them to survive so that someone will take care of Grayson if we fail."

Riley was clearly more freaked out than he had been two seconds ago, but I didn't have time to console him. I needed to save Maya.

I got out of the car. But the moment I did, I was grabbed from behind and was suddenly in a chokehold. A grunt escaped the man's mouth when I reflexively elbowed him in the ribs. His grip loosened but he didn't let go.

Cole and Riley were both trapped in chokeholds too, and with a start, I realized our attackers all had the same dazed expression on their faces. They had been compelled, and although it meant they wouldn't change their minds on completing this given task, they wouldn't focus on anything else either. Meaning that even though they might have been compelled to kill us, they probably hadn't been compelled to kill anyone else.

"Monique!" I cried, hoping she had her earpiece near her. "Jana! Jeremy!" I kept calling their names, and realizing what I was doing, Cole did the same. Riley, who was slowly running out of breath, seemed confused, but he did the same. In the meantime, I gripped this guy's forearm, trying to force him to let go. I couldn't, but at least I could keep him from fully choking me, unlike Riley, who was going under.

I suddenly wished we hadn't parked in the shadows. And I wished it wasn't a weekend so that people would already be up and moving, so that this attack wouldn't have happened.

Just then, I saw movement in the house through a window of the basement, and realized they were going to take Maya somewhere else while these guys tried to kill us.

No, I wouldn't let that happen. I had just found her. I couldn't let them take her away.

I was going to save her. Nothing would stop me. Not even some stupid brute holding me down. I was stronger than him. I knew I was. I was stronger than a lot of people on and off Earth. I was just distracted. Distracted by Maya. It was for that reason that I hadn't heard these guys approaching us. And it was for that same reason that I couldn't concentrate on getting him off me.

But I needed to.

With my body shaking and my heart pounding in my ears, I elbowed the guy once more, harder this time, and when his grip loosened, I pulled his arm away and flipped him over me. He landed on his back with a thud.

"What is it?" I suddenly heard a frantic voice say through the earpiece. Monique.

"We're being attacked! Come down to your house *now!*" I ordered, kicking the guy in the side to keep him from getting up. I then grabbed him by the head and turned it all the way back, snapping his spine.

Unfortunately, by the time I had killed him, another one of them showed up and caught me off guard. He threw me to the ground and began punching me.

"There's more where he came from," I heard a voice say behind me. I couldn't see him, but I recognized the voice immediately. "Grayson knows just how strong you are, Sam. He wasn't going to send just one to kill you."

Another guy showed up before I could throw off the first.

"Fuck you, Byron!" I seethed.

"You brought this upon yourself. If you had just done what I asked of you, I wouldn't have tipped Grayson off about what you guys were planning."

But Jana broke the camera . . . how had he found out?

I was finding it harder to think as the pain took over all of my senses, but I suddenly remembered the camera in Monique's room. We'd avoided her room, because we knew it was there, but I realized that we hadn't checked the rest of the house for cameras. Byron must have seen the HellCam coming through.

Damn it!

One of the guys tried choking me while the other continued to throw punches at my sides, holding me down in more ways than one. I felt myself starting to get lightheaded and panicked. I knew I couldn't exactly die as long as Nathan lived, because the bond that protected Maya protected me too, but who knew where the fuck Nathan was? For all I knew, he was already dead. Not only that, the bond itself could have snapped, it was so weak. I could die in a split second, just because of my stupidity. How had I let this happen?

Suddenly, one of the men was being thrown off me, and seconds later, the other one was off too, both of them slammed against a nearby tree. I couldn't tell if they were dead or just out but didn't stay put to figure it out. I noticed Monique getting out of Jana's car just as Byron turned around to look at her.

"Go!" Cole gasped. "He's taking Maya. Go save her!"

Jana and Jeremy got out of the car, and trusting they would have the situation under control, I ran toward the house. Not bothering for subtlety anymore, I burst in through the front door of the house and ran

212

down into the basement. There were only three guards upstairs, since the others were fighting outside, and I shot the other three, catching them off guard. The other two were dragging her out of the cellar when I came in, and the moment I saw her, I stopped in my tracks.

It had been so God-damn long since I had seen her in person, so long since I had spoken to her. And seeing her in the flesh for the first time since Friday threw me off. It made me think of all the memories we'd shared together and how, if Grayson had killed her, we would never have made any more. I didn't know what I would have done if I'd lost her. I would rather make more bad memories with her than good if it meant saving her life. I didn't care what we did together as long as she was with me.

I could have lost her. For the past couple of days, I'd spent every single moment with her on my mind, wondering if I would ever see her face again, ever hear her laugh again, ever be close to her again. Ever feel her love again.

I could have lost her.

But I hadn't. Now she was finally before me, struggling against the compelled guards as they brought her out of the cellar.

"Maya," I breathed.

She looked at me, and her expression immediately flooded with relief. "Sam!" she exclaimed and suddenly, the guards turned my way. But I didn't care that they noticed me. I didn't care about anything. All I cared about was the relief I felt seeing Maya alive, the relief I felt radiating off her.

The love.

But all of that left in a split second as suddenly, her eyes widened. "Sam!" she cried again, looking past my shoulder, but before I could turn around to see what had happened, I felt a sharp pain in my head and slipped into darkness.

I was awakened by the revving of an engine and then the sound of it speeding away. It took me a while to remember where I was, but the moment I did, I realized that the car speeding away had to be carrying Maya.

I sprang to my feet, my anger far greater than the pain in the side of my head. I ran up the stairs to see a black Sedan speeding down the street and turned to where Cole's Cruze was parked. The rest of the gang was still on the street. Grayson had more men than we'd anticipated. But our group was handling it well.

"You!" I yelled, pointing at Monique. She looked up from the man she was holding down with her newfound power. "Come with me." Without question—thank *God*—she did as she was told.

Having Cole's keys on me, I started his car and as soon as we were both in, we went blazing down the path the Sedan had taken. I quickly found it on a main road and followed close behind, weaving through traffic to keep up as we headed onto the main road.

It bugged me that I'd let my emotions get the best of me. If I hadn't paused to take in the situation, I would already have Maya safe. It was my fault that they were getting away, but I wasn't going to let them take her away from me again.

"I want you to stop that Sedan with your power, but only when it's safe to do so," I said without looking at Monique. "If Maya gets hurt, you're going to pay for it."

"You want me to stop it in the middle of street? There are other people around."

"I don't care," I growled.

"You're not thinking clearly. We don't want to draw attention toward us. Just keep tailing them until they make a turn. They can't keep going on Huron Church forever or they'll hit the border, and I'm fairly certain a struggling, or sleeping, girl in the back won't sit well with the officers."

She was right. They made a turn on Malden, trailing back into LaSalle. Thankfully, this place was much less busy than Huron.

"Now," I ordered. "But be careful."

"I'm not sure how to do this. I've tried moving things, not stopping them."

"You can do it. You have way more power than you realize, Monique. Just try."

I kept my eyes trained on the car as she did as I told her to, holding her hands out in front of her. A blue light shot out of them, but all it did was give the other car a speed burst.

"You idiot!" I yelled, flooring it. Monique was thrown back against the seat.

"I'm sorry! I'm still learning, okay? Cut me some slack."

"I don't have time for slack! Stop that car!"

She tried again as my impatience boiled over. I knew I could have avoided all this, and that made me even angrier than I already was. Gritting my teeth, I ran over a squirrel, not stopping for anything. I needed to keep up with that car.

"You just ran over a squirrel!"

"If you don't stop that fucking car, *you'll* be the one I run over next."

Maybe it was because I sounded threatening enough. Or maybe it was the fact that she had gained enough confidence and concentration. I don't know what exactly gave her the ability to do it, but she finally slowed the car in front of us to a stop. I wasn't sure how long she could hold it; the Sedan kept trying to pull itself out of her power range.

"Hold it," I ordered as I hit the brakes. I got out and stalked over to the car in front of us. The doors were locked, but I smashed through the driver's window with my bare fist and unlocked the door. Ignoring my bleeding hand, I dragged the jackass out, and before he knew it was coming, I snapped his neck. Monique came out just in time to hurl the other guy across the field beside us.

Ignoring Monique, I opened the back door of the car and helped Maya out. She had a rag in her mouth to keep her from screaming and handcuffs on her wrists. She could barely stand on her own, she was so weak, so I supported her with my arm, taking the rag out of her mouth.

"Sam," she sobbed, crying into my shoulder.

"Shhh, it's okay. I got you. They can't hurt you now. I won't let them." I looked at Monique, who was standing at an awkward angle, facing us and the man she'd knocked out at the same time. "Do you have a hairpin?" I asked.

She rolled her eyes and pushed her long, reddish locks behind her shoulder, revealing her earpiece. "Yeah, totally." But she walked over and pulled something else out of her pocket. I realized it was a pocketknife.

Why the hell did she carry that around?

I didn't bother asking but gently pushed Maya away from me so Monique could try getting the cuffs off with the knife. It took a while, but it worked, and immediately, Maya wrapped her arms around me, still crying. I let her sob into my shoulder, just glad to know she was safe in my arms and that I could hold her, rocking her to comfort.

I hated seeing her cry.

"What did they do to you?" I asked as I watched Monique take a seat back inside Cole's car.

"They were starving me. Grayson tortured me, asking me why I couldn't be killed, but I couldn't answer him . . . I didn't know myself." I thought I would be okay to hear what he'd done, but I wasn't. Rage boiled beneath my skin and I started shaking, wanting to find that man and tear him apart for hurting Maya. But when Maya buried her tear-soaked face into the crook of my neck, I forgot my anger, knowing that in that moment, I just had to be here for her. She was traumatized by all of this, and before I took any action, I needed to make sure she was okay.

"He's completely barbaric," she said.

It was an understatement, but all I said was, "I know."

"No, you don't, Sam. Listen, I didn't think he'd really kill me, or even try. The first day, I called him out on it. I told that if he really wanted to kill me, his partner would have done it in the motel the same day he kidnapped me."

"What did he say to that?" I asked, wondering myself, wondering if this was a trap.

"I was in Diviano for the first day, Sam. He told me he took me there so the enchantment would fry my brain. He wanted me to go through the pain, knowing you'd feel it too. But all it did was torture me to no end. I couldn't die."

I began shaking again, clenching my fists as I remembered the pain I had felt. It had stopped, I guess because I wasn't like other Divianans.

Now it was her soothing me, running her warm hands down my back. "He only moved me when the pain stopped, and he no longer saw any reason to spend his nights in the little shed he kept me in. And he couldn't find another Cloaker. He was so impatient."

"I'm sorry I let you go through that. I'm sorry it took me so long to find you."

"No, don't be sorry. It wasn't your fault. And . . . Sam?"

I didn't like the hesitant tone of her voice. "Yeah?"

"He's much worse than you think he is. Grayson is *not* a man. He's a terrible, terrible monster and has no mercy for anyone in his life, not even for the people he should love."

"I know."

"No, you don't." She pulled away, and I wiped away the fresh tears falling from her eyes, unable to stand the scared look on her face. "When I called him weak for not being able to kill me with his bare hands, he told me something."

"What?"

Now she was making me nervous. What worse deed could this man have possibly done? Taking Maya would always be the most immoral step he'd taken in my eyes.

"Your mother didn't die in a car accident, Sammy. Grayson killed her because she was getting in the way of killing Monique."

I suddenly felt like I was going to puke.

MONIQUE

Looking out at Sam and his girlfriend standing in a tight embrace reminded me of what Cole had told me. That Sam *did* care but was just stressed about Maya's situation. The way he looked at her when he got her out of that car made me realize just how much he felt for her, which gave reason to his impatience.

He still didn't deserve to punch people for it, but I decided to try clearing my head of all judgments, hoping to start fresh with him.

And his darling girlfriend.

It was clear that he loved her, which I hadn't really expected. I was sure he was a jackass like all the other guys I knew. I was sure his whole reason for having a girlfriend was all about sex, which was why I hadn't understood the impatience before. But this moment made me think that maybe he wasn't like that. Maybe he was different.

I was willing to try living with that possibility, despite how uncomfortable it made me feel. But in order to keep living, we had to move on from this moment, which didn't look like it was going to pass anytime soon. Sighing, I reclined the seat and waited for them to come to the car.

"You guys good over there?" I asked, really liking this earpiece.

"Yeah," Jana replied, breathing hard. "We just finished disposing of the bodies. We couldn't break the compulsion, even by knocking them out, so we ended up having to kill them. Byron ran like hell, though."

Oh shit.

I immediately sat up and looked out the window to see that the guy I had knocked out was no longer in the field where I'd thrown him. With my body trembling, I scoped out the entire area but couldn't spot him anywhere. Scared as shit, I got out of the car to warn Sam—who seemed too horrified by something Maya had said to have paid attention to Jana—but before I could, I was being smothered from behind. I immediately knew it was the guy we'd thought wouldn't be a problem any longer. He had my arms pinned down, so I tried biting his hand but didn't hurt him enough for him to let go. Feeling myself becoming lightheaded really fast, I tried screaming but only got out a little wail.

Fortunately, that was enough. Sam looked away from Maya to see me struggling, and came running at us, pulling the guy off with little to no effort. Before I knew it, Sam had snapped the man's neck.

"Thanks," I said, breathing hard.

"You say thanks when I kill a man for you but cry when I run over a squirrel?"

I narrowed my eyes at his accusing tone. "He was trying to kill me," I muttered. It was either me or him. But that didn't mean looking at the dead body didn't make me feel any remorse for the guy. He was compelled. He was merely a pawn in this battle. It wasn't like any of this was his fault. It was Grayson's.

All of these deaths were on his hands.

Sam rolled his eyes and walked back to Maya, sitting her down in the passenger seat of the Cruze. And then quickly, before anyone could show up on the street, Sam stuffed one guy's body in the trunk of the car and the other in the back seat, where I got stuck sitting when he decided to head back.

Once we were in the safety of some dense woods, we burned the bodies like Jana and the others had done, as the Oscubris prevented them from disintegrating. Once that was done with, Sam dropped me off at Jana's, where everyone else was gathered, before leaving with Maya to God knows where. I really shouldn't have cared where he went, though

I couldn't help but wonder if he had only planned on helping us until he saved his girlfriend.

SAM

"You need to go back," Maya said weakly from her hospital bed. I didn't look up at her when she spoke; I was sitting on a chair next to her cot, looking down at my phone and twirling it over and over in my hand.

"No, I'm staying to hear your test results, Maya. I need to know how much damage Grayson has done to your chances of survival," I replied, still unwilling to look up at her. I knew what I would see if I did. I would see the worry, the pain, and the heartache, and I didn't want to face all of her emotions just yet. I wasn't ready. I was too worried about what I would hear to deal with anything else. Not only that, I was still processing what she'd told me a mere five hours ago.

"You keep staring at your phone. Just admit it, Sam. I know you can't help what you feel."

I looked up at her then and found that I was right; a myriad of emotions was passing through her eyes, and I hated it. I hated the fact that she thought she knew how I felt about this. People really needed to stop telling me what to feel.

Putting my phone away, I said, "Maya, it's not what you think. If anything, I'm more pissed than ever. She's the reason my mother is dead."

She sighed, giving me an annoyed look. "Sam, you have to understand that it's not Monique's fault. She had no idea what was going on. She had no control of her fate. You think she wanted to be Keeper?"

"That's still not enough reason for me to not be pissed at her."

"Listen, if you're going to be mad at anyone, it should be Grayson. You're just channeling your anger toward Monique because she's easily accessible whereas Grayson isn't. You can take your fury out on her, but not on Grayson. Your pain and your anger are clouding your judgment, and you're not thinking clearly."

I looked away. I knew she was right, but I didn't want to believe it. I just wanted to put this pain and rage somewhere, even if it was all packed in a fist being thrown at Monique's face.

"Sam, just take a deep breath," Maya said calmly. I did as she said, but it didn't help. Sighing, she reached for my clenched fist, her warm touch working as an immediate pacifier. I looked back at her, and she gave me an expression full of love. I placed my other hand on the cot beside her and she squeezed it with one of her own, holding my cheek with her other. I sighed, relaxing against her touch, all my pain and anger replaced by the love I had for her.

"You will be fine," she assured me, caressing my cheek with strokes of her soft fingers. "You're going to get through this. *We* will get through this, together. I'm not going to let you feel any more pain."

"Neither am I," I replied. "I'm going to do whatever it takes to get you treated until you're well, to make sure you don't have to visit another hospital in your life. I'm going to go back and kill Grayson so he can never hurt us again. Then we're going to go far away from here, somewhere Cameron and Warren won't find us. And we'll be free to do whatever we please. You won't ever feel any pain, ever again."

Her amber eyes held so much sorrow, and I could tell she was still worried. But the moment I gently kissed her lips, all the worry seemed to evaporate. When I pulled away, she sighed and closed her eyes, holding both of my hands tightly. "I love you."

"I love you too."

MONIQUE

In the three days that Sam was gone, many people arrived at Jana's. Because there were so many, we relocated all of them to nearby motels. And since we were still without training grounds, only a few came over to train in Jana's backyard at a time.

"If *you* asked, we could get any place in Diviano to train," Cole said to me the second day.

I mused over that for a while. I wasn't exactly sure what I *could* do with my power, but figuring that I was protecting Diviano, I guessed I could do a lot. Plus, Sam had told me I had the most power on the entire planet. Not only could I get a place for a few hundred people to train, I could probably get the military to help out too, people who were actually already trained to fight.

220

The problem was, if I got the military on Diviano involved, it would attract the media's attention, and since the government covered up literally *nothing* in the papers, wanting all citizens to be fully informed, the news that Grayson was trying to kill us all would get out. If Grayson heard the news and realized what we were doing, then he would respond by building up bigger forces of his own, putting who knew how many others in danger. So we had to keep quiet.

"You're right," Cole said when I finished telling him and the others why I didn't think that would work.

"But can't we just *reason* with the government?" Jeremy asked.

"We don't have the time," Jana said. "Who knows how long it would take to reason with them?"

"Not only that," Cole added. "If word does get out, they'll lose the trust of their people, and they won't be willing to take that risk."

So basically, we were still without training grounds when Sam showed up at the house the day after. I had no idea why he was gone but didn't really care until his presence reminded me of something.

Mom had taken us down to a cottage she owned with Aunt Carrie a couple of times. It was in the middle of nowhere, and to make things even better, there was so much land there, and so many trees to shield the area. It would be perfect spot to train our small army.

When I asked Jeremy if he remembered where it was, he shook his head, so I turned to Sam, who had just sat down across from me.

"Hey, did Mom ever take you to her cottage?" I asked him.

He looked up at me and gave me a glare that I hadn't anticipated. I was taken aback, wondering what was causing this new hatred, worse than what he'd expressed when we first met. "*My* mom," he snapped. "She was *my* mom, not yours. Just because yours didn't want you doesn't give you the right to steal mine."

My heart sank. I saw Jana, Jeremy, and Riley looking up from what they were doing, but they were all too stunned to say anything. Just like me.

It was Cole who spoke up. "Sam!" he cried, commanding Sam's attention with a force I didn't think he'd ever use on his best friend.

I couldn't tell if Cole was going to try to get him to apologize to me or if he was just going to lecture him, but I didn't care what he was trying to do. By the time he had spoken up, I was already up and walking away, heading up the stairs with a hard look on my face. But the moment I was in the privacy of my room, I let the tears fall. And the moment I was in the shower with the water pouring noisily, I stopped choking the sobs back.

I already knew my mom didn't think I was worth keeping. That didn't come as a surprise to me. But he didn't have to remind me of it. He didn't have to vocalize the truth, especially since hearing it come from someone else's mouth hurt more. It made the words more truthful because it wasn't only me who thought them. Everyone around me thought it too.

Sam was just the only one inconsiderate enough to voice it.

I remembered thinking I would give him a fresh start when I saw how much he cared for Maya. I had thought that he was different from other guys. It was then that I realized he wasn't. In that moment, I realized that the problem wasn't the guys. It was *me*. I just drew negative attention—from Sam and every other guy in this world.

The sobs worsened, and the pain pulled at my sides as I thought all of this through. It wasn't even Sam's fault. There was something wrong with me, and that was why Sam was always mean to me. That was why the only interest guys took in me was sexual. Because I wasn't worth being seen as anything more. My own mother must have realized that the moment I was born. Maybe that was why she set me up for adoption.

So then . . . how was I pure? If I drew negative attention from everyone, why did the gem choose *me* out of all people? If my mom knew that I would turn out like this—one huge mistake—how could the gem not know? If it could somehow "see into my heart," couldn't it tell my future? Didn't it know I would be raped and would turn into a drug addict and an alcoholic? How could the gem choose me after all that?

As the realization struck me, my legs gave up on me, and I fell to the ground of the standing shower, curling up into a little ball. Wrapping my arms around my knees, I cried harder, hoping that crying would ease the pain, but it didn't. It did nothing to help me.

I needed my pills. They were the only thing that would give me immediate relief.

With shaking limbs, I got up and quickly washed up before getting redressed. I headed back into the room and rushed over to my bag to get my pills, only to find that I was out. They had been the only thing getting me through the past few days, and I had used them all up.

Fuck.

My hands were still shaking as I reached for my cell phone, dialing Tyler's number. I was so scared that he wouldn't pick up and I wouldn't be able to get my drugs, but to my relief, he picked up on the third ring.

"I need more," I said frantically before he could even give me a hello. "*Now.*"

"I'm home. Come get them."

I didn't wait any longer. I quickly got my license, grabbed an outfit he'd give me more drugs for, and decided to change at a fast-food restaurant on the way to his house or something. I didn't want to drag the others' attention toward me.

Unfortunately, the moment I stepped out of my room, I was being run down by Jana.

"What do you want?" I snapped.

"Don't take your anger out at me." She closed the door. "Are you okay?"

"I'm fine, just let me go."

"Go where?"

"Somewhere!" I nearly yelled, my hands shaking really noticeably now. God, how was I going to drive like this? I needed release. I needed relief. I needed happiness. I needed, I needed . . .

"What's wrong? Why are you shaking?"

"I'm running low, okay?" I hissed.

She widened her eyes, and her stance grew more stubborn. "No. You're not going back to him. You're going to stay here and deal with this like a grown-up. Drugs aren't going to help you."

"Well, they did a much better job than you ever could."

That struck her. I took advantage of her shock and headed out the door, not halting even when I saw the guilt in Sam's eyes as I walked past him.

I didn't care how unprotected I was. I didn't care about what I'd said to Jana. I didn't care about this stupid battle. I didn't give a shit about anything but getting my drugs.

I needed a fucking release.

SAM

"You know what? You're a total ass," Jeremy exclaimed once Monique went rushing out the front door.

"Yeah, you could try being a little nicer to her," Riley added.

I looked at him, clenching my fists. "You want another broken nose, dickhead?"

"Only if you want to add on to the guilt you're feeling."

"I'm not feeling guilty," I lied. He just smirked at me, and I despised him even more than before, for letting everyone know exactly how I was feeling.

Cole came to my saving. "Riley, Jeremy, go downstairs and work out."

Riley left immediately, but Jeremy stayed back, giving me a dirty glare. "I don't even know why Monique and Jana still insist on keeping you around. All you do is add to the pain she's feeling. All she wants is to be accepted, and all you do is hold her back from that."

He paused, standing up and clenching his fists. "You should have died after saving your girlfriend," he spat.

And then he left, stomping down the hallway to the door of the basement.

"What happened?" Cole asked. "I thought you were finally tolerating her. What changed all that?"

"Cole, I don't want to talk about it," I muttered, standing up. I wasn't ready to face his inquiry. I couldn't bring myself to tell him what Maya had told me, especially when I was so torn between the anger that shook me and the guilt that had my heart plummeting.

I couldn't think.

I headed out the front door, walking down the driveway. I was now in plain sight of anyone watching, but I didn't care. I'd already sorted things out with Byron, and he'd told me he'd let me know if Grayson was planning an attack. Plus he'd hired a bodyguard for Maya until we'd killed Robert. So I just continued walking down the road and eventually picked up my pace, breaking into a jog as I neared the end of the neighborhood. It was when I'd approached the last house to my right that I heard a conversation from within.

"An Xbox One!" a little boy cried. "You got me an Xbox One?"

A man laughed. "It's what you wanted. And what better time to give it to you than your birthday?"

"Thank you so much, Dad!"

The conversation brought memories as my feet carried me out of the neighborhood and onto a trail in a forest.

"Happy birthday!" Cameron cried, giving me a tight hug on my twelfth birthday. His ash-coloured hair brushed against my cheek, tickling me.

"Thanks!" I laughed.

"Dad got you a PlayStation 3," he said, grinning as he pulled away. "I wasn't supposed to say anything, but I couldn't help it. He's been keeping it a secret for months now."

"A PlayStation 3? Really?" Excitement filled me head to toe.

"Yeah. Just act surprised when he gets home from work, okay?"

I nodded, barely able to contain myself for the rest of day. I was practically jumping up and down in my seat at school too. I couldn't wait to get home.

Cameron and I caught the bus back, and we waited about an hour at home before Dad showed up. I'd expected him to give me a hug the moment he stepped through the door like he always did, but he didn't. He was angry, and I wasn't sure why.

"Get out," he snarled when he saw that I was the one who'd opened the front door. His teeth were gritted and his face was puffy in anger.

I frowned. "Why? Dad, what's wrong?"

"Do not call me Dad! You are not my son!"

"How am I not your son?"

He shook with anger and shoved me hard out the door. "Didn't you hear me? I said get out! And don't come back! You don't belong here!"

My eyes started stinging with fear-induced tears. "How am I not your son?" I asked again, frantically. Why was he kicking me out? How was I supposed to live? I was only twelve. "Look, Dad, I have your hair!" I exclaimed, lifting up a strand of the black hair on my head. "I have your hair, Dad! I have your eyes! I'm your son!"

I saw tears in his eyes, the eyes that looked exactly like mine, only much wiser. But his own agony didn't keep him from slamming the door in my face.

I ran faster, the cold, brittle wind immediately drying the tears that had surfaced in my eyes. The memory brought back the anguish, especially when I found out the real reason why he had kicked me out . . . why he thought I didn't belong.

My hands started shaking as I remembered the warmth of the hug he'd given me the night before, when I was about to go to sleep. Or the kisses he'd given me so many times before I decided it was "totally uncool" that he still kissed me. The love he'd showered me with before he found out the truth. Before he found out what I really was.

"You're a hybrid, Sam," Maya told me two years later after finding the truth out herself. "Your mom had a Wunissa perform a spell so your dad wouldn't know what she really was. But it eventually wore off, and he found out. That's why he kicked you out. He thought that would be enough to get rid of the danger. But now he's thinking about killing you."

It was in that moment that I knew I would never be accepted by him. I would always remain the oddity in the family, even if I *was* blood related to all of them.

I found myself back on Normandy, only farther down on the street, just as it started pouring. I picked up my pace, heading back to the house.

"All you do is add to the pain she's feeling. All she wants is to be accepted, and all you do is hold her back from that."

I gritted my teeth as I remembered Jeremy's words.

"All she wants is to be accepted."

The guilt washed over me harder than the rain.

"She didn't purposely put herself in the position that she's in. You can't blame this on her."

But she'd still caused me pain.

"Your mother didn't die in a car accident, Sammy. Grayson killed her because she was getting in the way of killing Monique."

This was her fault.

"She had no idea what was going on. She had no control of her fate. You think she wanted to be Keeper?"

She didn't. But she was.

I was breathing hard and thoroughly drenched by the time I got back to the house. I ignored Cole, who was still sitting at the dining table on his laptop, and changed into clean clothes. I'd caught my breath by the time I got upstairs, but my emotions were still a mess.

I felt a pinch in my side as I headed down the stairs. Thinking it was a result of running so hard shortly after eating, I ignored it and headed the rest of the way down.

Cole came to greet me in the living room. "Ready to talk?" he asked. I pushed past him and headed into the dining room. He followed and sat back down beside me.

"What happened?"

"Grayson told Maya that my mom didn't die in car accident. He was trying to find a way around Monique's protection, and my mom was leading him down the wrong path. When he realized what she was doing, he killed her."

I had been looking down at the table while I spoke, trying hard to stop shaking as the anger took over me again. But when he didn't reply immediately, I looked up to see him staring down at the table intently, formulating a thought in his head.

"Listen," he sighed, looking back up at me. "It sucks, I know. But it's not her fault. You can't take it out on her."

I knew it wasn't her fault. I knew I was redirecting my anger at a girl who didn't really deserve it. But everything that had happened in my life was because of her. And it was hard to ignore that, especially when focusing on the anger and the jealousy helped me drown out the guilt of my own unredeemable actions. It drowned out the fear that maybe this time, my mistakes would take me under the current. That I wasn't worth the mistakes I was making. That I was too much of a mess to handle any longer. It drowned out the fear that maybe this time, my mistakes would cause Cole to give up, cause Griffin to give up, cause *Maya* to give up, and that this time, I would be nothing more than a hybrid who just didn't fit in. Who no one would accept.

MONIQUE

I felt much calmer after I left Tyler's house and was able to think a bit more clearly too, so I made a quick stop before heading back to Jana's house.

In fact, despite Tyler's brutality, I was feeling happier and actually forgot about what Sam said to me earlier.

Which was why I didn't appreciate being reminded of it when I saw Cole and Sam sitting alone in the dining room when I walked through the front door of Jana's.

"It wasn't her fault," Cole was saying with a hushed voice. "She was eight years old. How was she supposed to know what was going on between Grayson and your mom?"

I closed the front door and interrupted their conversation. Glancing up at them from the corner of my eye, I locked the door and found Sam staring at a laptop screen while Cole lectured him. I would have ignored them if I wasn't curious as to what they were talking about.

So I dropped the bag with the change of clothes in it by the stairs and walked over to them. "What's going on?"

They didn't say anything. Cole just stared at Sam, who ignored him. I could tell Cole wanted him to apologize but I saved Sam the effort. "Unheard apology accepted. The guilt in your eyes says it all." I then turned to Cole, who didn't seem comfortable with the change in my attitude. I knew I was acting slightly different, since the ecstasy had left me a little effervescent and giddy, but I didn't care that he noticed. "Now tell me what exactly you were talking about, because I know it had something to do with me."

"Ask him," Cole said quietly, looking confused.

He got up, leaving the dining room.

I sat down next to Sam and kicked him under the table when he didn't start talking. It didn't seem to hurt him, but at least I got him looking at me. "I deserve to know what's going on, especially since you were such a dick to me."

Sam had this look on his face that I'd never seen before. There was guilt, but there was also pain and fear. He was stressed, and not just about this Grayson issue. He wasn't even giving me a mean smirk to hide his feelings. He was just sitting there, staring at me as he leaned his head on his hand, his fingers weaved through his hair.

"Why do you hate me so much?"

"You're the reason my mom's dead."

That wasn't something I expected. "But she died in a car accident," I replied, puzzled.

He shook his head. "Grayson told Maya something while he held her captive . . ." He trailed off, averting his eyes. Eventually, he continued talking. "Grayson killed my mom. She was trying to protect you and was getting in the way of Grayson killing you. So he killed her. To get to you."

I immediately realized the truth in his words. My mother had died protecting me. I was the reason she was dead. I wasn't sure whether that should have made me feel loved or guilty for taking her from this world. When feeling loved didn't sit well, given everything else that had happened in my life, I settled for the latter.

But the thought just made me want to throw up. Even the ecstasy couldn't keep me in an elevated mood after this realization.

And then I wondered, who else would die trying to protect me from Grayson? Wasn't I supposed to be protecting myself? Plus, if I couldn't even protect myself for the past nearly eighteen years, how the hell was I supposed to protect an entire planet?

The truth was, I couldn't, but I should have been able to. I was probably the first Keeper to need help protecting the gem. How pathetic did that make me? I was going to be using the population I *should* have been protecting to fight for me. And they could die for me just like Mom did, and for no victory.

Maybe I wasn't really the Gem Keeper. Maybe, somehow, the gem itself had made a mistake. Because not only was I unable to protect myself, I also wasn't pure.

And while I had been excited to find that I had a new purpose in life when I first found out I was the Keeper, I now felt that maybe, I *didn't* have a purpose. Maybe I was just one big fat mistake.

And then I really threw up. Right before I fainted.

~

"Are you sure we shouldn't be taking her to the hospital?" I heard someone ask as I slowly came back from the darkness.

What had happened? Who was talking? I wanted to open my eyes to see but I was too tired; it felt like they were glued shut. So all I could rely on at the moment was my sense of hearing, which didn't tell me who the voice belonged to. Instead, all I heard was the sound of quiet breathing, and shuffling feet.

"No, no. This is normal. Well, the fainting at least." That was Jana, and I suddenly realized I was on a soft, warm bed with a blanket around me.

"She has low iron," Jana lied.

"Divianans don't *have* low iron."

The accusatory tone belonged to Cole, and it compelled me to open my eyes to see him, Jana, and Sam in the dimly lit room with me.

The room. What room?

The guest bedroom.

Jana was sitting on the bed beside me and smiled when she saw that I was awake. "Hey, hun. How are you feeling?"

"What happened?" I asked. God. My throat felt like sandpaper. I winced and sat up, wanting some water, which Jana handed me right away.

"You *puked* on me," Sam replied, standing at the foot of the bed. "And then you fainted."

The turn of events came rushing back, and I groaned, closing my eyes again. Great. Now, not only did I know I was a complete failure, I had made a fool of myself too. "I'm sorry," I said, taking a sip of the water. My stomach churned uncomfortably.

"Yeah, I'm sorry too, for letting you sit that close to me." I heard him grunt and opened my eyes to see him running a hand through his hair. Cole was giving him a glare. "And I guess I could have explained things in a better way."

"You think?" I snapped, feeling a bit more awake.

"You tolerate him way too much," Cole said. I didn't reply, not knowing what to say, and drank more of the water.

"What was up with the puking?" Jana asked.

"Morning sickness," Sam joked.

My heartbeat spiked, but I tried not to let my fear show. He didn't know how seriously I took that. Even with the precautions I took with Tyler, it was something I constantly worried about. I took tests like every day because I was so paranoid about it.

I glared at him, then decided not to bother with him. He was going to make me puke again.

I answered Jana truthfully, "I have no idea."

"I think you're just exhausted," Sam said. "You've been running around all day for the past week."

"Since when did you become the MD here?"

"Since Jana told us you'd chop us up into little pieces and feed us to evil squirrels if we took you to the hospital."

"A squirrel would make a much better doctor than you."

"Even the one I killed?"

I glared at him, not appreciating his humor.

"I think the real reason she threw up is Sam," Jana muttered. Cole laughed.

"Can I just rest please?"

Jana gave me a reassuring smile. "Of course."

I smiled back at her, feeling incredibly guilty about what I'd said to her before I left for Tyler's. "Thanks. And I'm sorry," I added, knowing she'd know what I meant.

"It's all right; we'll talk later. Get some rest."

She hugged me before leaving, followed by Cole.

Sam stayed back, and I glared at him. "I want to rest," I sighed.

"I know."

The smirk had disappeared from his face. "Then why aren't you leaving?"

He opened his mouth but then closed it again. Finally, he sighed and asked, "Do you want me to shut the door when I leave?"

I nodded, knowing he had something else to say but not wanting to hear it right now; it couldn't possibly make me feel better. So I just ignored him as he closed the door and turned to my side, closing my eyes to get some rest.

CHAPTER 10

DEATH SENTENCE

MONIQUE

Whatever courage Sam had gathered up to tell me something that day disappeared by the time I got out of bed. In fact, his attention appeared to be constantly elsewhere. But he had remembered what I'd asked him about Mom's cottage. By the time I was up, Jeremy had already called Aunt Carrie, the legal owner since mom passed, and asked if we could use it for a nonexistent birthday party we were throwing for our nonexistent friend. She'd readily agreed but said that if it wasn't clean the next time she went there, she'd sue us. We knew she was joking, but out of respect, we decided to try our best to keep it clean.

Besides, it wasn't like we'd be using the actual cottage much.

Sam was still annoyed that we weren't telling Carrie the truth, but Jeremy refused to take any more shit from him. So instead of giving Sam a calm explanation, he snapped, "We'll get it under control, asshole. Monique doesn't want to worry her, so we won't. For once, just do the right thing and *shut the fuck up.*"

It made me smile, knowing that Jeremy was sticking up for me, and that he had everything under control. And he was right. If we didn't need to worry Carrie, we wouldn't. Plus, according to Jeremy, Aunt Carrie was in the hospital for a serious case of bronchitis anyway—which Divianans apparently *weren't* immune to—and it wouldn't have been right to ask her to help us in that condition.

After he told me all of this, Jana let me know she had found a Cloaker and we could finally send Jeremy off. We decided to let him know the day he was supposed to leave so he wouldn't have time to think of ways to convince me not to send him. But I was still dreading the conversation, so I threw myself into training to keep my mind off it. Fortunately for me, the day before we sent Jeremy off, Sam decided to skip the cardio and the weights; he had newer, more interesting things to teach me instead.

"Concentrate on me," he drilled me from the opposite side of the backyard a few days after the puking incident. Everyone else was up at the cottage; we were the only ones at Jana's. Cole had opted to train the majority of the people we'd gathered, since he had more patience for a whole few dozen of them than Sam had for one. So Sam spent his time with me, aiming to make me as strong as I could possibly be.

The problem with his command was that it was extremely vague; I had already been concentrating hard on him, watching his every move so that he couldn't make any surprise attacks on me. But in the moment, he looked completely relaxed; his hands were in his pockets, and his shoulders were set back with ease. In fact, he seemed a bit *too* comfortable. What was he trying to teach me that required such little effort on his part?

"What do you mean?" I asked, holding myself in a ready stance. I expected him to pounce at any second, and not wanting to be taken straight to the ground so that he could laugh at me again and remind me that someone could do that to me at any given time, I stayed fully alert.

"Concentrate here," he clarified, pointing to his chest. "Try to visual my lungs."

"What good will that do?"

He ignored my question. "Lift your arm." Rolling my eyes, I did as he said, knowing I wasn't going to get anywhere arguing with him. "Now direct your hand toward me. Twist it."

I twisted my hand, but nothing happened. No light was shining from my palms either.

"Concentrate, Monique. Imagine you're compressing my lungs, trying to choke me."

Frowning, I formulated an image of his lungs in my mind, pretending that I was compressing them, twisting them in my hand. But I could tell it was having no effect on him. All it resulted in was a killer headache.

"I can't do this," I cried, getting out of stance. My head was throbbing with pain, and I doubted I would be able to do anything for the rest of the day because of the headache. "It's hurting my head."

"Push through it. It'll take a while, but once you get used to it, you'll be able to do this without even thinking about it."

Taking a deep breath, I got back into stance and tried again but failed once more. My ears started ringing, and not able to take the unbearable pain, I collapsed on to the ground.

"You're really going to give up now, Monique?" he taunted instead of asking if I was okay. I noticed that he'd pulled his hands out of his pockets and had gotten into fighting stance, as if he were expecting me to pounce. "Are you really that weak?"

"No," I denied through gritted teeth. "I'm not."

"Grayson ruined your life, Monique. You can't let him get away with that. You said yourself that you wanted to kill him, but in order to do that, you have to train yourself to push through the pain. Everything we're doing in training *has* to become second nature to you by the time we go to take him down. But you can't fight him if you let yourself succumb to the pain, because let me tell you this—you *will* feel more pain on the battlefield. So get your ass off the ground and try again. *Get angry.*"

I thought of all the times Grayson had hurt me, all the pain he'd caused me. Driving Kay away, hurting Jeremy, killing my mom. It was all too much *not* to get angry at. He was the sole reason why I was hurting. Everything that had happened in my life was *his* fault. If it hadn't been for him, my mother wouldn't have died, Kay would have still been here. I wouldn't have turned to drugs.

I wouldn't have been raped.

Driven by fury, I got back onto my feet and immediately went back into stance. I devised an image of Sam's lungs in my mind once more, and when it was perfectly clear, I snapped my hand to the side as if I were twisting his lungs, compressing them. My hands lit up. His immediately flew to his chest, and his eyes bugged out. He looked like he was in a lot of pain. I smiled.

"Twist it further," he added in a raspy voice. I did as he said, twisting my hand further, but nothing changed. I frowned.

"Concentrate, Monique," he reminded me. I narrowed my eyes so that my field of vision contained nothing but his chest. Keeping the image of his lungs sharp in my mind, I thought of killing him, of killing Grayson and getting my revenge. Raising my head higher, I twisted my hand further, and Sam began choking. I immediately dropped my hand, and he straightened up, taking deep breaths of the fresh air surrounding us and then grabbing a drink of water from the bottles we'd kept to the side.

When he put his drink down, he turned to me and grinned. "That was amazing. I didn't think you'd learn that technique that quickly."

"I tend to surprise people," I replied, beaming smugly.

"Still not as good as me, though," he countered.

Suddenly, the grin on his face disappeared as he moaned in pain, collapsing on the ground beside me. He held his side in agony, his eyes squeezed shut.

I immediately dropped to my knees beside him, wondering what the hell was wrong, as I felt a burning in my own right side. It wasn't enough to have me on the ground, though, so I ignored it, thinking it was just another side effect of the ecstasy.

"Sam? What's wrong?"

Suddenly, he opened his eyes and let go of his side just as my burning stopped. He was breathing a lot harder than before. "I'm not sure. I need to make a phone call . . ."

He reached for his phone, and I could tell he wanted me to leave, so I did. But I stayed in the kitchen to hear what he said to whoever he was calling, grabbing a glass of water to drink while I listened.

"Hey Maya," I heard him say a moment later. "I was just calling to make sure you were okay."

I could hear her voice on the other end. "Yeah, I'm fine. I'm just tired. I was actually sleeping."

"Shit, I'm sorry."

"No, it's okay. But I'm really tired and I was wondering if I could let you go."

Sam hesitated before speaking. "Yeah, that's fine. I'll talk to you later."

"Thank you, Sam. I love you."

"I love you too. Bye."

I put away my glass of water, just as he came into the kitchen with his brow furrowed. "Is something wrong?" I asked. He shook his head as his eyes changed to a yellowish colour, and he grabbed his own glass of water. He was lying and clearly worried about something, but I knew he wouldn't bother telling me, so I let it go, and we went back to training.

The real trouble arose the next day, when I told Jeremy about the decision I'd made.

"You're sending me to Barrie?" he demanded, giving me a wide-eyed look. We were sitting in the living room, alone, since Cole, Jana, and Riley were up at the cottage. Sam was still here, but had agreed to leave me alone with Jeremy so I could talk to him about this.

"Look, it's for your own good," I began, but he wouldn't listen to me.

"If you're sending me away, you should be sending everyone else away too, if you want to be so protective!"

I sighed. "You're my little brother, Jeremy. I *need* to protect you. Besides, I already bought you a train ticket to Toronto, and a bus ticket from there to Barrie."

"I won't go."

"Jere—"

"No!" he yelled, getting up on his feet. "I can't believe you would do this. You're expecting me to live in complete isolation for however long this whole thing takes, and I won't know a thing about what's going on. I won't even know if you're dead!"

I then dealt the card I didn't want to use, but I knew it would be the only thing that would convince him to leave without a fight.

"If you don't willingly go, Jeremy, I'm just going to get Sam to compel you."

He pressed his lips together, his hands curling into fists by his sides. He was shaking with infuriation. Scowling, he shouted, "I hate you!" and then stormed out of the room, heading upstairs and out of my sight.

I sighed, putting my head in my hands in defeat. I hated it when Jeremy got pissed at me. But he needed to see that I was doing this with good intentions. I couldn't bear the thought of him getting hurt. He needed to leave, not only for his own safety but for mine as well; if all I was thinking about was Jeremy while fighting Grayson, I knew I wouldn't be focused enough to take him down. And I needed to survive this. I needed to save the people who were so willing to help out.

But would Jeremy forgive me, after this was all over and he could come back to Windsor? Or would he hate me forever for keeping him away?

Just then the front door barged open and Cole and Jana stepped in, carrying wild looks on their faces. I immediately stood up, knowing something was up, just as Sam walked in from the kitchen.

"Military base just got broken into," Jana said before I could even ask.

"In Diviano?"

Cole nodded. "In Farum. Took their weapons."

Sam frowned. "How'd that happen? Their security is really tight—"

"We have no idea," Jana replied. "But all of their weapons were taken. Hundreds. He's getting ready."

I suddenly felt like I was choking. "Okay, well what do we have?"

"Our hands," Sam responded bitterly. "Your bow and arrow. My two guns."

"I've been teaching the group hand-to-hand combat," Cole added. "I didn't think—" He cut off, turning around and pacing.

"Cole, it's not your fault," Jana assured him.

"It's not," I agreed.

Sam sighed. "The point is, we know *now*, and we need to get our own weapons."

"From where? Shops?"

"Can't buy them legally in Diviano," Jana said. "They don't allow the public to carry weapons. The only thing we can get are swords to kill Daeblo in vessels. And the black market won't carry the amount we need. They only get small shipments."

Cole sighed. "Stores here don't carry much either, and the weapons here aren't as advanced as the ones Divianan military bases carry. I'm assuming that's why Grayson didn't just use his own weapons from his hunter's shop. We need something more advanced too."

Sam turned to me. "Monique, get Cole's computer. It's upstairs, second guest room. Cole, I need you on it *now*. We can't get any weapons from Diviano. They had to have boosted their security tenfold. We need to search up military bases here on Earth, preferably ones that are close by."

"You want me to try to hack into their systems?" Cole asked.

Sam nodded. "Turn off any security. Monique and I will go in and steal everything we can get."

"What do you want me to do?" Jana asked.

I sighed. "Get Jeremy to gather his things and then continue training." With that said, I left to grab Cole's computer. When I came back down he was still pacing, and Sam was trying to get him to relax. Jana was heading my way, and she squeezed my hand gently before going to deal with Jeremy.

"Cole, your computer." I handed him his MacBook, and he went to work in the dining room.

Sam turned to me. "Are you ready for this? Cole can get rid of the technological security, but we still may have to face guards. You think you can handle it?"

"I hope so."

"We barely have any weapons, so we're going into this empty-handed. But we've got your power, which they won't see coming, so use that to our advantage. And remember, *control*. All you have to do is focus. Don't get scared, keep a clear head, and you'll be able to channel all your power effectively."

I nodded, taking a deep breath.

"Cole, you got anything?" Sam called, walking toward the dining room. I followed.

"Closest working base is about seven hours away by drive," Cole said. "Only looking into Ontario."

Yeah, there was no way we could pass the border . . .

"Can't we use portals?" I asked Sam. "I mean, you told me yourself you've both been using a permanent one in Diviano to get back to Earth."

He sighed. "Monique, we're trying to gather at least a couple hundred people here. Each person needs at least one weapon, and I'm hoping we can get more. If you think that the weapons will go through those portals *twice* and won't go everywhere and *break*—"

"We can hold them though, right?"

He rolled his eyes. "You got knocked down when you went through the portal. Could you stay standing while holding a hundred pounds on your back?"

I raised my eyebrows. "We're using backpacks?"

"Sacks, and I don't want to take any chances. Plus, if anyone sees us and the weapons . . . I can't always pin us down to an exact location since the portals can be shifty, and I don't want to be taken in. We don't have time for that right now."

"And flights are out of the question," I mused.

"Well, maybe not. I still have my compulsion and can get anything through. Cole, are there any—"

Cole was already furiously typing away. "Not for another day."

"Wait, *still?*" I asked, realizing what Sam had just said. "Do you mean we can lose our powers?"

He sighed. "No. I'll explain later. We *need* to get going."

"Sam's right," Cole said. "Take my car. I'll call you and let you know when I get the system down. And Sam, let Monique drive. She's been eyeing that thing for days."

"What?" I demanded, not realizing he'd noticed. Cole just smirked, and Sam dragged me away.

He handed me the keys. "Get your bow and arrow and start the car. I'll get the guns and the sacks." I nodded and left, getting my arrows from the backyard where I'd left them. When I got to Cole's car, Sam already had his guns and was waiting by the passenger door with the keys in his hand.

I snatched them from him. Opening the locks, we got in.

And the moment I sat down, I felt a burst of excitement surge through me.

"If you trash his car, he'll kill you," Sam said. "And then I'll bring you back to life and kill you again for wasting everyone's time."

I ignored him and started the car, loving the soft purr that sounded the moment I did. It was so smooth and . . . sexy compared to my roaring engine.

And I was definitely betting that it would go a thousand times faster without falling apart.

Oh how I hated used cars.

"Monique," Sam sighed. "Drive."

Right.

I pulled out of the driveway, heading off in the direction of the main road.

"Cole said to take the 401. We're headed toward Kingston." I didn't reply but did as he said, picking up speed as I drove.

"If we get pulled over, you can get us out of it, right?"

"Yeah," he replied.

Which reminded me. "So we can lose our powers?"

He sighed. "For the last time, no. We can *never* lose our powers. The only reason I can lose compulsion is because it's not *mine*."

I frowned. "What do you mean? You stole it from someone?"

"Yes."

"You can do that?"

"Yes."

"How?"

Again, he sighed. "Requires a spell. Complicated. Not important. Drive faster."

He was being evasive. I sighed, shaking my head, but I knew I was never going to get anything out of him so I dropped it and drove faster, keeping my eye out for cops.

Just then, Sam's phone rang. He picked it up and said, "Hey."

I could hear Cole responding. "I'm sending you a picture of the layout of their base. It's labeled, and it'll help you navigate your way. I'm close to cracking into their security system. I'll let you know when I've got it."

"Okay."

Sam hung up just as I met a car that seemed to be crawling along the highway. Sighing, I switched lanes and then checked the time. Six o'clock. Hopefully we'd be back by seven in the morning.

"So I have really good hearing," I said after a time of silence I didn't enjoy. "Is that a power?"

"Yeah," he muttered, seeming distracted. I glanced over to see him looking at the layout of the base. "I have it too."

"And it's *your* power. It won't fade."

He gave me a longsuffering sigh. "Yes, now shut up for a while, would you?"

I rolled my eyes but didn't argue. I just kept driving in silence.

JANA

"Listen, Jeremy," I sighed. "She's only doing this because she loves you."

"If she loved me, she would take my opinion into account here," he growled, throwing the tennis ball furiously against the wall as he sat on the edge of his bed.

"She has! She listened. It's just . . . if you're here, she's going to keep worrying about you and wondering if you're okay. She won't be able to think properly in battle, and that could get her killed. You don't want that, do you?"

"I'll be fine. I've trained with you guys. I can protect myself."

I shifted on the bed, placing a hand on his shoulder. "You'll be safer in Barrie. You'll have a Cloaker who'll protect you."

"This is stupid."

God, I had no idea how people dealt with their siblings sometimes. Stifling another sigh—and a shriek—I tried, "Jeremy, get your bags packed *now*. Your train leaves tonight, and if you miss it, I'm going to make *you* pay for the next one."

He stopped bouncing the ball and glared at me. "So that's just it? You're going to keep buying me tickets?"

"No. We'll buy you tickets for the next train, and Sam will come back in time to compel you. So if you'd like to have your free will, *start. Packing.*"

He shot up to his feet, giving me the deadliest look I'd ever seen on his face. "You're going to regret this," he growled.

Without another word, he started getting his things ready, stashing clothes into a school bag with exaggerated anger and frustration.

I rested my elbows on my knees, rubbing my temples. This boy was giving me a headache. "Jere, your sister won't be home in time to say good-bye. Do you want to talk to her while she's still on the road?" He didn't reply. "Jeremy!"

"No!" he shouted, turning to look at me. "You really think I would, considering she's sending me away?"

I bit my lip. I didn't want to say it—hell, I didn't even want to think it—but it was a possibility. "Jere, she might not—"

"Don't you dare say that," he snarled, turning away from me now. "Don't you dare complete that sentence."

I saw tears welling in his eyes and stood up, knowing just how he felt. I didn't like the sick feeling I got in my stomach when I thought of it. I didn't like thinking that I might not see Monique again after all this was over. But I needed to prepare myself for the worst.

"You can't say that," he whispered as I pulled him in for a hug. "She's my only family. She's all I have left."

Tears pricked at my eyes, but I kept them down; if he saw me crying, he'd lose any hope he could still have left. "I know, Jeremy. Which is why this is best, you know?"

"She needs to keep a clear head, I know. But if I'm not with her, I won't know if she's dead until it's too late. And I won't have any change of preventing her death."

"We'll all be here to prevent it, Jere. I promise I will try my best to protect her. I love her just as much as you do. But you have to stay strong and do what's best." I pulled away, holding him at shoulder's length. "So stay strong, okay? And know that we'll get through this."

He nodded, and I smiled. "I gotta go back to the cottage. Will you be okay?" Again he nodded, and I took a deep breath. "I'll see you later." I gave him another quick hug before turning around and walking out the door.

Cole was still working on his laptop to disable the military security system when I got downstairs. His brow was furrowed, and he was chewing on something in vivid frustration.

I headed toward him.

"Hey," I said. "Have you gotten anywhere?"

He shook his head. "Not yet. Just give me another couple hours and I'll be in."

He had that much confidence? "You really know what you're doing, don't you?"

His frown deepened. "I've been doing this kind of stuff for a while."

Not wanting to hinder his concentration, I shifted on my feet and replied, "Well, I should get going. I'll see you later tonight."

I turned around, but he called me back. "Jana?"

I faced him. He looked worried now. "Be safe."

I nodded and left.

When I got to the cottage, I found that things were a little bit disassembled. We'd left Riley in charge, but clearly he couldn't control a group of seventy-five. I sighed as I looked across the field of people we had gathered. There were of all ages really, since the ones we contacted had contacted others. But they all looked tired and restless.

"Hey," Riley said, jogging up to me when he saw me approaching.

"What's up?"

"They're all a little annoyed, mostly the new ones who aren't caught up yet as to what's going on. Plus, they've been at it for the past couple of hours without a break and are kind of hungry."

I sighed. "Okay, I'll order pizza."

I paused, scanning the crowd. A few people were practicing hand-to-hand combat, but the rest were taking a break, talking amongst each other. "Get them up and going until the food gets here. They haven't learned anything new since the early morning, and Cole's busy with our weapons issue. Sam and Monique are gone too."

"Will we be able to get them?" he asked.

"Hopefully. Just be prepared to go in empty-handed."

He looked nervous but nodded. I tried to give him a reassuring smile, but I was sure that I'd failed at the reassuring part. The truth was that Grayson now had a huge advantage and was still probably compelling more people to fight against us. *We* were now at a standstill, with no weapons and only a small handful of people still yet to arrive. We'd contacted all the people we knew, and this was basically it.

So about eighty-five against possibly more than two hundred. Our odds weren't looking too good, but nothing could be done. At least not yet. All we could do was just wait for Monique and Sam to return with those weapons. If they didn't, we were as good as dead.

I sighed. I really hoped this all worked out.

JEREMY

I was beyond pissed at Monique for sending me off to Barrie. I knew she had the right intentions and all, but it was ridiculously irritating, especially since she was completely cutting me off from social media and using the Internet while I was gone, ensuring that Grayson had no way to find me. I was going to be in complete isolation for who knew how long, and I would have no way of knowing what was going on back home. I wouldn't even know if Monique was alive until someone told me . . . or if I started dying. Knowing that I could have had my last conversation with her made my eyes sting, and talking to her again on the phone was just going to destroy the dam I was trying so hard to build in my eyes.

I couldn't do anything to help protect her. Now that I wouldn't be in the front line of battle, I was useless.

The only company I had on the train ride—and from there on out—was the Cloaker Jana had hired for me, who wasn't much of a talker. Nor was he very interesting when he *did* talk. I soon got bored with him, and since everyone else on the train seemed to be in their own worlds, I just plugged in my earphones and tried to catch some sleep.

Hours later, I woke up to find that we were stopping. I grabbed my bags as the Cloaker grabbed his, and the moment we could, we got off the train and called for a taxi to get to the nearest bus station. Another half an hour of silence later, we got there.

The place was busy when we got there, but soon a couple buses pulled in, and plenty of people left. The bus we were boarding was yet to arrive.

It was then, in the dark, that I heard two quiet pops, and a girl about five meters from where I was standing dropped to the ground. The girl beside her—the only other person there—dropped too. My eyes widened, and I looked around me. I realized too late that someone was standing behind my Cloaker and had aimed a silenced gun at his head. The next thing I knew, my Cloaker was dead.

What the hell was going on? Was this guy here to kill me too?

I wasn't sure, but ignoring the tremors that ran through my body, I bolted.

Within seconds, he was in front of me again.

Superspeed.

Shit!

He blocked my way inside the building, so I punched him in the face. His head snapped to the side. Spitting out blood, he turned back to me blankly and punched me back. The pain rang through me, but I ignored it as he spun me around, trying to knock me out by cutting off my air supply. With my breathing becoming harder, I bit his hand, but it didn't loosen his grip on me. All it did was give me the bad taste of his blood in my mouth. I cringed, as suddenly, my entire body began shaking even harder than it had been before. My stomach churned, and I felt my intestines tightening in on themselves. My knuckles suddenly grew, and the hair on my arms thickened. My entire body was aching. With a start, I realized what was going on.

My body was morphing.

I remembered the conversation we'd all had about powers one night back in Windsor, and Cole wondering what mine was. I remembered him telling me that everyone's powers presented themselves at different times in their lives, and Monique ensuring me that I would discover mine soon. She had completely ignored the issue after that, too focused on saving herself and others to put her curiosity at the top of her priority list, so I doubted she'd even thought about my power after that. If she did, she didn't voice it, and I didn't care, knowing she had much more important things to focus on.

But I suddenly wished that we hadn't just ignored this issue, because it would have made me more prepared in discovering my power. It would have kept me calmer as the searing pain shot up my body. My feet and legs changed shape, and suddenly my torso was changing too. I was becoming thicker, and when the man holding me realized what was going on, he let go of me, unable to control the convulsions that shook through me as I roared in pain.

Whatever was going on with my body seemed to last forever. But once it stopped and the pain ceased, I looked up to see a reflection of myself on a darkened station window.

My brown eyes were gone, replaced by the man's blue ones. My hair, which had been brown and short, was now blond and in a ponytail. My boyish face had been replaced by a more structured one.

I no longer looked like Jeremy Rolland Brooks. I now looked like my attacker, who seemed too shocked to even move.

My heart hammered even harder than before, and my breath came even faster. But I didn't hesitate a single second. Instead, I took advantage of my attacker's alarmed state and grabbed the gun he'd dropped. I realized I had no clue how to shoot this thing, but in the next second, I realized that I did, because I suddenly had this guy's memories, and I shot him in the leg to immobilize him.

I then ran the hell out of there, though without the guy's superspeed, and suddenly remembered—through his memories—that someone had been standing nearby in the shadows to surprise me just in case I got away. I *would* have gotten away, too, if it hadn't been for the fact that I had no idea how to control my power. I only got one last memory before I started morphing back into myself.

Grayson had sent these men. And he'd sent them to hold me hostage. I was his leverage. He was willing to put the life of his own son on the line to get to Monique.

As I roared in the physical and emotional pain of it all, I was hit in the head by a hard object, and the next thing I knew, I was drifting into unconsciousness.

MONIQUE

Six and a half—accounting for a couple of stops—hours of aggravating arguments and snoring from Sam later, Sam and I finally got to the military base, which seemed ridiculously protected, as we'd expected. The moment we got there, we called Cole on disposable phones. He'd already been in their system for a while. Because he could only keep the system down for short amount of time before someone noticed something was wrong, we had to be quick.

The first thing Cole did was disable the cameras located near the wing where the supply base was. Two guards stood near the entrance carrying heavy weaponry.

"This should be easy," Sam whispered, adjusting the ski mask on his face. We were hiding behind a thick tree among a line of others. It wasn't much, but coupled with the darkness surrounding us and the dark clothes Sam had grabbed before we left, I figured we'd be good.

"How?" None of this seemed easy to me.

"Your power, dimwit. Freak them out."

I took a deep breath and did as he said. Lifting my hands, I concentrated hard to channel the power within me. Closing my eyes, I imagined the snakes crawling to the surfaces of my hands from the back of my brain and soon, I felt them awakening. They slithered through my body in a way that made me cringe, but I fought through the discomfort. They were making their way to my palms, and soon I felt them warming up.

I opened my eyes. They were glowing blue.

"Control," Sam reminded me.

I *wanted* their weapons. I needed to get them unarmed. I wanted their guns to come flying out of their hands and slide into mine.

I moved my hands upward and the blue light glowed brighter, shining toward the guards. One of them looked our way and scowled, furrowing his brow. I sucked in a breath as he took a step toward us, but before he could get any closer, I whipped my arm up and drew it into my body. The gun came flying at us.

Sam grabbed it. The man gasped, and his partner cocked her gun. She held it up, stalking toward us.

"Ready?" Sam hissed. I nodded, getting ready to follow through with the rest of our plan.

I conjured up the snakes again as the man came closer, looking much more frightened than before. The woman was advancing much faster, but Sam stalled them both by grabbing a rock and tossing it to the side, away from where we were standing.

Their heads snapped to our left simultaneously. I used their distraction to build my energy to do the job. When I felt the snakes growing thicker, I took a deep breath and lifted my hands, pushing against the air in front of me in the direction of the guards.

Down.

They didn't make a single sound. We immediately moved into action, and as I grabbed the woman's gun, checking their pulses to make sure they were still alive, Sam called Cole.

"Get us in," he whispered.

By the time we reached the doors to the chamber, we'd heard a faint click. Sam tried the doors, and they gave in easily.

"Remember, we have five minutes at the most before they notice something's up and figure out what the problem is," Sam said as we stuffed everything we could into our sacks without damaging anything. The dark room had shelves upon shelves covered with all sorts of weapons, and we got through nearly half of it—probably about a hundred weapons or so—before we heard running footsteps approaching.

With one look at each other, we bolted out of there with our sacks. It was only when we stepped out of the chamber that we realized the footsteps were too close. They were right behind us.

"Freeze!" a man boomed. I noticed three other men behind him but didn't stop running.

And then I heard a gunshot.

Pain was suddenly shooting up my calf, and I cried out, my knees giving beneath me. The sack fell out of my hands, but Sam swept it off the floor in one quick motion and kept running.

They shot more bullets at him while I whimpered in pain, but he managed to dodge every single one.

I was still helpless.

My power.

Right, I still had my power. I turned onto my back just in time to see a man coming up to me. He was too close for me to conjure up my power in time, so I used my good leg to trip him, using that time to call for the snakes again.

They didn't show.

Oh no.

I suddenly found it hard to breathe.

They were going to take me in, and Sam couldn't come back for me, because he was already running from the two men chasing him.

Just then, the one I'd tripped got up on his feet, and another one showed up by my head. He dropped to his knees and pinned my arms down as the other demobilized my legs.

The memories flooded back.

Oh no. No, no, no!

"You're in some serious trouble, kid," the brunet said, curling his fingers around the edge of my mask. Panicking and fighting against the feeling of helplessness, I thought for a way to get out of this.

Arms, legs, head. All unusable.

But my hands weren't.

I unclenched my fists. I needed the snakes, but fear never brought them out. I needed something else.

Anger.

""She was my mom, not yours. Just because yours didn't want you doesn't give you the right to steal mine."

The snakes zipped their way to my palms. Soon, I was being shoved hard into the ground along with the military men, my power having pushed against the air without the light showing up in my hands.

It wasn't the distraction I was looking for, but it still freaked them out.

The brunet loosened his grip, and I immediately took the chance to elbow him in the gut. He groaned and fell back. I sat up, punching the other freaked-out guy in the face and shoving his arms away from me. Taking a swing at his head with my good leg to knock him out, I got up shakily as the bullet still lodged in my calf sent sharp pain up my leg.

I moaned.

It was only when I was on my feet—holding the wall I'd created since I could barely stand—that I realized I would never be able to get out of this crater. I had created something at least twelve feet deep.

"Shit," I fumed as the one of the guys—the one who had failed at removing my mask—stood up. I didn't have time for him. Lifting my hand, I conjured up the angry snakes and sent him into a probably painful sleep.

"Hey," I heard someone say, and I looked up to see Sam dangling some rope into the crater.

"Where were you?" I hissed.

He handed me a rope and I tied it around my waist, since I couldn't climb with my injured leg. "I outran them. They don't have the endurance we do. I was on my way back to you when I met up with them again and had to knock them out. The rope was in the chamber."

He pulled me out, and as I stood on my two feet again, the pain came back, worse than before.

"Easy," Sam said, grabbing me by the waist before I could fall. I immediately became ten times more aware of every single part of him and wanted him to let go, but I could barely walk. He helped me limp all the way back to the car.

"The bullet's still in there," I muttered. "But I think the wound is healing."

"I'm just glad your pants soaked up the blood. Otherwise they could have figured out who you were from the DNA. And we can't exactly go to the hospital here since they'll question how you're healing so fast, and we're not going to Diviano and leaving these weapons on Earth unattended." He paused, sighing. "I'll fix it."

"How, if the skin covers the bullet up?"

"I'll do it."

We approached the car, and I sat in the passenger seat. "Let's just get away from here first," he added. I nodded, so he began driving and soon after, he stopped the car on the side of the highway. Turning to face me, he said, "Okay, this is going to hurt, but it'll be better than keeping it in there."

"I don't trust you," I said, my chest tightening.

"I'll make it quick."

I gave him an even look, judging how he was going to do this. But I knew that I had no choice. Having the bullet lodged in there was excruciating.

I sighed. "Okay."

He put on the car's flashers. "Where exactly is it?"

"My calf."

"Roll up your pants." I tried but couldn't get them far without it being too painful. They were too tight. I hadn't wanted to use these, but Sam hadn't even consulted me; he'd just grabbed the first black pair he saw.

"Rip them."

Grabbing the bottom of the leg, I ripped the material so there was a slit going up to my knee. When he asked, I shifted to put my leg over the gearshift. He looked for dried blood and gently touched the area around it, sending a shiver up my spine. I tried not to show it.

But the pain was worse.

"Here?" he asked as I stifled a moan. I nodded.

"Close your eyes."

What? "Why?" I demanded, immediately suspicious.

He rolled his eyes. "Just do it, okay? Trust me."

I didn't, so I closed my eyes only enough to get a slit of light through. But it was enough to see him bringing out the knife.

Before I could stop him, he cut through my skin right next to the bullet. The layer of skin wasn't really thick, but it still stung like mad. I hissed, clenching my fists.

He lifted a little slot on the dashboard by pressing a button and pulled out a napkin, cleaning the knife before shoving it into one of the sacks. The bullet was still lodged in the leg, though. He reached forward to take it out, but I didn't want him touching me again.

"I'll do it," I said, pulling my leg back. I dug into the wound, holding in my cries of pain as I felt around for the bullet and pulled it out.

He handed me the dirty napkin, and I put the bullet in there.

"You're still bleeding. Put some pressure on that." I nodded and did as he said, about to throw the napkin and my disposable phone out the window into the field beside us. But before I could even open the window, he grabbed both from me, shoving them in the cup holder. "Ah, let's not. I want to make a stop for food along the way anyways."

He began driving, yet I couldn't help but laugh. "So you act like a dick in all ways possible but you care about the environment? How does that make any sense-?"

"I have to tell you something," he cut in, looking a little nervous. He'd had the same look on his face the day I puked on him, when he'd

251

hesitated in my room. Knowing for sure that this had to be the same thing, I dropped the environment.

"I know," I said. "So tell me."

He sighed, opening his mouth to speak but then closing it again. He was clearly having a hard time getting this out, and as my curiosity grew, so did my impatience. When he visibly tried to search for words, I urged him, "Just hit me with it, okay? This has been bugging me ever since—"

"You know how I told you that you couldn't be killed until your time as Keeper was up?"

"Yeah," I replied, already not liking the way this conversation was going. It gave me a queasy feeling in the pit of my stomach that I really didn't enjoy.

"When your time as Keeper is up, you're going to die."

That single sentence immediately had me choking on air. I mean, I guess it really shouldn't have. I should have been happy. I couldn't count how many times in the past four years I'd wished I could just die, even recently when I'd hurt Nathan. But now that my wish had suddenly become impending reality, I couldn't stand the thought of it. Yeah, my life could be a bitch, but I'd been hoping that after Grayson died, a little bit of peace could be restored into it. I was hoping I would be happier. I was hoping that my life would get better and that I would stop wishing to die.

Not only that, the fact that I was going to die in three years made me realize how much time I'd spent wasting my life away. What was the purpose of going through all the pain school brought? What was the purpose of killing Grayson when it would all soon be over anyways? Why was I even bothering with all of this? Why was I even trying?

"Why the fuck," I began, as my entire body began shaking, "didn't you tell me this the moment you told me about Diviano?"

He sighed again. "Do you think you would have listened to anything I said after that? Nobody wants to believe that their death will come that quickly, and it would have just made you revolt. You wouldn't have decided to fight and try to kill Grayson. You would have run away in fear."

"Because you know so much about death, right?" I snapped. I could tell from the look on his face that I'd clearly hit a sensitive spot, and

I should have felt guilty but I couldn't find the compassion to. I couldn't find the fucking *purity* to.

If I was so pure, why would the gem want to kill me?

"Why?" I demanded.

He seemed to know exactly what I was asking.

"Nature couldn't let you live with all the power you would keep with you even after you finished your time as Keeper. And the gem travels to the next Keeper, carried by the spirit of the previous one. If you lived, it would stop that cycle from continuing."

"You should have told me sooner. I have three fucking years left to live, and I'm wasting my life with you. I could be off in the Bahamas or something enjoying the rest of it but no, you *kept* me here by not telling me. Do you really hate me that much?"

When I raised my voice, so did he. "Do you realize I'm not the only one who knew about this? They were the ones who told me not to say anything until after this was all over."

I tensed, in more shock than I was before, if that were even possible. I immediately knew when he said "they" that he was talking about Jana, Cole, and Nathan, who had all known about Diviano for a while. And the fact that Jana knew this but refused to tell me sent my heart plummeting into a bottomless pit. She was my friend—my *best* friend. No, she was like my *sister,* and she had refused to tell me this. She kept it hidden from me.

Yet I was sitting here wasting my life away. Why was I even doing this? Why was I even helping kill Grayson? Why should I *care* when I should be living my life right now? Why the *fuck* was I still sitting there?

I needed to go. I needed to leave and never come back. I was done with this mission. I didn't care if Grayson ended up killing me. I was going to die soon anyway. I might as well have just handed myself over to him and made this all go by quicker.

But how was I supposed to leave now?

I looked outside the window at the smooth terrain beside the highway. We were speeding, but this was my only option. I couldn't go back to Windsor.

Slowly, and as quietly as I could, I undid my seatbelt, but he still noticed, and despite how quick I had been to unlock my door, he quickly locked it back up and stopped the car on the side of the highway, again with the flashers on.

"What the hell do you think you're doing?" he boomed, grabbing my arm before I could get out of the car. "You're going to get yourself injured! More than you already are!"

"I can't die, asshole," I replied bitterly, glaring at him.

"Monique, you're acting like a child."

My hands shook. I tried squirming out of his grip, but it was useless. "I don't fucking care! Let me go!"

"You're not thinking clearly."

"Yes I am! I'm thinking about how I'm no longer needed in any of this. You have enough people to take Grayson down by yourself. Now let. Me. Go!"

He set his jaw. "No."

I struggled, and he tightened his grip. When I tried to pry his hand off with my free one, he grabbed me by that wrist too. "Monique, think about what you're doing! You *just* helped me rob the fucking *military*, and now you want to leave? And you sent your brother to Barrie for a reason. You wanted to protect him, to keep him alive. But if you don't kill Grayson, there's always going to be a threat hanging over him."

I looked away, not wanting him to see the tears threatening to pool in my eyes when I thought of Jeremy. I was going to be leaving him alone in this cruel world after three years.

"You can't do all this and ditch."

"You have it handled. Just a few more people in your army and you'll be good to go."

"No, we need you."

"No you don't."

He sighed. "Monique, you are literally the most powerful person on this planet right now. If you don't protect these people, then who will? If people see you running, they'll realize that even you can't protect them. They'll lose hope. They'll think that we have no chance of survival. And if they lose hope, if they quit, then Grayson wins. We all die. *Every single one of us.* Including Jeremy."

I bit my lip, looking down at my lap. He was right. I was dying, and everything I'd done up to this point was useless. But everyone else still had a chance to live, including Jeremy. I didn't want to steal that from them. I had to stop Grayson, not just for myself, but for all these people. And sure, the others could just as easily kill him without me, sure I could let it be someone else's problem, but then everyone could do that. Plus, this was my responsibility. I was the Keeper, so I had to do this.

"And," he continued, "if these people realize you've run because you wanted to live the rest of your life in peace, they'll see you as incapable. As weak. Do you really want that?"

"No," I replied. That was the last thing I wanted. I didn't want people thinking I was weak. I didn't want anyone thinking that I couldn't do my job, that I couldn't protect them. And just like I didn't want Jeremy dying for me, I didn't want anyone else dying for me either.

I wasn't going to let Grayson kill any more people. I didn't care if I should have been enjoying the rest of my life. I knew I wouldn't be able to do that knowing that I was putting these people's lives in danger, letting a murderer run lose.

I needed to kill him.

But . . . what I still didn't understand was why it was me. I clearly didn't have a pure heart, since I had just been thinking about running away from all of this, letting everyone else die just so I could live the rest of my life in peace. So why the hell was I the Keeper?

I wasn't sure, but regardless, I knew I needed to go back and do what I could to stop Grayson. As much as I hated to admit it, as little prepared as I was, I *knew* that I had to be the one to lead these people into battle.

Sam put a hand on my shoulder, making me go rigid. "Listen," he began, but I cut him off, shaking his hand off of me.

"Just drive," I said quietly, putting on my seatbelt. "We need to hurry back."

He didn't say anything but turned and merged back into the highway.

Something was still bugging me.

"Why would you tell me this now when Cole and Jana wanted to wait until after it was all over?"

He pressed his lips together, his brow furrowing. "Because—" He sighed and gripped the steering wheel tighter, his knuckles turning white.

"Because you deserve to know, and this wasn't something I could hold from you any longer."

My throat tightened, and my eyes stung with tears threatening to spill down my cheeks. I swallowed hard, trying to drown the sobs. I didn't want this. I never wanted any of it. But there was nothing I could do about it. And it made it worse knowing that Jana knew about this and didn't tell me. I didn't want to talk to her again. I didn't even want to see her again either, but I knew avoiding her would be impossible, especially at a time like this. I would have to bear the betrayal I felt, and the pain, as I worked with her. But I wasn't sure if our friendship would be the same after this. This was too big of a secret to keep for this long, so I wasn't sure if I was ready to just jump back into that friendship.

At least Sam had said something.

"Thank you," I said quietly, trying not to cry. He didn't reply, but I wished he would. I wished he would change the subject, get my mind off it. Because everything was coming crashing down on me. Everything from Jeremy's departure—though I had planned it—to my own death sentence was too much to handle, too much to take in one day. It was too much pain, too much stress, too much death to comprehend, and it was breaking me apart.

The music from the radio did no good either. It didn't stop the tears from falling. It didn't stop the sobs from threatening to burst out. But I didn't want to cry, not in front of Sam. I didn't want him to know how weak I was. I didn't want him to take advantage of me when I was like this. I didn't want him to hurt me. So I did everything I could to keep quiet.

It was the longest drive of my life.

CHAPTER 11

UNDERESTIMATION

MONIQUE

By the time we got back to Windsor, my leg was fully healed, our disposable phones were in the trash, and I found it a little easier to breathe, as the gift of sleeping had given me some time away from my thoughts. But halfway through the ride, I had switched places with Sam, and when I neared Jana's house, I found my stomach in knots.

I didn't want to talk to her. But there was no way to avoid this.

Though it looked like nobody was home. Jana's car wasn't in the driveway.

Confused, I shook Sam by the arm, and he rolled his head toward me, blinking his eyes open.

"Wake up," I urged loudly, since he still looked half-asleep.

"Are we here?"

His voice was gruffer than usual.

Fuck.

I let go of his arm. "It's eight o'clock. It doesn't seem like they're in the house. Let me just go check."

Everyone was usually up by now. Actually, a lot of us had trouble sleeping, so we were usually up earlier than eight. But Jana usually didn't leave the house till nine.

"Okay."

I got out of the car and walked toward the front door. When I opened it and stepped inside, I noticed that it was too quiet.

"Jana?" I called. "Cole? Riley?"

When I got no answer, I pulled out my phone. But not really wanting to talk to Jana or Cole, I called Riley. He picked up on the second ring as I stepped back out of the house.

"Hey, you guys back yet?"

"Yeah," I replied. "Are you guys up at the cottage?"

"Yeah, we started earlier today. You guys should get here soon with those weapons."

I was already in the car. "We're on our way."

I hung up. "They're at the cottage?" Sam asked, and I nodded, heading back onto the 401.

When we got to the cottage, I saw lines upon lines of people all practicing a single defense tactic. Cole was standing and watching them all with his brow furrowed. Jana was off to the side underneath a huge oak tree, arguing with an older woman. It looked serious. Frowning, I left Sam to deal the weapons and walked toward them, even though seeing Jana had my hands shaking in anger.

"I'm just saying," the woman said, "I've never heard of a single Keeper needing help to protect the gem, and we're all putting our lives on the line for a job *she* should be doing."

Oh great.

"Her situation is different, and you're bound to come across some really messed-up people once in a lifetime. For you, that's now," Jana countered. "Just because not everyone is constantly thinking about world domination doesn't mean nobody is. It doesn't mean no one is willing to compel themselves an entire army to get to *one* person, *one* stone."

When I approached them and stood beside Jana, the brunette turned to look at me. "Look," I began, "if you don't want to help out, then don't. But don't ruin the hope these people have of saving their own lives.

I know this is different for you. But have some fucking empathy. If you were in my situation, you would want some help too."

The woman glared at me but walked back to the group to continue preparing.

Jana turned to me, giving me a longsuffering sigh. "Did you get the weapons?"

I nodded, trying hard to keep the tears down.

"Good. They've all been anxious to get them. By the way," she began, reaching into her sweats' pocket. She pulled out an iPhone. "I went to Diviano and got you this last night. Figured it would be useful. It's a knockoff," she added. "You have the same number. You'll have to pay your bills in Divianan cash, but just give me a hundred bucks monthly and I'll get it to the providers."

My jaw dropped. "A hundred?"

She gave me a sheepish grin. "The conversion rate's really high. And this thing uses a *ton* of magic. But it'll be worth it, I promise. Oh, and don't let any humans use it. Just touching this kind of magic could zap them dead."

"Okay." I looked down at the phone, not wanting to look at her. I knew she would notice that something was wrong, and I wasn't ready to confront her yet.

"Hey, have you heard from Nathan, by the way?" she asked.

I shook my head, looking back up at her, not wanting Jana to realize that something was up because I was avoiding eye contact for too long. "No, not since the day Riley showed up. Why?"

Her brow furrowed. "It's like he dropped off the face of the earth. He was coming here for a while, but he didn't show up yesterday. And he didn't show up today. I tried calling him but he wouldn't answer his phone."

I frowned. "I'm not sure why that is. I'll try calling him."

"Okay," she said.

Just then, Cole called her over, and she left after giving me a small smile. I immediately went to transferring my contacts to the iPhone knockoff, and when I was done, I walked over to where Sam and Jana were now talking. Cole had gone back to training the group of eighty-five we now had, teaching groups of fives how to use their respective weapons. So far, he'd only gone through ten people.

"I'll be back soon," Jana was saying when I approached them.

"Where are you going?" I asked.

"Airport. My friend needs me to pick her up if we want her help. She just flew in from Toronto."

"I just got a lead on a murder that happened in Diviano," Sam said, looking down at his phone. "I think you and me should go check it out. It looks like Grayson's doing. It's been twenty minutes, but the Daeblo should still be close to the crime scene, and if we can take him down together, Grayson will lose an important ally."

"Okay," I agreed. "But if the Daeblo is really strong, we should get Cole to come with us."

"Already spoke to him. He can't. These people are still unprepared, and Grayson's had a day extra with those weapons. Even if we do manage to take the Daeblo, Grayson will still have his army ready, and we need to prepare to face them."

Damn it. We couldn't take Nathan either, since we had no idea where he was.

"Take Iris," Jana pitched in. "She's been here the longest, and she's been taking martial arts classes since she could walk." She pointed to a small Asian girl roughly our age.

"Okay, but we should hurry," I replied.

"I gotta go," Jana said. "Be safe." I nodded, averting my eyes, and soon, she left.

Sam turned to me. "You sure you're ready for this? It's going to be very dangerous, even if it is three against one."

I raised an eyebrow. "Do I really have a choice?"

He shrugged, the corner of his lip tugging up. "Guess not. Bring your bow and arrows. We don't have time for me to teach you how to use any of the weapons we brought. Your arrows won't be much, but they'll be more effective if you keep shooting him with arrows rather than trying to use a gun and missing."

"Got it." I left to go get my weapon from the car, and by the time I turned around, Sam was talking to Iris. I walked over to them, on the other side of the group practicing their fighting skills, and realized that he'd filled her in on everything.

"Hi," she said, giving me a little wave. "I'm Iris. Sam explained everything, and oh! By the way, I have superstrength. It may not look like I have much muscle, but watch this." Grinning, she bent down, and to my surprise, she grabbed me by the calves and lifted me above her head. My eyes widened and so did Sam's, but before I had time to freak out about falling, she set me back down, laughing.

"You're confident about this," I commented as I regained my composure.

"I'm just saying, I think the three of us can take him down."

"What are you going to do? Lift him to death?" Sam muttered, creating a portal.

"Look, I would punch you and show you what I can do, but then you wouldn't be able to fight."

"Sam, we should hurry," I sighed, and he nodded, grabbing my hand. I grabbed Iris's and Sam took us through. I ignored the nausea as I was lifted off my feet and urged myself to stay standing as we landed.

I succeeded in remaining upright, but I noticed that Sam had ended up nowhere near me and Iris. Wondering where he was, I looked all around us and broke out in a sweat.

I had no idea where we were. All I could see around us was a whole bunch of trees. The only light was coming from the moon, which was shielded by the canopy of branches above me. Not only was it dark and the place unfamiliar, if we couldn't find Sam, how were we supposed to get home?

I didn't even have a virtencia on me.

"Do you have a virtencia?" I asked Iris.

"Yeah." She took a look at our surroundings and frowned. "Where's your boyfriend?"

"My what?" I demanded, raising my eyebrows. "Sam? He's not my—"

I heard a twig snapping to my left, and we both shut up. Iris pulled out a gun. I got my bow and arrow ready, staying on high alert for any movement. But I didn't see any.

I did, however, hear a quiet gasp and crack behind me. I immediately turned around to shoot whoever was there, but before I could, they snatched my bow from my hands. At first I thought it was Grayson, but when I focused more closely in the dim light, I realized it was someone I didn't recognize. Instead of Grayson's squared, hostile expression, I was now looking at a man with chocolate-brown eyes and jet-black hair with auburn highlights. I was pretty sure he was in his early twenties.

I then noticed Iris's body on the ground. Her head was twisted, her eyes wide.

She was dead.

Oh God.

The man cocked his head to the side, bringing my attention back to him as my heart went racing. He was gazing down at me with a predatory look in his eyes.

The gem started heating up against my skin.

I immediately turned to bolt but before I could take a single step, he gripped me by the wrist.

"You are one very pretty girl, aren't you?" he began in an overly calm voice. My heart beating faster, I tried to pry my wrist out of his grasp, but it was useless. "You're nothing like the other one. You're exactly the opposite."

The other one? I wondered briefly, but instead of letting myself focus on his words, I paid close attention to his body movement; if I didn't, I'd be unprepared and as good as dead, just like Iris.

But I needed my bow and arrows. I tried to grab them back from him, but he held them back, toying with me like I was a child.

"If I give this to you, you're just going to use it on me."

"Yeah, well, you're messing with the wrong girl, man." I narrowed my eyes and raised my hands to use my power on him, but for some reason, it wouldn't work. He wouldn't obey my commands.

He grinned. "Telekinesis doesn't work on me. I'm stronger than you, which is why you should listen to me very carefully. I could kill you in a split second if you don't do what I say."

My eyes widened. I swear to God, my heart was about to pop out of his chest.

I needed to get out of here. I squirmed within his steel grasp, trying to keep the horror of my expression but I from the wide grin on his face, I could tell I was failing.

"What do you think you're doing?" Sam demanded from behind me. I turned my head to see that although he looked a little shaggy, he seemed well enough to fight the man in front of me. While I wondered where the hell he'd been, I noticed that his hands were in his pockets and his shoulders were relaxed, but that didn't take the dangerous look out of his eyes as he glared at the man in front of me.

The man widened his eyes. He dropped my bow, released my wrist, and made a run for it. I quickly realized that if this man was working with Grayson, he didn't expect Sam to be here for some reason. I wondered why he was so scared, but before I could ask a single question, Sam had bolted off after the guy. I was about to join him, figuring that he had some sort of information, but before I could, somebody spoke from behind me.

"Monique," he said.

I shrieked, my body trembling, and turned around to punch whoever it was in the face. But before I could do anything to defend myself, my mouth was clamped shut by a hand, I was pushed against a tree, and suddenly I was trapped.

"Fucking hell. Shut up!" I couldn't see who the person in front of me was; it was darker now that the streetlight was out. I didn't even care who it was. I just wanted to get out of there.

I struggled against his hold, trying to free myself, but he wouldn't let me go. Irritated, I bit his hand, and he cussed under his breath, removing his hand from my mouth. Not sparing another second, I immediately began to shriek, "Help! Let me go! Please somebody help me!"

And suddenly I was free. I instantly ran, tripping on a rock and almost falling. I felt all around me with my hands as I ran and suddenly felt gravel under my feet. I slowed to a stop.

A light shimmered behind me again, and I immediately turned around again. I saw a shadowy figure approaching me. My breath hastened. I tried to remain calm this time but failed miserably.

"Who are you?" I demanded, shouting at the top of my lungs. I heard the streetlight flicker on behind me, shining some light onto his face. I saw the grey eyes first. The chilling grey eyes that seemed so familiar. But they looked much younger, much more innocent, and as the light flickered on and off again, I saw the rest of his face. It was Sam, but why did he look so much younger?

"Sam?" I called. I would have been really angry at him for scaring me so badly, but the thing was, he looked so out of it, like he wasn't even sure why he was there. It was like he was scared.

He stood ramrod straight, not seeming to have heard me. His eyes were suddenly red. He was glaring at me. He had glared at me before, but this was crazy. There was pure hatred in his eyes, pure regret. I was actually shocked by it, not believing the hatred I saw. But I didn't show it. I didn't show that I was scared of him.

Suddenly, I felt my body swirling and changing. It twisted and turned all over, but surprisingly, it didn't hurt—it just felt weird. And when it was done, I looked down at myself to see what had happened, and I realized I was somehow in the body of an old man.

"It's all your fault," Sam said, hatred and pain still filling his eyes. "If it wasn't for you, we'd still be in LA. We wouldn't be stuck here in the middle of nowhere, in the middle of a fight." To my surprise, I saw tears in his eyes. "You ruined my life."

"Monique, it's all fake," I heard someone say in the distance, and for some reason I thought it was Sam, but I couldn't see him, not the older him, and the one before me now stood silent.

I felt myself going back to my own body, and suddenly the younger Sam was gone too. In his place stood Jeremy.

"This is all your fault," he began in a monotone voice before I could yell at him for being here. "If you hadn't left me alone that night, I'd still be alive. My death is on your hands."

"None of it's real," Sam's voice continued.

Jeremy disappeared too, leaving Mom and Grayson standing before me. Grayson was glaring at me as usual, but Mom looked sad.

"You're so gullible," Grayson said. "I can't believe you fell so hard for my trick."

"Don't listen to it. Listen to my voice. *Focus* on my voice." Again, it was Sam's desperate voice, but I ignored him as Mom began talking.

"Monique, run. Run away with him. It's the only way to survive. Forget about us and just leave. Find Alice. Find her, go to her. Take him with you. Don't let him go!"

She and Grayson disappeared and were replaced by two figures: Sam and me in the foyer of my house.

"Monique, are you listening to me? I said it's not real!"

I ignored Sam's voice at the back of my mind as I noticed copy Sam reeling copy Me in, cutting off something copy Me was saying with a kiss. We—or they—continued to kiss, and as the vision faded, I was suddenly standing against the tree again, but instead of being shoved against it, I was standing freely. Sam was standing in front of me, and in the little light there was, I saw that he looked slightly crazed.

"Nothing you saw was real, Monique," he whispered. Why was he talking so quietly? "Do you believe me?"

I wasn't sure, but I nodded anyway. "Good. Now I want you to do me a favour and don't say a *single* word." I was about to question why when he rolled his eyes and clamped his hand down on my mouth to keep me quiet.

"Stay *very* still," he whispered, widening his eyes and keeping his hand clamped to my mouth. I was still breathing hard, shocked from the visions, but I did as told, too freaked out to do otherwise.

It was quiet, the only sounds coming from the rustling leaves, the lamenting wind, and my erratic breathing. But in a split second, that all changed. The next thing I knew, we were surrounded by the howling voices of unseen people and sand blowing through the air. Not wanting to get any in my eyes, I closed them and felt Sam pushing me harder against the tree. I opened my eyes for a brief second and saw sand flying past us like it was possessed by some sort of spirit, forming the shapes of hands, mouths, and other body parts. Sam had squeezed his eyes shut and was shielding me from the sandy wind with his body. After a while, I realized that he wasn't even breathing, and I wondered how he could manage that.

My attention was dragged away from him by the sand hovering near my face. A hand formed, and before I could move away, a finger caressed my cheek. I felt a familiarity in the touch, something I should have found odd but didn't. *Take care of him, sweetheart,* a soft, quiet voice sang in my head. I realized it was my mom's. *He is not as strong as he appears to be. He deserves some love, love I cannot give him any longer.*

It didn't take me long to figure out who she was talking about.

But he hates me, I thought, as if she would hear me.

It turned out she did.

He does not hate you, honey. He is confused and scared.

I wanted to ask her what he was afraid of, but before I could, her hand drifted away with the rest of the sand.

I swear to God, my heart was racing faster than Usain Bolt.

My heart was hammering harder than before. Oh *jeez,* I needed to breathe. This was all too much in such a short amount of time. First the visions, now this sandstorm or whatever it was and my dead mom talking to me. It was so freaky.

Sam opened his eyes but didn't pull away from me automatically. Instead, he looked all around us, moving just his eyes. I figured he was making sure nothing else would jump out at us. As much as I didn't want anything else to pop up, I was uncomfortable with his touch and began squirming beneath it. He looked back at me and glared at me but slowly lowered his hand from my mouth. He looked around us once more, and when he saw we were alone, he pulled away from me, letting me go. Putting a finger to his lips, he signaled for silence, and I readily listened to him, freaked out about what would happen if I didn't stay quiet. He grabbed my hand, and although I wanted to object, I knew it wouldn't be appropriate in our situation. So I just bore the nervousness his touch was giving me until we were out of the forest.

Once out, he commented, "Well, you look like shit."

"That's pretty reasonable, considering we were just in a *fucking* sandstorm," I retorted. "What the hell was that anyway?"

"Spirits," he explained. "When we die supernaturally, we burn into ashes, and those ashes get sent here. That wasn't sand; it was the ashes of the dead, controlled by spirits that seek on the living for food. You could say that our body flesh keeps the spirits alive. They rely on the senses of sound and touch, which is why we had to stay still and quiet."

"That's freaky as hell."

"You were freaked out even before the spirits attacked us," he continued before I could ask him what had happened to the guy he was chasing. "I know you had a vision of some sort. What did you see?"

"Nothing, just shut up," I muttered. I didn't want to talk about it.

Unfortunately, he didn't. Looking around to avoid any surprise attacks, he asked, "Monique, are you sure you're okay? You're pale."

"Why the freaking hell do you give a crap?"

"What? I'm just ask asking—"

"Just shut up," I ordered.

But he didn't. "Look, that forest is full of spirits, just like the ones we saw. Anyone who goes in there has visions. I had a feeling you'd have one too when I found you in there. But they're not real. Nothing you see actually comes true."

I didn't reply but kept a lookout with him.

"Monique, what did you see?" he asked again, and irritated, I finally answered him.

"You really wanna know what I saw, Sam?" I exclaimed, having had enough of him. "I saw you and me making out, okay? Happy?"

He raised an eyebrow. "Seriously? That's all that bothered you?"

It wasn't. Jeremy's death revelation bothered me a lot more, but that was something I didn't want to speak about. The moment I vocalized it, it would become harder to convince myself that it wasn't going to happen.

I wasn't going to let Jeremy die.

"Yeah, now can we get out of here? The Daeblo clearly isn't here."

He sighed. "He was. I just didn't—" He paused, pressing his lips into a thin line and shaking his head. "I looked around everywhere for a body, but I couldn't find it. I figured you two were either following me or looking too, but then I saw that man. I thought he was just there to cause trouble. I didn't realize *he* was the Daeblo until later."

"How'd you realize?"

"He was scared, and I wasn't sure why, but his eyes didn't change colour. And then I saw Iris's body. It didn't disintegrate. And then I realized why we didn't land in the city we were supposed to. He had to have messed with the magic of the portal. That's why I went after him, but he teleported and got away."

"Well shit," I fumed. "We had such a perfect opportunity too."

He sighed. "I know." Just then, his cell phone rang. Looking annoyed, he pulled it out of his pocket and answered it.

"You better have something good," he said with an authoritative tone of voice.

Who was he talking to?

I stayed quiet so I could hear what the other guy was saying. "I've found them. They're in an abandoned warehouse in LA."

Found who?

"Give me the address and I'll be on my way."

The guy on the other end obeyed, and Sam immediately hung up. "Who was that?" I demanded.

He sighed. "Let's walk, okay? I'm going to LA, and I need to get to a portal. I'll explain on the way."

And he did. Apparently, since Byron had tipped Grayson off, Sam took it upon himself to make sure he didn't do anything like that again. He hired a Tracker to look for Byron's family while Sam trained me. Finally, after the past week or so, the Tracker had found them.

The portal Sam had been leading me to was within the village Cole and Jana had scoped out to find Grayson.

More specifically, it was in a house within the village.

My breath hitched.

"Whose house is this?" I asked as we walked through the forest-like front yard to get to the front door.

"A friend's."

I tried not to freak out, but I guess he realized that I was scared, because he turned to me and demanded, "God, why the hell are you so scared? What's your problem?"

You, I thought, but I didn't say anything as I was suddenly immersed into the darkness, the moon successfully hidden by some tall plants. Luckily for me, I adjusted well and was able to see Sam reaching for the door and unlocking it.

He had a key?

Why would he have the key to a friend's house?

As he went inside and lit a candle—since this fucking place didn't use any electricity—I also noticed the empty look to the house. It had the basic necessities, a kitchen, a dining table, and couches all in plain view. But no one appeared to be home, which scared me even more.

I tried to control my nervous shaking as I followed him inside. He shut the door behind me before leading me down a narrow corridor, just past the sitting room. He then opened a door to our left to reveal what looked like a portal.

"You sure you're ready to go to LA? I don't know what kind of security Grayson has set up at this location."

"I'm going," I said with confidence.

So he took my hand, and we stepped through. Again, I got a queasy feeling in the pit of my stomach, but I ignored it and landed in a motel room.

"Whose room is this?" I asked.

"Maya's."

"Where is she?"

"Doctor's appointment. There's a car dealership down the road that gives rentals. We're heading there."

So I followed him out into the dry, smoggy air of the city, which was much warmer than it had been inside. Still in the jogging pants, sweater, and T-shirt I had been wearing when we robbed the military, I decided to take the sweater off and ditch it at the motel just before Sam locked the door. I kept my bow and arrows concealed in a large duffel bag on my back and walked with Sam down the packed sidewalks to this rental place. Within the next half-hour, we left the place in a small Toyota, heading on our journey to save Byron's family.

JANA

I knew Monique was going to kill me if she ever found out what I'd really gone out to do. I could tell she was already pissed at me for some reason, but she'd be more pissed if she knew I hadn't told her that it was really Jeremy who'd texted me, telling me that his Cloaker was dead and that he was in danger. But I didn't want her to worry. Knowing her brother was in danger would just cloud her thinking. I just hoped she hadn't seen the worry in my eyes as I left.

I needed a quick way to get to Barrie, but knowing I could only use the permanent portal Sam and Cole had been using to places I'd already been, and since I' never gone to Barrie or Toronto, I had to opt for other options. When I found out there were no flights heading from Windsor to anywhere in or near Toronto until tonight, I looked up train tickets, but I'd already missed the one that had left today. The only options I had were driving or taking the bus.

I decided to take my car, since it would be quicker.

I had just gotten onto the 401, which was pretty much empty this time of day, when a police car tailed me. I groaned in exasperation as I drove my car to the shoulder of the road. Impatient to get to Barrie, I prayed the police officer was a straight male and got ready to flirt my way out of the situation. I had just finished adjusting the neck of my shirt when the he knocked on my window.

I rolled it down. "I'm sorry, sir, is there a problem?"

I made sure to bat my lashes a little, but it seemed to have no effect on him.

"Ma'am, I'm going to have to ask you to step out of your car."

I stifled a sigh and tried to smile as I got out. It was only when I had shut my door and peered a little closer at the male in front of me, trying to read his expression, that I saw the dazed look in his eyes.

Compelled.

My eyes went wide. Stifling a gasp, I turned to jump inside the car, when he grabbed my arm and the back of my neck in one swift motion. Before I could fight back, he took advantage of this deserted part of the highway and smashed my head into the side of car.

I immediately began fading, falling into fearful unconsciousness.

MONIQUE

The location, like the Tracker Sam had hired said, was an abandoned warehouse that was locked shut from the outside. We picked through it easily, however, drawing no attention to ourselves, by taking the deserted alley to go in through the backdoor. Actually, it all seemed a little too easy, and as we made our way through the darkness with only a flashlight to guide us, trying to find Byron's family, I looked back at everything that had happened the past weeks.

It wasn't just today that seemed easy, I realized, but everything else as well, starting from the day I found out Mason and Donna were dead. Finding Riley had been too easy—but Grayson had wanted us to find him so I let that one slide. But finding Byron had been too easy as well. Yeah, getting Maya out had been more of a challenge, but the fact that Byron gave us information so willingly, instead of just telling Sam to find his family first before giving him anything, seemed suspicious. At least, that's what I would have done.

But the deal breaker was this place. It didn't even appear to be the least bit guarded and was too easy to find. Not only that, I suddenly noticed that Grayson was doing all of his business on Earth. I pondered why, trying to find a connection to the rest of this mess, when I remembered something I had reminded myself of not too long ago.

Divianans got *all* the information the media could obtain. They didn't hide anything. So if Grayson was really planning on compelling an army, he wouldn't do it on Diviano. He wouldn't want to draw attention. He would do it on Earth. All attacks would happen on Earth.

But if he didn't want to draw attention, he wouldn't want to form an army at all, even on Earth. There was no way in hell he could cover that up for so long. Somebody would eventually find out. So what if he used it as a distraction? What if he was actually just going to attack Sam and me when we were alone, like right now? It would be the perfect opportunity, as we would have no one to help us fight. Everyone was training, getting ready to face Grayson's armed forces. Jana was picking up a friend from the airport, and Nathan was God knew where.

Suddenly another thought dawned on me. I stopped Sam in the middle of our search, placing a hand on his shoulder. "Where did you find this Tracker?" I asked.

He raised an eyebrow at me. "Why do you care?"

"Just answer me!"

"Byron paid for it, since it's his family. He's paying for Maya's bodyguard too, as long as Grayson is alive."

I was fairly certain my theory was right, but I had realized it too late. The next thing I knew, I had been struck down, and slowly, the world around me started spinning as I drifted into unconsciousness.

COLE

I didn't know half the people I was training. There were about eighty-five of them, and I only could remember the names of about twenty, give or take. I was used to that, though, since this wasn't my first time training people. I had a part-time job at a gym, where I taught aikido to a group of people.

There was a difference, however. Back at the gym in Toronto, I got to know everyone eventually. Here, I still felt like a stranger to most. Not only that, I was losing my patience day by day, because I had no idea when this was going to end. Sam had told me that Byron would tell him when Grayson was planning to attack, but we'd barely heard from him at all.

It was nearly noon at the cottage. I'd finished training the whole group on how to use the weapons they chose and was watching them shoot target boards Riley and I had set up.

Riley was now practicing with swords—which Jana was able to get through the black market—with a blond guy he'd become fairly close with. He was one of Jana's friends. His name was Argent, but he told us all just to call him Ace.

"It's what my friends call me," he'd told Riley and me.

Friends, whom he never mentioned otherwise. Friends, who never showed up to help.

I was kind of suspicious of him but I shouldn't have been, since Jana told me to trust Ace with all my heart. And I trusted her. Plus, Ace seemed earnest and did no harm. Actually, he helped me train the others, knowing quite a few fighting tactics himself.

But I noticed that while the others—when taking breaks—talked amongst each other about their lives outside of this place, Ace just remained beside Riley. If Riley wasn't there, he wouldn't talk to anyone else.

"He's just very selective about who he chooses to spend his time with," Jana had explained very simply one day. It made sense, but there was just something about him that I didn't like.

And then Sam suggested I might be jealous, since Ace and Jana seemed to have a pretty tight history together. Just as friends, but still.

Jealousy wasn't an emotion I was used to feeling.

Ace and Riley pulled apart when I walked past them. "Hi, Captain," Ace greeted cheerfully.

"I told you not to call me that," I said for probably the hundredth time since we'd met. He would continue anyway, telling me it suited the way I trained everyone.

Ace and Riley both laughed. "Back to work," I said, realizing too late that my command did fit a captain's role. I rolled my eyes, annoyed at myself for it, but let it go as I tried to keep track of everyone's form.

That was until I felt a sudden ringing in my ear. I remembered the earpiece and looked at Riley to see that he had heard it too.

"Help me," Jana whispered.

She sounded so desperate. Where was she? What had happened?

"Where are you?" I asked.

Her voice came out weaker than before, and it made it harder for me to breathe. Was she dying? She couldn't be dying. I wasn't going to let her die, not on my watch.

"I don't know. I'm—I'm tied up. It's dark . . . and cold."

She was going to have to give me a lot more than that.

"Look for a telltale sign," I urged desperately, no longer focusing on the people in front of me. "Look out a window."

I heard her taking in a deep breath. "It's foggy," she breathed.

Well, it wasn't foggy here.

"Is there a Cloaker near you?"

"I'm alone."

"I'll hire a Tracker," I said immediately and walked away to make the call. As I did, I pointed to Ace, knowing he was the only one here capable enough to monitor the others. Despite his lack of social skills, he was the only one with enough knowledge.

"Argent!" I called. He looked up at me. "Take over."

He nodded and left Riley's side to supervise. I didn't pay another thought to him but tried my best to keep my mind clear as I prayed to whatever God was up there that I would be able to save Jana. That I wouldn't lose what I now desperately wished I hadn't willingly stalled.

273

SAM

My memory was cloudy when I woke up to find myself in a dimly lit room. From the look of the makeshift beds and canned food lying in the corner where the stairs were, it looked like some sort of storm cellar. But I wasn't on one of those beds. Instead, my hands were tied to the bedpost, which was chained to the wall.

In front of me was Monique, who was slowly opening her eyes. It was seeing her that brought back the memory of what had happened.

We'd been set up.

The moment I realized it, anger and adrenaline surged through me. With my palms sweaty and my body shaking, I tried desperately to break the bedposts. But it was as if they were made of steel. Monique tried doing the same, grunting out, "Where are we?"

"I have no idea," I replied. "But we need to get out."

"Well no shit. Jana?" she called. "Cole, Riley, anyone?"

We got no answer through the earpieces. The magic fueling them could only work so far, and we were out of range.

Fuck!

"How did I not think of this earlier?" Monique growled, still struggling with her bonds. "How did I not figure it out? It was too easy, *way* too easy. All of it. I'm *such* an idiot!"

Despite the fact that I agreed, I didn't say anything. She was already pissed, and so was I. Besides, it wasn't just her fault. We all had a fault in this.

This couldn't get any worse.

Until it did.

Just past Monique's bed was a door that opened in that moment. In walked Maya's bodyguard, holding her unconscious body in his arms.

If I had been angry before, I was going to burst into flames now. This was the last straw. I should have realized it. I should have seen through Byron's bullshit, like Jana had. But instead I trusted him blindly, all because of the story of a sick child who probably didn't even exist.

I should have realized it.

"Let her go!" I yelled, but judging from the bodyguard's dazed expression, it would be no use.

He was being compelled.

Before I had time to process all this, someone else walked in through the door. At first I was relieved to find Nathan here, come to save us. Until I realized that he looked dazed too.

I remembered how after a while, he had stopped showing up to train. We hadn't thought much of it, and because none of us paid much attention to him, it had to have been easy for Grayson to pluck him off the streets and compel him for whatever Grayson wanted to use him for.

Suddenly I heard a shrill shriek that belonged to Monique, who now was thrashing violently, so angry at the sight of Nathan that she was digging into her skin with the ropes that held her back.

"You monster," she snarled, and I realized she was looking at who was just now coming in.

Grayson.

"Monster is a fucking understatement," I seethed, looking at Maya's still body. She looked like she was dead, and it killed me to see her like that again.

I didn't need any more reminders of her fate.

"At least I am a monster with the brains you lack," Grayson replied. I snapped my head toward him to see that he looked much bulkier than I remembered and held himself with much more confidence, much more power.

Power he'd received by killing those innocent kids.

"What the hell did you do to him?" Monique growled, looking at Nathan.

"Him?" Grayson asked, grinning sadistically. "I just compelled him, that's all. He'll be fine soon, once his task is complete."

"What task?"

His response was a maniacal laugh.

Monique visibly tried to use her power on Grayson. I knew she thought she could hurt him enough with it to make him untie her. But, her power did nothing. She tried once more but failed again, getting angrier and angrier by the second.

"It's useless," Grayson said. The grin on his face made my blood boil. I clenched my fists, trying desperately to get out of these bonds.

"Byron informed me about your telekinesis power, so I inhibited it when I attacked you." Fucking Byron! "Gave you a little dose of magic."

His smirk widened as Monique's scowl deepened.

"Let. Him. Go," she snarled, motioning toward Nathan with her head. As if that would do anything. She continued trying to win him over with useless threats, while I wondered if Grayson knew that Nathan was the person keeping Maya alive, since Jana had gotten the bond created again, just to be on the safe side.

He had to know. With all the cameras in the house and Byron having tricked us, he must have known.

But then . . . why were we here?

Was he going to kill Nathan in front of us and then kill Maya here too?

The thought sent shivers down my spine.

"You know what's funny, Monique?" Grayson began, bending down to her level as if he were going to father her. "Watching you and your little friends running around thinking you're winning. You had so much confidence that you were beating me, but that's exactly what will cause your demise. I'll admit, you guys were smart to have figured out where I was keeping Maya. I didn't expect that." He gave her a bitter smile. "But that was your only lucky streak. You were blind to everything else. Finding Riley? It was too easy, wasn't it? And the kid is malleable. I knew the moment he met you, he'd side with you. So telling him that I didn't want you finding out I was building an army? Score one for me. He thought I was building one. He wanted you to be prepared. When in fact, there is no army."

He stood up, pacing around. "It got you building one, though, didn't it? Split you up, all of you busy with different tasks. Kept you distracted. Instead of everyone focusing on making sure *you* were prepared, making sure you both gained more strength, they focused their energy on a whole group of people. People you weren't going to bring along on a mission like this because you needed them for a battle that wasn't going to take place."

He smirked, and as the words sank in, my anger rose. How could we have fallen for this?

"And then you sent Jeremy away. You basically did all the work with that one. The cameras weren't there anymore, but just like you had Cole hacking into my computer, I had a man of my own. Took merely an hour to figure out you were sending him away. Took him less time to realize when and where. And of course, when I sent my men, Jeremy did put up a fight, but he's locked away now. Getting Jana out of the way with a frantic text from 'Jeremy,'" he air-quoted the name, "was even easier. So now she's locked up too. Cole and Riley are busy training. Now tell me, Monique. Who will be here to save you?"

Monique was breathing hard, and I could see tears in her eyes. Worried. She was worried. Jana and Jeremy were being held captive, and there was nothing she could do.

Grayson's grin widened as he walked in circles around Nathan. "Your lover here was the easiest to kidnap. After all, he was walking around the streets at night, feeling worthless after you turned him down. And Maya," he sighed, walking over to her.

I gritted my teeth. "Get away from her!"

He ignored me. "Byron screwed up, but at least he gained your trust, Sam. Made it very easy to figure out who her bodyguard was and compel him."

"Why'd you do all this?" Monique demanded, her voice shaking.

He turned his attention back to her. "Because I wanted you two here alone, see?"

"Why?"

He shook his head, clucking his tongue. "Are you really that stupid, Monique? I brought you here to make a deal." He walked over to her and bent down on one knee again, looking at her intently. "You have three options. One is to simply hand over the gem. The other is to tell me who it is I need to kill in order to end Maya's life. If you choose that option, I will give you a ten-second headstart to get the hell out of here."

"And the third option?"

"Nathan dies."

So Grayson didn't have a clue as to who was bonded to Maya. Why hadn't Byron told him? Why withhold that information?

I could tell that Monique was thinking the same thing, but instead of letting Grayson know that something was up, she demanded, "What's the purpose of killing Maya? What do you get out of it?"

Grayson laughed. "Of course Sam hasn't told you."

"Told me what?"

It was then that I realized Grayson was going to expose my secret, something that I'd meant to keep hidden from Monique. If we got out of here, I wasn't confident that she wouldn't go against me and use it as advantage. I couldn't let her find out.

But there was nothing I could do, nothing I could say to stop the truth from coming out. The only thing that would make Grayson shut up was unconsciousness, which wasn't going to happen as long as I was tied up.

"It's Cole," I blurted in attempt at distraction. Thankfully, Grayson turned to me. I continued, "We bonded Maya and Cole."

It was a good lie, since Cole was nowhere near here and it would give us some time to get out of these bonds somehow and warn him of what was coming. Plus, Cole was no doubt with the army we'd gathered. He had protection.

Grayson just smirked. "Nice try. I know it was Jana who got a Wunissa to create the bond, and I know for a fact that she didn't meet Cole until afterward. And *you* would never tell me who it is."

"Why do you want to kill Maya?" Monique demanded again.

"Why don't you just kill me already?" I interjected. "The only reason you want me dead is so that you can kill Monique, right?" I was letting out a lot of information that I didn't want Monique knowing, but if it meant saving Maya's life, I would yell it at the top of my lungs if I had to. "So what does Maya have to do with this? Leave her out of the equation. Just kill me already."

I knew he couldn't. Bonding Nathan with Maya had left me protected as well. I could only die if Nathan died, because of the bond Maya and I shared. But I was buying time. I didn't care if he tried to kill me, as long as he didn't touch her.

Grayson turned back to look at me again. His smirk, which had looked taunting before, now looked malicious. Diabolical. He had something wicked cooked up for me.

"I'm not a fool, Sam. I know how bonding works. Besides, what could be more pleasurable than doing this?"

He stood up and took a knife out of his pocket as he walked over to Maya, and immediately, my anger was replaced with fear. "No," I begged. "Don't touch her." But he ignored me. "No, don't touch her. Don't—arghh!"

He had sliced through the skin on her abdomen, leaving me scared and in pain as well. But it hurt more to see her whimper, and she woke up in the pain.

"Let her go," I hissed through gritted teeth.

And then the pain amplified. Slowly, my skin started burning. I groaned. "What the hell is this?" I snarled.

"Oil extracts of the plant muertem. Pretty harmless to humans, but it can kill a Divianan in large quantities. The knife is coated in it." He sliced Maya's other side. I screamed, now withering in pain, pushing against my restraints as I tried desperately to get away. To ease the pain. To save Maya and go.

"See, while you thought Maya was so safe, I had actually taken her into my own hands again. Only this time, even *she* didn't know it. Compelling her bodyguard was the best thing I could have done. While she slept, he experimented with different poisons, and Byron watched to see which one would affect you the most. I tested this one using the plant from the forest. But when Byron watched from a camera in the backyard you conveniently missed and noticed you withering in response to it, I decided to steal from the chemical plant in Mediralis. They grow the plants with a more concentrated level of the poison. And you didn't hear about that burglary because you guys were too caught up with my men robbing the military at the same exact time. You didn't suspect a thing."

I remembered the pain I had felt that day, and how Maya had seemed like she was trying to get rid of me. I realized she had meant to send me a message indirectly, trying to warn me that something was wrong. But instead of taking it as danger, I took it as the fact that I *had* fucked up and she'd finally lost patience with me.

I grit my teeth in anger, at myself and at Grayson.

"See what this is doing?" Grayson asked, now looking at Monique as he sliced through Maya's skin again. I growled, trying to hide the pain.

"It's called the Diveratus Mundoversum bond, formed by a curse between lovers of two different worlds. Maya's human. Sam's not. So everything that happens to her will happen to him. If I kill her, he dies."

He sauntered over to Monique, looming over her like a tower. She didn't even try to hide her fear. "So tell me who Maya is bonded to."

Her fear didn't stop her from standing up to him. "Over my dead body."

Grayson laughed, walking away. "Oh really?" And before I knew what he was doing, he had pulled out a silenced gun and shot Nathan in the head.

"No!" Monique shrieked. She was trying now more desperately than ever to get out of her bonds. Tears welled in her eyes, but I could tell she was trying to keep them down. "You monster!"

Grayson just continued laughing. "Still don't want to tell me?"

She was still struggling to get out of her bonds, and fear was evident on her face, as well as pain, but she visibly put those emotions to the side and growled, "You lost your leverage, you ass."

"Not exactly. That was just a show. I know you didn't care as much for him as you do for some others. Remember how you put Jeremy in danger, and how I got Jana alone?"

He pulled out his phone, dialed a number, and then put it on speaker. He then pulled out a second phone and dialed another number. In seconds, he had it on speaker too. "Hello Jana. Hello Jeremy."

Monique shrieked as Jeremy pleaded with someone not to hurt him. "Let them go!" she cried. "Please!"

"Not unless you give me the gem or tell me who it is that is bonded to Maya. *Now.*"

Monique didn't say anything. She just stared up at him with her forehead creased in fear, and I prayed to God she wouldn't tell him it was Nathan. Even with the kid dead, if Grayson didn't know he could kill me and Maya, he wouldn't try.

I looked at Maya, who was whimpering in the arms of her bodyguard. She was looking at me with tired eyes, and I sent her a look that said, "I love you." She sent it back, knowing this was going to be the end. I knew Monique wouldn't let Jeremy and Jana die, not for Maya, not for me, and she didn't understand the bond she and I shared. She didn't know that her life was tied to mine. But Grayson knew, and he was going to take advantage of her ignorance to kill all of us.

I couldn't let that happen. But before I could let her know, Grayson started talking again.

"Hurry Monique. Tell me where the gem is, or who to kill to get to Maya. I'm losing my patience."

When Monique didn't talk, looking petrified, Grayson sighed. "All right. As you wish. Kill her," he ordered to whoever was with Jana.

"No, wait! Wait!" Monique screamed. "Wait, I'll give you the gem!"

What?! No!

Grayson smirked. "Stop," he said, talking into the phone.

Monique set her jaw. "Let me out of my bonds and then I'll give it to you."

"I'm not stupid," Grayson replied. "If I let you out, you're just going to run. Just give me its location."

"I'm not stupid either. The safest place for the gem is on me. It's here, in this room."

What the hell was she *doing*? She was going to give him the gem? Was she stupid? I gave her a pleading look, trying to catch her eye, but she wouldn't look at me. She just stared down at her hands with a look of shame and defeat written across her face.

Panic shook through me. If Grayson got the gem, I would lose Maya. I would lose the only thing that could breathe any life back into her. It hurt much worse than knowing thousands of lives would be lost; none of this was Maya's fault. She didn't deserve to die. I couldn't let Monique give him the gem, but I couldn't do anything in these stupid bonds.

"Where on you?"

"In my pocket. Just let me go. You're going to kill us anyway, and I'd rather not feel violated in my last moments."

But he ignored her request, searching her pockets. With each passing second, I was finding it harder and harder to breathe, praying that he wouldn't find it, that Monique had lied, or that someone would come in and save us. But I was out of luck. A moment later, he paused, and a wicked grin stretched across his face.

He pulled it out.

The gemstone.

Grayson's eyes brightened when he saw it, greed taking over his expression. I could tell that he thought he was a genius, but I realized something in that moment that he didn't.

Monique was acting.

The stone in his hand wasn't the gem. Somehow, she had prepared for this moment.

Grayson wasn't stupid, but his greed was making him blind. He would have realized the gem were fake if he'd paid a little more attention to his adopted daughter. If he had, he would have realized like I did that she would rather a few of us die than all, which was why it wouldn't make sense for her to give him the gem at all. But for eighteen years he was so fixated on his end goal that he'd completely overlooked her brilliance.

But the thing was, we had no way out. If he tried to destroy the fake gemstone right here and now and nothing happened, we'd be back at square one.

Fortunately, Monique had another plan.

When Grayson had leaned over to grab the gem from her, she'd taken the gun from his holster without him noticing. She couldn't exactly aim the gun right at him, because of her bonds, but I saw her using the butt of the gun to loosen a part of the rope. When I saw Grayson about to turn and look at her, I stalled him.

"You're a cruel monster. I can't believe you're willing to kill so many people for power."

He focused back on me, his grin wider than ever. "It's not like you don't want the same thing."

I didn't want Monique to know why I wanted the gem, or that I wanted it at all, but I had to talk. I had to say something so that he wouldn't notice her, so I continued, "I never wanted it for power. My reasons are much more selfless, and you know that."

"Killing thousands of people for the sake of one isn't selfless. It's pathetic."

"Well, he's not as pathetic as you," Monique said, and I looked over to see that she was free of both of her bonds. She now had the gun aimed directly at him. But I knew she had never used a gun before, and I could tell she wasn't confident enough to shoot him. But before I could come up with anything—even some stupid lie—that would build her confidence, Grayson lunged at her.

With tear-filled eyes, she dropped the gun and kicked him in the abdomen as he came toward her. His body hit the wall behind him with a loud thud. She didn't waste another second. The next thing I knew, she was on her feet, kicking him like crazy.

"You bastard," she snarled.

Before she could throw her sixth kick, Grayson lifted his hands with his teeth clenched together and blocked Monique's blow. Shoving her to the opposite wall with a force that left a dent, he grabbed the replica from where he'd dropped it and raised it in the air.

"You think just because you're untied you can beat me? I still have the gem. You'll be dead in a second, and I will be immortal forever."

And then he smashed the replica on the ground hard enough to crack it open. But nothing came out. None of the blood that was supposed to be in there came out, and that was when he realized that he had been tricked.

He looked up at a still crippled Monique with his eyes blazing. "You're going to pay for that, bitch."

And then he lunged at her, but having taken enough time to heal, she was quick. Rolling out of the way, she pulling something out of her back pocket and whipped it at me.

A pocketknife. She'd cut the rope enough to loosen it, but nicked me in the wrist doing it. Ignoring the blood, I freed myself from my bonds just as Grayson grabbed at Monique's throat. She kicked him away from her again, buying herself more time to heal and get up on her feet.

Suddenly, blue light flickered from the surface her hands. She looked down at them, realizing she had her power back just when I did. With a smirk, she looked back at Grayson, who was still recovering on the other side of the room. "Guess my power's back," she taunted.

On that note, she lifted him high above the air with one hand and then threw him heavily against the far wall, cracking a good chunk of the cement. With a broken arm, she winced as she made her way to where he was now wheezing.

"This is for all you did to me, you sick monster," she snarled, shoving her foot into his neck. Relentlessly, he tried grabbing at her with weak arms but it was useless.

She continued, "This is for Mom." She threw a punch in his face and then lifted him to his feet by the collar of his shirt. "This is for my sister." Turning him around, she held his arms behind his back and smashed his face into the wall. "Nathan." Again, she smashed his face in. "Mason. Donna." Again. His eyes were now fluttering shut as he bled out. "And this is for everyone else you've killed or hurt in your life, including me."

She was beating him into the wall hard and fast, and I knew she would kill him. But I also saw the tears starting to overflow. She wanted her revenge. But she wouldn't be able to live with herself if she killed the man she'd always called father. She'd never committed murder. It would destroy her.

I was already feeling some of the guilt seep through.

She couldn't do this.

Snapping into action, I pulled her away from him just as I heard something crunch. His heartbeat was already slowing. She'd already killed him. But I grabbed the gun and shot him in the chest anyway, watching as his body slumped to the ground in a pool of blood.

It was over. She'd killed him.

But she'd never know.

CHAPTER 12

INVISIBLE BONDS

MONIQUE

The man who had been holding Maya dropped her the moment Grayson died, but Sam was there to catch her. The dazed look left the man's eyes, and he looked at Maya. "I'm sorry," he apologized, observing his surroundings with wide eyes. "Where am I?"

I had no idea so I couldn't give him an answer. I just looked at Nathan's body, which hadn't disintegrated. "It was the Oscubris he used," Sam explained before slowly letting Maya down on one of the beds. "You okay?" he asked. I didn't hear her response and didn't turn around to see if she'd nodded. I kept staring at Nathan, feeling sick to my stomach as I realized that I could have saved him if I had just pulled my move earlier. I could have saved him if I hadn't turned him down, if he wasn't walking the streets aimlessly, if he wasn't so upset. I could have saved him if I hadn't reacted the way I had when he told me he had feelings for me. But I hadn't saved him, and now all I could do was stare into his dark, lifeless eyes and pray that he was in a better place, despite how sick thinking that made me feel.

"Let me see the cuts," Sam said quietly behind me, and the moment he mentioned them, I remembered the pain I'd felt when Grayson was torturing Maya and Sam, the dull ache in my sides that still existed.

"They're not as bad as yours. Sam, you need to get yourself to a hospital."

"So do you."

"He infected you with muertem. If you don't get yourself taken care of, you're going to die."

I turned around. I wasn't going to let anyone else die on my watch.

"You," I snapped at the bodyguard, ignoring the pain in my sides. "Take the girl and get to a hospital *now*." He still seemed a little dazed but nodded, and I immediately pulled Sam away from Maya.

"Take off your shirt," I ordered. He was still looking at Maya, watching the bodyguard handle her. I snapped my fingers in front of his face, and he looked at me, but he didn't seem to have heard what I said. Impatient, I lifted his shirt and saw that his abdomen was slowly turning purple.

This was bad. *Really* bad.

I didn't have a virtencia on me, and apparently Sam was stripped of his. I looked back at Grayson's dead body, which hadn't disintegrated either—probably due to the fact that he'd used Oscubris on others—and saw one in his pocket.

And then I saw the phones that were still on the ground and heard someone talking.

"Where am I?" a male asked.

"Jana? Jeremy?" I called as Maya and her bodyguard left.

"I'm okay," I heard Jana say through one of the phones, and I breathed a sigh of relief, despite still being angry with her. "Cole's on his way. What happened?"

"I'll explain later. Jeremy?" I heard whimpering through one of the phones, and my heart started beating faster. Was he hurt? "Jeremy, where are you?"

"I don't know."

"Where's your Cloaker?"

"Dead."

"Okay, I'll send someone to find you. Just hang in there."

And then I cut the call with both of them and turned around to find that Sam was on his knees, holding his side in pain. I immediately snapped into action and handed Sam the virtencia. "Can you make a portal?" I asked him as I made a mental note to learn how to do it myself in the near future. Silently, he nodded and made a portal. I grabbed his hand before heading through, landing in the middle of a busy street. It was bright daylight, and people were milling around, going about their daily business. I looked around, trying to look for a hospital or an ambulance, but didn't see anything.

And then Sam groaned, doubling over in pain. I didn't think twice before wrapping his arm around my neck and wrapping mine around his waist to hold him up.

"Where'd you land us?" I asked.

"The capital. First place I thought of." He was wincing, clearly trying to hide the amount of pain he was feeling.

"I need help over here!" I shouted, desperate to get to a hospital. I was surprised by the response I had gotten, something I didn't think I would have gotten back on Earth. When I'd shouted, people looked at me and immediately rushed to help.

"There's a hospital fifteen minutes from here," one man said. "I can take you in my carriage."

I nodded, and a few others helped Sam get into the carriage. It was in this moment, with these people acting so selflessly, that I began to think of what could have happened had I not decided to make that replica of the gem when I made my trip to Tyler's house. What could have happened if I didn't think it could have been useful in the long run. What could have happened had I not been able to grab the gun from Grayson without him realizing it. What would have happened had I not been so skilled at getting out of knots, though I'd never be thankful for how I'd learned.

And what could have happened had I decided to run away the day I found out my life was going to end in three years—if I had decided I didn't care about anyone but myself.

"We're almost there," the man controlling the carriage said when Sam hissed in pain.

"Your arm," Sam mumbled, leaning his head on my shoulder. His energy level had quickly depleted and I was left feeling queasy but I bared with it.

I looked down at my arm. It was broken but I'd barely registered the pain until now. "It's fine. It's healing."

He seemed to want to say something else but before he could, we reached the hospital.

The hospital was lit with electric lights, not candles, since they sacrificed a bit of environmental cleanliness to save lives. It looked exactly like a normal hospital back in Canada, but when we brought Sam into the emergency room, they immediately took him in. I noticed that there were very few others waiting to be taken in as well. It wasn't at all like the overcrowded emergency rooms back home. They had to have been very well staffed.

As they took Sam in on the stretcher, I followed, and Sam quickly slurred, "Call Cole. Check up on Maya."

I nodded. His eyes began fluttering closed. Stopping in my tracks, I did as he said and pulled out my phone, dialing Cole's number. But he didn't pick up. I remembered that he'd gone to save Jana and called Riley instead.

"Where are you?" I asked.

"Down at the cottage. Are you and Sam okay? You've been gone a while."

"Listen, Grayson's dead. We don't need to go through any more training."

"What? How? What happened?"

"I'll explain later. I need to talk to Cole, but he's not picking up his phone."

"He left it here. He was in a rush."

Fucking hell. "Okay, I want you to do three things for me. If Cole is in range, let him know that Sam's in the hospital, in Diviano. It's called Pelagipul, the main one in the capital. And then I need you to get a Tracker and find Jeremy. Can you do that for me?"

"Yeah, got it. What was the third thing?"

I sighed. "Do you know how to make a portal?"

JANA

I was so lightheaded from the earlier blow that I didn't even try to fight it when my attacker came in and put a gun to my head, seconds after Cole told me he was getting a Tracker to find me. But when he got a call and put the phone on speaker, I started to freak out, realizing that he was being compelled by Grayson to kill me. I wasn't exactly sure what happened after that, having passed out for a while, until I heard Monique crying for me and Jeremy.

I was just glad that whatever had happened, she sounded okay.

Now the guy who'd held the gun to my head had dropped it, and the dazed look in his eyes was gone. He disconnected the call when he realized it had gone dead and looked at me with confused grey eyes, while before they'd been brown. He was Divianan.

"What happened?" he asked.

I shook my head. "I don't know."

Suddenly, I heard a door being torn down above us with a huge crash as it hit the ground. "Jana!" I heard someone call, and with relief, I realized it was Cole.

"Down here!" I called and then turned to the guy beside me. "Untie me please," I begged. I wasn't sure what had happened exactly, but I knew that the compulsion was no longer present. He was free to think for himself.

He did as I asked and freed me from the bonds holding me to the pole in the center of a basement. It was precisely that moment that Cole came running in, a gun in his hand.

"What did you do to her?" he demanded, pointing his gun at the man.

"Stop!" I cried, noticing the man's petrified expression. "He was compelled. He's not now."

Cole looked at me and lowered his gun, helping me to my feet and supporting me with his burly arms. "You okay?" he asked.

My heart was racing, but now for a completely different reason.

I nodded. "He didn't hurt me. I think he was waiting on a call."

"Okay, let's just get out of here."

There was still a panic in Cole's eyes that was slowly dissolving, though not quickly enough.

I wanted to get out of here as badly as he did, but I felt as if something else was necessary. Still in the circle of his arms, I turned my head to look at the still-fazed man. "Are you okay?"

He nodded. "Yes. But I don't remember much."

"What's your name?"

"Henry Atwood."

"Where are you from?"

"Tecumseh."

"We're *in* Tecumseh," Cole said. "Is this your home?"

"Yes. There was a man," he added. "He knocked me out."

I knew he had to be talking about Grayson. "We'll take care of him." I turned to Cole. "Let's just get going."

Cole promised him again that we would take care of Grayson and that he would fix the guy's door, and then we left, heading up the stairs and out of the house into a clearing sky. It had just finished raining, and Cole's Cruze was dotted with the free shower.

"Thank you, for coming to get me."

He suddenly stopped walking and held me back as well. "Go out with me."

I was kind of startled by the request. I mean, I'd had a hunch that he would ask, but now? "What?" I blurted, unable to conjure up more of a response due to the butterflies in my stomach.

"Will you go on a date with me?"

He seemed more nervous than when he'd first asked, so I said, "I would, but at a time like this?"

"Who knows if we'll ever get through it, Jana? I don't want to miss our chance."

I realized just how right he was. But before I could respond, somebody spoke inside my ear. Realizing it was the earpiece and that it was Riley talking, I diverted my attention away from Cole to hear what he was saying.

"Grayson's dead."

I breathed a sigh of relief. "What happened exactly?"

"I don't know. Monique didn't give me the details. She was in Diviano and needed to get to LA, so she cut the call pretty quickly."

What was so important in LA? I pulled out my phone to call her but realized it was dead.

"Is she okay?" I asked.

"She's fine, but Sam's not. He's in the hospital."

Cole's eyes widened. "Which hospital is he in?"

"Pelagipul, in the capital."

"Okay, we're heading there right now."

Cole forgot our conversation and made a portal with his virtencia. We landed right outside of the hospital and rushed in, asking a lady at the front desk where Sam was.

"He's in the critical care unit."

Critical care? Would he be okay? I personally didn't care as much as Cole did, and I really wanted to check up on Monique, but I stayed by his side; I felt I owed it to him. Plus, I didn't exactly know where she was, and none of the phones here would let me call her on Earth. Cole had apparently left his on Earth as well.

We went up to the third floor and spoke to the nurse at the front desk there.

"The doctors are still working on taking the muertem out of his system, so I'm afraid you can't see him right now, but he will be fine. He's lucky he got here quickly."

Cole settled with that information and waited outside Sam's room while I went back to Earth to find Monique. I hadn't ever been to LA, though, so I ended up in the middle of a busy sidewalk, but everyone seemed too busy to notice that I'd just appeared out of nowhere.

Except one teenage boy.

"Hey, how did you—"

I smiled at him, a bit flirtingly, hoping to distract him from what had just happened. "What's your name?" I asked him.

"Teagan."

"Hi, Teagan. My name's Jocelyn. Let's take a walk shall we?" He seemed too confused to object but didn't begin walking, so I simply locked my arm with his and led him to an alleyway. "Do you have a phone, Teagan? Mine's dead."

I gave him a smile to urge him out of his hesitance, and he handed me his phone, unlocking it for me. "Thank you," I said, right as we got out of sight of others. I quickly took notice of the fact that there were no cameras around and punched him with enough force to knock him out.

I quickly called Monique, knowing her number by heart. She picked up on the second ring. "Hello?" she said, sounding confused.

"It's Jay," I said. "Where are you?"

"In LA."

"Where in LA?" When she named the hospital, I replied, "I'm coming." Hanging up, I used the kid's data connection to find directions, memorized them, and then called Teagan's dad.

I didn't give him a chance to talk. "Hello?" I said in a scared, ditsy voice. "This is Teagan's friend. He was just punched and knocked out by a man who stole money from his wallet."

"Where are you?" I gave him the street name, and he said, "Okay, I'll be right there."

Cutting the call, I took some money from Teagan's wallet and gave him his phone back, praying to God that the police didn't scan his stuff for fingerprints; I only took twenty bucks.

It was quicker getting to the hospital by walking because of the traffic, although it still took me a good twenty minutes to get there. By the time I did, my feet were killing me. Luckily I found the room Maya and Monique were in fairly quickly and silently thanked the inventor of elevators.

Maya was lying on the hospital bed with her eyes closed. She appeared to be sleeping, but also in pain. She seemed so frail, so much weaker than I remembered. Despite not having seen her in so many years, my heart fell looking at her expression, and in that moment, I realized just how much I'd missed her.

I wondered if she even remembered me.

Monique was sitting on a couch beside the cot, staring off into the distance. "How is she?" I asked.

Monique looked up at me and sighed. She answered my question, but I could tell from the distant look in her eyes that she was thinking about something else entirely. "She only needed stitches. She'll live through this. There wasn't any internal damage."

"What happened exactly?" I asked, sitting down beside her.

"Did you know about this whole thing—love between people of different worlds and how it bonds them?"

"Yeah," I replied. "It's complicated, but it's really just a curse set out to protect potential offspring. Most of the time, when we procreate with humans, our offspring come out defected and quickly die off. Can you tell me what happened now?"

So she explained everything. When she told me about Nathan, I was left dumbstruck.

I hadn't expected that. Why hadn't I seen that coming? Why hadn't I paid more attention to where Nathan was? Why hadn't I realized that he would be in more danger after Monique rejected him? He had a huge thing for her . . . I should have realized that he would have been sulking. I should have realized that it would have made him easier to kidnap.

My heart fell as the guilt washed over me, and my eyes pricked with tears. I was such a shitty friend. If I had paid a little more attention, he would still be alive. But now he was dead, and there was nothing I could do to fix it.

I dried away the tears, noticing that Monique was looking down at her hands.

I needed to make sure she was okay.

"How are you holding up?" I asked.

"Okay, I guess," she replied, but I knew she was lying. I put my hand on her shoulder to give her the support I knew she needed, but she didn't even turn to look at me. She continued staring aimlessly at her hands, with an expression of hopelessness written across her face.

"Monique," I called, wanting her to talk to me, but she wouldn't respond. Something was wrong, something she wasn't telling me, and I had no idea what.

MONIQUE

I didn't want to talk to Jana, which was why I ignored her when she tried to get me to open up. I wasn't ready to discuss the issue yet, not knowing how to start, not knowing how she'd defend herself, and not knowing if she even cared. But that didn't mean I didn't want to cry. It just meant I had to hold it in. I didn't want her to see me cry, not when she'd betrayed me like this.

After a long moment of silence between us, my phone rang. I pulled it out of my pocket to find that it was Sam calling.

Had he already been discharged?

"Hello?" I answered, ignoring the dull ache that still resided in my sides.

"Hey, it's Cole. Is Jana with you?"

"Yeah, she is. Did you want to talk to her?"

"Actually, I wanted to talk to the both of you."

The door of Maya's room was closed, so I put my phone on speaker. "What is it?"

"Byron called."

Just hearing his name made me want to throw up. He was such a traitor. "What the hell did he want?"

"It turns out that Grayson figured out he was hiding something when we managed to save Maya the first time. So he killed one of Byron's kids and threatened to kill the other if he didn't tell him what we were planning. That's why Byron let Grayson know that Sam was Tracking down his family, and Grayson compelled the Tracker to lead Sam where he did. What he didn't tell Grayson was about Nathan, worship the guy for that. It saved all of our lives."

It suddenly all began to make sense. "Is the rest of his family still in captivity?"

"No. Byron had installed cameras inside the warehouse, and once he realized that Grayson was dead, he sent another Tracker to find his family. They're with him now, but he just called us. He kind of sent us a death wish."

"What for?" Jana asked, mirroring my confused look.

"He said that if we had just gotten his family out before jumping to save Maya, his child would have lived."

"Well great," I muttered.

"I would be on the lookout for him."

"How's Sam?" Jana asked.

"He's okay. They're going to keep him here for a few more days, but they've gotten the muertem out of his system. He's in stable condition, though. He's healthy enough to pull through."

Was it Sam's health or the amazing health care on Diviano? Either way, I found myself being kind of glad that he was okay, something I didn't expect from myself.

"How's Maya?" I heard a small voice ask through the phone. I realized it was Sam.

"She's okay," I assured him. "She's stable too. Just had to get stitches, but they're going to keep her here for some treatment she chose not to let me know about."

I had been deathly curious but let it be. Besides, I didn't mean anything to her. Despite her thanking me for coming to check up on her and taking Sam to the hospital, I wasn't her friend, and I had no right to nose around.

"Okay," he replied, and then after a while, "Thanks for checking up on her."

"Yeah, no problem."

"We'll see you guys soon," Cole said. "Stay alert."

~

After my arm had fully healed, Jana and I made sure Maya didn't need anything before we took off to take care of the bodies the bodyguard had carelessly left back at the warehouse. They had been left untouched, since no one was aware of what had been going on in earlier in the day, thanks to the silencer on Grayson's gun. It hurt me to see Nathan's lifeless eyes, and I could tell Jana was just as upset about this. But she didn't carry the guilt that I did. She didn't know how I felt.

"You know people can be resurrected from the dead, right?" Jana asked after we decided to burn his body somewhere here in LA, where no one would think to look. We were taking it out in a rental car Jana had paid for with some stolen cash. However, it didn't cover the entire price so I covered the rest, thankful that I'd had my wallet in my pocket when Sam and I had left to go to Diviano.

"I know," I sighed, remembering Sam telling me about that power. "Let's just hope that never happens."

Resurrection was nearly impossible anyway, she explained as we left the city, finding a vast enough deserted area to burn the body in.

"It's a long, complicated process that not many people with the power are willing to go through, especially for someone as old as Grayson."

"Why does age matter?" I asked.

"The parents of the deceased are involved. That's all I know."

I was so grateful that Grayson's parents were dead.

Once we finished burning Grayson's body, we returned the car and went back to the warehouse, carrying Nathan's body in a portal Jana made with Grayson's virtencia—the one that I kept since I'd left mine at Jana's house before leaving for Diviano. I had stolen one from someone while at the hospital when Grayson's was out of power and used that one to get us back to Jana's house, where we found Riley coming in with a very beaten up looking Jeremy.

"Oh my God!" I cried, rushing up to him, completely forgetting about Nathan. Jeremy was limping with his arm around Riley's tired shoulders. I took Jeremy's other arm and put it around mine, helping Riley carry him to the couch in the living room.

Once he was sitting down, I noticed his black eye and the cuts on his wrists.

"Are you okay?" I asked.

He glared up at me, but his attention was soon diverted to Nathan's body behind me, and his eyes went wide. "W-what happened?"

"No, you first. I need to clean your cuts."

Jana immediately left to get the first-aid kit.

He wouldn't look away from Nathan's body as he told his story. "I was at the bus station. Some guy shot everyone who was there, including my Cloaker. I bit him to try to get away, and when I got a taste of his blood, I realized I was what Riley calls a shape-shifter."

"What?" I demanded in utter shock.

"It's really self-explanatory," Riley teased, and I rolled my eyes.

"How was the process of morphing?" Jana asked. She'd come back with the first-aid kit in her hand. She handed it to me, and I got to work on disinfecting Jeremy's cuts as he continued talking.

"It hurt like a bitch, but shifting didn't get me out of the situation at all. I knocked out the guy I morphed into but ran away to find someone else waiting for me. And I don't have control of my power yet, so I morphed back really quickly, and the other guy knocked me out after recognizing me. When I woke up, I was tied up in ropes. This happened when I tried wiggling my hands out of the knots." He held up his wrists. "Now you go."

"It was Grayson," Jana began. I explained the rest of the story as I wrapped Jeremy's wrists up so his cuts wouldn't get infected.

"I'm sorry, Jeremy," I sighed after I was done, noticing the melancholy look in his eyes. "I thought you'd be safer away from here. I didn't want this to happen to you."

He sighed too, leaning into my arms as I sat down beside him. "I know. But you have to promise me that after today, you won't push me away like that again."

"I won't. I promise. And I never break my promises."

It didn't matter that we still had another threat lingering in the air. No matter what happened, Jeremy would stay by my side so I could protect him. I needed to take better care of him, and keeping him close was the only way I could. I wasn't going to let him get hurt ever again. Or anyone else for that matter.

~

After Jana and I called a funeral home so they could prepare Nathan's body for cremation on a later date, we contacted his parents, who had been on vacation this entire time. We weren't sure if Nathan had told them what he'd been up to, but we decided to lie about the cause of his death regardless, to avoid evoking more hatred in our direction. It was really depressing announcing the death of their son. The pain was unbelievable and the guilt was even worse, but I was so sick of crying that I just treated myself with a little Scotch while we dealt with the situation.

After taking care of Nathan's death, Riley scoped out our old house for any more threats. When he confirmed there were none, Jeremy and I settled back in. We were glad to have our house back, safe for the time being. We were also glad Grayson had installed a security system a few years back, which we decided to keep on at all times now.

The real problem was figuring out how we were going to pay the bills. I'd already decided to opt out of school completely, since I wasn't going to live long enough for it to benefit me anyway. I got my job back at the restaurant and had asked for more hours, but even if I *was* working fulltime, my paycheck wasn't going to cover everything, especially with university coming Jeremy's way.

Thankfully, Cole was a huge help in that department. He quickly figured out the account numbers and passwords to all of Grayson's bank accounts and gave them to me so I could use his savings whenever I wanted to.

Other than that, Jeremy offered to get a job to help out, but I wanted him to focus on school. Although it would definitely help, we decided that we would take each day as it came. Besides, we had bigger things to worry about, like the fact that Byron wanted us dead.

The morning after, Riley decided to take off. He had stayed the night at our place and was leaving to go to LA that day. As he went out the front door, he smiled and said, "Keep in touch."

"I will," I replied, smiling back at him. I wasn't sure why exactly he wanted to keep in touch, but I was pretty sure it had something to do with who he'd thought I was when we'd first met. I was curious, so I decided to keep my word.

It was after he left that Jana called me over to her place. I didn't want to see her, and now that I didn't have to, I ignored her text and decided to grab myself something to eat for breakfast, trying hard not to think about Nathan. But before I could even figure out what to make, she decided to come knocking on my front door.

I didn't want to open it, but I also knew that giving her the silent treatment wasn't going to work. She would work herself back into my life somehow, sooner or later.

So I sighed and opened the door, but blocked her way in. "What?" I demanded, shifting uncomfortably against the door frame. I still felt that dull ache in my side, but it wasn't really painful so I merely regarded it as another side effect of the ecstasy.

She raised an eyebrow at me. "Mind telling me what's been making you all crabby at me?"

I took a deep breath, knowing I'd have to tell her eventually, and crossed my arms. "My death sentence," I said.

Her eyes widened.

"When were you going to tell me?"

"Right after—how did you find out?"

"Sam."

Her eyes narrowed.

"Oh, don't get pissed at him. He did the right thing telling me. Unlike you and Cole, who wanted to keep it hushed."

"At least let me explain!"

No reason would be good enough for not telling me that I was going to die, but I wanted to know why she'd thought it would be better to let me know later rather than sooner. So I let her in.

We sat down in the living room and I gave her a cool gaze, waiting for her to talk. She was fidgeting with her hands as she began, "I knew you would lose your motivation to fight if you found out you were going to die."

"That's not enough," I replied. "It was your job as my friend to give me a reason to fight, like Sam did. It was *your* job to make me understand that this fight wasn't just about me."

She sighed. "I know, I'm sorry. I promise I'm going to try harder—"

"Do you even care at all that I'm dying? When I told you I was the Keeper, there was no fear in your voice. When you came to take Jeremy from Carrie's house, there was no fear in your eyes, no concern. It's like you don't even care at all that I am dying."

"I do care! How could you accuse me of not caring?" Her voice rose, clearly offended by what I'd said. But she didn't have the right to be. "You've been my best friend since we were in diapers, Monique! I love you! So of course I care!"

But I couldn't believe a single word she said. What reason did I have to believe her? If my mother didn't think I was worth keeping, why would Jana love me? She had probably just been my friend all these years because she'd had a vision that told her I would be Keeper, so she could help me kill Grayson in order to survive. It wasn't like she *needed* me as her friend. She could have made so many others. She was so popular.

She sighed, and lowered her voice when she spoke again. "Monique, just because you don't believe your life is worth living doesn't give you the right to think that I believe the same. It doesn't give you the right to think that I couldn't care less about you dying."

It was like she'd read my mind, just like she always did, and suddenly I had nothing to say. But I still wasn't sure. Why would I be worth it? I was so fucked up . . .

Suddenly, her phone rang, and she looked away from me to answer it. "Hi Cole," she said quietly.

I could hear him talking on the other end. "Hey, are you at home? I wanted to come see you."

"Um, no, not right now. I'm in the middle of something. I'll call you later, okay?"

"Yeah, that's fine. But if you're with Monique, could you just tell her that Sam wants her to stop by?"

I frowned, wondering why Sam wanted to see me. I could tell from the look on Jana's face that she was thinking the same thing. "Yeah," she said. "I will."

"All right, bye."

"Bye."

She hung up and turned back to me. "I'm sorry," she sighed.

"It's okay," I replied, because I had nothing else to say to her. I didn't know what to believe and what not to. I wanted time to think, and I was only going to get that time away from her. Telling her it was okay, even though it really wasn't, was the only way to get her to leave.

It just hurt so much knowing *she* hadn't told me, since I thought she was my best friend. Hell, I considered her my sister, and she'd once told me that she considered me one too. The fact that that could have been a lie too just hurt like crazy, and I wanted all this pain to just go away.

"I'm going to go see what Sam wants. Let yourself out."

She nodded as I made a portal with my virtencia, feeling a weird buzzing in my head as I channeled the power that I needed to do this. Soon, I headed through, ignoring the sick feeling I got as I did. I landed on my feet just inside the entrance to the hospital and headed up to the third floor.

I knocked on Sam's room door before entering and caught Cole slipping through a portal of his own. I ignored it like it was the most normal thing in the world, and it was in that moment that I realized how much this whole experience had changed my perception of normal. It was ridiculous.

Sam was sitting upright in his cot. His dark hair was messy and his grey eyes stormy as he watched me walking in.

"Hey," I said, eying the band on his wrist. I looked around for a chair and found one in the corner of the room, beside an open window, breathing in fresh air and sunlight.

I pulled the chair closer to Sam's cot and sat down as he replied, "Hey back."

"Why did you want to see me?"

He gave me a lopsided grin. "Always getting down to business, right?"

I raised an eyebrow at him, waiting for him to talk. I had better things to do than deal with him, and the quicker he got on with what he had to say, the quicker I could begin asking him the questions I had stored up. They were questions I had pushed to the side all night, being too busy dealing with other shit. But now that I had time to breathe, I also had time to think.

When I didn't answer, he sighed, rolling his eyes. "I just wanted to thank you for getting me to the hospital. I would have died if it wasn't for you."

Judging from the look on his face, he was uncomfortable thanking me. That wasn't much of a surprise, though, considering how much he hated me. Although he'd been pretty civil toward me lately.

"Yeah, don't mention it."

I wasn't really comfortable with this whole thing either. I wasn't comfortable with appreciation period.

"Although, I'm not sure why you did," Sam continued. "I expected you to leave me to die, considering I didn't tell you that you were dying until recently. Plus, you know I want the gem."

I gave him the only response I could, not knowing myself why I'd felt such a sudden urgency to save his life. "You forgot that I'm the Keeper, and I'm supposed to have a pure heart." I replied bitterly, thinking about Jana. "I wasn't going to hold it against you."

It wasn't like we were friends, and he had no obligation to tell me, like Jana had.

"And I have enough faith in your humanity to know that no matter what reason you have for wanting the gem, you'll see just how crucial it is that you let it go. Especially since you have a friend like Cole to slap some sense into you. I'm not worried. I don't see you as a threat."

I could tell from the look in his eyes that he was hiding something, but I didn't question him. I didn't care enough to try to get it out of him. I honestly *didn't* see him as a threat.

"So when did you get that replica made?" he asked after a moment of silence.

"The day you decided to be an even bigger dick than you had been previously, telling me my mom didn't think I was worth keeping."

I saw regret and guilt lingering in his eyes, but he didn't apologize. Instead, he said, "Fine, I'll admit it. That replica was genius."

I laughed. "Yeah, thank Jeremy for that; it was his idea, remember? I just thought it could come in handy if I was ever stuck in a situation like that."

"And you kept it a secret."

I shrugged. "I figured if no one knew about it, it would be more believable, which was why I stalled in surrendering it to Grayson."

But it got Nathan killed.

Wanting to think about something else, I asked, "How did they get rid of the oil extracts?"

He had a calculating look on his face. "I don't know. They put me under because they had to cut open my abdomen." As if talking about it made him remember the pain, he grimaced, the calculating look gone.

"Are you okay?" I asked.

"Yeah," he replied tightly. "I'll be fine." He was shifting. I removed a pillow they'd placed beside him so that he could move easier.

"Thanks."

"No problem."

He was staring at the mark on my wrist, and to my surprise, he grabbed it as I was pulling my arm away. He traced the vines of my mark as he spoke, sending shivers down my spine.

"You should hide this. You don't want people finding out you're Keeper."

"I will."

I could hardly breathe.

He looked up at me. "Byron's out to kill us."

"I know."

"It's my fault."

He was looking back down again. "No, it's not," I assured him sincerely. "We all knew what he wanted us to do. It was just a matter of priorities."

"Just be careful, okay?"

I was surprised that he even cared, but I figured that it had to do with the fact that if I died, we were all pretty much screwed. So I replied, "I will."

When he didn't say anything for a while but continued tracing my mark, I took it as my cue to start asking my questions. "Maya's sick, isn't she?"

"Finally whipping out the questions?" he murmured.

"You had to have already realized just how many I have. This is only the beginning." He sighed. "Answer me. I shoved my curiosity down long enough, but now I'm not going to leave without answers. You owe it to me."

"Yes, she's sick."

"And she's dying?"

His finger stopped at the center of my mark, and he swallowed hard enough for me to hear. "What makes you think that?" he asked.

"I heard what Grayson said to you. I know you think I was too focused on getting out of my bonds. But he said that you wanted the gem to save someone's life. I'm assuming it's hers, and that if you become immortal, she will too. So she won't die from whatever illness she has."

"Monique, you don't know what you're talking about. You're delusional."

"No, Sam, it's *you* who's delusional. You keep thinking that you're successfully hiding behind closed doors, keeping your secrets safe in that little room. But that door has cracked, and your secrets are slowly being let out. I don't know everything you're hiding, but someday those cracks are going to grow, and I'm going to see everything clearly."

He finally looked up at me. "As if you're not doing the same thing."

The apprehension worsened. I swallowed hard. "My doors aren't cracking," I retorted, unable to stand the thought of that actually happening.

"No, not yet, but they will."

"Whatever I'm hiding isn't any of your business."

"And Maya isn't any of yours."

I sighed. He was right. "No, she's not, but there's something else I care more about, something I already know you're not going to give me the answer to."

"And what is that?"

I paused for a moment, taking in his expression. He was trying to keep an impassive cover on his face, but I'd come to recognize the flittering of his eyes as fear.

"My life is tied to yours, isn't it?" I asked. "Otherwise, Grayson wouldn't have bothered trying to kill you. My protection is you."

He rolled his eyes. "That's ridiculous. Grayson wanted me to die because he saw me as a threat. He hated me for training you, for making you more difficult to kill. That's the only reason he wanted me dead."

"You're the one who explicitly stated it."

"I was stalling, making things up. I didn't want him touching Maya."

His jaw twitched. His eyes changed to a yellowish colour.

He was lying.

I sat back. I distinctly remembered his entire conversation with Grayson. And I could tell by his defensive response that I'd hit the mark. I still needed more clarification about what this all entailed, but I knew I wouldn't get it from him, so I let it go, deciding I would soon search for more information myself. I wasn't exactly sure where to start, since I doubted information on Keeper protection would be easily accessible. But I also knew that I could access anything I wanted.

I was the Keeper.

And I had just saved the lives of all these oblivious people around me.

He finally let go of my wrist. I let out a breath I hadn't realized I'd been holding in this entire time. The corner of his mouth tugged up a little when I did, but he didn't say anything. Not wanting to stay in that room a second longer, I replied, "I should get going."

"Your virtencia isn't going to be powered up."

"I have two on me."

"Okay. Take care of yourself."

I stood up and opened up a portal. "Yeah, you too."

I meant it too. But I shouldn't have. He was an ass to me and always had been, so I wasn't sure why I cared.

Whatever the reason, I just hoped that I wouldn't ever see him again unless it was necessary. He made me uncomfortable. Just the sight of him gave me a feeling I didn't like. I wasn't sure what it was, but I knew that from here on out, I would avoid him as much as I could.

SAM

I was so glad when Monique had left my hospital room. Being in her presence made me feel as if I was suffocating, especially when she was also prying me for answers. I knew she had seen through my crap, but I hadn't known how else to lead her in the wrong direction. So I just prayed to God that she was kept too busy to discover what was really going on.

Roughly six hours after she'd left, I was discharged, to my relief. The moment I left the hospital, I went to go see Maya in LA, urgent to meet her.

She looked so frail, lying in her hospital bed. The pain of seeing her like this was much worse than the physical pain I was still feeling.

The portal had just made that worse.

"How are you feeling?" I asked when she fluttered her eyes open to see me walking in.

"I'm okay," she said quietly. I sat down beside her. "Better than you must be feeling."

"I'm fine," I lied, trying not to show her how much pain I was in. The medication the doctors had given me wasn't enough to numb it, since my body didn't function the same as other Divianans' did.

"You're a poor liar."

"I'm also in much better condition than you. What did the doctors say?"

She grimaced. My heart dropped.

This couldn't be good.

"They think my injuries could have affected my chance of survival." My throat tightened. "But they need to run a few more tests to see where I'm at before coming to a solid conclusion."

"I'm sure you'll be fine," I assured her, though I wasn't so positive myself. I could tell she didn't believe me from the look in her tired eyes. "And if it's necessary, I'll get more money, and we'll go to a better doctor. I'm not going to let you die. I promise."

But I wasn't sure if that was a promise I could keep. And it bugged me that I didn't have a clear answer. It bugged me that I didn't know enough to help her. I bugged me that I couldn't save her, that the cure to her disease wasn't lying in my hands, that I had no idea how long I had with her before she died.

She sighed. "Sam, you're driving me *nuts* with all your fidgeting."

I looked down at my hands. "I'm sorry."

"It's all right. You should get some rest, okay? I'll be fine for the night."

I didn't want to leave her alone. "I can stay the night here."

"No, I *want* you to leave and get a good night's sleep. If I know you're not taking care of yourself, it's just going to stress me out even more."

I got up. "Okay," I sighed. "I'll leave. Call me if you need me here, okay?" She nodded, and I tried to force a smile, leaning down to give her a lingering kiss. I pulled away unwillingly and squeezed her hand before creating a portal and heading to Diviano.

When I got to the house I shared with Griffin and his fiancée, I realized it was nearly midnight here. I expected them to be asleep, but when I passed by their bedroom, I was glad to find that they weren't home. It gave me the place to myself, which meant I could do whatever I needed to without being overheard.

Walking into my room, I lifted the carpet from the corner of the floor and opened up the trapdoor that led to a secret room that had been used for shelter when the Palidia attacked a hundred years back. I closed the door above me and headed down the stairs, flipping an emergency light switch on the way. The basement was dark, a single room with damp grey cement walls. There was a lot of moisture in the air, and I was betting there were plenty of bugs down here too, considering we never cleaned the place. But it was just what I needed.

I looked at him, the man Monique and I had bumped into the night Grayson captured us. Although he'd escaped from me that day using teleportation, I had still been able to rip off a piece of his shirt and hired a Tracker to quickly Tracked him down after killing Grayson. Cole had captured him with the help of some of his friends before I left the hospital and kept him down here until I was discharged and could interrogate him.

The chains were restraining him from moving, and his head was hanging low. His eyes were closed, and his hair was wet from the moisture in the air. He was breathing hard.

"It's the chains, am I right? They're killing you, restraining your teleportation power. How are your burns?" I asked idly, grabbing a chair. I held a knife in my hand and began sharpening it while I waited for him to respond.

"Go to hell," he seethed.

"That's an ironic threat, coming from you."

He laughed weakly, lifting his head up to look up at me. "Do you have any idea who you're messing with?"

I rolled my eyes, eyeing the knife in my hand. "You're a Daeblo, I get it. But the thing is, Captain *Ego*, I know someone who is friends with someone who knows a Wunissa. And this Wunissa just so happens to have exactly what I need to cut out your tongue so you can't make snarky commentary at me. Fortunately for you, I have a few questions I need to ask you first."

He grinned sardonically. "Let me guess, you want to know how I know you're a hybrid."

"What else would I want?"

"I've been alive for thousands of years. Don't you think I would notice if someone, the only person who would be able to kill me on the face *all three planets,* were to be born? You are the first hybrid I've seen in *five hundred* years. I don't know how you've managed to survive for eighteen years, but I swear once I get out of here, I will make it my life's mission to have you killed."

"And why won't *you* kill me?" I asked, raising my eyebrows at him.

"Because I want to see you suffer," he spat. "I want to watch you run as they hunt you down, hunt your dad down and kill him and then kill your mom. But wait." He paused. "She's already dead."

He grinned, and although I'd planned on containing myself, I couldn't help it. As the pain bubbled up inside of me, I punched him in the face. Blood flew out of his mouth, but that didn't wipe the smug look off of his face. "What? Are you hurt, poor baby? Too bad she's not here to console you. The only person you have left is that blonde. Maya, is it?"

"How do you know about her?" I demanded, my heartbeat spiking. If he knew about Maya, he could hurt her.

"How does it feel?" he asked instead of answering my question. "Knowing that the only sure way of saving your girlfriend's life is to end the lives of thousands of Divianans?"

"I will tear your heart out—" I began, but he didn't let me finish.

He laughed. "Good luck trying to find one. I lost mine the minute your world was created. You, on the other hand, have a heart that is beating deliciously, and I would *love* to tear through your skin and eat it."

"You're *disgusting.*"

"I feed on the living, remember?"

"Who else knows about me?" I demanded.

He visibly thought about it, cocking his head to the side as he looked around the muggy room. "*Well*, there's your pretty little girlfriend, your friends Griffin and Cole, and let's not forget your father. How does *that* feel by the way? Having your father search the face of the Earth to find you and kill you before somebody finds out about you? Must be exhausting. This is the second time you've moved in the past year, isn't it? I had a father like that, a thousand years back. He didn't like the way I was abusing my power on Earth, but then he joined me and relished it. Don't you ever wish you could get along like that? Maybe he would have even helped Maya."

I didn't reply. He'd been spewing out so many words that I just didn't know what to say anymore.

And then he said, "What if I told you that there's another definite way you can save her life, and it's sitting right under your nose?"

A cure? Was he bluffing? "Tell me what it is," I demanded, my hands shaking. I'd been searching for a cure for years now. I couldn't let this opportunity pass by me.

"And why should I?"

"Because if you don't, I will tear you apart until you do."

He laughed. "You can't threaten me. But I could give what you want. At a certain cost, of course."

"What do you want me to do?" He grinned at me but didn't say a single word. It was his silence that made me realize what he wanted. "I'll die though," I replied. "Is there anything else you want me to do?"

He shook his head. "There is only one thing I want from you, and that is your consent. Fortunately for you, you already know the consequences. You should be well informed from your army days about what you're getting yourself into. The others agree blindly, driven by the thought of power, but you just want one thing, and I will give that to you. Just give me your consent."

I couldn't believe I was actually considering this. I had spent years of my life killing people who'd given their consent to Daeblo, and now I was considering doing it myself. But I was desperate. All I wanted was to save Maya's life.

"How do I know you're not lying?"

He grinned. "You don't. But let me ask you something. How much pain are you in right now?"

I'd blocked it out, focused on him, but the moment he mentioned it, I felt the agonizing pain inside my core that would have made me cry out if I hadn't been trying so desperately to seem tough.

"A lot of internal damage has been done. Specifically to your kidneys," he said. I didn't understand. The doctors had told me I was fine. "But of course the doctors let you walk, because they themselves believed you were fine. After all, that's what they were compelled to believe."

My breathing came harder as I realized that either way, I was going to die, and Maya would die with me. Forget going to the best of the best, we were both going to die, either from the damage to my kidneys, her illness, or this third way—by Possession. The only difference was that Possession would give me more time. Maya would die with me, unless I broke things off with her and prayed to God that she moved on, that she fell out of love with me. And if by doing this, he'd give me the cure to her disease, then I'd do it, even if it meant dying myself.

So I bent down on one knee and recited, "I, Warren Vega Junior, give you my consent to take full control of my body anytime you please till the day I die. I understand that this means I mustn't ever fight back and will surrender to your Highness whenever deemed necessary by you."

I looked up at him and he grinned wickedly, but instead of giving me the answer I'd done all of this for, he closed his eyes. My body immediately dropped to the floor without my consent. My eyes closed without my command, as fear coursed through my veins. Pain shot up my arms and legs, into my spine. I roared through the never ending process, feeling as if my limbs were breaking and would never stop.

Until suddenly, I felt nothing.

When I opened my eyes, I was on my feet, and the Daeblo's former body hung unconscious from the chains, not breathing. My legs began moving on their own accord to the stairwell just as a voice spoke in my mind—*his* voice.

Brace yourself, Warren Vega. The worst is yet to come.

Printed in the United States
By Bookmasters

Printed in the United States
By Bookmasters